IT STARTED WITH PARIS

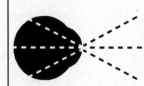

This Large Print Book carries the
Seal of Approval of N.A.V.H.

IT STARTED WITH PARIS

CATHY KELLY

THORNDIKE PRESS
A part of Gale, Cengage Learning

GALE
CENGAGE Learning·

Farmington Hills, Mich • San Francisco • New York • Waterville, Maine
Meriden, Conn • Mason, Ohio • Chicago

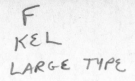

F
KEL
LARGE TYPE

LIBRARY OF CONGRESS CATALOGING-IN-PUBLICATION DATA

Kelly, Cathy.
    It started with Paris / Cathy Kelly. — Large print edition.
      pages cm. — (Thorndike Press large print women's fiction)
    ISBN 978-1-4104-8349-2 (hardback) — ISBN 1-4104-8349-5 (hardcover)
    1. Female friendship—Fiction. 2. Life change events—Fiction. 3. Large type books. I. Title.
    PR6061.E484I86 2015
    823'.92—dc23   2015028133

Published in 2015 by arrangement with Grand Central Publishing, a division of Hachette Book Group, Inc.

Printed in Mexico
1 2 3 4 5 6 7 19 18 17 16 15

For Matt, my godfather, with love.

PROLOGUE

Love is an ideal thing,
marriage a real thing.

GOETHE

He had the engagement ring in his pocket. He was terrified it would fall out — all through the ride up in the Eiffel Tower elevator, with people pressing against him, he thought of what he'd do if he lost it. Proposals on the Eiffel Tower should not be memorable because of the would-be groom crawling around on the floor feeling for a ring box.

No, the memorability was the venue, with Paris sparkling around them, with other people smiling at the joy of it all. Paris was the city of love — not the city of *I had the ring and it fell out someplace — let's find it, for heaven's sake!*

Ever since they had got out of the cab, smiling with relief because the Parisian cabdrivers were all race-car drivers at heart, he'd been clutching the box in a death grip, having secretly taken it from its hiding place in the camera bag.

Too distracted by the sights to notice, she kept beaming at him, her cheeks flushed the same color as her peony-pink scarf. Even cold and with a runny nose that was taking a pack of tissues an hour, she was beautiful.

Doe-eyed, his mother had called her, and as usual, his mother was right.

She did have the look of a deer, but a happy deer. A deer who grazed in Santa's paddock and who expected all things in life to be magical.

Even among the Parisian beauties, with their hauteur and their chic clothes, people still looked at her admiringly: she wasn't tall, but she was slender, with the bearing of someone who'd done ballet for years and still walked as if she was about to go onstage in her teenage dance school corps. And she was his. His girlfriend, his about-to-be fiancée . . .

He said a fleeting prayer, something he hadn't done in years, and asked for help. *Let her say yes, please.*

He'd told nobody he was going to ask her to be his wife.

Not his father, though he'd nearly said it to his mother, because he'd been sure she'd hug him and say, "Go ahead, I love her like a daughter, you know that."

His friends might say that he had loads of time to settle down, but then they'd have recalled how luminous she was, easygoing as a person and easy on the eye, and how clever she was yet never showing off her cleverness.

None of those were the reasons he was asking her to be his wife. He simply loved her and had ever since they'd met all those years before when they'd been put at the same table in preschool.

Turning those big dark eyes on him, she'd shown him her newfangled eraser with the strawberry scent and gravely told him he could borrow it anytime because she liked the dots on his face.

"Freckles," he'd informed her. "You get freckles when you're special."

"My daddy says I'm special but I don't have fleckles," she'd said, sounding shocked at this betrayal.

"I'll draw some on," he'd said, getting out his pencil.

The first two freckles had hurt too much so he'd stopped and hugged her the way his mother hugged him.

"Will you be my best friend?" she'd asked him, sniffing.

She'd had him at her feet then and ever since.

The Eiffel Tower elevator came to a discreet halt; holding the ring box in one hand as if it was a grenade, he managed with his height and big frame to make a space for her to get out without being squashed. The tourists in

Paris were maniacs, he decided: all mad to see everything *first.*

"Thanks, love," she said when they finally made it out of the elevator. "I thought I was going to be flattened."

She hugged his arm and he felt the surge of protectiveness he always felt for her, even though she was anything but a fragile little flower of a person. Small or not, she had plenty of toughness in her.

"Look," she said now, holding his free hand and racing over to the railings to gaze at Paris spread out in front of them. It was as if the tower were the center of the universe.

He looked and saw nothing.

Let her say yes. Let it be like a movie where she loves it and says yes and the other tourists clap. She could say no, she might say we're too young and we have plans and —

A tour guide was pointing out the different arrondissements and areas of interest to a group, and she was listening in.

A Spanish couple asked him if he'd take a photo of them with their camera. Looking over to where she was eavesdropping on the tour guide, he saw her grin and wink at him. This was always happening to him. With his tall frame, smiling, charming face and the chestnut hair that looked as if someone had just ruffled it, he was the picture of honesty.

Afterwards they walked around the observation deck and she pointed out landmarks.

10

"Do you think that's where our hotel is?" she asked, squinting.

Their hotel wasn't the bijou beauty near central Paris they'd been promised. The bedroom was bijou all right, so bijou it was easier to climb over the bed to get to the door than risk your kneecaps on the bed frame.

And it was near central Paris only if you happened to be an Olympic athlete gearing up for a run. But now was not the moment to ruin things with such matters.

Unable to take it anymore, he grabbed her by the waist to stop her, turned her to face him, then sank to his knees. The box — *thank you!* — was now in his pocket and he pulled it out, held it up the way he'd seen it done in the movies a hundred times, and said, "My darling, will you —"

"YES!" she shrieked, throwing herself at him and hugging him. With him kneeling down, there was a reversal of their usual height difference and she had to angle her head to kiss him.

"Really?" he said, hardly believing. He knew she loved him, but *this* — this was everything, and they were young and —

"Yes, yes, yes!!!" she said, and then kissed him as though he were dying and she needed to bring him back to life.

He sank into the embrace and felt his heart pulse with sheer joy.

She'd said yes.

Touristy approval emanated from the crowd and people began to clap and shout approval. Someone was taking pictures, but he didn't care at this intrusion into their moment.

"You will?"

"I will. Show me, show me."

He opened the box with its antique diamond ring inside: an emerald-cut diamond surrounded by two rows of tiny diamondettes or whatever they were called when they were incredibly small and probably not big enough to qualify as actual diamonds. He'd spent two months searching antique jewelry shops all over Waterford and even Cork, trying to find the perfect ring for the woman he loved.

She breathed in and held out one small hand, and he slid the ring slowly on to her finger. It was the right size, he was sure; he'd measured one of her costume jewelry rings, and according to the ring guidelines it was a J. "Perfect for this delicate ring," the jeweler had said happily as he'd pushed it a quarter of the way down his own little finger and tried to see it through her eyes.

"I love it," she said in wonder, one hand still on his shoulder, the other held aloft as the ring caught the Parisian sunshine.

The Spanish couple came up and asked if they wanted them to take their photo.

"You make a handsome pair," said the man.

So they posed with the Parisian skyline in the background, arms around each other's waists and her left hand held proudly out to the camera to show off her engagement ring.

Other people looked on in approval at the tall, strong man with the messy hair and the slender girl in jeans and pristine white tennis shoes, her silky dark hair worn in a ponytail. They looked good together, they fit somehow.

"You will have beautiful children," said the Spanish man, smiling as he handed back the camera.

They both laughed at the thought.

Children!

That was years off.

"Who will we tell first?" he asked, when the crowd had dwindled and it was just them again.

She looked thoughtful. As he watched her, he realized he still had that gloriously joyous feeling inside. He'd known she'd say yes — he knew her so well — but even so . . . she'd said *yes. Yes!*

He'd never forget this moment, ever.

ONE

Love is a flower which turns
into fruit at marriage.
FINNISH PROVERB

At her desk on the fifth floor of the mermaid-green glass office block where Eclipse Films had their offices, Leila Martin sniffed the rose tea that her assistant Ilona had carried in for them both on a tray.

It smelled beautiful; even the packaging was beautiful: 1940s pretty, with a china cup painted in watercolors on the front and swirls of steam emerging, tiny roses drawn in the swirls.

"You'll love it!" said Ilona, arriving back in the modern office, this time with her arms full of notepad and tablet. Ilona was always bringing things in to her boss: chocolates, biscuits, a Hungarian herbal tea her mother swore by but that smelled like cat litter mixed with patio yard sweepings.

If Leila didn't know better, she'd swear Ilona was trying to cheer her up. But then

Ilona knew — because Leila had told her firmly — that Leila had absolutely no need of cheering up.

It was business as usual at Eclipse. Leila Martin wanted people to know that she didn't do heartbreak or any of that type of thing. She was pretty sure she had them all fooled.

She stared back at her rose tea.

It was healthy too. Probably lowered stress levels or boosted immune systems or did *something* proven in scientific tests by a fleet of people with PhDs coming out their ears. It just wasn't coffee.

Worse, it wasn't coffee like Leila's favorite cup of the day, which used to be the one her husband brought her in bed in the morning and which she could hear him brewing in the classic espresso maker that shook volcanically on the top of the stove and was probably the oldest thing in their apartment.

Since Tynan had left, no coffee tasted right.

Nothing tasted right.

Six months of having to do it herself and Leila still couldn't make it just the way he had. How could a person go their whole life making their own coffee, enjoying drinking it in trendy cafés, and then fall in love with their husband's coffee, so that when he left her for another woman and another city, she was practically allergic to the taste of anything else? It made no sense at all.

16

When she'd been fifteen and living in the country town of Bridgeport, she and her best friend, Katy, had adored the very concept of coffee, spending their pocket money ordering skinny cappuccinos and Americanos in the café near Poppy Lane, where Leila lived.

Katy lived on the outskirts of Waterford city, a stone's throw from Bridgeport. Leila hadn't been able to wait to get out of what she considered a desperate backwater and live in the big city. Fifteen years later, both the city and coffee left a bitter taste in her mouth.

"A latte's quite nice," Katy had urged the last time she'd been up in Dublin for a weekend with Leila. They'd found seats in a smart café and Katy was running a finger up and down the menu, dithering over syrups and double shots.

"No," Leila said gloomily, "I hate lattes. All that milk. I don't know what it was about that damn French coffeemaker yoke, but it worked for him. Not for me. He jinxed it. I'm back on the tea. Builder's tea, Earl Grey — you name it. Has anyone ever checked whether a marriage breakup has a chemical effect on your taste buds? That's the only answer. Or else he's got a wax dummy of me in London and he's sticking pins into its mouth."

It sounded so ridiculous, they both laughed: the thought of the slick, modern Tynan believing in any sort of religious practice, including voodoo. He was an atheist, believed in nothing but the dollar, he said, which used to annoy the hell out of Katy, given that the Irish currency was the euro.

"If there's any wax dummy to be made, you should be the one making it," Katy said.

The two women had been best friends since they were in primary school. Both on the short side, one blonde, one brunette, and a force to be reckoned with when together, the partnership felt a bit lopsided to Leila these days. Katy was gloriously happy with her first love and Leila was very much unhappy.

Worse, Leila knew Katy thought she should be *rejoicing* that someone as disloyal as Tynan had walked out of her life and their one-year marriage.

Katy had said that — and more. The statute of limitations on criticizing appalling husbands was somehow up now that six months had passed. Katy wanted her friend to move on. Unfortunately, moving on was proving harder than she had hoped, and both of them knew that Leila would take the cheating Tynan back in an instant should he turn up on her doorstep repentant.

So Katy comforted during late-night phone calls, mopped up tears via supportive text messages and tried to hold off on criticizing because the once-strong Leila Martin had been made vulnerable and fragile by love.

18

That day, Leila ordered green tea and they settled in cozy coffee shop chairs to talk about the only thing Leila ever wanted to talk about.

"I know this sounds ridiculous now, but when we got married, it felt safe, final. As if the years of dating all the wrong guys were over and at last I'd come home to Tynan. He was The One. And — this is almost the worst bit, Katy — I pushed him to get married. He'd have been happy the way things were, living together, no bit of paper to show we were officially man and wife."

Katy, who'd heard it all before, patted Leila's knee in solidarity.

"We all do dumb things for love," she said, a variation on her previous themes. "And he wasn't The One. The One doesn't dump you for a twenty-something with thighs skinnier than her knees."

Sometimes this made Leila laugh. Not today. She barely heard, lost in reliving her mistakes. It was such a relief to be able to talk about her pain. Pretending she was utterly fine when she was at work was making recovery even harder.

"I rushed us both into it because I wanted to be with him so much. I wanted him to be mine. If only I'd taken it more slowly, waited . . ."

She'd been sure that Tynan wanted the same things in life as she had: he'd swung

19

her around on their wedding day with the band playing a cheesy version of "It Had To Be You" and he'd had eyes for nobody but his blonde bride, whose face was lit up in a way that owed nothing to the careful application of cosmetics. They'd been so happy; she'd have bet her life on it.

How had she not seen?

"You OK, Leila?" Katy said. "You've gone off into the Twilight Zone."

"Yeah." Leila nodded. She managed a half smile for her best friend. "Thanks for listening. You should be charging. What's the going rate for counseling these days? Sixty quid an hour? You deserve to be paid for sitting through this, because I can't tell anyone else or they'd think I'd totally lost my marbles. This is not how people expect me to behave."

With everyone else — her colleagues, her mother, her sister Susie, who had enough on her own plate as it was — she smiled stoically and murmured that it was his decision and she was fine, really. It was what she thought people wanted to hear from a strong, ambitious woman of twenty-nine with a brilliant career.

She couldn't say that Tynan had made her feel like the crazy teenager she'd never been, and that she'd run blindly into his arms, convinced he was her destiny. He was loving, sexy, handsome, funny, kind — he'd even bought her the perfect coffeemaker.

"You should stop trying to pretend it doesn't hurt," Katy said. "It doesn't make you look weak to say you're upset. I'm sure Bill Gates would cry if his wife dumped him."

"Bill Gates is far too smart to have married someone who'd dump him," Leila retorted. "I have never felt like a loser before, but I feel like one now. And I still want him. That makes it worse."

"Listen!" said Katy sternly. "If Tynan could run out on you like that for some young hipster girl he met through work, then he wasn't good enough for you in the first place. Better you find out now rather than ten years down the line. He's done you a favor. In a few years, you'd be throwing *him* out."

Would she? Leila wondered sadly. She could never have seen a time when that would happen. He was like a force of nature, a passionate, devil-may-care man who'd come into her life like a tornado. She'd never have thrown him out. She loved him too much.

He'd taken his stuff and nearly all of Leila's self-confidence. Would she ever get it back? Who knew? But for now, she was off men. In fact, not just for now — forever.

A few weeks ago, on the six-month anniversary of Tynan's leaving, Leila had thrown out the little French coffeemaker and started on an odyssey into herbal teas. As grand

21

gestures went, it wasn't much, but it was a start.

Now, at her desk, she stared at the rose tea whose virtues Ilona had extolled.

"It's my favorite," she'd said, a trace of her exotic Hungarian accent in her voice. "Jasmine is lovely, but the proper stuff is expensive and rose is calming, don't you think?"

At twenty-three, Ilona looked up to her boss and mentor with unflinching devotion, despite the fact that Leila was only six years her senior. Leila had taken her on as junior in the publicity department two years ago. Ilona's grammar had still been a bit shaky and she'd worried about her ability to write proper emails, but she'd wanted desperately to progress in the company.

What would Ilona think if she knew that the boss she admired was not a strong professional woman but someone who'd felt entirely broken for the past six months?

Of course, she would never know. Nobody would know.

We wanted different things, Leila had told people blandly.

Ilona started running through their to-do list.

They'd been busy since Leila arrived at nine on the dot, even though she had been out late the night before at a work event. Leila Martin had not become one of the most valued members of Eclipse Films' staff by

22

taking time off.

She was good at what she did — managing director Eamonn Devlin wouldn't have hired her otherwise. She had worked hard to get where she was, devoting hours to the job and giving up weekends when required. Plus she looked like a magazine illustration of a successful media PR rep, with a wardrobe of chic trousers and elegant silk shirts or T-shirts, and never a streaked blonde hair out of place. While careful not to outshine whichever star she was accompanying, she had indefinable style and looked smart enough to make people notice her.

This morning, fifth on the to-do list was an email from a young actress's manager setting out her hotel requirements for when she arrived in Dublin to attend the premiere of a movie that was barely a nod away from straight-to-video in Leila's opinion.

"*Yellow orchids, not white,*" she read out. "White is so last century, isn't it, Ilona? *Muslin curtains on the windows in her suite.*"

"I'll check what sort of curtains they have in the presidential suite in the Centennial," said Ilona, pen poised over her notebook.

"They can swap to muslin, no problem," Leila said. "When the white orchid/muslin curtain/Zen garden on the terrace thing was big, they bought lots. Plus, I think they have enough Zen white sand in the basement to make one hell of a sandcastle. Phone Sergio and kindly ask him if housekeeping can get the muslin curtains up. Right, next."

"Omigod, you know everything," said Ilona admiringly.

"No," said Leila. "It's only that you get used to being asked for crazy stuff."

They continued to run through the list of requests relating to every detail of the actress's visit. It was one of those aspects of a publicity director's job that could be very time-consuming and required vast diplomatic skills. Publicizing films for Eclipse was a joy in so many ways: Leila spent time in the film world, met some of the world's most fascinating and talented actors, directors, and producers, and saw them without their public masks on.

The true professionals flew into the country, did their job with sparkling expertise, and flew out again without having requested more than wheat- and lactose-free meals in their hotel suites, approval on big interviews, and sometimes a driver for the day to see some of the sights.

And then there were the people who were determined to prove that they were so special, normal rules didn't apply.

Hideously expensive scented candles, vintage champagne on every available surface, and new Frette four-thousand-euro-a-pair sheets were commonplace among this tribe. Ditto raw food/green juices on call 24/7, rare

24

fruits, and calorific desserts that might not be touched but that had to be there just in case the juicing got boring.

However, there were limits. When one would-be star demanded that Eclipse supply puppies to cavort at her photo shoot, Leila put her foot down. She would not allow anyone to indulge themselves at the expense of animals. A phone call to the manager of the star in question had done the trick. "Tell her we follow ethical PETA rules," Leila told him calmly. It worked a treat. Nobody wanted to get on the wrong side of PETA.

Drugs were another no-no.

"Not on our dime or our time," Eamonn Devlin said to his team when a wild young actor — not in an Eclipse movie at that moment, thankfully — trashed a hotel room in Paris while under the influence of crystal meth. "Anyone who wants it can source their own coke/OxyContin/whatever."

When Devlin spoke, people listened.

Muslin curtains and specific flowers, however, were perfectly commonplace.

"Irish music CDs, for Irish atmosphere/ dancing," read Leila in amusement. "This is sweet, really. You'll have to get an iPod and download some jigs and reels."

Ilona blinked at her.

"Sorry — ask Marc or Sinead," Leila said. "You've turned into such an Irish girl, I forget you're Hungarian and don't know all our insane ways."

"Not insane," Ilona replied. "I'm proud to be Irish. Or I will be, in another year."

"You need to have the Irish dancing part of the induction, then," Leila said solemnly. "I Irish-danced for eight years and have all the medals. I'll show you sometime."

It wasn't easy, but she managed not to grin. Ilona, who never quite knew whether Leila was joking or not, gaped at her wide-eyed.

"OK, I'm kidding. I have a few Irish dancing medals, but neither love nor money would get me to dance now. I was never *Riverdance* quality. I was one of the ones who shuffled down the back of the line for the complicated treble steps. I got the medals out of pity.

"Right, back to the list. A choice of mineral water and Coke Zero. This is almost easy, Ilona. No temperatures for the drinks, no requirements for specially imported vodka or newly installed toilet seats. This girl is either a nice, classy person or else nobody's told her what some folks ask for. She might be one of the normal ones — or as normal as you can be when you're famous all around the planet and get papped as soon as you step outside your home without full makeup." Leila grinned. "I'm so glad I work on this side of that world and not the star side."

"Me too," agreed Ilona fervently.

Once they'd finished working their way through Leila's to-do list, Ilona headed off with her notepad and Leila turned to her computer, already filling up with a dizzying number of emails. It was almost a pleasure to come across spam in her inbox — at least those messages she could just bin, not bothering with a reply. If only they were all spam, she thought wistfully.

At five thirty that evening, one hundred and fifty miles southwest of the Eclipse offices in their modern glass office block, Susie Martin left the hospital in Waterford, got into her car, and drove off slowly in the direction of Bridgeport. She always found hospitals vaguely scary, even when she wasn't sitting in the ER waiting for news of her mother after a serious car accident. Coffee from the machine in the waiting area had helped, but even so, she felt shaky and not herself. Seeing her mother bruised and in shock had added to the stress of watching people with cuts, broken bones and pale, pained faces waiting alongside her.

Still in a state of anxiety, Susie waited till she got back to the outskirts of the city and into one of the parking slots at a small convenience store before she rang her sister.

Leila never failed to take her calls, but Susie always had the feeling that she was interrupting her sister's life: a life full of movie stars, premieres and important meetings. Susie herself kept her phone on silent when she

27

was at work in the telecoms call center, although she left it on her desk in case Jack's school or Mollsie, the babysitter, rang. At home in the evening a caller might interrupt her helping Jack with one of his kindergarten projects — like making a dinosaur out of kitchen paper cylinders, tinfoil, and recycled bits and bobs — but that was it. No one would ever ring her and find that she couldn't talk at that exact moment because she was running a press conference for a Hollywood A-lister with thirty journalists and a cadre of TV reporters in attendance. Leila's life was big, while hers . . . hers was very normal.

Instantly Susie felt the surge of guilt at even thinking such a thing. Her life contained Jack: precious, joyous, special Jack. The light of her life.

But the guilt couldn't stop the knowledge that she was lonely. Lonely for the sister she'd once been so close to before Tynan had wrenched Leila away. And lonely at the thought that she'd never feel romantic love again, because she willingly gave most of her time to her precious son, the rest to her mum, and that left no time over to even think of having a man in her life.

Plus, men her age didn't exactly line up to date single mothers, did they? They were avoiding women with ticking biological clocks, not leaping into relationships with readymade mothers who couldn't fly off to

Barcelona for a weekend just for the fun of it.

She unclicked her seat belt and sat waiting while her sister's phone rang.

"Susie," answered Leila in surprise.

"It's Mum," said Susie, not bothering with formalities, "she was in a car accident."

She heard the sharp intake of breath.

"Is she — ?"

"She's OK. Very lucky, the doctor said." Susie got out of the car and went into the store, phone clamped to her ear. "She's fractured her hip."

"Oh God . . ." muttered her sister.

"Her poor face is all bruised — which obviously isn't the worst thing, but she looks so terrible. Some old fella in an ancient Fiat plowed into her at a red light. He wasn't going very fast or it would have been a lot worse. She's pretty shaken up, though."

"Poor Mum," said Leila weakly, and Susie could hear the huskiness of tears in her sister's voice.

Susie picked up a shopping basket. Hurrying through the store, she grabbed some milk and groceries for dinner, although who knew when she'd be eating, because first she had to pick up her mother's dog and then drive to the babysitter's to collect Jack. She threw in a jumbo bar of chocolate as well. That was the low-carb, low-sugar diet out the window.

"Susie, are you listening?" said Leila.

"It's a bad line," Susie replied, realizing Leila had been asking questions. "I'm stressed," she added with some irritation. "It's my half day at work, so I had to get Jack picked up from school while I was at the hospital. Before I collect him, I have to go over to Mum's to get Pixie, as I promised that we'd have her while Mum's in the hospital. So I have to walk the damn dog too, *and* she'll probably eat the couch if she's left on her own because Mum lets her do whatever she wants . . ."

"I'm sorry," said Leila quietly. "I know you have to do everything. You're brilliant, Susie. You really are. I'll be there to see her as soon as I can. What are they going to do? Is she going to be OK?"

"I think so," Susie said, still testy and hating herself for it. She and Leila had once been so close — like twins, people used to say — and now she was snapping at her sister. "Sorry, I'm a bit shaky," she added out of guilt. "They're doing X-rays because she'll need surgery and probably a pin inserted. They won't say exactly till the orthopedic team decide. She was on a gurney for ages and was in agony until they finally gave her an injection."

"Oh, Susie, poor Mum," Leila said, and began to cry. "If I ring the hospital now, will I be able to talk to her, do you think?"

"I don't know," Susie said. "She didn't have

her cell phone. You can ring the nurses' station, but I don't think they'll bring the phone to the bed —"

Leila appeared to have stopped listening, because she interrupted.

"I think she'd be asleep due to the meds," she said. "I'll talk to the nurses."

"You could try, but she might be in surgery. I'm not going in again tonight. They said they'll phone me afterwards. I have to get Jack. He's never slept over at Mollsie's."

"Mollsie?"

"My babysitter," said Susie, with a certain grimness. Even the girl at the desk beside her at work, a girl who lived for partying, knew Mollsie's name. Susie's sister, Jack's godmother, didn't.

Susie felt the familiar anger flood her, anger fanned by the fear and anxiety of a day spent in the hospital worrying. "I can't believe you didn't remember that, Leila. Mollsie and Mum are the people who help me with Jack. There *is* nobody else."

For a second there was silence on the phone.

Susie hadn't meant the statement to sound quite so stark: that she was alone with a small child because his father hadn't been interested, and that her once best friend, her sister, wasn't around for her anymore.

But it was said now, it couldn't be unsaid, and she wasn't sorry.

31

She understood that Leila was broken-hearted, but Tynan had taken Leila away from Susie and their mum long before he'd run off. And though he was gone, Leila still hadn't come back to them.

"It's five forty-five now," Leila was saying awkwardly. "I'll leave the office in half an hour, go home to pick up some things, and I can be at the hospital by nine."

Susie sighed to herself. Leila had always hated being in the wrong, so she was simply ignoring her sister's comments.

Fine.

"Mum won't be able to talk to you," she said evenly. "She could be in surgery."

"I think —" began Leila.

Susie was at the checkout now.

"I have to go, Leila. Bye."

"Bye," said Leila, but Susie had already pushed the "end" button, so her sister was left talking to dead air.

There were a few missed calls on Susie's phone when she got back to the car. One from a work friend and two from Mollsie telling her that Jack was fine and not to worry. Jack loved his mother's half day, when she could pick him up from school instead of Mollsie and they'd have an adventure: the park in summer or hot chocolate and a DVD snuggled up in front of the fire on wintry afternoons.

The stress of the day blasted through her, and Susie sat in her parked car and wept.

She was only thirty-one, and yet sometimes she felt ancient. Compared to the other single women at work, she *was* ancient. Most of the people in the call center were young, doing this job as a stopgap. They had wild weekends, booked amazing holidays on the Internet, and came back with stories of trips to places she'd only seen in photos.

Susie spent her money shopping wisely for food, buying clothes in cheap shops, saving up for Christmas and their rare holidays. She couldn't remember the last time she'd had a wild weekend — probably with Leila and Katy before Tynan had come along.

When Jack was asleep, long eyelashes sweeping over still chubby cheeks, she looked at him with such love and gratefulness that he was in her life. Yet this small boy with his hopes and dreams was her responsibility, and there was no one with whom to share it. She wouldn't trade her life with Jack for the world, but it was tough sometimes, no doubt about it.

And lonely. She'd felt lonely ever since Tynan had come into her sister's life. Susie had taken one look at him — all lean and handsome, carefully styled so as to give the impression that he'd just flung on his clothes, though she could tell he'd spent hours in the bathroom fixing his hair, practicing his moody look — and known he'd break Leila's heart.

He'd tried to charm Susie that first time they met in Bridgeport.

"How come a gorgeous girl like you isn't beating men off with a stick?" he'd asked, patting her knee in a way that was half affectionate, half flirtatious.

"I've got a big stick," she'd said grimly. "I've beaten them all away. All the losers and users, anyway."

Tynan had looked at her thoughtfully. He was too clever to rise to her comment, but she could tell that he knew she'd assigned him to the loser-and-user category.

He'd flicked his charm onto her mother then, and afterwards Susie had warned Leila about him.

"He'll dump you, Leila," she'd said earnestly. "You're not even yourself around him. It's like you're . . . like you're someone else, someone you think he'd like. You can't change yourself for a guy."

Her eyes had taken in the un-Leila-like tight black jeans and spindly heels, the clingy top, the rock-chick tousled hair and more eye makeup than normal.

"I like how I look," Leila had said furiously. "You're just jealous because I've finally found someone and you haven't."

The sisters had stared at each other in sudden silence. They didn't do harsh words in the Martin family. Dolores spoke gently to everyone. Nobody screamed or yelled at anyone else. The sun was never allowed to set on anger. But this, this was something different, something nasty brought in by damn Tynan.

Susie knew her sister might eventually forgive her for what she'd said. But when Tynan had done exactly what she'd known he would, Susie hadn't felt any happiness that this horrible man was gone from Leila's life. She'd felt only the loss of the sister who'd never come back to cry on her shoulder and say "I'm sorry, I know you wanted what was best for me."

That loneliness was the hardest thing to bear.

Leila bit her lip and stared out of her office window at the Dublin skyline. Down below was buzzing with people already leaving offices for home. In the distance, it was still bright enough that she could see the Wicklow Mountains, a faded purple blur where she and Tynan had once climbed the Sugar Loaf with some of his friends.

She wouldn't cry. All she'd been doing lately was crying, and she wasn't going to start in the office just because Susie had made her feel guilty on purpose. It wasn't her fault that her job was miles away from Waterford and that she couldn't nip over to take care of Jack at a moment's notice.

She had a full-time job, a career. Susie had to understand that.

Then she thought of her mother lying on a gurney in the hospital, scared and in pain, and she had to bite her lip really hard. Susie was there for Mum and Mum was there for Susie and Jack.

Leila wasn't there for anybody anymore. Tynan had managed to drive a wedge between her and her family, and Leila had been in too much pain to fix it. Now she didn't know how.

Eamonn Devlin looked up as Leila burst into his office.

"What's wrong?" he said, instantly interpreting the expression on her face.

"My mother's had a car accident. I have to go home right now. I know I'm leaving you in the lurch with the *Octagon Rising* movie people coming into town —"

Devlin held up one big tanned hand. A week's skiing in France had made him look more piratical than ever. His dark skin, combined with coal-black hair and eyes, had made Leila wonder the first day she'd met him if he'd be able to pull off hoop earrings and a parrot on one shoulder. He was tall, well built in a rugby player sort of way, and devastatingly handsome — and he knew it, using it to great effect with visiting talent.

More than one actress had wanted to succumb to Devlin's charm, but Leila was pretty sure he was too canny to actually have a fling with an actress. That way madness lay — and probably a one-way ticket to the Antarctic office. If Eclipse *had* an Antarctic office.

Right now, he studied Leila carefully through the long dark lashes on those black eyes. She often wondered if he could see through her carefully constructed persona to the person underneath, the woman cowering behind the carapace of professionalism, the woman on the verge of crying at her desk every day. But no, how could he? She was a good actress.

"No worries, Leila," he said calmly. "You go. Ilona can take over for a couple of days, can't she?"

Leila nodded. Ilona was clever and dedicated. She'd love the chance to run things in her boss's absence.

"I can brief her, but really, she's good to go on her own," she said. "We'll have to fight to keep her, you know. She'll want to progress in the industry."

"She's not you, Leila," Devlin said brusquely. "Update me with how long you'll be away, right?"

"Right." Leila saluted, swiveled on her heel, and walked out.

Eamonn Devlin watched as she left, expensive suit jacket and trousers finished off to perfection by the even more expensive heels. He often wondered how she walked mile after mile in those damn platform things. It was a short-woman thing, he decided. Determination that no boss would tower over her.

Did she know that *she* was the one he'd do anything to keep? Probably not.

He caught one last glimpse of her blonde hair falling in a curtain down her back before the door closed, hiding her from sight. Apparently she had it blow-dried professionally several times a week. Or so he'd read in a magazine profile. One of those "how I manage to do what I do" articles, where she'd sounded lively, fun, and wildly efficient, professing to love clever black ensembles and spicing up her clothes with big architectural jewelry. Perfect nails and hair completed the package, along with her BlackBerry and all the latest technology in her big career-woman bag. All in all, it came across as a carefully crafted lie to cover up the real person, the sort of construct only a rather brilliant publicist could pull off.

The piece, which had been written before her husband left, was accompanied by a photo of her in trendy designer clothes, sitting on a beige velvet couch in a hotel, wedding and engagement ring prominently displayed. With the gorgeous hair and clothes, she'd looked the part, but neither the articles nor the photo captured who Leila really was:

funny, kind, brilliant at what she did, so lovely to that sweet Hungarian girl she was mentoring.

Few people could smile as warmly as Leila. Her face lit up and those rounded hazel eyes shone with happiness or humor. Since that bastard of a husband had left her, though, there hadn't been much smiling.

She was in serious pain, even though she thought she was hiding it. He wished he could do something, but she wouldn't accept help. Any help. Especially not his. He was the boss; it wouldn't be right.

Devlin turned his head back to the figures on his computer. Women: impossible. There was nothing more to be said.

On a small housing estate in Waterford, five hours later than planned, Susie finally parked with an excitable Pixie in the front, clambering down to the footwell and back up on to the seat, a routine she'd kept up since Susie had put her in the car.

"Stop!" Susie begged. It wasn't that she didn't like dogs, but she felt so close to the edge already, and having to babysit Pixie, who didn't appear to understand either the word "no" or the concept of doing her business outside, was really the final straw.

Somehow she clipped the dog's leash back on and led her up Mollsie's neat front path with its perfect grass verge and nicely trimmed shrubs lining the way.

She'd barely got to the door before Mollsie opened it.

Mollsie was everyone's idea of what the perfect babysitter should look like: neat and tidy as her garden, her face an oval of warmth and eyes that missed nothing but shone with kindness. Nobody ever noticed what Mollsie wore or how her curly gray hair was styled. Such things were secondary to the sweetness of her personality.

"You sure you don't mind the dog?" said Susie, almost sinking against the door with exhaustion.

"I love dogs," Mollsie said, reaching out to rub Pixie's ears. "Jack will be thrilled to see you, won't he?" she said to the dog, who instantly fell, like everybody else, under Mollsie's spell and threw herself with delight against her new friend's legs.

"Come on in and have some supper. You must be worn out."

"No," said Susie. "I don't want to intrude. I thought if Pixie went into the garden she might pee or something . . ."

"Great plan. Now, you have to eat. I have chicken pie heating and some mashed potatoes. I know it's not the diet food you like," Mollsie added, leading the way, "but you need nourishment after the day you've had. Tell me everything."

"Mum!" Jack launched himself out of the

kitchen at his mother. Then he stopped. "Pixie!"

"We're going to be minding her while Granny's in the hospital," Susie said tiredly.

"Amazing!" said Jack, on his knees and receiving a thorough Pixie face wash.

At least someone would be happy to have the dog in their apartment, Susie thought, though how she'd manage during the day was another story.

"What sort of a dog is she?" asked Mollsie fondly.

"Spaniel, a bit of something else . . . wildly disobedient . . . Is there a name for a dog like that?"

"Normal," pronounced Mollsie.

Susie relaxed as Mollsie ushered them all back into the kitchen, let the dog out for an exploratory sniff of the garden, and began to heat food for Susie, all the time keeping up a stream of idle chitchat about how broken hips were much easier to sort out now and her mother would be back on her feet in no time.

Jack snuggled up beside Susie as she sat on the couch.

He was a beautiful child, everyone said so: with Susie's fair hair, but almond-shaped brown eyes and olive skin that made him look like a creature from a fairy tale. He was a good kid too, but despite Mollsie's best efforts, he'd gotten stressed because his mother was late. Susie did her best never to be late.

She was determined that, though Jack might lack a father, he wouldn't miss out on anything else. Jack ate the best of everything and had much more expensive clothes than anything Susie wore.

"He tells me everything, you know," Mollsie laughingly told Susie early on. "Some people are astonished by that, but with kids, it all comes out. Arguments, crisps for dinner, you name it."

"No crisps for dinner or arguments in our house." Susie grinned. "Except when Jack won't eat his vegetables."

Mollsie pretended surprise. "He tells me he eats vegetables all the time at home and that's why he doesn't have to eat so many here."

Jack giggled. "I hate green things."

"You don't say," said his mother, smiling.

Susie rarely even had a cup of tea at Mollsie's, aware that the older woman tried to look after both the children in her care and their parents. But tonight, the thought of chicken pie and someone to cook it for her was too much.

As Susie ate, even Pixie calmed down after killing a sock and lay quietly on the couch.

"There's holes in it now," Jack said, holding the sock up gingerly as Pixie admired her handiwork proudly.

"There were holes in it before," Mollsie said, "so it's fine."

Finally Susie rounded up her son and the

dog and said good-bye.

"See you tomorrow," she said.

Jack hugged Mollsie.

"I can take care of him for you over the weekend when you're visiting your mother," Mollsie said. "And Pixie can come too. Not when I've other children, I'm afraid, but she's safe with Jack, isn't she?"

"Safe with Jack, yes. She loves him. Unsafe with socks and shoes," Susie said ruefully, already wondering how long it would take her to Pixie-proof the apartment. "Thank you, Mollsie."

As they drove off, Mollsie stood at the door watching the car. She'd taken care of many children over the years, and there were always a few parents who wriggled their way into her heart. Susie was one of those. She had an air about her of someone who'd been let down and was so determined that it wasn't going to happen again that she would never let the circumstances arise.

But, Mollsie thought as she closed her door against the winter night, everyone needed help. No woman was an island.

Two

Loving is not just looking at each other, it's looking in the same direction.

ANTOINE DE SAINT-EXUPÉRY

Headmistress Grace Rhattigan liked being the last person to leave Bridgeport National School in the evening. It was a peaceful time to catch up on her endless paperwork, when the last teacher had vacated the staffroom and all the children — from the tiny ones to the sixth grade, who considered themselves very grown-up indeed at age twelve — had gone.

The cleaners had usually finished up by four thirty, although they'd been later leaving today as an explosion of yellow paint in kindergarten had taken some time to eradicate.

"It really *is* everywhere, Roberto," Grace had said to the head cleaner earlier as they both surveyed the corner of the classroom where an innocuous plastic bottle of paint — nontoxic — had been shaken and splashed

44

joyfully at the walls by a five-year-old called Jamie.

"No problem, Mrs. Rhattigan," said Roberto. "We will clean so no yellow can be seen. Kids, they do these things." He smiled to show that it was no trouble at all and only to be expected.

Grace was so fond of Roberto: he worked two jobs, she knew, to keep his large Brazilian family, and yet he was unfailingly obliging and greeted all events with a smile.

If only everyone in the school was the same.

"Look at this mess! Jamie said he wanted his sunflower to be on the wall instead of on paper," Miss Brown, the kindergarten teacher, had said crossly earlier when she'd shown the headmistress Jamie's rather larger than intended flower.

"He certainly thinks big," Grace replied, gazing at the corner where yellow paint covered a sweep of window, a decent amount of the adjoining wall, and every crevice of a shelf of books and jigsaws. "Maybe he's going to be a famous artist, known for giant canvases."

Grace was always full of hope for the children in her care. They were all precious beings, with great talents and lovely characteristics, provided they were nurtured the right way.

"Or he might be starting graffiti early," added Miss Brown, sounding knowing.

Orla Brown was one of the youngest teachers in the school and she could do with a lesson in child care from Roberto, Grace couldn't help thinking. This was her first year as a teacher and she was still on probation. In her interviews with Grace and the school board, she'd been the epitome of the smiley kindergarten teacher in her floaty pink skirt and flowery blouse. In reality, she had a hard streak that Grace was growing to dislike intensely.

Grace drew herself up to her full five foot seven, and put on the sternly cool headmistress voice she found worked marvelously on certain people.

"Orla, let's set our sights higher than that," she admonished. "If we tell Jamie he's going to be spray-painting walls down by the train station in the future, that's as far as he'll aim. There are plenty in his family who'd expect no more for him, but we won't be doing that here. No." She surveyed the yellowness. "He's an artist in the making. We have a huge responsibility for the children here, Orla. We must aim high for them, particularly when nobody at home will be. Do you understand?"

It was not a question — it was a command.

Chastened, Orla had said yes, she understood, but Grace wasn't so sure.

There were people who had a gift for education and there were those who didn't.

If a teacher believed a five-year-old boy was en route to a lifetime of nothing more than spray-painting rude words on walls, then that teacher had no place in Bridgeport National School.

As soon as she returned to her office, Grace found her big desk notebook, the one she kept under lock and key, and reluctantly added a note to Orla Brown's file.

When she herself had been a preschool teacher, over twenty-seven years ago, Grace could recall looking at each one of those little faces as if they were the country's hope for the future. Happy and fulfilled adults, the best mothers and fathers ever, good-hearted people, even captains of industry and enthusiastic entrepreneurs. She'd seen it all in them, and she still did. People who thought differently did not make the best teachers.

Sitting at her desk, with no noise apart from the ticking of the large clock on the wall, Grace's thoughts ran to the framed childish sunflowers halfway up her own stairs.

Sunflowers were kindergarten; twinkling stars and happy Santa Clauses made with cotton wool were from first grade; and penguins and butterflies adorned with dropping sparkles were second grade. As a teacher, she'd been well aware how the various pieces of artwork and stories that Michael and Fiona brought home would mount up over the years, but it hadn't stopped her from keeping them all.

On the walls of the stairs and landing she had a gallery of their most precious pictures, from two sets of splodgy sunflowers to Fiona's beautifully realized watercolor of the hills surrounding Bridgeport when she was in high school and taking art for her final state exams.

"Ma," Michael used to beg occasionally, "take them down. They're embarrassing."

"Oh no, they're not embarrassing, I promise you."

"No, Ma, really," he pleaded. It was hard for a grown man who could bench-press decent weights in the gym to have his sparkly Santa Claus displayed on the stairs. What would people think? Luckily, the person whose opinion most mattered to him thought they were adorable.

"You love them," Fiona would tease her older brother, "because Katy loves them too. She's always cooing over your finger-painting and sighing about how cute you were."

Michael was twenty-nine now, an engineer who lectured at the nearby Institute of Technology. Proud as she was of his academic successes, Grace was even prouder of the fact that he'd grown into a good man. Despite his burly frame, there was a deep loveliness to her son, a gentleness belied by his size.

As she tidied up the last of her papers, Grace glanced toward the phone. She'd been waiting all day for a call from her son. She wondered whether she could have been mistaken about Michael and Katy getting engaged during their trip to Paris. Michael hadn't actually said anything, but Grace wasn't a school principal with a degree in child psychology for nothing. Usually she could read her son like a book — which wasn't too difficult, given his inability to keep things from her. Several times over the past few weeks he'd blurted out questions about her and Stephen and their marriage.

"What age were you when you and Dad got married?" he'd asked during one visit, his face telling her that he regretted the words as soon as he'd said them.

Pretending innocence, Grace had replied: "Twenty-three, but it was different then, darling. Not like today, when people live together and know each other's foibles. Back in prehistoric times, we were babies at twenty-three, all fresh and shiny from school or college and knowing nothing. It's better the way your generation does things — live together and discover if you're suited before committing to marriage, like you and Katy."

Michael and Katy had lived together since college. They had a two-bedroom town house on the Bridgeport side of Waterford, and Katy commuted daily to Bridgeport Woolen Mills, where she worked in the marketing department. She'd done a business degree to help her understand, and eventually take over, her father's business, but there was nothing in her of the spoiled only child.

"Talking of Katy, are you two coming for dinner on Sunday?" Grace had asked her son innocently, as if she'd made no connection between the questions about marriage and the girl he'd been dating since they were teenagers.

It was lovely to know that neither Michael nor Fiona was scared of marriage, put off it for life by their parents' divorce. She and Stephen had worked hard to ensure that they weren't affected. Being civil when it felt as if there were no civil words in the world; smiling when the children passed from one parent to the other; talking to each other as calmly as if they were discussing a blocked drain instead of a family being split up.

For years afterwards, Grace had wondered whether the breakup had been her fault. If she'd only been a more compliant sort of woman. If she'd been able to compromise, leave her teaching job in Bridgeport and move to Dublin, where Stephen would have had his pick of fabulous ad agency positions . . . but then Stephen hadn't been one for compromise either. They'd clashed — both of them young, full of dreams and plans. Grace had argued that neither career was more important than stability for the children, and that meant remaining in Bridge-port.

Somehow, amidst all the arguments, they'd come up with the idea of a trial separation. A crazy idea that seemed to grow on them.

Grace had hoped it would make him realize what he was leaving behind. He'd miss being at home; he'd come around to her way of seeing things.

And then, two years later, along came Julia, and suddenly there was no point in Grace wondering if they'd done the right thing or not. Julia had made all the second-guessing redundant.

"I'm so sorry," Stephen had said. "I never thought . . . She was there and you weren't."

It didn't hurt anymore. Not after fifteen years. But it . . . Grace searched for the word. It *stung.* Yes, that was it. It stung that their marriage hadn't worked, and yet Stephen had now been living happily with Julia for thirteen years. Julia had managed what Grace couldn't. That, too, stung.

Julia was so very different from her. Childless by choice, it seemed, effortlessly cool, intellectual in a way Grace had no interest in being; she was as far apart from Grace as it was possible to be. Grace's social life didn't involve book clubs — she had tried one once when the children were younger, but it hadn't worked out. Wine had been produced too soon, everyone present was a mother, the

51

conversation had inevitably turned to children, and by ten they were all tired, worn out with half a bottle inside them. Not one single conversation had gone on about the book.

Julia's book club, however, had progressed through the Irish classics, great American literature, Australian writers, and Booker Prize winners, and was now casting around for fresh territories to cover — Grace knew this through Fiona; Stephen would never confide such details. Any more than he would tell her about the foreign films he and Julia went to see, or their visits to the theater and their annual trip to attend the opera in Vienna.

Grace's social life revolved around her children, friends from school, and some of the mothers she'd known from when Michael and Fiona were small. Her best friend was Nora, who ran the Hummingbird Nursing Home in town. It was a world apart from Stephen's current life, and even though she knew she shouldn't be comparing, she somehow still did.

"Why do I do that?" she'd asked Nora many times. "Why do I wonder if I had been more like Julia, more laid-back and sophisticated, would we still be together?"

Nora, wise as Grace and still married to her childhood sweetheart, Leopold, said she thought it was just one more part of being human: imagining what *might* have been.

"The path not chosen — it haunts us all," she said. "We all wonder, Grace. Listen, as I've said before, you had children and a career: you were thinking of both of those things when you told Stephen he should move to Dublin without you. Besides, you are very sophisticated.

"Sometimes," Nora went on, "I wonder if I hadn't stayed in Bridgeport, married Leopold, and set up the Hummingbird, would I be singing in the Royal Albert Hall once a week and living in a posh flat with suitors coming by with flowers daily?"

"I can't imagine you with a different life," Grace said.

"Neither can I, really," Nora said. "But I still dream about it from time to time. People dream, sweetie; it keeps us sane. But you're you, not Julia. She's never had the joy of children. And let's face it, you'd go stone mad if you were out at the cinema and theater every night. As for the opera, even though you listen to it for me when we're in the car together, I know it's not for you. You're a Fleetwood Mac girl, and if you were blonde, I swear you'd dress like Stevie Nicks."

They both laughed.

"Principals can't wear trailing shirts and too many bangles, or have long, long hair that hints at someone having run their fingers through it," joked Grace. "Though I might try it one day for fun."

53

■ ■ ■ ■

It was nearly six, and a typically freezing January night, as Grace drove home through the streets of Bridgeport. Even in the bitter cold, with wet roads and the possibility of black ice around the corner, it was still a beautiful place to live.

She recalled the times she'd flown into Waterford Airport and looked down on her beloved hometown from above. Clinging to a peninsula close to Waterford city, it called to mind a starfruit placed on the mouth of a river: the town with its five fingers splayed out and the silver thread of the River Dóchas leading to the harbor. The river divided the town into two, the opposite sides joined by the Old Bridge and the New Bridge.

Well over a hundred years ago, Bridgeport had evolved from a fishing town into a resort where wealthy people frequented the big Edwardian hotels that lined one side of the harbor. On the other side of the water were the fishermen's cottages, now painted in sherbert colors, at least a third of them turned into restaurants capitalizing on the local fishing industry. In the late 1980s, half a Viking boat and some Viking gold had been dug up from the river delta at low tide, and the canny lord mayor had insisted on having an interpretative center built, to put Bridgeport firmly on the tourist map. The New Bridge was speedily renamed Thor's Bridge and the short winding path along the headland on the west side of the town became the Valkyrie Walk. A long-drawn-out argument had been going on ever since, with the Ancient Order of Hibernians insisting that it should be called the Nuns' Walk, as the path was reputed to have been used by sisters making their way to morning prayers from the old convent that adjoined a long-abandoned monastery on the headland. Those whose businesses relied on the tourist trade felt Vikings were a far better bet than nuns when it came to drawing vacationers to the area.

The argument had been rumbling on for years, with battle reenactment days interspersed with silent retreats, both of which brought in tourists.

As Grace drove, she tried to remember whether she had anything in the fridge for dinner. Healthy eating was all well and good; at school she operated a strict lunchbox policy that banned crisps and permitted chocolate or sweets only on Fridays, but the lunchboxes of five- to twelve-year-olds were a far cry from the provisions of a divorced headmistress. Eating properly took planning, and sometimes Grace simply didn't have the time or energy for such a thing. She kept meaning to order her groceries online, but somehow she never got around to it.

"I don't see how this healthy business is all that good for you," Nora had moaned the week before, when they'd been having their once-a-month Friday-evening get-together — or witches' coven, as Nora's husband called it. "There's no cake in it, for starters. People need cake," she added firmly.

"*You* can live on cake and it doesn't go near your hips," Grace pointed out with a wistful sigh, regretting that she'd started the conversation. "If I so much as look at a piece of cheesecake, five minutes later I'm wearing it. I used to be able to eat like a horse."

Nora could carry weight, being nearly six foot tall and still built like an athlete, despite being the wrong side of sixty. Grace, who was a shade over five five and with slender bones, came from a family where the women piled on the pounds once they hit menopause. The weight settled implacably around their middles and refused to move.

At fifty-four, and with a wardrobe of clothes she was determined to carry on fitting into, Grace had begun to realize that genes were powerful things. In theory, she had no problem with her changing shape — people aged, bodies were bound to change; it was the way of the world. But she felt mildly irritated when garments like her lovely russet silk skirt, the absolute favorite thing in her wardrobe, no longer fit.

She and Nora had examined the skirt to see if careful seamstress work might make it wearable again, but the consensus had been no.

"I'll have to buy new clothes now," grumbled Grace.

Nora laughed. "You have to be the only woman who doesn't like clothes shopping."

"I'm too impatient," Grace said. "It takes hours and you come out with one blinking sweater for all your trouble."

"*You,* impatient? Never," added Nora sweetly. "Go into one of the big shops in Waterford and get a personal shopper. It's all different now. Nobody tries to make you buy expensive things. You just tell them what you want to spend."

"I'd hate that. No, I'm going online," said Grace. "If I look like a madwoman in something, nobody but me and my own mirror will know, and I can send it back."

While she was at it, she might as well sign up online to get her food delivered, she decided as she drove into town, trying to figure out where she'd stop to shop for dinner. Planning was all it would take. Less planning on school and more around her own life.

She decided that she couldn't face the supermarket, which had somehow turned into a dating zone in the evenings, full of single people with baskets eyeing up other single people with baskets.

Since the divorce, Grace had spent far too much time thwarting the efforts of well-meaning friends hell-bent on setting her up with men; the last thing she wanted was to encounter flirtatious or uninterested glances over the avocados. She didn't know which was worse — being eyed up or being considered too old to eye up. Maybe it was a good thing her russet skirt no longer fit — it did make her look a bit schoolmarmy. Her favorite magazines were always warning of the dangers of making yourself seem older than you were by slipping into comfy clothes. Still, did it matter how a person dressed? What you were like on the inside and your enthusiasm for life was what mattered, surely?

The mini-market at the bottom of Westland Street had no time for such shenanigans. It was the sort of place where office workers nipped in to grab frozen pizzas, milk, and tea bags, too tired after a hard day to care what anyone else was doing.

"Mrs. Rhattigan, hello," said the cheery ex-pupil behind the cash register when Grace had finally filled her basket.

"Hi, Maxine, how's college?"

"Great," Maxine said, ringing up Grace's purchases with speed: fresh pasta stuffed with cheese and ham, pasta sauce, lettuce, balsamic vinegar, and finally, evilly, two of those yogurt-pot-sized cheesecake desserts. All wildly innocent purchases.

That was one of the drawbacks of the job, Grace thought with a private grin. A headmistress daren't buy a bottle of vodka and chicken nuggets for dinner, else it would be around town in a moment.

"Thanks, Maxine," she said with a big smile as the girl helped pack her groceries. "Your mother told me you got great results in your Christmas exams."

Maxine returned the smile.

You never forgot the children, that was the thing about being a headmistress. Whether they were beaming examples of sweetness or naughty little monkeys forever being caught messing around in class, it didn't matter. If a child had been through her school in the twenty-four years she'd been there, ten as a teacher and fourteen as headmistress, then Grace remembered them.

Not all her past pupils were doing as well as Maxine. As Grace left the mini-market and drove home, her thoughts turned to the discussion she'd had that day concerning Ruby Morrison.

She'd known there was a problem as soon as Derek McGurk, headmaster of next door's Bridgeport Technical School, asked to see her urgently. As the respective heads of the town's two biggest schools, they ended up having most of the same kids pass through their doors; some were no trouble at all, while others had files the size of house bricks to catalogue their many transgressions, warnings, and suspension notices.

It was both a blessing and a curse to Grace that she felt so bound up in the lives of her little students. Just because a pupil had left her school at the age of twelve and gone on to the grown-up world next door didn't mean she could forget about them — or stop worrying about them. Derek was wily enough to realize this and often got her involved when confronted by a problem he didn't know how best to tackle.

During her lunch break, Grace had walked the few hundred meters to Bridgeport Tech. As always, she was struck by the difference between the senior school and hers. Here, the scent of teenage sneakers mingled with sweat and deodorant and a hint of forbidden cigarette smoke; Derek and his staff did their best to stamp out smoking, but their efforts were about as successful as trying to plug a giant hole in the dyke with an ice lolly.

"Hello, Derek," she said, sitting herself down on the most comfortable seat in Derek's modest office.

"Coffee?" Derek asked, poised over his favorite toy, a gleaming black Nespresso machine, bought by himself and not from school funds, as he told his guests every time he offered them a drink from it.

"That would be lovely," Grace said. "One of the little green ones?"

Grace knew that Derek had romantic notions about her and that nothing gave him greater pleasure than to invite her into his inner sanctum. She'd spent years pretending not to notice how he complimented her whenever he saw her. One day, she was sure of it, he would be brave enough to ask her to dinner. But even though as a principal she was supposed to know all the answers, she had absolutely no idea how to wriggle out of that one.

"You look wonderful today, Grace," he said, eyes shining at her like a faithful dog.

Inside, Grace quailed.

"Thank you, Derek," she said, in her most professional tones, thinking that if she'd known she was going to be visiting his office that day, she wouldn't have worn the gold silk blouse that Fiona had bought her because she said it brought out the honey flecks in her blue eyes. She wouldn't have indulged herself with a splash of Opium perfume either, which her ex-husband used to say was unadulterated female pheromones in a bottle that no man could resist.

"I'm sure you're as busy as I am. Let's talk about what's worrying you, shall we?" she went on.

Ruby Morrison, now almost seventeen, was the daughter of Jennifer and Ryan Morrison. Until about a year ago she'd been a model pupil, but now she was locked into a down-

61

ward spiral, sitting silently in class and not taking part in any discussions. She was doing little or no homework and had gone from being an A student to someone who failed every test. Earlier that day she'd been sent to the principal's office for not turning up for history class, despite being in school.

"It's the fourth time she's missed class in this way this month, and we're only just back after Christmas," Derek said. "Her form teacher has asked her what's wrong, but she won't say, says she's fine. When the teacher pushed, she said school was boring. Nothing more. You can only do so much, Grace, if they won't even talk to you. Which is why I thought you could help."

Grace had been listening with sadness. Ruby had been one of the good ones, the kids who were a pleasure to teach. She did her homework happily, got on well with her peers, and was eager to be picked whenever an older pupil was required to deliver a message to a younger grade's teacher because she loved the little kids.

Grace could picture Ruby perfectly: pointed chin, solemn gray eyes that saw everything, and the same midnight-dark hair as her mother, Jennifer.

Jennifer had been a different kettle of fish: one of those women always ready to see insult in everything and fire off a letter of complaint.

"Have you spoken to her mother?" Grace asked.

"I haven't. Her form teacher has, but all she got was the usual: Ruby is an angel and so what if she skips class. Why are we complaining about Ruby when there are hoodlums in the place — you know the kind of thing."

Grace did indeed. There were always the deluded parents who refused to believe there was any sort of issue with their own son or daughter and that the problem was everyone else.

But Ruby? Ruby wasn't the sort of girl to skip class. Something was going on, either at school or in the girl's home life, to have brought about this change.

Ruby's little sister, Shelby, was still under Grace's care: a gentle nine-year-old who was shy, her teacher said, but biddable and artistic.

"Bullying?" she asked.

Derek didn't bridle. "You know the work we've put into the bullying program," he said. "You can't see the paint on the walls for anti-bullying posters. We've had the whole class working on it in social and personal studies all month. It's not that — it's something at home. Nobody can reach her, not the form teacher, nobody.

"You've got a great network in this town, Grace," Derek went on with a hint of envy.

63

"You know everyone. Could you discreetly find out if there's anything going on there? Ruby's mother isn't easy to deal with. If we knew what was happening — money problems, whatever — we might be in a better position to help."

Knowing everyone and everything was a real boon. Grace knew that Ruby and Shelby's parents had split up, but that was four years ago. There could be no trauma there, surely? But then the length of time since the split was no guarantee of improved relations. Some couples carried separation or divorce like a precious wound and refused to ever let it heal. Grace hoped that wasn't what was happening here. But what *was* happening?

She hadn't stopped fretting about Ruby since she left Derek's office. The little girl with the gray eyes had been one of those special children, the ones who touched a teacher's heart and would always have a place in it. Teenagers were so vulnerable, delicate creatures held to earth by fragile threads that could so easily be broken. She and Stephen had done their very best to shield Michael and Fiona from the effects of their divorce, and thankfully both had grown into happy, confident adults. But little Ruby . . . what had happened to her?

Grace parked the car, gathered up her briefcase and bag of groceries, and hurried up the path to the front door of the pretty cottage she'd bought when she and Stephen had finally divorced. Inside, she turned on lights, closed curtains, and then flicked on the television news; sometimes, when she was feeling down, a blast of headlines about the world's problems put things into perspective.

It was at moments like this that she wished she still had someone to share things with. Someone to whom she could say, "I'm tired and worried and I don't know if I can do this job for much longer because it's hard, and I'm soft."

But there was nobody, not even a mouse. Since she had put down poison a few weeks ago, the scrabbling under the sink cabinets had stopped.

"Sorry, mouse," she said in the general direction of the cabinet as she boiled water for her pasta. "I feel mean now. If I were a Buddhist I wouldn't have done that. I'm sort of sorry I did. You deserve a life too. Just not under my kitchen cabinets."

She flicked on the kettle and wondered what was wrong with her. She'd been single for a long time now and had grown used to it; comfortable in her solitary state and perfectly happy to wake up on Saturday mornings with only herself to please.

But lately — and she wished she knew why — she'd felt a strange loneliness inside. She'd told nobody about this, not even Nora. Certainly not her children. She didn't want anyone's help because nobody could help her. She simply wished she understood what had happened to bring on this melancholy. Why, after happily spending years on her own, was she now wistfully looking back to the days when she'd been married to Stephen and busy with Fiona and Michael? Was it thinking about her son finally getting engaged to his childhood sweetheart?

Whatever it was, she decided firmly, she needed to get over it.

THREE

The heart will break, but broken live on.
                    LORD BYRON

Leila drove home quickly, her mind barely on the road, inhabiting instead the unknown hospital ward where her mother lay scared and in pain. She'd get in and out of her apartment in twenty minutes, she'd decided — twenty minutes to eat a snack, pack, and be off.

If only she could talk to her mother . . .

She rang as she parked, but after being shuttled around three departments, she was finally told that her mother was in surgery.

Leila burst into tears. *Surgery,* and neither of her daughters were there. This was not the way families should do things.

"Give me your number," the kind voice said. "We'll keep in touch with you about your mother's progress."

"I'm in Dublin; I'm driving down now," Leila said tearfully.

"Drive carefully. You don't want to end up

in the bed next to hers, do you?"

Somehow Leila managed a wry laugh. "True," she said. "I wouldn't be much help that way."

She had to quiet down the feeling that she hadn't been much help with her mother for a long while. And as for Susie . . . No, she wasn't going to think about that at all.

Leila's apartment was the sort of place she'd dreamed of living in when she was a schoolgirl in Bridgeport all those years ago. The Martin home had been a seventy-year-old fixer-upper that they'd never had the money to fix up; its distinguishing features were bad linoleum, old wallpaper, and a couch so decrepit that if you sat on it incorrectly, one of the springs might bite you.

The three Martin women had cleaned for all they were worth, but the house always looked tired and old. As a result, Leila had longed for a home with modern decoration and not an old piece of furniture in sight.

Her open-plan apartment was on the top floor of four. She'd had it redecorated when Tynan moved in because he didn't like her "girlie" wallpaper. Now, the whole place was minimalist in the extreme, painted in neutral colors with one feature wall a dark gray — which had seemed wonderfully chic a couple of years ago, with the decorator waxing lyrical about it, but now reminded her of a mortuary.

These days, everything about her home felt cold and empty.

It wasn't as if Tynan had been at home to welcome her when they were married. He'd often stayed out till four in the morning, checking out some band or other. But at least there had been the prospect of him coming home at some point, a warm body sliding into the bed beside her. And the signs of his presence would be there: his breakfast dishes sitting on the drainer, the washing machine full but not yet turned on because he'd forgotten to push the button in the rush out the door. There had been proof that another human being lived here. Now there was only emptiness and the sense of failure that tugged at her every day.

She threw her bag on to the couch — modular, expensive suede, also mortuary gray and one of Tynan's favorite pieces — shrugged off her coat and heels, and hurried into the minuscule kitchenette to make a quick snack. If she was driving to Waterford, she'd need some sort of boost.

The kitchen cabinets were ruby red — her favorite color, she'd realized far too late. Too late for the designer to liven up the rest of the apartment, anyhow. Over the past six months, Leila had been trying to de-mortuarize the place, but it was all too neutral for splashes of ruby cushions to bring it to life. The nubbly red throw she'd bought didn't suit the suede couch. The red candles looked a bit too romantic when lit.

One day she'd redecorate, she muttered. All she needed was money and time.

She found a ready meal in the freezer, stuck it in the microwave, and went off to pack.

"You, wall," she said as she walked past, gesturing at the empty spaces where Tynan had removed his framed band posters, "you're history. I must have been bonkers to let you come in here. You almost smell of embalming fluid." She glared at the wall, wanting to take her fear and upset out on something.

She'd paint it herself. White. And hang pretty pictures on it. Something Tynan would have hated.

In her bedroom, with the king-sized sleigh bed that was ridiculously big for one, she threw some clothes into a weekend bag, changed into jeans and a dark comfy sweater, and made sure she had chargers for all her electronic gadgets.

In the bathroom, she simply swept the top shelf of the cabinet into a bag, added her toothbrush, and she was done. Time was of the essence: she wanted to be with her mother when she woke up from the operation.

The microwave pinged and she went into the kitchen, took out the tuna bake, and, without bothering to tip it out of the black plastic carton on to a plate, gulped it down where she stood, leaning against the sink. It was her favorite meal at the moment. She'd been eating it most nights since she'd gone off the chicken risotto.

"Delicious," she said to the microwave. "Thank you, honey. What would I do without you? Go insane and start talking to the wall, probably."

A glass of water later, she flicked the lights off.

"Don't forget to put the trash out," she called to the microwave as she left.

It didn't answer. It never did.

As soon as she was in the car, her day began to get even worse. It had started to rain and the traffic had gone into meltdown.

"Oh, come on! I have to get to a hospital!" she yelled at the unmoving line.

Sitting in the jam out of the city made Leila realize with another giant pang of guilt just how long it had been since she'd made the journey to Bridgeport. Nearly two months, she worked out; she'd gone right after the launch of the big Christmas kids' movie in late November, and it was now January. She hadn't made it home for Christmas because she was with a girlfriend in Paris; there was an Eclipse conference in Cannes just after New Year, and it had seemed like a very good idea to spend her first Christmas without Tynan somewhere else. The hotel in the Marais had promised gastronomic delights

71

and even a first-class gym to burn off the calories in luxury — not that either of them had set foot in the gym.

"Santa won't come if you're not home," Jack had said tearfully on the phone when he'd heard the news. "You have to come, Auntie Leelu, you have to!"

"I can't always come," Leila had said, angry with Susie for telling Jack what was happening. She was already feeling guilty about not seeing her mum without her sister making things worse. Why couldn't Susie be one of those parents who made up adorable fibs for children, like *Leila can't come because she has to work on something really important, but she'll send you an extra-big pressie to make up for it?*

"I'll give you an extra-big present to make up for it," she tempted.

"I don't want a present — I want you," said Jack in a fierce voice.

"Wait till you see what I'll bring you from Paris —" Leila had begun, but Jack had put the phone down and she was left talking to the air.

Kids remember the promises had been the tagline of the big Eclipse Christmas movie, and it had hit Leila just then that there was a good deal of truth in that sentence.

The general craziness of work after the holidays had kept her from making it back to

Bridgeport, and now she had the Parisian toy-shop gifts stowed in the back of the car. They would be a distraction for Jack, what with his beloved gran being in the hospital. That would be OK, wouldn't it?

She stopped once to get a cup of tea and to phone the hospital again. They told her that Mrs. Martin was in recovery.

"Thanks," Leila said, suddenly not really wanting her tea anymore.

An hour and a half later, she reached the hospital and was directed to a ward with eight beds in it. She would have walked past her mother's bed if the nurse hadn't told her it was the one beside the door. The frail creature swathed in bandages and attached to a drip, her face full of darkening bruises, didn't look like her mother at all. Her normally golden head of hair was all gray now, only hints of gold at the ends. She looked well over seventy instead of sixty-three.

Leila, who prided herself on never crying, felt the tears running down her cheeks.

"The bruises make it look worse than it really is," the ward nurse said gently. "I know that this is serious and it's going to be a slow recovery for her, but many people in car accidents have much worse injuries, ones they'll never recover from. She's had a lucky escape."

Leila nodded. She knew the nurse was right. But her mother looked so old, so fragile, not the strong woman she'd once been. That was the shattering revelation.

Could an accident do that to a person?

"She's not in pain, is she?" As she spoke, Leila held the hand without the drip attached. The skin felt papery, no hint of hand cream, no scent of her mother's perfume. Just the sense of age and the smell of the operating theater.

"No, she's not in pain," the nurse soothed. "She's on a morphine drip. But she'll be up in no time. We'll have her out of bed for at least a few steps tomorrow."

"Tomorrow?"

"We get patients on their feet quickly in case of clotting," the nurse said. "Just a few steps with a walker. Then she'll be having physiotherapy and there are exercises she'll have to do. In a week, you'll be surprised at how well she's doing."

"She won't be confined to bed?" Leila could hardly imagine her mother walking.

"No, she'll be out of here in a week to ten days, and then on to a nursing home for convalescence. She'll need physio and the gym, you see."

Leila's disbelief must have shown on her face.

The nurse patted her arm kindly. "It's all a perfectly routine part of the recovery process. Tomorrow will probably be the worst day — the first day after the operation often is —

but it improves every day after."

Tearful, Leila nodded. "You've been so kind," she said.

"Leave your number with the nurses on the desk when you leave; we'll call if we need you."

"Can I stay for a while and just sit with her?"

"Of course."

Leila found a chair and pulled it close to the bed. Before she sat, she bent and kissed her mother's forehead, noticing more wrinkles there than she recalled from her last visit. Even in sleep, with her face relaxed, the web of fine lines showed her mother's age. Her lovely hair looked as if it hadn't been washed for days, the gray curls clinging to her skull. The hand with the drip inserted was badly swollen, which Leila assumed was from the crash.

"Mum," she murmured, stroking the other hand, "I'm sorry I wasn't here earlier, but Susie looked after you. She had to go home with Jack."

Thinking of the phone call with her sister, Leila felt more tears trickle down her cheeks. In her own pain about Tynan, she'd ignored her family. Susie was angry with her, she'd let her nephew down, and Mum no longer even went to the hairdresser to have her hair dyed. What had happened, and why hadn't she been there to see it?

The unsettled feeling stayed with Leila as she drove out of Waterford to Bridgeport. She was on automatic pilot, not looking out for changes in the town the way she'd found herself doing on previous visits. Ever since she left for good, it was as if she wanted her home to stay exactly the way it had been when she was growing up. Tynan had teased her about it.

"You're like the long-absent emigrant who thinks everyone in Ireland's stuck in a forties movie, going to country dances and staring at big cars like they're spaceships. Everything changes eventually, baby, even where you grew up."

Since Tynan went out of his way to avoid setting foot in his childhood home — even though it was in Dublin and his mother still lived there — Leila had been tempted to tell him that he had damn-all knowledge of things changing, but she hadn't.

"Change is good, Leila. Get with the program."

He was right, of course. She reminded herself of that as she took in the new developments and tried not to let them upset her. Like the supermarket that now sprawled over the fields where her class had gone on nature walks, beloved by all students as a way of escaping the classroom. The trees where they'd laughed and chatted as they tried to get bark rubbings were no longer there.

At least that first sight of the town, coming into view as she drove over the headland, seemed unchanged, still dominated by the two bridges: an Edwardian one of great beauty, and a modern cantilevered creation with one steel stem reaching up into the sky and taut wires streaking out of it to hold the whole structure up.

Leila remembered how she and Susie and Mum used to laugh at the traditionalists and the Viking lobby arguing over the names of the bridges. There had been a time when her father had joined in the laughter, but it seemed so long ago, she could barely remember it.

Dad had been ill for so long and Mum had held the family together. Until Leila had left and somehow it had all changed.

As she drove along the riverside, past the old stone warehouses and grain stores from the days when Bridgeport had been a fishing and trading town, she noticed that most of them had been converted into modern apartments or shops. On the other side of the Old Bridge, things were exactly as she remembered: the line of golden nineteenth-century houses facing the river, with half the town arranged in row houses behind them, steep roads leading up to the cathedral and the cathedral close, a tranquil square occupied by wealthier townsfolk like doctors and lawyers.

The Martin house was on higher ground, so she negotiated the row houses until eventually she turned left into a small road mostly made up of cottages dating back to the 1950s. She'd walked every inch of Poppy Lane thousands of times in her life: to school, back from school, to catch the bus to Waterford city with Katy and Susie, to her job in a fast-food restaurant so she could earn money and study, and later to the train to Dublin and college, to the airport so she could explore the world. At night and from the comfort of her car, the lane looked older and shabbier than she remembered.

But the sensation was that of driving into her own past.

Number 15 was halfway down the street. From where Leila parked her car, under a streetlight, it seemed that the garden looked distinctly less cared for than it used to.

It's because it's night, she told herself as she walked up the path, fishing in her pocket for her key.

Flicking on the hall light, she set her bag down, shut the door, and looked around. After she'd left home, number 15 had finally been redecorated, the old paisley wallpaper replaced with a floral one her mother liked. The last time Leila had visited, the house had looked pretty and neat, with her mother's precious plants in pots all over the place: ferns, orchids, and spider plants with trailing spider babies hanging down perilously.

The plants were still there, she saw as she moved into the living room with its pair of two-seater couches facing each other, but they were neglected now. Withered leaves hung limply from dried-up earth. Every surface seemed to be covered in a film of dust. She reached out a hand and ran it along the mantelpiece, sweeping up a tidy pile.

And there was a smell too . . . Rotten chicken, perhaps?

She went into the kitchen, where the smell was more intense. Opening the fridge, she found the source. She shut the door quickly and glanced around. The kitchen was far from clean, which was so unlike her mother. Even when the house had been a shrine to old wallpaper and museum-quality linoleum, it had been spotless.

But now . . . Leila looked at the floor: clearly it hadn't seen a mop in a long time. She thought of her mother on her knees, attacking the old linoleum with a scrubbing brush. "It's the only way to get it properly spick-and-span, Leila," she used to say.

What had happened to change her mother so drastically?

Grace's house phone rang loudly, interrupting her as she was switching off the living room lights.

"Mum, it's Fiona. I know it's late, but I thought I'd phone and say hello. Has Michael rung yet?"

Grace had let her daughter in on the Katy-and-Michael-getting-engaged theory.

"No, he hasn't," Grace sighed, walking into the kitchen with the portable phone jammed against her ear. Suddenly she felt so tired it was all she could do to fill the kettle for a cup of herbal tea to bring up to bed. It was only just gone nine, but she'd had a busy day. "They're coming home tomorrow, so either he asked and she said no, or he didn't ask," she said wearily.

"Mum, don't be mental!" said Fiona. "There's as much chance of me winning Miss World as there is of Katy saying she won't marry Michael. Even though he wouldn't admit it, you know as well as I do that the whole reason he brought her to Paris was to get engaged. They're love's young dream. If I didn't adore them both, they'd make me sick, what with all the hand-holding and ear-nuzzling. They're like grooming chimps. Besides, they're already married — well, I feel as if they are, anyway," Fiona added. "Living together for five years qualifies as marriage in my book."

Grace laughed. Fiona had always been able to make her laugh, even during the dark days after the separation when Grace wondered if she'd been stark raving mad to agree with Stephen that yes, their marriage was essentially over, because how could they live separate lives with him in a flat in Dublin and her with the children in Bridgeport?

Fiona was a programmer at a hip tech firm in Dublin and appeared to have an endless supply of clever male friends to bring to family events. The anxious mother in Grace longed to see her daughter find one particular man she could settle down with, but she tried not to let on. Tonight, however, she was too tired to rein in her curiosity.

"Found anyone you want to groom like a chimp yet?" she asked, hoping it didn't sound as if she worried about her only daughter being alone at the age of twenty-seven. At the same age, she herself had been married with one small child and pregnant with Fiona.

Fiona, as usual, laughed it off.

"I'm choosy," she told her mother. "And no, it's not because you're divorced. Even if you and Dad were still happily married, I'd be choosy."

"Don't be choosy for too long, darling," Grace said, grateful that Fiona hadn't taken offense. There had been occasions when she'd got annoyed at her mother for touching upon what was clearly a sensitive topic. "I'm not trying to be intrusive, love, but I'd like to see you happy and settled with someone special . . ."

"Mum! That's entirely hypocritical coming from someone who lives on her own and hasn't dated since blue eyeliner was in fashion."

"I have dated, as you well know," Grace replied, thinking of the handful of men she'd gone out with briefly over the years. It was strange how you became so used to one individual that you compared every other man with him. Somehow none of them had ever quite measured up to Stephen. It was going on three years since she'd been on a date, and deep down she felt there was a hint of cowardice involved — not that she'd admit it to anyone.

"Besides," she added, "blue eyeliner is in again, according to some brave souls in the staffroom."

"Dating is in again too," Fiona reminded her sweetly. "There's no reason you can't give it a try, Mum. I don't know why you aren't on one of those online dating sites, looking for someone else. Just 'cause you and Dad split up doesn't mean you can't find true love. Dad has Julia. It *is* possible to find it more than once in your life."

Was there a wistful note in her voice, or had Grace imagined it? The guilt that sometimes hit Grace swamped her now.

"Maybe Michael's going to ask Katy to marry him tonight, over dinner." Fiona changed the subject swiftly and Grace knew it was her fault. She shouldn't have stuck her nose in. You couldn't push people into falling in love.

Or stop them when they were falling out of it.

Grace brought her tea up to bed after turning off all the lights, including the fake Tiffany one she knew Stephen had hated.

She adored her cottage. It was very different from the three-bedroom house she'd shared with Stephen when they were married. His tastes had run to modern things — unusual light fittings made from Perspex, walls of glass, and big modern canvases — while Grace had been more of a woman for vast comfy couches in front of the fire and toile de Jouy wallpaper in the bedroom, with the bed covered in plumped-up beribboned pillows.

She certainly had that now, she thought wryly as she carried her cup of tea and her phone into the bedroom. It was a bower of prettiness, for sure — but there was nobody to share it with, apart from when the window cleaner peered in every few months and had a good look around.

"That's a lovely room you have up there, Mrs. Rhattigan," he'd said once.

"Thank you, Jimmy," Grace replied crisply, trying to ward off this conversation. It wasn't that she thought she was a man magnet by any means, but over the years she'd found that when you were a divorced woman, the most unlikely men decided you were desperate for affection and threw themselves at you. They were always deeply offended and often rude when Grace discreetly threw them back.

"I was thinking my wife would love that sort of wallpaper," Jimmy went on. "It's coming up to her birthday and I could surprise her if I did up the bedroom. What would you call it? I never saw it before."

"I'll write the name down for you," said Grace, relieved. What had she been thinking of — imagining that Jimmy fancied her?

In bed, she ran through the day in her head, and then found her gratitude diary and wrote in it:

1. Having two healthy children.
2. The nice phone call from the multiple sclerosis charity saying thank you for the children's fund-raising last month.
3. Hector the debating teacher bringing homemade blackberry jam into the staffroom and giving everyone a pot because he was ill before Christmas and hasn't been in since.

She paused. What else? She'd worried about Michael and Katy, about seventeen-year-old

Ruby Morrison, about upsetting Fiona by asking about the men in her life.

That last worry was a nagging, anxious one, hiding in the recesses of her brain and ready to slither to the surface at weak moments. Why did a lovely girl like Fiona have no steady boyfriend? Like Grace, she was slim and dark-haired, and though Grace didn't have a vain bone in her body, she knew she wasn't bad-looking. Fiona had the same oval face, large, intelligent hazel eyes, and obedient silky hair the color of polished mahogany. She was funny, interested in other people the way Grace was, interesting to talk to . . . It made no sense that she hadn't been snapped up.

As for Fiona's suggestion that Grace try online dating — well, that was crazy. Grace was happy as she was. Fine, so the house could seem lonely when she arrived home on winter nights, but weren't single women the fastest-growing group in the Western world? She was normal, that was all.

She stared at her gratitude diary hopelessly. There had to be five things in it. Five.

She was so lucky; she had family, friends, a job she loved, and a pension. She didn't worry about every penny or how many slices of bread there were in a loaf the way some mothers in the school had to because of job losses in the recession. Compared to them, she had loads of things to be grateful for.

Finally she gave in and wrote:

4. I still have a job and a house and enough money to pay my bills.
5. Jimmy the window cleaner is not secretly lusting after me, which is an enormous relief.

Not the ideal things to write on a gratitude list, but they would do.

FOUR

Something old, something new, something
borrowed and something blue.

ANON

Katy Desmond had the radio on low as she
and Michael drove home from the airport.
He could sleep anywhere and was tired from
the plane, so she said she'd drive.

She liked driving, was an excellent driver
— even her father, a wildly critical person
when it came to most people's driving, said
so. Most of all, she liked the fact that she was
marrying a man who wasn't threatened by
her taking the wheel. She'd never seen her
mother drive her father anywhere. Even after
he'd had a few drinks at a dinner and Birdie
hadn't, Howard Desmond would insist on
being in the driver's seat. In the car and in
life.

He was an entrepreneur with the Midas
touch. Thanks entirely to him, Bridgeport
Woolen Mills were known all over the world,
and according to her mother, these days

Howard needed three phones to keep on top of it all. Katy knew that she was one of the few people to whom her father deferred, but it was the deferral of besotted love.

She'd never have been able to work with him in the business if he'd bossed her around the way he did everyone else.

They had some ferocious arguments in the office, when the rest of the staff flattened themselves against the walls and listened in awe as Katy argued with the boss. She often won the arguments too.

As she explained to Leila, "Dad just needs someone to stand up to him, and once he sees your point of view . . ."

". . . *eventually*," Leila liked to tease.

"Eventually," agreed Katy. "But he loves innovative ideas." She knew that his liking her innovative ideas was due to her being his daughter, but still. People needed to stand up to Dad. She wished her mother would.

When they'd been kids, Susie, Leila's older sister, thought it astonishing that Katy could ask the powerful and controlling Howard for anything, literally anything, and he'd get it for her. Susie, used to a life of secondhand everything, couldn't understand why Katy didn't ask for enormous birthday presents, given that her father would have happily bought the world for her if only she'd asked.

"You could have had a pony if you wanted it," Susie had said on Katy's twelfth birthday, when she'd been given a new bike. Susie, who was two years older and loved horses, desperately wanted a pony, but there was little money for such things in the Martin home. Their father was an invalid with a serious back condition, which meant he spent much of his time in bed. Their mother had had to become the breadwinner, and money was tight. Besides, Katy knew that even if they'd had the money for a pony, the fact that both girls helped their mother to care for their father meant there would have been no time to ride it.

"I don't want a pony," she'd pointed out.

But because his little girl ought to have the best of everything, and a pony was on his mental list of Things Girls Should Have, Howard had bought Katy a pony the following year. Unfortunately, she'd soon found that the adorable animal she'd spent six months riding wasn't even vaguely under her control when he got spooked and decided to bolt around the training arena in the stables.

"You should get back on the horse," Daddy had said crossly, when she'd announced that she was giving up riding.

"I did," Katy replied spiritedly. She hadn't a fearful bone in her body. "But I think I'm going to try something new. *You* ride him if you want."

Eventually cars had replaced ponies, and naturally, as soon as she was old enough to get her driving license, Katy had been given a brand-new red Mini Cooper with gleaming leather interior.

"If you weren't my friend, I'd hate you because you get *everything,*" sighed Susie as she and Leila were driven around Bridgeport by Katy at a jerky fifteen miles an hour on the car's maiden voyage.

"But now we can go places without waiting for the bus," said Leila happily.

"Or lifts," said Susie, who still couldn't drive because she had no money for lessons and because her mother never had time to teach her.

"Yeah, lifts," agreed Leila, glancing swiftly across at Katy from the passenger seat.

She and Susie practically never got lifts. Their mum was so busy looking after their dad that they didn't like to bother her, and in any case the Martin family car was so old that extra journeys might have pushed it over the edge. The only thing holding it together was a combination of rust, spray paint, and their mother's prayers. Every journey was taken with the sense that at any moment the car might come to a juddering halt in the middle of the road and never go again.

"It's an adventure," their mum used to say cheerfully on the rare occasions when she drove the three of them anywhere.

"I love adventures," Katy would say, being loyal to her friends.

She was lucky, she knew, looking over at Michael snoozing happily in the passenger seat. She'd grown up with enough money so that finances hadn't ever been a problem. The Desmond cars were replaced every other year. Dad would never have tolerated a member of the family driving an old banger like the Martin car.

Michael moved in his sleep.

"Are we there yet?" he asked, and Katy laughed.

"No, go back to sleep, darling."

Birdie Desmond, wife of the great and charismatic Howard and mother of Katy, was searching for her phone. She wanted to send a *Darling, hope you've both enjoyed Paris* text to Katy and Michael, although she wasn't sure when their flight got in. Was it first thing, or were they at the airport in Paris still?

A small, slight woman with a head of long silvery hair, at first glance Birdie could have been taken for any age between sixty and eighty. In reality she was on the cusp of her sixtieth birthday.

Her few friends bemoaned her lack of interest in self. She did nothing to conceal the ravages of life, her skin windblown from spending so much time in the garden — or perhaps from constant exposure to the full-blown gale of being at Howard's beck and call. She didn't seem to care about such things, but she was happy enough, they decided. Wasn't she?

Birdie found Howard's American phone on the windowsill in the den — he now had three phones: one for Europe, one for Asia and Australia, and one for the U.S. He was always leaving them under cushions in his armchair after having a Scotch and soda before dinner, and then forgetting about them.

But then, she reasoned, Howard had so many things on his mind. And she had so little in comparison.

"I wish *I* could sit at home all day and relax," he would say in the evening when, whiskey in his hand and the scent of dinner in the air, he'd put his feet up on the low table in the den and stare out at the beautifully maintained garden.

Birdie, who did most of the gardening herself, cleaned the house with help from the youthful Morag from the village, walked Thumper, her beloved dog, and spent hours rattling tins for a score of needy charities, as well as shopping for and cooking Howard's meals, would say nothing.

Howard was so clever with the business and it was thanks to him that they had this lovely house, she'd remind herself. Think of all the people who had nothing. The people who'd lost their jobs and could barely feed their families. She knew enough about that from her charity work. No, she had so much to be thankful for.

She and Howard lived in the rambling Vineyard Manor, an old but perfectly updated house with five glorious acres of garden, where Birdie spent so much of her time. The problem with a house this big was losing things — like her phone when she wanted to text Katy. She often wasted ages in the morning phoning herself on the house phone in order to track her cell down, listening carefully for buzzing noises because she always muted the sound at night.

She finally found it in the china bowl near the front door that held the keys.

"I'm going to tie you to me with gardening string," she muttered at it as she checked her messages. There was a text from Katy and she opened it happily.

Mum, ring me when you get this. We've just gotten home from Paris. Good news, not bad!

Birdie's mind instantly went to their engagement. What else could it be? Michael had been hell-bent on taking Katy to Paris for the thirteenth official year of their relationship — despite young love starting in the most innocent way in junior school, Howard had insisted that both of them were sixteen before they were allowed to go out properly.

Heart beating with excitement, she rang her daughter's cell phone.

"Katy, lovey, how are you? What's the good news?" she said as soon as the phone was answered.

But it wasn't her daughter. It was Michael.

"Birdie!" he responded with pleasure. "Katy's in the shower. We were on such an early flight, she only had five minutes in the hotel one. Give me a moment and I'll get her."

"Everything's all right, is it?" Birdie asked, the words flying out of her mouth before she could stop them. "Sorry, I realize Katy said it wasn't bad news, it's just I worry . . ."

"It's all fine," said Michael gently. "I promise I'll always take care of her for you."

"Thank you, I know," said Birdie, feeling stupid.

Where did this fear come from, this constant anxiety that something bad was going to happen? Her brothers weren't like that, although they'd been the apple of their father's eye while Birdie, shy and quiet, hadn't.

"Stop being such a little mouse, Birdie!" he'd roar with irritation, which naturally had the opposite effect.

"I had a bad night's sleep, Michael," she lied now to cover her silliness, because that was all it was really: silliness.

But there was no response from the other end, only muffled sounds, as though Michael had clamped his hand over the phone while he interrupted Katy's shower. Birdie could make out the hiss of water, and then it suddenly ceasing.

"Mum," said Katy, "I'm putting you on speakerphone. Michael and I have some news."

Birdie sank on to the bottom step of the stairs in the hall. Thumper, the family golden retriever, backed in beside her, angling his too-wide rear against her and looking back beseechingly. *Pet me, pet me.*

"We got engaged! Michael asked me to marry him —"

"And she said yes!" Michael broke in joyously.

"What else could I say?" Katy said, laughing.

"That you wanted to hold out for a better offer!" Michael joked.

"Mum, there is no better offer, is there?" said Katy.

"Lovey, I am so happy for you, for both of you," Birdie said tearfully. "He's a good man."

"Careful, he can hear you!" warned Katy.

"I know, and he's still a good man, one of the best," Birdie told her daughter. "This isn't good news, it's wonderful news. Have you set a date?"

"Well . . ." said Katy slowly, "we want to do it soon, not wait for three years or anything. I was thinking of June, because it's my birthday. I know that's only five months away, but we can do it, and then . . ." She paused before blurting, "We want to take a year off to travel.

Backpacking, see the world before we settle down for good."

"Oh," said Birdie, feeling the fear again. Her heart fluttered in her chest: the frantic rattle of sheer anxiety. Such dreadful things happened to young people on gap years.

"We'll be fine, Mum. Perfectly safe. I'll be with Michael, remember. He's built like a tank, who's going to hurt us? I'll text and email all the time," Katy added gently. "I promise. I know you worry."

"Of course you'll be fine," Birdie said, holding a shaking hand over her heart as if she could somehow calm its wild thrumming. "I am sorry I didn't travel myself," she added bravely. As if she'd have had the courage.

"We have a favor to ask, though, Birdie," said Michael. "Katy wants the wedding at the Vineyard — I know it's a big ask, to have a wedding in your house, but —"

"But nothing!" said Birdie, forcing the fear out of her head. The wedding: she would concentrate on that. "We'd love it. Your father will be delirious. He'll probably build a special wing!"

Birdie and her daughter laughed, both of them picturing Howard rushing around with assistants trailing in his wake, struggling to note his every command on their tablets or notebooks.

Beside a towel-clad Katy in their bathroom, Michael smiled but didn't laugh. He suspected that in Howard Desmond's eyes, not even the Élysée Palace would be grand enough for Katy's wedding. He had also long suspected that he, a humble college lecturer, was not grand enough for Katy either.

"We're only just back home," he said. "We thought we'd take you, Howard, and my mum out to dinner to celebrate on Friday night. I'm going to phone my father, but I don't know if he'll be able to make it on such short notice."

"He'll be there in spirit," said Birdie kindly. "I can't wait. Is your mother happy, Michael?"

"You're the first to hear, Mum," said Katy. "Grace won't mind, you know she won't. We're going to phone her now and then I'll phone Dad."

"You told me first?" Birdie held tightly on to Thumper's solid body for support. "That was so lovely of you both, thank you."

"Love you, Mum," whispered Katy into the phone.

Grace's cell phone buzzed discreetly on her desk. She ignored it, even though she could see from the picture on the front that it was her son.

She felt a frisson of pleasure all the same.

He and Katy *had* to have gotten engaged, because it was so rare for Michael to phone during school time: he knew better.

Even lunchtime was dodgy for receiving phone calls; left unwatched, the naughty contingent of the sixth grade would probably take it into their heads to escape en masse down to the forbidden park just off the schoolyard and play among the empty beer cans of an older generation.

None of these thoughts showed on Grace's fine-boned face as she faced the couple across the desk from her.

"Awful pity you don't play poker, Grace," Nora had sighed many a time. "With a face like that, you'd wipe the floor with everyone else."

"I tried strip snap once," teased Grace, and Nora threw back her head and laughed till she shook.

"Really?"

"Do school principals generally admit to playing strip snap?" Grace demanded.

"I've heard a hell of a lot worse," Nora said back. "A bit of strip snap is nothing, honey. I bet you kept your clothes on too."

"Wouldn't you like to know," said Grace with a grin, tapping the side of her nose.

"Ciaran's such a sweet boy at home," continued the mother in front of her now, desperate to convince Grace that this whole bullying allegation must be a mistake. "I can't see him hurting anyone really, can you, Kev?"

Kev sat with his big muscled arms folded and glowered at Grace, who decided that the time had come to end this going-nowhere interview with two parents who weren't hearing what she was saying.

"Ciaran has hurt five children this term in incidents ranging from pushing to kicking, culminating in yesterday's biting incident in the playground. It is highly unusual for children to bite when they're eight years old. Biting occurs among the smaller children, yes, but not in second grade. This is very serious, very serious indeed. The child Ciaran hurt was badly injured and is very upset. There were five witnesses, including his teacher, Miss Lennon, and the parents' garden committee, who were walking around the yard discussing the planned flower beds."

Kev's arms unfolded and he sat up straight. Witnesses: this changed the whole thing.

"Ciaran clearly hasn't learned that it is wrong to hit or bite other people, particularly ones smaller than he is. The child he hurt yesterday is both much smaller and from a younger grade," Grace added gravely.

She didn't know if any of this would penetrate Ciaran's father's head, but she had to try. It wasn't the child's fault that nobody had taught him to behave; he undoubtedly only practiced what he saw at home.

"I've talked this over with the board and we've agreed that we must suspend Ciaran for a week," Grace went on. "Now, if you could leave, and take Ciaran with you, that would be good. Here's a copy of the school bullying policy — which I have given you on four other occasions."

She paused. Was it worth telling them that the board had discussed expelling the child, something that had never happened before in her time? Probably not. She could only hope that the family realized exactly how serious this was.

Without another word she got to her feet, opened the door to the corridor, and ushered them out. It was a relief to close the door behind them. She'd had such a busy start to the day that she hadn't had a moment to herself to either wonder about Michael and Katy in Paris or give any more thought to what she could do about Ruby Morrison.

She'd slept badly, dreams about her son and daughter and little Ruby overlapping until she woke at four thirty knowing more sleep wouldn't come. To counteract this, she'd been drinking coffee all morning, which would stop her sleeping all over again tonight.

She quickly emailed the board members with detailed notes of the meeting with Ciaran's parents, then phoned the school secretary.

"Mary, can you hold all calls for ten minutes, please?" she asked.

" 'Course," said Mary. "Should I put a note on your door saying you're not to be disturbed?"

Grace's office was easily accessible to all, which was how she liked it. The children knew they could come to see her if they had a problem, any problem. But she knew that Mary would stand at the door like a sentry if required. Mary was wasted in a school, Grace thought fondly. She'd have been far better employed in a military facility, taking no backchat from rookie soldiers and four-star generals alike.

"No, Mary, it's business as usual. I just want to make a phone call in peace."

"Righto."

Mary never asked anything personal. Another of the things Grace loved about her.

Michael answered on the first ring. "Ma! Can you talk?"

"No, love, I've got a few of the fifth grade in here right now and I'm doing fingernail extraction for homework offenses. You know, the usual Tuesday morning carry-on in a busy school . . ."

"Funny, Mum," he said, and she could picture his smile. Michael's face was an open book, revealing everything he was thinking. She loved his smile so much: it took over his whole face, from the crinkles around eyes that were just like Stephen's to the broad grin that reminded Grace of her own father, who'd also been a gentle giant.

"We've got news for you — I'm putting you on speaker."

"Yes," breathed Grace.

"No, you should say it to her yourself, not on speaker," Grace could hear Katy whispering. "She'll want to hear it from you."

"Just tell me," Grace said evenly. "I've several possibilities in my mind, from lovely ones like weddings and babies, to terrible disasters like you're both stuck in a French jail and a gendarme's holding your phone in through the cell bars and the bail has been set too high and —"

"Mum, you're totally mad, you do know that, don't you?" Michael said.

"You told me often enough when you were a teenager," she retorted. "I prayed we were past that stage . . ."

"Oh, stop teasing your mother, Michael," said an exasperated Katy. "We're engaged, Grace!"

"I asked her on the Eiffel Tower and she said yes," Michael chimed in.

"The Eiffel Tower," whispered Grace. She breathed in and out slowly. "That's wonderful news," she said quickly. "Darling Katy, you're already part of the family. I'm thrilled you're getting married. You were made for each other — and I don't say that lightly."

"Do you think Fiona will be a bridesmaid?" Michael asked. "You know she hates girlie stuff." There was a note of alarm in his voice as he added: "She can't wear jeans to our wedding, I mean, really she can't."

"I'll get her into a bridesmaid's dress," promised his mother. "It might have to be made of denim, though, or some indigo wash."

They all laughed at the thought of Michael's sister clad in a denim dress, with her biker boots peeking out from underneath. Fiona hadn't been separated from her jeans since she was about six and first discovered the lure of denim.

And then the three of them were talking fast, discussing the date and the venue, and Grace had to reach into her desk for her tissues to wipe her eyes.

"It's truly wonderful news," she said finally. "I love you both, you know."

Through the opaque glass of her office door she could see several small shapes in the school's gray uniform: children being sent up either for being in trouble or on an exciting errand to show Ms. Rhattigan how well they'd done in their spellings or essays or maths.

"I have to fly. Little people at my door and they'll burst in any moment. Delayed gratification is not a child thing. You're home now?"

"Yes," said her son hurriedly. "Just got back. We'd like to take you, Birdie, and Howard to dinner to celebrate on Friday."

Grace heard the subtle change in her son's voice when he said Howard's name. She understood it. For all his bonhomie, Howard was not always easy company. His need to be in charge of everything was at the core of his personality, and he could barely last five minutes without interrupting someone.

Getting married wasn't just marrying one person: marriage meant moving into a whole new family, as Grace knew from her own experience. Even now, Stephen's mother still phoned her for a chat. Lesley Rhattigan had never quite recovered from her son's separation and subsequent divorce.

"You married for life, in a church, in God's eyes!" she'd cried after Stephen had told her about the separation, and then she'd phoned Grace to beg them to reconsider.

"Whatever he's done, can't you take him back?" she'd begged.

"He hasn't done anything, Lesley," Grace had said quietly. "Neither of us has. Our marriage is simply over, that's all. We want different things. I can't hold Stephen back any more than he can hold me back from what *I* want."

It had taken years for Lesley to recover from the blow. It was only thanks to Grace and Stephen's combined efforts at bringing up their children, ensuring that she was still very much a part of their lives, that she eventually reconciled herself to the fact that the marriage was over.

"It was all down to you, Grace," she acknowledged now. "You were always a lady, always the sensible one. You kept it civilized."

"Stephen was responsible for that too," Grace would say. As he had been.

In her large office outside Mr. Desmond's much bigger, oak-paneled office at Bridgeport Woolen Mills, Roberta could hear Howard whooping and hollering on the phone. Good news for sure. Either he'd won the lottery — and Roberta knew he didn't believe in gambling, calling it dumb luck — or he'd something very special lined up. Whatever it was, she hadn't heard him that happy since he'd won the enormous deal with the Canadian department store chain to supply them with Bridgeport products.

"I love you!" he roared, and Roberta stared down at her computer, wondering how to play this one.

Acting was useful when it came to being an executive assistant. Acting deaf and sometimes acting blind and dumb too. She was like those three wise monkeys rolled into one: she saw no evil, heard no evil, and spoke no evil.

"Roberta!" roared Howard's voice over the phone intercom. "Come in and bring your big pad."

A big deal needed a big pad in her boss's mind. Roberta often felt like telling him that you could write big ideas in tiny letters and they'd still be big ideas, but she needed this job and if she could stick it out for another eight years, she'd have put enough into her pension to find something where the stress levels were better.

The moment she woke that Tuesday, Leila had dialed the hospital, even though it was still only six in the morning.

Her mother had had a good night and was dozing.

"She's on a morphine drip, so she'll sleep a lot, plus she needs to rest," the nurse said. "She'll probably be taken off that today, though. If you come in now, she'll still be out of it."

"How about twelve?" said Leila.

"Whatever suits," said the nurse.

An hour before she was due to leave for the hospital, her cell phone rang. Her first thought was that it would be the nurse, ringing to say her mother's condition had suddenly deteriorated. To her relief, it was Katy, bubbling over with excitement as she announced her engagement.

"I'm so glad you're not in a meeting, Leila. You're only the sixth person we've told, after our parents and Fiona," Katy had said, and Leila decided that this was not the time to explain how things were in her world, that she was not at work in Dublin but in her mother's messy kitchen in Bridgeport.

"I'm so happy," she said, the rattle of tears

in her voice, and it was all Katy could do not to cry too.

"Why are we crying?" she asked.

"Happiness does strange things to you," muttered Leila, sitting on a kitchen chair. She was wearing a pair of elderly running shoes and leggings she'd found in her old room, along with a sweater that might have been Susie's. The floor looked too unclean to walk on in bare feet and she had no slippers with her. She had been working out some nervous energy by cleaning the kitchen before heading into the hospital, but she was leaving the floor till last.

"Now, details — when, where, how?"

"Bridgeport, reception in our house, early June, and you as a bridesmaid. I was thinking orange floral sofa fabric with lots of gathers around the waist and giant puffball sleeves," Katy teased.

"OK, it's in my mental diary and I am honored. But I am not looking like a sofa-cum-pumpkin. I want to be a goddess," Leila declared.

"You already are," said Katy. "Thank you, Leila. It wouldn't feel like being married if you weren't there."

"Try and keep me away," said Leila. "I am so happy, darling. Michael is just right for you. He's a beautiful person, inside and out."

"I know. I'm really lucky. If only he could come up with some hunky cousin we've never met to be best man, then we'd sort you out too."

Leila snorted with laughter. "I have sworn off men forever, Katy. I spend my life shuttling gorgeous movie stars around, guys that women all over the world dream about. Only I get to see them throwing tantrums because the pine nuts in their salad weren't toasted correctly or the makeup artist didn't have the right shade of base to make their nose look smaller for the press conference photos. They may be the hottest men you've ever seen, but at heart they're wildly insecure, self-centered idiots, who are *always* shorter than they look on-screen."

"That's work," Katy pointed out. "You need a hot civilian."

"There are no hot civilian men. It's either hot dysfunctional actors or not quite so hot but equally dysfunctional ordinary guys. It's a no-win situation."

"The right guy will appear one day," Katy said, and they both fell silent. Katy knew that Leila considered the departed Tynan to be the right guy.

"Sorry," said Katy.

"It's fine," Leila said. "I still . . ." She paused. This was something she could only say to Katy. Not to Mum and certainly not to her sister. "I still think about him every day."

"Sorry, I shouldn't have pushed you about

meeting someone new," Katy said, contrite. "He's a bastard, Leila. If I ever meet him again, I'll kick him where it hurts."

"No chance of that now he's in London with *her.* But thank you for offering."

"You can talk to me about it," Katy said. "Just because I'm Ms. Happily in Love, that doesn't mean you can't tell me stuff. I'm your best friend."

"I know."

"One thing before I go," Katy said. "Susie — should I ask her to be a bridesmaid too? I don't want her to be offended if I don't, and you know she might be."

There was silence as they both considered this.

Three friends never worked, Leila thought. Three was a crowd. She and Katy had been in the same class, and her older sister's innate shyness meant she'd hung out more often with them than with people her own age.

But their lives had gone in entirely different directions. While Katy and Leila had been having fun, going to concerts, having exotic holidays, Susie had become a mother.

Katy had staunchly said things like "It won't make a difference to the three musketeers," but it had.

And they all knew it.

"It's up to you," Leila said. "It's your wedding — you don't have to be responsible for everyone else's feelings." Even as she said it, she felt disloyal. With their blissful relationships and challenging jobs, they'd both abandoned Susie. But she was Susie's sister, and that changed everything.

"You're no help at all, Ms. Bridesmaid, with your therapy-speak," groaned Katy. "Blast it, I'll tell her and see how she reacts."

"Your mum must be thrilled."

"Delighted," Katy said happily. "I can see I'm going to have to rein Dad in, though. Once he heard we wanted the wedding at the house, he got thoroughly overexcited. We'll have him as a wedding planner if we're not careful."

"I expect him to behave like Franck from *Father of the Bride,*" Leila said, trying to rally but feeling her own misery rising. "Talking of parents," she said, not wanting to rain on her friend's parade but desperate to share her own news and be comforted, "I wasn't going to tell you, but I'm actually in Bridgeport right now."

"What?"

"Yeah, Mum was in a car accident yesterday."

She heard Katy gasp. "I'm so sorry — I've been wittering on about the wedding . . . why didn't you tell me straight off?"

"This was your moment," Leila pointed out.

"Yeah, but you're family and so's your

mum. That comes first. Is she badly hurt?"

"She fractured her hip and they had to operate yesterday evening to put a pin in it. And her poor little face is all black and blue. She looks so old all of a sudden, Katy. So frail. I'm always hearing about how people get infections in the hospital, like MRSA, and with Mum looking so weak . . ."

Finally Leila allowed herself to break down and cry as she hadn't done on the phone with her sister. "She looked so bad in the hospital last night. Ten years older at least, and the bruises, Katy. I almost didn't recognize her. The nurses say she's doing well, and people get over hip operations fine, but you can't be sure, and I love her so much, I can't stand to lose her . . ."

"Leila, darling, they do their best to tell you the truth in hospitals. If they say she's doing well, then that's the truth. Last night — did they want you to stay?"

"No, they sent me home. She'd had the operation and she was resting."

"OK then, that's a good sign. When my granny was dying, they told Mum to stay. And when your dad was dying, they told you to stay too, didn't they? This is different. You have to be positive. Should I ask my mum to come in with you?"

"No, I'm fine, but perhaps if she could visit Mum another time . . . ?"

"Of course. Once we're sorted out here, I'll

come around to see you, right? I'll text. Is Susie there?"

"She had to go home to Waterford. I phoned her this morning and she seems to think I can handle it all from now on. You know: she's done her bit and now it's my turn."

"Oh," said Katy, understanding. "Well, you *can* handle it. Listen, I'll be over later, but text if you hear anything new in the meantime."

"OK. And you can text me if you see any sofa material for my dress," added Leila.

"Wedding schmedding," said Katy. "Your mum comes first."

With a flurry of fond farewells, they hung up.

"Was she pleased?" asked Michael, walking in from the kitchen where he was making lunch before going in to work.

"Thrilled." Katy put her arms around her fiancé, saying the word happily to herself in her head: *fiancé*. "But upset. She's in Bridgeport, about to head off to the hospital — Dolores had a car crash yesterday and she had to have surgery for a fractured hip."

"Ouch," said Michael, wincing. "Poor Dolores."

"Plus Susie's having one of her moments. She's gone home, leaving it all to Leila," Katy said, faint irritation marring her face.

"Hey, kiddo, she has a son to look after. She's not fancy-free. She's never had the easiest time of it, even when we were kids," Michael said. "You and Leila were always more like sisters, and then things worked out so well for you both. You've got a great job in the family business and Leila has a fabulous job and the glamorous marriage."

"Tynan's gone, so she hardly has that now," Katy said, the tone of her voice showing exactly the regard in which she held Leila's ex.

"No, but she did have him for a while and it all looked wonderful," Michael went on. "Rock-star parties, heading off to gigs around the world, a husband who looked like he was in a band himself. It's got to be hard, seeing your two best friends happy and successful when you're a broke single mother like Susie, working in a call center for minimum wage."

"But she has Jack," protested Katy. "He's adorable."

"She's still on her own," Michael pointed out. "Nobody to take responsibility for any of it *ever*. That's tough. So of course she has to race home to take care of her son — and her mother — because nobody else is doing it."

Katy sat for a moment regarding the man she was going to marry.

"That's what I love about you," she said finally. "You surprise me all the time. I'd never thought of it that way."

113

"I've seen it that way for a long time," he replied. "I feel sorry for Susie. Always did. She was never as smart in school or as confident as you and Leila, and no matter how gorgeous Jack is, it's a lot of responsibility and worry being a single mum. Plus, you guys never see her anymore. Leila's too busy to make it back here. You're able to catch up with her in Dublin, but when was the last time Susie did that?"

Katy nodded. "You're right. We have to do something about Susie. She's definitely got to be a bridesmaid."

At that, her new fiancé laughed loudly. "This wedding will make all lives better," he boomed in an Old Testament voice.

Katy grinned. " 'Course it will. It's going to be absolutely wonderful. Everyone loves a wedding — and this will be *our* wedding, so it'll be doubly wonderful."

Even saying it, she felt a hint of remorse at how she'd blindly not seen things from Susie's point of view at all. Jack was always so beautifully dressed and adorable when they saw him: Katy had never really thought about the effort that went into taking care of him without a partner to help. And Susie was undoubtedly the person who had to be there for her widowed mother because Leila, heartbroken and miles away, wasn't.

Katy reached over for Michael's hand.

"I love you, you know," she said.

"Hope so," he replied. "Secondhand diamonds never make much money compared to what you paid in the first place."

FIVE

Being someone's first love may be great,
but to be their last is beyond perfect.

ANON

Vonnie Reilly crouched down till she was at eye level with the top of the wedding cake and looked at it carefully, moving the icing turntable so she could examine each inch.

Chocolate ganache was chocolate and cream mixed in precisely the correct way to get the glossy, almost mirrored finish her chocolate poppy cake needed. This cake, three round tiers covered in Valrhona chocolate, waiting for the application of wreaths of watermelon-red flowers, was perfect.

"It's good?" said Joan, standing close by, peering at the cake along with her boss.

"It's good. Very good," Vonnie said, smiling as she straightened. "Well done. I wasn't as good on my third attempt. It's smooth as silk."

Joan laughed. "You! I have never seen you mess up a cake, never."

"Never," agreed the small all-female team in the Golden Vanilla Cake Shop kitchen.

Vonnie grinned, thinking of her early attempts at cake decoration. Nobody here had ever seen any of those cakes, because by the time she'd opened the cake shop, she'd perfected her technique in every way.

Studying the curve of a rose to get the petals just so, working with food dyes to create exquisite shades seen in nature, coming up with new flavors with lemons, almonds, lavender, and raspberries, developing her own delicious dairy-, egg-, and gluten-free cakes: these details had been Vonnie's meditation.

She'd been baking her way through grief, and the one thing she could say with any conviction about grief was that sheer time made it a patient teacher. Years of grief had turned a non-cooking woman in the most agonizing pain into a person who could live again simply by virtue of the clear, simple rules of baking and decorating.

Unlike life, you knew where you were with cakes.

It wasn't just cakes, of course. Shane had kept her heart beating. Trying to be a good mother to a young son and not a woman deranged with loss over the death of her husband had helped her survive. But there was no doubt about it: hours bent over sugarcraft had stilled the anguish inside in a way she'd never have believed possible. The calmness of making her cakes and setting up her business in Bridgeport, the town where she and Joe had been so happy as visitors long ago, had helped her to be a mother again when she was barely surviving as a person.

Running a cake shop in a small town in Ireland had never been in Vonnie Richardson's life plan. She'd only taken one year of home economics in seventh grade back home in Brookline, Massachusetts, and she'd hated it. There had been lots of boring theory about vitamins and food groups, and absolutely no making muffins.

The old home economics teacher used to bake all the time, which had swayed the girls in Vonnie's grade.

"Imagine, cookies and doughnuts for lunch," they'd drooled happily.

It turned out that the new teacher, Miss Lusak, had a thing for fish. Fish pie, fish chowder, doing inventive things with smoked fish, and even one quahog shell cleaning class, after which Vonnie had begged to give up the subject.

Mother hadn't minded, as long as she kept up piano.

Vonnie knew she had the long fingers for piano — "Like mine, darling," her mother would say proudly — but she wasn't musical.

She was like her mother in many ways: tall, slender, with almost Scandinavian coloring of creamy blonde hair, fair lashes and cool gray eyes. But Violet Richardson was a passive woman, content to let life happen to her, happy with the life she and her husband enjoyed. Having her precious manicures when she could afford them, getting her hair done, watching her figure: all that was enough for her.

Vonnie, despite loving her mother and father hugely, wanted more.

She wasn't sure *what* until she was eighteen, met Joe Reilly, and fell in love.

She was waitressing for the summer at Wilma's Family Pancake House. Joe, a couple of years older and working two jobs to finance his second year at Boston U Law, was a short-order cook. At first, his easy line of patter annoyed her.

"Hey, Blondie, I've got pancakes with bacon, one egg, sunny, and two rounds of plain pancakes, maple syrup only."

After a few days of this sort of chat, she replied coolly: "My name's not Blondie, it's Vonnie." She'd whisked back her flaxen hair, aware that the looks she'd inherited from her mother meant she resembled a classic Boston rich girl and not the well-brought-up poor girl she really was.

"Vonnie's short for what?" said Joe, undeterred.

"Short for *stop wasting your time,*" Vonnie said, whisking the plates off.

"A bit of chat helps the day slip past," Joe remarked, turning back to his griddle. "That's what my mom says."

Vonnie went to her tables, delivered the plates, swept away empty glasses, refilled coffee mugs, and headed back to Joe for her next order. He was cute, despite the cook's hat. Cooks at Wilma's wore black tees, black pants, and white aprons. Joe was tall, with a muscular grace, and the dopey hat couldn't disguise the coal-black hair curling down underneath it.

He swiveled and saw her looking.

She'd have known he was Irish even without the name: incredible blue eyes, the fabulous bone structure of the darker-skinned Celts, heavy black eyebrows, and a mobile mouth made for talking and touching skin . . .

Vonnie, known for being cool, blushed.

For the first time, Joe's he-man demeanor failed and he looked hopeful. That hopeful look made Vonnie reconsider. He might be full of blarney, but at that moment he looked just as nervous as she was.

"And what would your mom say if she saw you distracting the waitresses from their jobs?" she asked quietly, leaning over the counter.

"She'd be thrilled. She wants me to settle down with a genuine all-American girl and have so many kids we can't remember their names."

Vonnie laughed out loud at such marvelous honesty. "That's not how my mother wants it."

Her mother's wishes were way more complicated.

"Honey?" A customer behind her smiled and waggled a coffee mug.

"Coming right up," Vonnie said, grabbing the coffeepot, filling the customer's cup, and then doing another expert sweep of her tables. She needed this job but she was drawn back to Joe.

"What does *your* mother want?" Joe said, taking longer than was strictly necessary to get the plates ready.

"A professional man with a good job," said Vonnie, without thinking.

Joe held up his spatula and said in his best Boston-Irish accent: "Ah sure, love, amn't I just the type of man you're looking for?"

"Will they like me?" asked Vonnie anxiously three weeks later, when Joe took her home for Sunday lunch.

She hadn't been inside many of her dates' homes, and the only boyfriends she'd brought home were sons of family friends, the sort of men her mother approved of. But Joe's life seemed to be so involved with family that taking her home was entirely natural to him.

"They'll love you," he said, kissing her cheek as they stopped in his old Miata at the intersection. "I'm presenting them for your approval, not the other way around."

"Joe! Stop kidding."

"I'm not kidding," he said, turning down Riverside Avenue, where a long line of clapboard houses trailed off in front of them. "If you're going to marry me, you're going to see a lot of the Reillys, all five siblings, in-laws, out-laws, grandkids, and Mom and Pop. I need you to like them."

"I'm not marrying you," she said.

"Living in sin, then, as my Granny Irwin would say. Whatever suits you. But my mother is going to be keen on the whole Catholic baptism thing when the children arrive, and it's harder to organize that if you're not married." Joe considered this. "Or maybe it's not? I'm on the black sheep side of the family when it comes to the Church. They might have changed the rules."

"They have not," hissed Vonnie, whose knowledge of Catholicism was limited to a sweet girl on her street whose parents went to daily Mass and engaged in complicated giving up of sweet foods before Easter. She was slightly afraid that the Reillys, with two Irish parents, would be saying the Rosary every night. How would she fit into that?

He'd told her all about his family, right down to the dog, who had been rescued by his animal-loving sister, and who quivered with fear when anybody new came into the house.

Vonnie hadn't told him much about hers. By comparison with the Reillys, her family seemed colorless.

Joe's home was a large gray clapboard house, the front of which told the family's life story. Two overflowing flower beds quivering under the weight of camellias and scented roses spoke of Joe's mother's devotion to the garden, and a homemade rocker on the porch was evidence of his dad's love of woodwork.

A small tricycle in the front yard said that Joe's married sister Sorcha was visiting with his niece and nephew. A rusty car smaller than the Miata up on blocks in front of the garage made it plain that his youngest brother, Sean, was hoping to get mechanic help from Joe's dad. His oldest brother's Mercedes station wagon was neatly parked close to the sidewalk, declaring that Liam and his pregnant wife Grainne were there.

"The baby's not due for another two months, but Liam thought he'd get the station wagon instantly," Joe said, eyes twinkling. "Being Liam, it had to be a Benz." Liam was a corporate lawyer in a blue-chip Boston firm, but Joe was an idealist — he wanted to work for the district attorney's office. "The side of good," he liked to say. "I like to wind Liam up by saying that. Works every time."

Inside there was the aromatic scent of roast

dinner, sports coming from somewhere, and a definite shouting match going on upstairs.

"Claire, I want my curling tongs back now!" shrieked a female voice. "Face it, your hair's going to burn off if you curl it anymore."

"That's Amy," whispered Joe, grinning. "Sixteen and a half. Hormones on full alert. It's like being backstage at a beauty contest with those two fighting over the cosmetics equipment."

"You'd want to have heard the argument when Claire bought the professional nail kit," said a voice. "I thought we'd have to call the police to break it up, but your Uncle Charlie was already here. Vonnie, hello. We've a full house today — they're all dying to see you."

A tall, slim woman in blue jeans wearing a sunflower-yellow blouse that went with her shock of truly Irish red hair was standing there, looking younger than a mother of six adult children should look.

"I'm Geraldine Reilly, mother to this man," she said, managing to reach up to ruffle Joe's hair and embrace Vonnie at the same time.

Vonnie smelled baking, floral perfume, and a hint of fabric softener. Geraldine had Joe's incredible eyes but her skin was pale and freckled. Her accent was still Irish, untouched by thirty years living in Brookline.

"We are so pleased to see you. Joseph

doesn't normally bring ladies home to meet us."

"Ma!" said Joe.

"Which means you're special, which means we're delighted to have you here." Geraldine took Vonnie by the arm and led her into a sprawling, well-loved kitchen with a giant oven, an oak table set for lunch, and a large seating area where several men were sitting on two old beige couches screaming at a TV set.

"I can't believe he missed that ball!"

"Told you he should be off the team."

"People," said Geraldine, not raising her voice, "Vonnie's here. TV volume down, please."

The sound was turned down and all the men, including a small boy who'd been hidden by the couch, stood up, smiling with genuine pleasure.

Pat Reilly, Joe's dad, hugged her.

"We're delighted to have you here, Vonnie. Dinner's nearly ready, and no game till it's over, boys."

Vonnie beamed back and thought how nobody in her home had ever hugged a guest. Even her grandmother and her mother exchanged cool kisses in the French manner: a hint of a peck on the cheek. Here, great bear hugs seemed to be the order of the day.

Even the trembly dog, a miniature fluffy

thing called Sparky, allowed himself to be petted.

"He loves you! He never does that with anyone and he's a very good judge of character," said Amy, the dog rescuer.

Joe smiled contentedly, as if he didn't need a dog to tell him anything about Vonnie. He sat beside her at the big table and held her hand under it as though he thought she might run off at any moment.

Vonnie had been given Joe's little niece Chloe to hold. The baby had stared at her with big solemn eyes for a full minute and then burst into loud, outraged tears.

"She still makes strange with people," sighed her mother, Sorcha, scooping her up. "Finn would let anybody hold him. Nobody can babysit this little honey except Mom."

"Wise child," murmured Pat, kissing his wife on the cheek.

Vonnie did her best to remember the names and, eventually, figured them all out. Amy was the youngest and had hair blonder than Vonnie's, though hers was dyed, she revealed.

"I'd kill to have hair as blonde as yours," Amy muttered darkly. "I'm not that dark, but the roots . . . if you don't keep up with the roots, you look like trailer trash."

"Amy, my own mother lived in a trailer when the house in Mayo burned down," Geraldine calmly rebuked her daughter as she handed around roast potatoes. "We called it a caravan. Never criticize anyone till you've walked a mile in their shoes."

"Yeah, and they're a mile away and you've got their shoes," laughed Sean.

"Sorry, Ma," he said, after a quelling glance. "It *is* funny."

Claire was next, eighteen, with red hair that refused all hair dye, as she told Vonnie dramatically.

"She did try, but it went orange," revealed Amy.

"And you wanted to borrow my Abercrombie jacket when exactly?" Claire said, a steely glint in her eyes.

"If I had hair like yours, Claire, I wouldn't dye it," said Vonnie. "It's beautiful, like a wood dryad's."

"You've got yourself a woman of learning," said Pat admiringly. "Joe done good."

Vonnie went the same bright red color Chloe had been when she'd begun to cry. Fortunately Pat began carving the turkey, and amid the plates being moved up and down the table and the ensuing arguments over the stuffing and people taking too many roast potatoes, almost nobody noticed.

"You get used to the nonstop chattering and teasing," said Sorcha, with four-year-old Finn beside her, eagerly eating mashed potatoes and his own mini portion of turkey. "Life in the Reilly house can be a shock to the system, though. Marcus." She smiled at the slim, olive-skinned man at the other end of the table, a now-contented Chloe on his lap. "Just kept silent for the first six months he was coming here."

"That was because nobody could hear him because you have to shout to be heard," said Sean, and then said "Ouch" loudly.

"No kicking under the table, Joseph," Geraldine said, not turning a hair as she delivered roasted squash topped with feta cheese and pine nuts to the table.

"We're not that bad," Joe said, looking imploringly at Vonnie. "I know you're not used to the whole big-family thing."

Vonnie turned to him, eyes shining, and said: "I love it."

Used to the reserved life of her own family, she found the Reilly clan utterly fascinating and welcoming. They laughed, argued, and made up, and no matter what, the whole family would congregate in the kitchen to eat together several times a week.

Geraldine was the center of it all: wise, funny, and gentle, and overseeing her grown-up family with such love and affection.

Geraldine was a nurse, Pat told Vonnie proudly when the dinner dishes were cleared away and Joe, Liam, and Sean were making headway with the cleaning up, with much joshing and splashing going on.

"She works with the local seniors' organization in her spare time," he added fondly.

"Ah stop, love, will you?" said Geraldine, exasperated. "He makes me sound like Mother Teresa, and I'm not, honestly, Vonnie. It's just helping out a little. You have to do something, don't you?"

"That's incredible," said Vonnie, thinking of how Violet hadn't worked since she'd got married. Their house was beautifully kept as a result, and Violet herself was always pretty, but other people's problems weren't really on her radar. She might buy the Girl Scout cookies at the door and was always keen to go to a charity dinner with their friends, but she didn't actively help anyone.

Vonnie didn't mean to start comparing, but she couldn't help it.

Pat was a mechanic. He'd have liked to have joined the police force, like his brother, but he had a bad leg. A fall as a child back home, never quite mended properly.

Geraldine stroked his cheek fondly. "I wouldn't ever sleep a wink if you were a cop, Pat. Always waiting for the knock on the door and the officers holding their hats in their hands."

By the end of the summer, Vonnie was hopelessly in love with Joe, whose passion for life — and for her — shone out of those incredible stormy-sea-blue eyes.

The following year, she graduated from

129

high school and was accepted at Boston U to study modern languages.

"It sounds so thrilling." Her mother's tinkling voice could be heard as she held a little tea party. She'd asked if Vonnie wanted to invite her "new friends," as she called Sorcha, Amy, and Claire. Violet hadn't met them, but Vonnie had spoken of them so happily, and Violet was, after all, a lady.

"No, Ma, it's fine," Vonnie said, unthinkingly.

"Ma?" Violet was horrified. "Veronica Richardson, I have never been so shocked in my life. I did not raise you to talk to me in such a manner. I know exactly where this language comes from, and don't tell me I'm wrong. It's that Joe Reilly. Well, I expect an apology this instant."

Vonnie stared at her mother, feeling the combination of love and pity she'd come to know so well.

Geraldine Reilly would laugh if one of her kids called her "Mother"; she might tease them, then everyone would sit down at the table and talk about their day. Claire would worry a little over her forthcoming exams and her mother would gently unruffle her feathers; Pat would say that a lovely old Camaro had come into the shop today and if he was twenty years younger he'd swear he'd buy it because it was a beautiful ride and in immaculate condition. He and Geraldine would smile at each other across the table, because it was just wishful thinking and the old station wagon was far more suitable to their needs.

Amy would have a story about a kitten she'd seen on the way back from school in the upstairs window of the Evanses' long-for-sale house, and even though she and Leandra had tried to get in, the door was locked and they'd had to listen to the kitten mewling plaintively for ages. Once, Vonnie and Joe had gone on a perilous rescue mission with her to free eight puppies that somebody had been trying to kill by dumping them on the edge of the freeway off-ramp. "The cruelty," said Joe, his expression furious . . .

"I'm still waiting for my apology, Veronica," said Violet, face white with strain.

Vonnie could see how truly shocked and upset her mother was. A woman whose whole world could be rocked by the wrong form of address from her daughter. It was what it was, Vonnie thought sadly.

"I'm sorry, Mother. It was a mistake."

She briefly touched her mother's cool, soft hands.

It was like living in two worlds and slipping between the two; except that the more she saw of one world, the less she could survive in the chilly formality of the other.

Two years passed, with Joe and Vonnie moving into an apartment of their own in Brookline — they'd have loved a district closer to the university but they couldn't afford it.

Thanks to a part-time summer internship, Joe was on track for a job with the state attorney's office.

Violet had her first angina attack the night Vonnie told her that she and Joe were moving in together, and an ambulance had to be called.

In the hospital, Vonnie and her father sat drinking horrible coffee as they waited.

"It's not your fault, Vonnie," her father said. "You have to live your own life. It's hard for her, that's all. She doesn't approve."

Despite her upset and guilt, Vonnie felt a surge of anger. "She doesn't see how amazing Joe is, Dad," she said. "She can't see beyond the fact that his parents are Catholics and came to Brookline with nothing. Why does that matter so much to her? This is supposed to be the land of opportunity."

He looked at her sadly, and she saw a man with his future long behind him; a man who wore his weariness lightly.

"Your mother didn't grow up with the sort of life and opportunities we gave you, sweetheart," he said. "She wants more for you."

"I know, Dad," sighed Vonnie.

Granny Lawrence had been a lady, but Grandpa Lawrence had been a vicious drunk.

There hadn't been money for manicures or trips to the hairdresser in that house.

Vonnie got up and hugged her father.

"For her sake, I wish both Joe and I had gone to Harvard and were off to live in Beacon Hill, but that's not the real world. I wish she could be happy for me."

"She will, darling, I'm sure she will."

"I love your eyes," Vonnie murmured one night as they lay together in bed in their small studio apartment. Wrapped in sheets, body to body and exhausted after lovemaking, she felt as if she could never be happier. She traced the coal-black eyebrows and the strong planes of his face, still gazing into his eyes. "A stormy blue, that's what they are," she said.

"The same blue as the Atlantic, Ma always says," Joe murmured.

"The Atlantic's supposed to be cold," said Vonnie, her fingers moving down to stroke the strong column of his neck. "There's nothing cold about you or your eyes."

"That's when I'm with you," he said, leaning against the pillow and gazing at her with such love. "I'm filled with fire. Fire to be with you forever, fire to marry you and make you happy, to have loads of kids, to be the best public defender this state has ever known."

"Marriage?" she said, pretending surprise for a moment. She knew he was going to ask her and she knew she was going to say yes instantly.

Joe planted a kiss on her forehead and a longer, lingering one on her lips. Then he slipped out of the bed and Vonnie groaned in dismay.

"You're not going to do more work? I thought you'd stopped for the night."

"Just getting something," he replied, rifling through his college sports bag.

When he turned, he was holding a small navy leather box in one hand.

Vonnie sat up, letting the sheet drop. Nakedness never bothered her around Joe; he was so comfortable in his body that any lingering hang-ups she might have had had vanished.

At the side of the bed closest to her, he dropped to his knee and opened the box, holding out a single-diamond ring in a simple round gold setting. It was small, the opposite of the jaw-dropping Tiffany ring her mother would have liked. But Vonnie loved it on sight.

"Will you marry me, Vonnie?"

No words came out at first. She didn't *have* any words, she who'd been a formidable debater, who'd been told she had poise and confidence in school. Instead she reached around his neck and pulled him to her, kissing him.

He held on to the ring.

"Is that a yes?"

"It's a yes, a definite yes," she said.

"Hand," he commanded, and he slid the ring on to her long, patrician ring finger.

They both stared at it contentedly. Vonnie didn't feel any of the dizzy happiness other women talked about. She felt instead the bone-deep joy of everything being just perfect.

"It looks right there," Joe said, angling his head to look at the ring. "I wanted something you'd like, something simple and elegant."

"Like me?"

"Yes, like you."

She leaned forward and kissed him.

"Can we tell our grandchildren this story?" she added. "That you proposed to me stark naked in a small walk-up apartment in Brookline?"

"Should I have chosen a fancy restaurant?" Joe pulled back the covers and slid his long body in beside hers.

"No," whispered Vonnie. "Not at all. We'd never have been allowed back if you had. You have to dress for restaurants."

He laughed.

"You did it perfectly, Joe," she said. "Never change."

Denise O'Brien stood outside the Golden Vanilla Cake Shop and swept a critical eye over the premises. In keeping with the old-fashioned winding street, the shop window was decorated in mellow golds, with antique-looking glass cases inside which sat elegant cakes of every hue: traditional cakes trimmed with ribbons and pale roses; cakes that looked as if they'd been dipped in watercolors, pale primrose at the top, with the lower tiers deepening to a heady saffron. Flowers, tiny brides and grooms, even a miniature sparkling silver palace decorated them.

Her daughter Eve stood at her side, hands clasped together. "Isn't it beautiful? Like a fairy-tale cake shop."

Denise allowed herself a snort. Far from fairy tales Eve had been reared. Still, if Eve wanted this nonsense, Denise was prepared to be a little pliable. Just a little.

"No sparkling silver palaces," she said sternly. "What would people think?"

What people would think was an important factor in many of Denise's decisions.

They went inside, Denise ignoring the tinkling bell over the door as more of the fairy palace flummery.

On one side was the straightforward shop part of the business, where cake-making supplies were sold; on the other, where she and Eve were obviously supposed to sit, was a shrine to cakes of every sort, from flower-bedecked bridal ones to birthday cakes shaped like cars. Glass cabinets done up in the distressed cream fashion that Denise *hated* housed the creations, while in front of an equally distressed cream desk were armchairs with loose covers and faded floral cushions.

Clearly the Golden Vanilla Cake people were into that Californian shabby chic, Denise decided with a disapproving sniff: cream hearts on ribbons dangling from the cabinet handles and a chandelier with colored glass overhead. What was wrong with nice Irish furniture in place of this distressed rubbish?

Eve had insisted that the Golden Vanilla Cake Shop was the best option because it catered to every allergy possible, and — this had been the clincher — it was always being written up in the press as being the last word in wedding cake elegance because of the innovation and brilliance of its owner.

When Eve had finally got engaged — and it had taken so long, her mother had almost given up hope — Denise had envisaged sourcing everything for the wedding from *outside* County Waterford. Anyone in the county could have a cake from here. But for an O'Brien wedding — the first proper O'Brien wedding, because Pierce marrying that awful Glenda-Louise in Las Vegas hardly counted — Denise had entertained visions of herself and Eve traveling to Dublin for dress fittings and cake discussions in posh establishments.

She'd been looking forward to discussing all the arrangements at her weekly bridge night; it would be one in the eye for Eleanor Fitzsimons, who'd carried on as if her daughter's wedding last year was quite the last word in style.

However, it had transpired that Eve's future mother-in-law was a celiac and therefore couldn't eat a proper wedding cake with wheat in it, so this place with its list of cakes that could be made to order without flour, dairy, or eggs was the ideal choice. Or so said Eve.

"It's so exclusive too, Mum, I thought you'd love that . . ."

Thwarted in the early stages of the planning, Denise had been determined to let her displeasure be known. And yet she couldn't fault the owner of the cake company, a tall, pale-skinned woman with what had to be natural blonde hair tied back in a severe plait. Denise patted her own dyed blonde hair in its bouffant curls from the morning blow-dry and felt envious of this elegant creature with her strange coloring and effortless poise.

Vonnie Reilly had greeted them with such cool composure that Denise wasn't sure it would be wise to snipe about how a local company might not be up to the mark for such a high-class wedding. Besides, it was clear from her accent that Vonnie was American, so perhaps all was not lost. An *American:* well, that made a difference.

Unusually for her, Denise began to feel

overdressed in one of her nicest knit suits with her pearls and the Roger Vivier pumps she kept for special occasions. Vonnie wore slim black trousers and a gray sweater that made her look like a model from a Scandinavian furniture ad. Her only jewelry was a slender beaten gold wedding ring that emphasized long fingers with short, perfectly clean but unpainted nails. She had to be forty or thereabouts, Denise decided beadily, but as to whether she was rich or poor . . . there was no sign of it from how she dressed, that was for sure.

Denise liked knowing where people stood on the social scale. Assessing accents no longer worked — people with the most dreadful accents turned out to have giant houses and jewels to beat the band. And the same with dress. But Vonnie Reilly seemed to have that upper-class American thing going on: a cool elegance, politeness, a hint of ancestry going back to the *Mayflower.*

Not knowing quite where she stood, Denise decided to play it carefully.

"Mrs. O'Brien, Eve, would you like tea or coffee?" Vonnie asked, sitting behind the desk on which sat a very pretty flower arrangement.

"Coffee for both of us," Denise answered in her faux voice, the one she used for answering the phone. No need to ask her daughter what she wanted: Eve always had what Denise had.

So that was the way it was, Vonnie thought to herself as she phoned through to the kitchen and asked for a cafetière, three cups, and the wedding platters to be sent in.

After six years running the business, Vonnie knew that every wedding had a queen bee — a member of the bridal party who had been waiting long years for this opportunity to seize control of arrangements with the zeal of an army general.

Often it was the mother of the bride. Or Momzilla, as Lorraine — one of the younger members of staff — liked to call them.

"There's a Momzilla on the phone wondering if anyone else has had the orchid-decorated cake recently, in case they both end up in the society pages and the sense of their wedding being *utterly individual* is lost."

"One day you will forget to press the mute button on the phone and our business will be ruined," Vonnie would say, taking the phone from Lorraine's hand and soothing the mother-of-the-bride in question.

Lorraine thought that marriage was a deluded venture, even though she made her living out of it because wedding cakes formed a large part of their business. "It's the twenty-first century, why marry at all?"

"You're absolutely right," Vonnie would reply, deadpan. "Let's close the shop in-

stantly. Why are we making cakes that con-
tribute to this insanity?"

"Smarty-pants," Lorraine would laugh
good-humoredly. "I meant for people my age.
People in their twenties. Marriage is like
women not having the vote or something."

"Or being a sheep," Vonnie would interject
helpfully.

"Exactly." Lorraine would smile and go
back to making sugar roses.

Lorraine was as gifted as Vonnie herself
when it came to making flowers, and nobody
could make orchids the way they did. Sometimes the blooms looked so real that people
thought they were actual flowers placed skill-
fully on the cake, until Vonnie gave them a
mini sugarcraft orchid to handle.

She watched Denise O'Brien scanning the
room with gimlet eyes. Yes, Momzilla. The
poor bride herself was at least Vonnie's age,
forty, and clearly in her mother's shadow. At
least she wasn't going to be a Bridezilla,
marching around with a clipboard as if
producing a multimillion-dollar action movie.

Vonnie knew that the brides who already
had children and demanding jobs were less
likely to go down this route. Working-mother
brides appeared to have little time to worry
about soft coral versus pale peach sugar paste
ribbons, and were good at the high-speed
decisions.

"Oh, blast, go for coral. I can't remember

the exact shade of the bridesmaids' dresses, I don't have time to drop a bit of fabric in, and to be honest, in the grand scheme of things, it really doesn't matter. If I don't have this report in by Friday, I'm fired, wedding or no wedding" had been the phone message left on the shop's answer machine at seven that morning by a forty-three-year-old bride with three children, a high-flying career in an accountancy firm, and no time for hand-wringing.

Clearly that wasn't going to be the case with the O'Brien/Sylvester wedding. With Mrs. Denise O'Brien playing queen bee, there was bound to be hand-wringing over every last detail.

Mrs. O'Brien's mouth had been set in a hard line since she stepped into the shop, and she seemed to have brought enough bad energy into the space to make even the sugar-craft flowers wilt a little.

Not for the first time, Vonnie wished she had a special wand for dealing with those few bad-tempered mothers of the bride who had no idea of the misery they spread. But none of this showed on her face as she handed out books of photos from which Eve and her mother could make their selections. As a professional in this field, Vonnie had more than once thought that an ability to act in front of customers was a great boon.

The coffee arrived, and with it a tray of

samples of the various types of cake available for both ordinary and gluten-intolerant guests.

"Thanks, Inge," said Vonnie to the girl who brought it all in.

Inge nodded. "I'll just get the profiteroles," she said, and left them to it.

"They're so sweet," cried Eve happily, picking up a tiny morsel with a simple buttercream swirl on top.

The swirls were every color imaginable, the fillings ranging from chocolate to fruit with biscuit cake thrown in, all served on the shop's pretty antique cream platters. The whole thing could have been photographed for a magazine just as it was. Vonnie was very keen on perfect presentation.

"That stuff's what they serve at children's parties," said Denise rudely, pointing a ruby-red-tipped finger at the biscuit cake samples.

Six years ago, Vonnie would have been thrown by such a comment, but the past had changed her. Rudeness no longer unnerved her. People were rude for such strange reasons: insecurity, anxiety, or an inability to express themselves any other way. It rarely had anything to do with the person they were being rude to. Once you'd cracked that, Vonnie thought, you understood the whole thing.

"You'd be amazed at what people like to eat nowadays," she said in the placid tone that had earned her legendary status among her staff. "The beloved fruit cake has had its day in the sun and many people want a simple sponge or chocolate cake, or our angel food cake. Or our very special biscuit cake. Have a taste. We use the best chocolate. Children don't get *this* at parties, I guarantee that."

With her great gray eyes clear and bright, she looked at the older woman in a way that made Denise O'Brien falter.

For years, Denise had delighted in being able to say what she wanted to people who ran shops and businesses. She was accustomed to going into the butcher's and loftily telling him not to give her fatty beef like last week, thank you very much. But this serene, calm woman, who looked as if she'd remain unflappable if a volcano erupted on Bridgeport's Main Street, was holding out a plate of cakes in a manner that indicated there would be no ordering around here.

"I'll try it," said Denise, recovering. She bit into the cake, and the chocolate and shortbread exploded into a symphony of taste in her mouth. She felt about three years old, experiencing her first Easter egg all over again. "Goodness, it is nice," she said, unwilling to praise too much.

"It's gluten-free too, so your future mother-in-law can eat it," Vonnie told Eve.

"This?" Eve spoke for the first time in ages.

144

"But it's lovely. I thought it would be dry and crumbly."

Vonnie smiled. "Not the way we make it," she said. It had taken months to get the recipe just right. The lack of gluten in the careful combination of flours meant the biscuits could be dry, but Vonnie had worked through the recipe endlessly until she'd ended up with biscuits everyone adored, either in or out of the cake.

"I've always loved biscuit cake," Eve went on, almost dreamily. "Could we have the whole cake, three tiers, of this?"

"One tier, Eve," interrupted Denise, shocked. "One tier. People expect proper fruit cake. It's traditional."

"But Vonnie says traditions are changing," said Eve, clearly emboldened by the variety of cake in front of her and the way Vonnie was standing up to her mother. Nobody stood up to her mother — it was dizzying to watch.

"They don't change that fast," Denise snapped. "This is a fad. Vonnie, I'm sure there was no such thing as chocolate biscuit cake for weddings in your day. You're married." She gestured at Vonnie's sole piece of jewelry, the wedding ring in beaten gold. "I bet you didn't have children's cake for your wedding?"

"I try not to remember my wedding," said Vonnie, her face closing.

"Divorced?" asked Denise, a penciled-in

145

eyebrow arching.

Some demon got hold of Vonnie's head. "Yes," she said. "It's easier now that he doesn't have the restraining order against me, obviously. The neighbors hated the armed police turning up. Right, Eve, which cake would you like — since it's your wedding?"

"What did they go for in the end?" asked Lorraine, when Vonnie had shown the O'Brien women out of the shop and returned to the kitchen.

"They went for general disagreement," said Vonnie shortly, still wondering what had come over her. It was an inviolable rule of business not to annoy the hell out of the clients at the first meeting, but she didn't care. Denise and her fake snobbery had got under her skin. And how dare she ask about Vonnie's own wedding?

Lorraine, who had been deep in concentration, decorating a cake with a spray of winter red roses, heard the tension in her boss's voice and looked up.

"What's wrong?" she asked.

But Vonnie had gone, exiting the kitchen via the rear hallway off which the toilets and storerooms were situated.

In the small loo, she splashed cold water on her face because she needed something to shock her back to the present and she'd already had too much caffeine. Any more and her heart would jump out of her chest.

The icy water splashed onto her collarbones and down her front. It took ten minutes for the water heater to work in winter, but there were certain circumstances when that came in useful, Vonnie told herself grimly. There was nothing like cold water on a cold day for bringing you back to yourself.

She must have been mad to think of falling in love again. After loving Joe so much, after living through his death, she didn't think she'd ever be totally human again. You only got one chance in life. It would never work, never.

Besides, Jennifer was working very hard to see to that. There could be no second chances for Vonnie.

"Vonnie, you in there? Those people you just saw — Eve O'Brien's been on the phone to say she loves the chocolate biscuit cake and wants that for all three tiers of her cake," yelled Lorraine.

Vonnie blinked at herself in the mirror. There had been a coup in the O'Brien car on the way home, clearly. Maybe she should try being mad more often in front of tricky clients.

"Take a message and I'll call her back," she said.

She was in no doubt that Eve's mother, the difficult Denise, would eventually be on the phone herself to change the order, probably on the grounds that her daughter had taken leave of her senses. But still. Vonnie didn't care either way. Life was too short.

Staring at herself in the bathroom mirror, she did some deep breathing. It was unlike her to be so anxious, but Ryan had said he would talk to Jennifer before the weekend. He was going to tell her about the house on Poppy Lane. It was a game-changer, for sure.

Vonnie thought of how she *might* have explained her personal circumstances to Mrs. Momzilla O'Brien:

I'm a widow, my husband died in a car crash seven years ago and I thought my life was over. But I kept going for my son — you keep going for your children, don't you? I came to Ireland because Joe and I had always dreamed of living here. He had relatives here and we'd visited twice. Being here helped. The memories of Joe were strong but didn't overpower me. I baked my way out of misery and from somewhere, I don't know where, I got the idea for this shop because I needed a job.

Then, even though I wasn't looking — because why would I look: I'd met and lost the love of my life — I met Ryan. He's amazing. I didn't think I could fall in love again, but I did. He's separated with two daughters and . . .

The mental story stopped.

There was such a big difference between

separated and divorced. Ireland's divorce laws made people who'd split up jump through so many hoops to finally divorce. It was all so different and slow compared to back home. But Ryan was special; she loved him, even though she'd honestly never thought she'd love again.

If Momzilla O'Brien was normal, she might have patted Vonnie's arm and said tearfully, *Isn't that lovely for you, pet. You've been through so much, you deserve your bit of happiness.* But this mother of the bride looked far too bitter for that.

And Vonnie's second chance at happiness still threatened to elude her, because even though Ryan was a wonderful man and she was stunned every day at finding love again, his not-yet-divorced former wife was determined to stand in their way.

Six

I will remember always that marriage, like life, is a journey, not a destination — and that its treasures are found not just at the end but along the way.

ANON

Jennifer Morrison knew she was going to be late for the makeup-demonstration-cum-coffee-morning at her neighbor's house, but she couldn't drag herself away from the television. This was the best bit, the DNA test where the love rat was revealed on television and everyone got to hiss at him for pretending he hadn't fathered a child with another woman.

She'd loved all those confessional TV shows from *Jerry Springer* onwards, and today's cable show had two women glaring at each other as the TV host waved a piece of paper in his hand.

Face sad, he addressed the man's wife: "This DNA test proves he cheated on you and lied when he said he'd never had sex with this woman; that he certainly wasn't the father of this woman's child. He's your husband. What do you want to do with him now?"

The audience growl grew, like wild cats fighting over meat.

Ryan used to hate those shows.

"It's vigilante justice," he'd say. "The audience probably want to hit those guys over the head with their handbags before they can reach the parking lot."

"He shouldn't have lied," Jennifer would say.

To her, it was simple: love was defined in very strict terms. Once you stepped over any of those lines, you deserved what you got, even if it was an outraged audience shrieking at you and threatening abuse.

Which made it worse that her breakup with Ryan lacked the simple right/wrong split.

Ryan hadn't cheated.

He hadn't got anyone pregnant, hadn't found another girlfriend, hadn't played any of the roles Jennifer would have been comfortable with.

"I can't live with you anymore, Jen," he'd said. "I'm sorry, but it's the truth. We're too different. We fight all the time. I seem to make you angry by just breathing. I can't live my life like this."

Jennifer had stared at him.

Yes, they fought, but didn't everybody?

What was wrong with that?

"Ryan, babe, don't talk rubbish . . ." she'd begun.

But he was steadfast. Their life was one long argument. He didn't think that was love.

"I can't stand arguing. Did you know that? I hate it when you just want a fight, and no matter what I do, I can't make it work. We'd be better apart. We could share custody . . ."

Here, *finally,* was something Jennifer could grasp on to.

"You are not taking away my girls!" she'd shrieked.

"But, Jennifer, we share everything to do with them. I take them to school every morning —"

Rage and pain fought to have their say in Jennifer's brain.

"I don't care, they stay with me."

Ryan had wanted mediation to organize the split amicably; Jennifer had thought it was a load of claptrap and wasted no time telling the mediator so.

"Don't tell me we need to think about our girls' futures and not our own battle," she'd hissed at the woman they'd waited a month to see, who had been calmly discussing how they could dissolve their marriage with the least aggravation possible. "He left us, isn't that enough? I have to cope with that and he can see them when I'm in the mood." Which would be never.

"Oh, honey, did you have to say that?" her mother had asked afterwards. Mom was a great one for never letting the sun set on her anger, although she could shout just as well as Jennifer when she wanted to.

"Yes, I did," Jennifer said. "So?"

"Ryan is great with Ruby and Shelby. He adores them, you know that."

Her mother sounded weary, which was how she sounded in all phone conversations these days.

"Aren't you on my side?" demanded Jennifer.

"We're talking about your daughters. When it comes to them, we don't need sides."

"You're not the one who's been dumped," Jennifer said fiercely. "Ryan has taken enough from me. He's not taking them too. He should pay."

Three years on, she would say the same thing if she had the chance.

Sure, he paid maintenance, paid for the big house in The Close, did everything by the book, and was never more than a moment late dropping the girls back from his legally agreed weekends with them. But he wasn't paying the way she wanted him to pay. Instead, he was dating a WASPy blonde American cow who ran a cake shop — although on her website she didn't look like she'd ever so much as licked a wooden spoon once.

Worse, said blonde cow got to spend every second weekend near Ruby and Shelby, even though Jennifer had done her level best to scupper that. Legally, she hadn't a hope, her lawyer said.

The lawyer's bills were expensive, and apparently Jennifer couldn't get Ryan to pay them, so she backed off.

Her mother, who tried to get her out of the house and living again, wisely said nothing when Jennifer imparted this information to her.

Nobody else wanted to know how angry Jennifer was feeling. She knew her anger had driven friends away. People expected her to get on with her life and find a job, find someone else, be happy. But she couldn't.

She finally switched off the TV when vengeance had been done on the show and hurried upstairs to run a brush through her hair. She didn't look in the mirror: she hated what she saw these days. She lived in clothes bought from catalogues or online: shapeless black garments with elastic waistbands, accessorized with large costume jewelry and eyeliner. Her own purdah. No amount of makeup was going to change that.

The demonstrator was well into her spiel when Jennifer made it across the green to another of the big houses in The Close. The woman was extolling the benefits of a new moisturizer made from what sounded like raw superfoods and angel's milk.

Jennifer grabbed a coffee and two pieces of chocolate Swiss roll from the buffet table and sat down.

"Our hostess, Nuala, has been trying this product for weeks now," the demonstrator said, letting Jennifer's neighbor take the floor.

Nuala had utterly disarmed Jennifer a week before by inviting her to the party.

"It'll be fun. Coffee, cake, and no need to buy. Plus you get fabulous samples. I promise you, it's an amazing range. Really works on those laughter lines."

Laughter lines, Jennifer thought afterwards, wishing she'd just said no. What bloody laughter lines? She had great rivets of misery in her face, not laughter lines. Still, it was a morning out, and she didn't get many invitations these days because she'd fallen out with so many of her old friends. People thought they had the right to tell you where you were going wrong and give you advice at the drop of a hat — and Jennifer hated advice, hated being pitied. So although she'd once been the life and soul of all parties, invitations were now thin on the ground, and here she was listening to Nuala and the makeup company rep singing slightly different songs from the same hymn sheet.

At least the models in the brochure were women of her own age and not the usual dewy-faced children companies hired to sell wrinkle cream to forty- and fifty-year-olds. Given the way makeup advertising was going, Ruby was probably the right age to advertise moisturizer to her mother's generation.

Ruby was in the same class as Nuala's daughter Cliona, who used to be a great pal but was never around their house anymore. None of Ruby's friends visited the Morrisons' house these days. Even Ruby wanted to be out all the time.

By the end of the morning, Jennifer had been persuaded to buy the damned moisturizer as well as a massage oil.

"For someone to rub into you . . ." the demonstrator cooed as she totted up the bill.

Yeah, the postman if I bribe him, thought Jennifer grimly.

"Oh goody, I love being rubbed with oils," she said in her most sarcastic tone.

She stayed till the bitter end because she wanted to talk to Nuala alone. Ruby was being so weird lately. Jennifer wondered, was it just teenagerdom and hormones? She'd been difficult enough as a teenager herself — probably God playing a trick on her and letting her get a taste of her own medicine.

"How's Cliona?" she asked idly, because she didn't want Nuala to know she was unsure of herself here. Jennifer hated people having the upper hand.

"Great," said Nuala, tidying up.

She sliced up some carrot cake.

"Do you want to take some home for the girls?" she asked. "But then you bake far better than I do."

"I don't do it so much these days," Jennifer said, which was partly true. She loved baking, but she only did it now when she was angry. Which was, admittedly, a lot of the time. But buying calorific desserts in the supermarket was easier.

"And Ruby?"

"Oh, you know, tricky," Jennifer replied. "Not keen on inviting anyone home anymore. I expect they're all the same now . . . ?"

The look Nuala gave her made Jennifer instantly furious with herself for letting her guard down.

"Cliona's always been a bit of a home bird. We're lucky that way," Nuala said.

Jennifer felt like flinging the plate of cake in temper. Nuala looked so smug. *Her* daughter loved to stay home and play happy families, she seemed to be saying. *It isn't so easy when your husband's broken the family up,* Jennifer wanted to shout, but then it would be all over both The Close and the school that Jennifer Morrison was falling apart: *Put on tons of weight, let herself go, and now she's shouting at coffee mornings.*

Nuala should try living with what she had

to put up with.

Jennifer tried, she really did, but it was so hard. Hearing the girls chatter about life with bloody Vonnie drove her insane. It had been fine when Ryan had lived alone on nothing but takeaways, but since he'd taken up with that damn woman, he'd had a life. Jennifer had no damn life.

At least Lulu, her mother, was on her side, her only ally, albeit a constantly nagging one.

"Come on, Jennifer, you've got to get out and about, start seeing other men, darling," she was forever telling her. "You're only young once. You can't give up just because your marriage failed. My girl never gave up on anything in her life."

Jennifer managed a watery grin, but inside she was thinking that she was nobody's girl anymore. Nobody's anything. Nobody's wife, anyway. It was hard being a brilliant mother when you were in pain and felt rejected.

She took a slice of cake and looked at the brochure with its creams and serums. She'd buy it all. She'd ring Nuala's makeup person, who was now gone, and tell her she'd changed her mind, that she wanted more than two products. Ryan shouldn't think he was going to squander their money on another woman. Not if she had anything to do with it.

The radio in the school staffroom was tuned

to a lunchtime talk show on which a panel discussion was under way about people giving up hectic all-hours jobs in favor of part-time work where they could enjoy home life.

Grace sat with a much-needed cup of tea and listened along with everyone else not on yard duty.

"Are we killing ourselves for nothing when we could be having more relaxed, stress-free lives?" asked the radio host.

In the studio, putting one side of the argument was a woman who'd once run a fabulously successful company but said she'd never had the chance to put her children to bed. Realizing that she'd spent more time on aeroplanes than curled up on the couch with her family watching movies, she'd sold the business and bought a house in the country. Now she kept chickens and pigs, baked her own bread and spent every waking minute with her children when they weren't at school.

The other side of the coin was represented by a younger woman who felt blocked from rising in her chosen career because of inherent sexism and said she was never having children because that would totally ruin her prospects.

"Prospective employers can't legally ask if you want children in the near future, but you know for damn sure they'd like to," she said. "So I say it up front. I'm a career woman with no time for children."

The search for favorite chocolates in the big box brought in as a treat for Mary's birthday stopped.

"Sounds a bit drastic," murmured Ms. Higgins, drama, who had fabulous platinum hair, a long-term partner, and no children as yet.

"I'd love to have a scatter of chickens, make my own bread, and not have to spend half my life marking copybooks, but I don't have a wildly successful company to sell off," complained Caroline Regan, who somehow managed three children, a job, and a busy working husband who was never home in time to do anything more than turn the dishwasher on. "She's talking rubbish. You need money to have that sort of life. It's not as if you can just give up on everything and live off your own eggs and bread. Besides, you have to have the money to buy the flour, and money to feed the hens, and money for the children's education. Where do you get that if you don't have a big company to sell, tell me that?"

Grace sent a sympathetic look toward Caroline, who had two children sitting state exams that year and the harried expression on her face to prove it.

"Why would you want to live in the countryside and keep chickens?" young Ben Kennedy wanted to know. "You'd go mad. No people, no bars, no parties. The only way to talk to people would be on Facebook or Twitter, and you can't exist on that — you need real people to go out with."

"One day," Caroline warned him, "one day you'll know what I'm talking about and you'll wish you could live in a cottage with nothing but fields outside."

She had a point, Grace thought. The things you wanted when you were twenty were definitely not the things you wanted thirty years later, but nobody could tell you that: you had to find it out for yourself.

What Grace and Stephen had wanted at twenty-five and what they'd wanted at thirty-five had turned out to be wildly different.

In their early twenties, they'd been happy to have jobs at all. Grace was teaching, Stephen had a junior copywriting job in a Waterford ad agency, and they thought they were blessed with their two-bedroom row house in the city with its painted walls and sanded floorboards because they couldn't afford carpets.

They had cheap foreign holidays where they lazed on Greek and Spanish and Turkish beaches or went exploring. They went to a different restaurant every night in order not to miss out on anything, and made love with passion on the rackety beds with the buzz of plug-in mosquito devices in the background.

By their late twenties, they had two small

children. Grace was working at Bridgeport National School and she was blissfully happy. Tired, but happy.

Stephen hadn't been happy. He had more mountains to climb.

The argument about a rural life complete with livestock and no stress versus city life and bars aplenty was still going on in the staffroom.

"What would you *do* all day if you lived in the middle of nowhere?" Ben demanded. "You'd go stark raving mad."

Ben lived in Waterford city and spent his wages on adventure sports: surfing, scuba-diving, parachute jumps. Amazing-looking women went along to these things too, in search of adventurous boyfriends.

"I'll tell you what you'd see living in the middle of nowhere," said Caroline, tearful now. "You'd look out the window and see nothing, and nobody would be asking you for anything or giving out to you because you hadn't washed their special jeans in time for the weekend."

Grace made a mental note to have a chat with Caroline later. Sometimes all she could do was listen, but when you were down to your last nerve, having someone listen quietly could be very soothing.

She searched through the chocolates for her favorite hazelnut in caramel, pocketed one, said "See you all later" to the other teachers and patted Caroline on the shoulder in a gesture of solidarity on the way out.

It was Grace's turn to cover the second half of yard supervision today, as the teacher on duty had to race off to the dentist. She enjoyed the job as it gave her a chance to watch the children play and she could keep up with how they were all getting on. The way they played was a good sign of what was happening in their lives — much the same as break time in the staffroom, for that matter.

Her coat buttoned up against the January cold, she walked around the edge of the playground, taking in the clusters of children, watching that the little ones were happy and trying to make sure her worrisome gang in fifth grade weren't attempting any foolhardy behavior involving giant leaps off the wall and onto the netball court.

She was thinking about Michael's news when playtime ended and she made her way back to her office. Before getting down to work, she took the opportunity to phone her ex-husband. Over the years she'd got to know Julia, but she still preferred to ring Stephen on his cell phone. It was partly because his job in advertising meant he could be any-where, so phoning him at home might be a waste of time, but also because she felt like an interloper calling the home he shared with another woman. Stephen had his own life now and Grace wouldn't dream of encroaching. It was one of her rules, the rules she'd made up when they'd first separated, because if they were to be apart, then it had to be properly apart. No running back to each other out of loneliness.

"Hi there," she said. "Did Michael tell you the good news?"

"Hello, Grace, yes, he did," replied Stephen. "He sounds so happy, and I'm very fond of Katy, but . . ."

After nearly thirty years, Grace had come to know his every nuance of speech, so the moment he hesitated, she could tell exactly the words he was searching for.

"Please don't tell me you think he's too young to get married?" she demanded.

Stephen Rhattigan sighed. "I can't help it. Nobody tells you that when you have kids of your own they don't stay kids forever. Stupid, I know. Some part of me still sees him as a schoolboy with messy hair and dirty knees."

"He's twenty-nine, nearly thirty, Stephen, a lot older than we were when we got married," Grace pointed out. "And don't jump in and say look how well *that* turned out simply because we got divorced. We were kids when we married. The difference between us and young people now is vast. They're wiser, they've grown up more quickly despite our best efforts. He's the perfect age."

She thought for a moment about the impact divorce had on the way parents saw their children. The parent who spent the most time with the kids saw them as they were: grown-up, moving away, ripping the umbilical cord. The one who'd gone to live somewhere else — like Stephen — could go on carrying that fantasy vision of eternal children in their mind. Grace knew exactly how adult and mature her son was, while Stephen, who'd left home when Michael was a spotty, often silent, fifteen, didn't.

But there was no point in saying all this. It would sound like a recrimination along the lines of *I did most of the raising of our kids.*

"You're right, I know. I just think he seems so young sometimes," Stephen was saying.

"Well, he's not. Plus, he and Katy live together and we didn't," Grace said firmly. "Living together is a great way to figure out if you're suited."

"Your father would have had to be carried off in an ambulance if we'd suggested it," said Stephen. "It was bad enough when we went on holiday to Greece the first time."

Grace smiled, remembering her dear departed dad saying that his own mother would spin in her grave if she knew that a good Catholic girl like Grace was going on holiday with a man before they got married.

"I told him we'd have separate beds — and we did," she said.

"Everyone did in our apartment block because they were all twin beds, no doubles,"

165

laughed Stephen.

"Remember when we arrived, at three in the morning, and we could hear the entire busload en masse dragging beds across marble floors so they were together?"

"It's odd to think that our kids are doing the same things now that we did. Do you suppose they look upon us as old fuddy-duddies who've no idea what it is to be young?" Stephen asked, with a hint of wistfulness. "I don't feel old," he added speedily, "but advertising's a young business."

"Nonsense, you're not old," said Grace briskly, wanting to shut off this line of maudlin conversation. "Now, are you and Julia coming to dinner on Friday night? Katy's father has imposed a three-line whip. I think he wants us all to understand that he's masterminding this wedd—"

"He is not," interrupted Stephen with irritation. "That man brings out the worst in me: he's a total control freak. Look at poor Birdie. She's afraid of her own shadow and can't do anything without running it by bloody Howard."

"Stephen, I have news for you," said Grace sternly. "The groom's family have nothing to do with the wedding except turn up on the day. If Howard wants to mastermind it all like he's hosting a G-20 summit, he will. Except I doubt Katy will allow him to get away with that. She's no shrinking violet, our

166

lovely daughter-in-law-to-be."

"I wish she'd shrink her father," Stephen said. "Do crimes of passion count between two prospective fathers-in-law?"

"Only in France, where passion is a legitimate defense, and only on the day of the wedding itself," Grace told him jokingly. "You'll have to hold fire till then."

"No court would convict me," said Stephen. "All I'd do is show them his YouTube speech about being a self-made man and how rich he is now, and I'd be acquitted. Sheer irritation needs to be a legal defense in this country."

Grace ignored this. "So, are you coming to the dinner?"

"I'll have to get back to you," he said.

Grace felt a moment's annoyance. Even when they'd been married, Stephen could never say yes to any invitation straightaway. Never commit, he'd say, in case a better offer comes along.

"Fine," she said. "Tell me when you get around to deciding." Then she hung up quickly, lest she was tempted to say more on the subject.

Stephen and Julia probably had a sheaf of invitations to choose from for their Friday night's entertainment, unlike Grace, who had no plans. She didn't know why, but the thought of her ex-husband idly choosing what to do annoyed her.

Perhaps she should have a go at Internet dating, as Fiona had suggested. Grab life with both hands and live it positively.

Being positive was important if she wanted to live a fully grateful life.

She thought of all the things she'd have to write in her gratitude diary tonight — about the joy of having Michael happy, the joy of him marrying Katy, who was truly lovely. Grace remonstrated with herself: there was no point in focusing on negative things like loneliness if she wasn't going to do anything about them, was there?

After hearing Katy and Michael's wonderful news, Leila had spent a distinctly unglamorous morning cleaning her mother's kitchen thoroughly and using up an entire roll of black trash bags to collect rubbish from all over the house. The dead chicken smell had been eradicated, thanks to open windows, liberal use of antibacterial cleansers, and as many scented candles as Leila could find.

Pixie, her mother's spaniel, had obviously been using the living room carpet as her personal toilet, and the scent of dog pee in there refused to budge.

Check cost of new carpet, Leila wrote on a notebook page, which was already full of house-related tasks. Or she could always see if the old floorboards would be up to baring. Floorboards were so lovely and rustic.

Work tasks filled two further pages.

She'd checked her work emails and had been on the phone to the office by nine to delegate whatever she could and talk to Ilona about the forthcoming movie premiere. Devlin had been out of the office all day, so Leila sent him an email full of bullet points on everything she'd organized.

My mother has a broken hip and I need to be with her at the hospital for a few days. It will also take some time to organize a nursing home for when she comes out of the hospital, she wrote, then her fingers stilled over her laptop keyboard.

It sounded so cold and uncaring. When Dad had been confined to bed with the series of back problems that had plagued the latter half of his life, her mother had done everything for him. She'd been his carer, devoting her life to him, and now Leila was blithely offloading the whole responsibility for her mother to someone else. It wasn't just the care of her mother now either. The house on Poppy Lane had always been immaculate, but it looked as if it hadn't been cleaned for months. The big question was why? What had happened to turn her mother from the house-proud woman she remembered into someone who never cleaned at all?

Leila picked up the piece of paper with Katy and Michael's wedding details written on it.

She'd drawn inexpert wedding bells and flowers around the date, and she felt happy for her friend because Katy was finally marrying the man she loved. But the contrast was unwelcome. Everything was wonderful in Katy's life, while Leila seemed to have made a complete mess of hers. And it wasn't going to improve anytime soon.

But then she remembered her mother lying in the hospital and told herself off for being selfish. The only thing that mattered right now was making sure that Mum was all right.

She made it to the hospital shortly after twelve, having stopped briefly at a shop in town to buy a new dressing gown — there'd been no clean dressing gown at home, so buying a new one seemed the best option — and some antiseptic wipes. She'd also picked up some magazines and a little arrangement of white roses that wouldn't need a vase so would require no looking for one in a busy hospital. And she hadn't been able to resist an engagement card for Katy and Michael: a silly one of two adorable cartoon mice.

As she was making her way out of the store, she noticed her mother's favorite lily of the valley perfume on display. Smelling the tester made her feel tearful, conjuring memories of the once-vital woman now helpless in a hospital bed. How had her mother aged so much without her noticing? She bought a flacon of the perfume to take in with her,

170

hoping its familiar fragrance would revive the mum she'd known.

It was outside visiting hours but she figured she'd be allowed in on the basis that she needed to see her mother's doctor.

"What was the name of the doctor you spoke to yesterday?" she asked Susie on the phone once she'd parked.

Susie, outside the telecom office, was sneaking a bummed cigarette to try to de-stress herself and wasn't in the mood for a call from her younger sister.

"I don't remember," she snapped. It was cold and she pulled her coat around her.

Leila counted to five. "That's fine," she lied. "I'll find out who it was when I get in there. Susie . . ." She hesitated. "Have you been to Mum's lately? I mean, did you notice it was getting a bit messy?"

"The house was a tip when I picked the dog up last night," Susie said shortly. "She'd crapped all over the hall and I had to clean it up."

Leila shuddered. The hall was parquet flooring, with endless crevices. Thank goodness she'd found those old running shoes.

"She crapped all over my kitchen last night too, as well as howling like mad for about two hours before she went to sleep. If I could afford it, I'd put her into kennels. God knows what state the place will be in when I get home after she's been shut up all day."

"The thing is, it's not like Mum to have the house dirty, is it?" Leila went on. "How long has this been going on?"

Susie exploded. "It's not my job to police *our* mother," she snapped. "In case you hadn't noticed, Leila, there are two of us. But just because I live nearby, I'm the one who gets lumbered with everything while you swan in a couple of times a year, hug everyone, and then swan off again to your fabulous job. I'm supposed to deal with it all, but I'm a single mother as well as a daughter, and I have a job. It may not be as glamorous as yours, but I can't afford to lose it."

"Susie, all I'm saying is that you should have told me something was wrong," Leila said, careful to keep any hint of recrimination out of her voice. "This isn't normal. Mum's always been so tidy, there's got to be a reason for her letting everything slide. The upstairs is a complete mess — her bed is covered in dog hairs, the sheets look as if they haven't been changed in weeks, and . . . well, it's dirty."

"You're here now," snapped Susie, "you fix it." And she hung up.

The hospital was a hive of activity, nurses walking around in soft-soled shoes and the scent of strong disinfectant in the air.

Leila had to navigate her way from one ward to another to find her mother because she'd been moved overnight. Stopping to rub sanitizer gel into her hands, she hurried through the double doors and there, sitting up in bed but still looking fragile and bruised, was Dolores Martin.

Even though she had seen her only last night, Leila felt tears sting her eyes. Her mother looked so beaten and old, and yet she wasn't old. Old was . . . well, old wasn't her mother. Old was more than Dolores Martin's sixty-three years.

"Mum" was all she managed to say before she burst into tears.

Somehow she managed to unload all her packages onto the floor beside her mother's bed before leaning in to hug her gently, careful of her injuries.

"Oh, lovey, how nice to see you," said Dolores, looking half happy, half on the verge of tears. "One of the nurses said you'd been in last night and rung again this morning."

"I didn't want to come in early and wake you if you were sleeping," Leila said, pulling up a chair.

Awake and in daylight, her mother looked a little better, but the bruises on her face had bloomed into sinister-looking purple things.

"How do you feel?"

Dolores grimaced. "Sore and stupid. All these years I've never had an accident, and now this. I'm a bit shattered. Once you do anything to your hip, you're finished," she

173

added, a tremor in her voice.

"You're not shattered," said Leila, who'd been warned by the nurse that her mother was very emotional as a result of the shock. "People can injure their hips at any age. We're going to get you right as rain, Mum. You'll be back walking Pixie before you know it."

Her mother's face clouded over. "How is Pixie? I know Susie has her, but she's too busy to look after a dog and —"

"Nonsense, Susie loves Pixie."

"She might, but it's a responsibility, and Susie's stretched enough as it is."

"Susie won't mind," said Leila, not sounding at all convinced.

"Can't you take her? You love dogs," her mother pleaded. "I'll be in here for a while and then, well, I'll have to go to a nursing home, won't I, to recover, and Susie has enough to do without having to walk my dog." Her bottom lip was trembling and the tears began rolling down her cheeks.

"Now then, Dolores," said a slightly stern voice, "you're not getting upset, are you, pet? We don't need that."

Leila turned to see a mature woman in nurse's uniform at the foot of her mother's bed. "Time to check your blood pressure. Is this your other daughter?"

"I'm Leila. I was hoping I could stick around until the doctor does his rounds so I can hear what he has to say about Mum's injuries."

"You've missed them for today," said the nurse. "Come back tomorrow before ten, that's when they do their rounds."

"But couldn't I phone someone . . . ?"

"Doctors don't give out numbers. They'd be on the phone all day. Do you want to wait outside while I'm with your mother?"

For fifteen minutes Leila paced the corridor, looking for doctor-ish people to pounce on. This was ridiculous. She wanted information about her mother's condition — surely that wasn't too much to ask?

Eventually she peeked back in to see the curtains had been opened again around her mother's bed. Mum was lying back with her eyes closed.

Feeling a lump in her throat, Leila tried to fend off the tears by busying herself. Her mother's clothes from the day of the accident — well, what remained of them — were in a bag in her locker, and Leila took them out before arranging all the things she'd brought.

That took about ten minutes.

Perhaps if she sat here long enough a doctor would come by?

In a bed across the way, an older woman was visiting a very elderly lady who wore a jaunty silvery wig on her tiny birdlike head and a sweep of glittery lilac eyeshadow on each eyelid.

"There's a nice coffee bar downstairs," the

175

tiny lady with the wig whispered across at Leila.

"Thank you," said Leila, getting up. She was cheered by seeing the other patient. Look at her: she had to be at least ninety, and even though she was in the hospital, she was smiling, well enough to bother with her wig and her makeup. She was still going.

Age was just a number, Leila told herself as she waited in line for her coffee. Her mother needed to be reminded of that fact.

With coffee and a newspaper, she sat beside her mother and watched her sleep for another three hours. Occasionally Dolores woke up and smiled sleepily at her before dropping off again.

Leila found herself touching her mother's wrist from time to time to reassure herself that she had a pulse.

"Is all this sleeping normal?" she asked another passing nurse.

"It's probably the pain meds," the nurse said.

"She wouldn't die, would she?" Leila asked fearfully, all thoughts of age being a number now gone.

"No, love," said the nurse kindly. "She's doing well. I expect she'll be brighter tomorrow, on less medication as the time wears on. So she'll be more alert."

"OK," said Leila.

The nurse looked at the board at the end

of the bed. "Selina is looking after her today. Stop at the nurses' station to talk to her."

Selina was a wise orthopedic nurse who'd seen more broken and fractured hips than she'd had hot dinners.

"Your mother's going to be fine," she said briskly. "Dr. Noonan says surgery went well, although her hemoglobin's low, that's why she's a bit pale. She might need a transfusion, we'll see after today's bloods. But she should be on her feet later, and if all goes well she'll be out in a week. Will you be around to take care of her, or will it be a nursing home?"

Leila blinked. She certainly had enough information now. "I work in Dublin," she stammered.

"Nursing home then," Selina said. "You look exhausted. Why don't you go on home and have a rest? We have your contact details, don't we?"

"Yes," said Leila. "I gave them last night."

"Fine. We'll phone if there's any change."

Leila stared at her. Selina made it all sound easy.

Leave and don't worry. All will be fine.

No mention of guilt and anxiety or that worry over what else was wrong with her mother.

"Thanks," said Leila.

She washed her hands with some more of the sanitizer and felt it burn into the new cut from her earlier housework. Rubber gloves would be a good plan, she thought absently as she left the hospital.

She reached her car and wished there was someone to phone to tell them how bad she felt. She couldn't call Katy in her happy affianced glow. No point ringing Susie and getting the head bitten off her.

These were the moments when she missed having Tynan in her life, when she needed someone to say, *Don't worry, it will be all right.* Even if it wasn't going to be.

She was back in her mother's house with a bag of groceries when her phone rang: Devlin, back in the office. He hadn't replied to any of her earlier emails, which must mean something had gone wrong. Her mind racing through the possibilities, she answered.

"Devlin," she said, "what's up?"

"Hello, Leila. Nothing's up, I just wanted to check in and see how your mother's doing."

For a moment Leila was at a loss for words at this unDevlin-like behavior. He sounded solicitous. She wished she could sob on the phone about how awful it all was, but that was out of the question.

"She's not bad. In pain, obviously, but there's nothing seriously wrong."

The dirt of the kitchen came to her mind but it was all too impossible to explain, and besides, Eamonn Devlin was hardly the person with whom to discuss it. Why had she even thought of confiding in him? She must be going totally mad.

"I'll be back at work as soon as I can," she said quickly, "so don't worry."

"That's not what I phoned for."

If Leila didn't know better, she'd have said he sounded hurt. But that would be entirely out of character. Devlin didn't do hurt.

"Of course not," she said easily. "You're very kind to phone. She's fine —"

"And how are you?"

This time she was at a loss for words. Devlin was asking how she was. He'd never done that, not even when Tynan had left. At the time, he'd stared at her a bit as if trying to work out what to say, but he'd never said anything.

Then the realization struck her: he needed to talk to her about something important and he was trying to do it in a roundabout way. The subtext of this conversation was undoubtedly *abandon your sick mother and get into the office.*

"I'm fine," she lied briskly. "How about I come up on Thursday and work Friday too? Mum will be in the hospital for another few days. I can come back down here over the weekend."

"There's no need," he said.

"No, really," Leila insisted. "See you Thursday — and thanks for asking about Mum. You're very sweet, bye."

Sweet, thought Eamonn Devlin as he slammed down the phone in his office.

She thinks I'm *sweet.*

He glared at his phone and wished he could throw it across the room, but the last time he'd done that, he'd made a hairline crack in the plate-glass window which had cost a small fortune to fix.

He felt like firing everyone, or at least shouting at them all, but you couldn't do that sort of thing anymore, as Leila had explained during a recent working lunch when he'd confided in her about a member of staff who was driving him mad due to total inefficiency.

"I want to shout at him every time he comes into my office and tells me about his latest disaster," Devlin had said, relief coursing through him at finally being able to get this off his chest.

Leila never flinched when he said things like this: he could tell her anything about work and she'd take it on the chin.

"Shouting will not make Jimmy any faster at what he does, and he might well take you to a tribunal for bullying," she'd said in exasperation, even though she knew Devlin was aware of all this. "And you can't fire him."

"I know I can't fire him," Devlin had

180

growled. "I wouldn't, you know that. He's a good man, even if he is crap at his job, and his wife is pregnant. Statutory redundancy would be no good to him."

Leila had grinned and said she'd known he was a softie underneath it all.

"Don't tell anyone," Devlin had muttered.

There were no problems at Eclipse, nothing going wrong, and Ilona was handling Leila's job quite well in her absence. But she wasn't Leila. It wasn't just that Leila was brilliant at her job, it was . . . Well, he liked having her around. Nothing wrong with that, was there?

Dolores Martin lay in her hospital bed and sleepily watched the pale evening sun on the wall opposite. She'd woken at five and had been lying there since, not in pain, just watching everything carry on around her. Strange, but she liked it here, liked the peace of it all and the sense that she was safe and being cared for. The nurses were kind, even if they were busy a lot of the time. She felt far too tired to read but knew that if she changed her mind she had the magazines Leila had left for her.

One of the other women nearby hated hospitals in general and St. Anne's Ward in particular, and said so loudly as often as she could.

She was, Dolores ascertained, another

person with a hip injury. Although she looked to be much older than Dolores, she had a mane of dark hair — dyed, surely? For the past hour she'd been complaining loudly about her dinner: "It's a disgrace, I'm telling you! The food is diabolical. How can a person get better on this muck? I rang my bell ten minutes ago but has anyone come to see me? No, I might be dying on the floor but nobody comes. When my son hears about this . . ."

If Dolores had felt stronger, she might have told the woman to be quiet. Clearly she wasn't dying on the floor, and even if the apple pie and custard wasn't the best she'd ever tasted, it was sweet and comforting. But the other woman was so loud and angry, and Dolores couldn't bear the thought of confrontation.

Instead she whispered to the nurses: "You're so lovely to us, pay no attention to that horrible woman in bed six. You're angels. I don't know how you do it all."

And she *didn't* know how they managed: checking vital signs, writing up charts, giving people their tablets, always with a gentle word for the patients.

"How are we doing now, Dolores? A bit brighter?" said a lovely Indian nurse who was like an exquisite little doll and seemed to speed through her work with the swiftness of a bird. "You've got some color in your cheeks. You'll be right as rain in no time. Don't you worry, my dear. You'll be back home with that lovely daughter soon."

The thought of going home frightened Dolores. She didn't want to leave this haven. Here, there were people around, taking care of her. At home, there would only be her, and she couldn't go back to that. She'd gone downhill so fast and she hadn't been able to tell anyone. Not the girls, that was for sure. They'd been through enough, growing up with their father an invalid. She wasn't going to be a burden to them. Not under any circumstances. Susie was struggling with her life and Dolores felt huge guilt at not being able to help her and little Jack more, while Leila — Leila was obviously still broken-hearted over that rat Tynan. No, whatever happened, Dolores wouldn't call on them for help: they needed to live their own lives.

SEVEN

There is only one happiness in life:
to love and be loved.

GEORGE SAND

Joe's aunt Maura lived in the sort of house Vonnie had always dreamed of owning. It sat on the outskirts of the town in an acre of wooded land with a farm to its rear. In the summer, sheep gazed with mild interest through the fence, while Maura and Tom's two rescued whippets blinked back as they lazed in the sun.

The house itself was small, two-story, and lured you in with its wisteria-clad porch and the bow windows that looked like sleepy eyes smiling out at you.

Since Maura had retired, she'd had more time to spend puttering around the garden and walking along the beach with Tom and the two dogs. Today, though, Tom was hard at work in his shed, judging by the droning noise of the lathe that Vonnie could hear as she stopped the car.

"He's making me a new bedside table," Maura said, standing at the open front door and smiling at Vonnie as she walked up the path.

"I thought he made you one last year? The oak one with all the shelves."

Vonnie leaned in for a hug. She was taller than Maura but still felt the comfort of a child with a beloved adult when they embraced. She wasn't sure what she'd have done when she first moved to Ireland if it hadn't been for Maura and Tom.

"He says I have too many books and magazines all over the place and this way, because the new one has more shelves, it will all be tidy."

The women grinned at each other.

Tom liked an excuse for his work. It would be no good spending hours making something if it wasn't strictly necessary. Perfectly adequate shelves were often deemed to have some structural flaw to allow him to search out a few nice bits of ash or walnut. Maura's kitchen cupboard doors were whisked on and off with dizzying regularity because of allegedly dodgy hinges and handles that needed redoing.

Maura, one of life's serene souls, put her feet up when the sawdust flew, and admired each new piece of furniture.

"Do you truly like it?" Tom would ask.

"It's beautiful, love," Maura would reply.

"I'm the luckiest woman in the world."

"Tea?" said Maura now.

"Yes, please," said Vonnie, though they both knew she wasn't there for tea really. She was there to cry and say all the things she wanted to say to Ryan but couldn't, because he was under enough stress already. Like were they mad to think of moving in together when he had a furious not-quite-ex-wife in the background who'd make hell when she found out their plans.

Maura had been like a mother to Vonnie since she'd lived in Bridgeport. She'd never asked why Vonnie had fled Boston a year after Joe died. Never queried if it was wise for her to move away from Joe's beloved family — or even her own admittedly distant parents.

"It's killing us that she wants to go when she and Shane are all we have left of Joe, but she has to find peace somewhere," Geraldine had said on the phone from Brookline. "She needs to grieve, and if moving to Ireland will help, then she has to do that. They had their best holidays there, she says. Vonnie knows her own mind."

Her sister had always been the wisest of the family, Maura knew. The whole Reilly clan were reeling from Joe's tragic car crash, and still they were gathering around Vonnie, taking care of her. In the years since Vonnie had married Joe, she had become like a beloved daughter rather than a daughter-in-law.

Maura knew from phone calls and emails from her sister that Vonnie spent more time with the Reillys than with her own parents.

"Ah, sure, her mother's a good woman, but she's a bit too concerned about how things look," Geraldine would say, because she rarely said a bad word about anyone. "Not the best one for saying the right thing to someone who's suffering. Not her fault, God love her, but she just can't connect."

When Joe died, Vonnie's mother hadn't been able to help her devastated daughter. Vonnie's wild grief was outside Violet's frame of reference. People did die of broken hearts, and the love match between Vonnie and Joe had been so vibrant that it was almost a palpable thing. Upset and frightened, Violet simply hadn't known what to do.

In the year following Joe's death, Vonnie and Shane had practically lived in the Reilly house in Brookline, until it had all become too painful and Vonnie had said she needed to get away: "To be somewhere we were happy, somewhere different where I don't expect Joe to walk into the room twenty times a day."

The whole Reilly family had been to Ireland several times during Joe's youth, and Maura remembered her handsome nephew's zest for life, evident even when he was just a child. A photo of Joe and Vonnie taken in this very house on Vonnie's first trip to Ireland had sat on the mantelpiece for years, but Maura had put it in a drawer when she'd heard Vonnie was coming.

Now, six years later, she wondered how she'd lived without Vonnie and Shane in her life.

"Tonight Ryan's going to tell Jennifer that we're buying a house and are going to move in together."

Vonnie, settled with tea she didn't actually want at Maura's kitchen table, blurted out the thing that was weighing so heavily on her mind. "Poppy Lane. I still love the sound of it — it's like a fairy-tale address. I wish I had a fairy-tale crystal ball to see how Jennifer's going to react."

"I'm not sure you need a crystal ball for that," Maura replied.

"No," agreed Vonnie. "Probably not. I should be glad the gun laws are a lot stricter here than at home, or she'd be paying a visit to my house tonight with an assault rifle."

Despite it all, Maura laughed.

"I think you need police clearance or to be in a gun club or something official-sounding," she said.

Vonnie played with the sugar in the bowl. "Jennifer would find a way around those pesky rules. *Hell hath no fury* and all that. Remember what she was like the first time

Ryan introduced me to Ruby and Shelby?"

Such had been Jennifer's rage that she had prevented Ryan from having any contact with his daughters for a month, until her own mother had gotten involved and persuaded her to let the girls see their dad again.

Until that point, Vonnie had thought the difficult thing was going to be helping Ryan's daughters adjust to there being another woman in their father's life. She had not foreseen Jennifer's volcanic reaction.

"But it's life. It happens all over the world every day," she had said to Ryan. "People split up. Families merge. There's no point sitting at home and eating yourself up with bitterness about it."

"Yeah, well, there might not be any point in it, but that's how some people do things. People like Jennifer, in fact," Ryan had said, sounding worn down.

It had taken the threat of legal action to change Jennifer's mind. But she still hadn't eased up. Her next move had been to drag the girls into it, which enraged the normally calm Vonnie.

Shelby, then a tender seven, began parroting things to Vonnie like "Mum doesn't like us to have pizzas on weekends because it's junk food," or "We have to phone Mum to ask if we can see films because they might not be suitable."

As if Vonnie didn't know what sort of movies a seven-year-old could watch.

"Let's ask your mom, good plan," she'd say brightly. Dealing with cranky customers had made her able to deal with a cranky Jennifer.

Things hadn't changed, though.

"She still doesn't keep that bile away from the kids," Vonnie told Maura, finally giving up on the tea. "She's like the CIA, interrogating Ruby about everything that happens when they're with us. I heard Ruby on the phone to her friend about it. We'd been to see a film, but Ruby told Andi she daren't tell her mother or 'she'll be furious.' What sort of mother doesn't want her children to enjoy themselves just because they're with someone else?"

"I'd say give Jennifer time, but it's been two years since you and Ryan met," Maura said. "Look, love, some people just don't like to take responsibility. Jennifer appears to be that sort of person: it's easier to blame Ryan, you, and the universe for her problems than to admit that she's lost in a pity party and needs to get out by herself."

"I wish there was a way I could make it all better," Vonnie muttered. "Ryan's heart is broken over this, and . . ." She didn't know if she could say this out loud; so far she'd only said it in her mind. "Maura, I wonder if we're crazy to move in together. Or even to have a relationship. Jennifer is so determined to ruin it, and I'd rather walk away now than go through more pain. Please," she said, "tell me honestly what you think. I can't do this to Shane, not after losing his father. It might be better to cut and run now."

Maura reached out and took Vonnie's hand with its short, unpainted nails and long, slender fingers.

Vonnie leaned forward in her seat, eyes closed. She couldn't bear to feel pain again or to have her beloved Shane hurt.

"Ryan's the best thing that's happened to you in a long time. Jennifer will try to ruin it all, you *know* that. So don't let her."

When Vonnie had gone back to work, Maura texted her sister in Massachusetts.

Vonnie was just here. Afraid crazy ex-wife is going to go ballistic when she hears about Poppy Lane.

It was breakfast time for Geraldine, and she always replied quickly.

How's she holding up?

Not bad but said she thought about not moving in . . .

Can I take out a contract on crazy ex?

Not legal.

Darn. Should I fly over for moral support?

Not yet. Will tell you if you need to.

In the small study nook in Brookline, Geraldine Reilly got on the computer and began looking at flights to Ireland. She missed

Vonnie and little Shane so much — not that he was so little these days. On their frequent Skype calls, she'd seen how much he'd grown in the last year. He was the image of his father now. He played hurling, he'd said proudly, and had held up all the medals he'd won with his team.

He was at that vulnerable stage: not quite out of the sweetness of childhood, but growing taller and stronger, and with that deeper voice that had never lost its U.S. accent. Looking at him was like looking at a mini Joe. It still hurt. It always would, Geraldine knew. Nobody lost a son and got over it. Not ever. But the pain changed somehow. It was always there, but she had learned to live with it, for the sake of the rest of her family — and for Vonnie and Shane.

She had to do that much for her son. Not seeing her beloved grandson all the time was painful, but she wanted what was best for Shane and his mother. Ireland had helped heal Vonnie. That was good enough for Geraldine. When her other grandkids muttered that they wished Shane lived in Boston, Geraldine said that people needed to find their peace in the world and that didn't always suit other people and they'd better get used to it.

In private and early on after Vonnie's flight to Bridgeport, Pat sometimes asked Geraldine if they should have tried harder to get her to stay close with Shane.

"We're here for them, Pat: on the phone, email, holidays," Geraldine had pointed out. "We love them and we can't keep them like birds in a cage. You do have to set something free if you love it."

"I thought that was a fridge magnet motto," Pat said miserably.

"Fridge magnets say wise things sometimes," Geraldine pointed out. "Besides, the poet Rumi put it better: *Rise up and go on your strange journey to the ocean of meanings.* Or something."

Joe would never come back; all she could do now was care for his family: that was her gift to him.

Pat had kissed her on the cheek. "What a lot you know, my wise woman."

Vonnie drove away from Maura and Tom's house inwardly raging over Jennifer and her blinkered view of life. Nobody had handed life to Vonnie on a plate, she thought furiously. It was the same for Shane, who'd had to deal with having his father die when he was just five.

As the therapist she'd seen for a few months had told her: "Grief is not something you can put a bandage on. Not even for your son. His father has died and there is no protecting him from the fact that he will not be seeing him again. Painful as it is for you to witness, he must learn to live with that."

The therapist never used euphemisms like "passed away." No, it was all straightforward and clear in her office. *Death, pain, grief, survival,* and *good enough mother* were her watchwords.

Joe was dead. Vonnie and Shane were not. They would survive. It would be painful, but they would do it.

"You're a good mother, Vonnie, but you must not cocoon Shane so that he never has to feel pain. That will do him no good. It's better that he learns to deal with this. The same goes for you."

Vonnie wondered why Jennifer didn't understand that life could be hard but you just had to learn from it and move on.

Vonnie hadn't been looking for love when Ryan had turned up two years ago. She'd honestly thought that part of her life was over. Besides, Ryan was almost the complete opposite of Joe.

While Joe had been fit, he was a lawyer, a man at home among giant law books. By contrast, Ryan was an outdoorsy sort of man, son of a market gardener, now with his own cycling and triathlon sports store business and with plans to open another one. But like Joe, honesty shone out of him like a beacon.

He'd told her that he was separated from his wife and had two darling daughters: Ruby, who was then fifteen, and seven-year-old Shelby.

"What happened to your marriage?" asked Vonnie, who wanted no gray areas.

It was their second date and she needed the truth before agreeing to a third. She had gone through enough pain without falling for a man who wasn't what he said he was.

Ryan kept his steady blue eyes on her. "I left. I couldn't stand the arguments. It wasn't that Jennifer was a danger to the girls or anything," he added, seeing a flare of anxiety in Vonnie's eyes. "But she's pyrotechnic when you're married to her. I did think of having an affair to make her throw me out, because that would have driven Jennifer entirely mad, but that was the coward's way out. I simply had to leave."

"You wanted to be thrown out?" asked Vonnie, thinking she must be crazy not to get up and leave right then, but something was compelling her to stay. For the first time since she'd met Joe, she'd felt an attraction to a man: she watched Ryan gesticulating as he talked, speaking with his hands as well as with his mouth, the way so many Irish people did.

She'd wondered what those hands would feel like holding her, what she'd feel kissing him. Her sense of sexual attraction, long since dulled, had sparked into life the moment she'd met him. There was a raw physicality to him, like there had been to Joe, even though they were two very different men.

And there was truth in this man — Ryan was no Casanova, she knew it somewhere deep inside herself. There had been no other woman involved in the breakup of his marriage.

Ryan nodded, as if he couldn't quite trust himself to speak. "I love my daughters so much I'd kill for them if I had to, but I couldn't stay with Jennifer. We should never have married in the first place," he admitted. "We weren't in love, not really, not in the let's-actually-stay-together-forever way. She's funny, Jennifer: she's got this deadpan sense of humor. Compared to lots of girls, it was easy to fall for that. All our friends were getting married at the time — we actually got engaged at a friend's wedding, mainly because we'd been together ages and marriage seemed the next step."

"That's sad," said Vonnie, head instantly full of memories of Joe and what she'd felt when they'd gotten married. How could you get something like that wrong?

"Yes," Ryan said. "It is sad. I had no idea when I stood in that church what marriage meant. It's not like dating someone for ages — it's hard, it takes work. The fun and the humor don't last when you've got a mortgage and a small baby. Neither of us knew how to do that. We argued all the time, but I thought we should stick it out for Ruby. Shelby came along just when the arguments were becoming nonstop. I did think of suggesting counseling, but why sit in a room with someone and try to fix what's unfixable?"

Vonnie had no answer to that.

"How are things with you and Jennifer now?" she asked.

Ryan paused so long, she wasn't sure he'd heard her. He was perhaps lost in regrets about his marriage, she thought, until he answered.

"Dreadful," he said flatly. "As soon as I left, it turned into Armageddon. I tried to get her to come to a mediator to organize the split, but she walked out after one session. She says I've ruined her life. She's going to hate it that I've met you."

Vonnie had felt a flicker of fear run through her.

Ryan made her heart sing in a way she'd thought would never happen again. She hadn't meant to let him in — she couldn't take a risk, not with Shane to look after, plus she couldn't take any more pain — but he'd gotten in anyway.

"How can she say you've ruined her life?" she asked. "Life isn't easy for any of us, but we have to try."

Jennifer's marriage might have ended in bitterness, but Vonnie had had to identify her darling husband's dead body in a cold morgue.

"She can't blame you for everything," she went on. "It takes two to make a marriage fail."

"You tell her that someday," said Ryan with a wry grin. "Moving on is not Jennifer's thing."

He was worrying too much, Vonnie decided. They lived in the twenty-first century, after all: people married, divorced, and life went on.

"It will work out," she'd told Ryan. "I know it will."

As she drove back to the shop, Vonnie prayed that she'd been right. This was a huge leap of faith for her and for Ryan. They'd both been hurt by life; they didn't want to rush into a short-term relationship and have it all fall apart a few years later.

She so wanted this to be forever for both of them.

But nothing was forever, was it? Vonnie's thumb idly stroked her simple gold wedding band. She still wore it and Ryan had never asked her to give it up.

She knew she had to, but she was waiting until the time was right.

Ruby Morrison settled herself into the corner of the dusty window seat in the attic bedroom of the Wards' old house and squashed her school coat into a cushion behind her so she could sit comfortably and stare out at the pinprick lights of the town spread out below her. She tried not to think about the insect life that was probably dangling in the old curtains behind her head. She hadn't turned the lights on as she'd climbed the winding apple-green wooden stairs that led from the second floor to the attic aerie. But she wasn't scared. When the Wards had lived here, Ruby had often come around to play with their daughter Lesley, so she knew the house well. Nobody had been to view it for ages, so nobody had seen the broken pane in the French window by which Ruby let herself quietly in.

The Ward family had been gone a year now and still nobody had bought the house.

"Doesn't surprise me in the least," Ruby's mother had said. "It's a buyer's market and people want somewhere tasteful and clean."

Mum had never liked Ruby playing with Lesley Ward: "common," she used to call her, and Ruby knew it was because Mr. Ward had a white van and his wife wore skintight jeans and spindly high heels and had hair extensions. There would follow a diatribe on downmarket people ruining the nice reputation of Bridgeport.

Ruby had long since learned to tune out whenever her mum went off on one of her rants. That was partly why she was here now instead of sitting in her own home pretending to do her algebra homework. She didn't want to be there when Dad phoned with the news that he, Vonnie, and Shane, Vonnie's eleven-year-old son, were moving in together. He'd said he was going to do it before the weekend, and Ruby felt sick every time she thought about it.

She hadn't seen the house on Poppy Lane, just the pictures of it on her father's phone last weekend. He'd been so excited, telling her she could have her pick of the bedrooms and he'd paint it any color she wanted.

"I'll be close to you and Shelby now," Dad had said, with such pure happiness in his face that Ruby knew she couldn't ruin it all by saying that her mother would go through the roof when she heard.

Ruby spent a lot of time not saying what she thought — it was the divorced kids' code, sort of like the Mafia one from the old movies her dad liked. *Tell nobody anything. Play dumb.*

"It'll be wonderful to have you nearby, Dad," she'd said. Which was entirely the truth.

The rented apartment where he'd been living since the split was an hour's drive away in the city, so he could never pick her or Shelby up from school or have them to stay during the week. Ruby had grown used to missing him. Every second weekend was really only twice a month when you thought about it. Not enough time with someone you'd loved your whole life. Or too much time when you were interrogated about it for days after.

What did you do? McDonald's again? Did he cook for dinner or get in takeaway? I hope you didn't stay up too late. What did you watch on TV? I don't want Shelby watching unsuitable things and your father never knows . . .

The questioning had intensified when Dad started going out with Vonnie.

At first Ruby had made the fatal error of being honest, thinking it would put her mum's mind at rest. "She's really nice, Mum. She's got a son of her own, so she understands us."

Her mother's face had gone white with anger and she'd snapped: "What? Your father let a complete stranger spend time with you and he didn't discuss it with me first?"

"You muppet," said Andi, her best friend, on the phone later. "You should have said Vonnie's a hag, it will never last, and you hate her."

"Yeah," said Ruby glumly. "I am a muppet."

Admitting that she liked Vonnie had caused a nuclear meltdown. Mum had stopped their dad from seeing them. It went on for a month; the only contact they had with him was when he phoned Ruby on her cell just before bedtime. She'd pass the phone to

Shelby, who was only seven at the time, and they'd be in floods of tears by the time they finished talking to him. Even Dad sounded like he was crying.

Eventually Ruby had called in to see Granny Lulu, Mum's mum, and told her how much she missed her dad. Granny Lulu had gone right off Dad, no doubt about it, but when Ruby had pleaded with her and told her how much it hurt not to see him, Granny had decided to step in.

She'd turned up at the house later that same day, shooing Ruby and Shelby out of the kitchen. There'd been a lot of screaming and yelling; Granny Lulu could scream nearly as loud as Mum, and the pair of them made so much noise that Ruby thought it was a good thing the big five-bedroom house in The Close wasn't stuck onto another house, else the neighbors might think someone was being murdered and phone the police.

"Is Mum scared of Granny Lulu?" Shelby had whispered as they sat on the top step of the stairs, trying to listen.

"Mum's not scared of anyone," Ruby had whispered back.

"Why do they have to be so loud?" Shelby was doing her best not to cry as she leaned her chubby little-girl body against her sister for comfort.

"Grown-ups do things that way," Ruby said without thinking.

"Dad doesn't."

"No," agreed Ruby. "Dad doesn't. We won't either, will we?"

Shelby shook her head solemnly.

Whatever had been said in the kitchen, afterwards they'd been allowed to visit their dad again. And ever since then, Ruby had followed the code: *Say nothing.* Questions about Vonnie got a combination of lies and half lies from her.

But the code wasn't going to save her this time. Nothing that had happened in the past would be as bad as what was about to happen, Ruby knew. Nothing. When her mother heard the news about Dad, Vonnie, and Shane and the house on Poppy Lane, it was going to be World War Three with knobs on.

She finished her chocolate, scrunched up the wrapper, and wished she'd bought another one. One chocolate bar was never enough.

Her phone pinged with a text from Andi.

Wot happened? Ur mum gone mental?

Hvnt been home yet. Going now. Cross ur fngers 4 me.

Ruby got off her seat, hoisted her rucksack and headed down the stairs. She wondered whether her mother might be diverted from her rage if she took the bus into Waterford city, didn't answer her phone, and appeared to have gone missing. Probably not. Eventually she would have to go home, and her mother would fly into a mega-rant — as if it wasn't bad enough that her former husband had betrayed her by moving into a house with another woman, now her selfish daughter was letting her down by running away. *Nobody ever thinks about me,* she'd yell.

Ruby looked at her watch. Six thirty. Time to face the music.

Leila phoned Susie with some trepidation.

"Is there any way you can come and visit Mum on Friday?" she asked. "You could stay in Poppy Lane and I'd be back on Saturday morning to take over visiting."

"I thought you said the house was a pit?" Susie snapped. "I can't bring Jack there."

"Susie," said Leila, and she didn't bother to keep the temper out of her voice, "we're talking about our mother. And I'm cleaning the house. It'll be so clean and tidy, it will squeak by the time you get here on Friday. I have to work Thursday and Friday and one of us needs to be there. I still haven't managed to talk to a doctor. The nurses say she's doing fine; a physio has been to see her and they've told her a nursing home would be a good plan for when she's out of the hospital, so I am assuming all is going well. But she's . . ."

Leila paused. There was something wrong and she simply couldn't put her finger on it. The whole issue of the house was worrying her. Could her mother have developed early-onset dementia? Could that be it? How else to explain a wildly house-proud woman allowing her home to fall into such a state?

The thought of dementia made her feel as if she was falling headlong into a wormhole, so she closed the idea up in her head.

"She doesn't seem totally herself," she said, "but everyone says it's the medication."

"Fine," Susie broke in, her voice heavy with resignation. "I'll come and stay overnight. But I am bringing that dog and I will be leaving her with you. You can figure out what to do with her."

"I can't keep a dog in an apartment," Leila said, thinking of her carpets.

"Well, I'm not looking after her," snapped Susie. "I have enough on my plate as it is. It's your turn now."

She hung up, leaving Leila staring at the phone sadly. Right now she could only cope with one major worry at a time. Susie would have to wait.

Vonnie didn't know which would be worse — being with Ryan when he phoned Jennifer and told her the news, or not being with him and having to wait to hear how it had gone.

In the end, Ryan decided it for her.

"I'll phone Jennifer after work," he said. "Then I'll drive over to you and stay the night. OK?"

"Fine," said Vonnie tightly.

After work, when she picked Shane up from the babysitter's, he wanted to chat about his day and ask her about hers, the way he usually did. Vonnie knew that hormones would soon start to rage through her darling boy, and if everything her friends said was true, he'd start grunting and never want to chat with his mom again, which horrified her. They couldn't be right, surely? But for now, he loved being with her, loved hearing about her day and who'd wanted what cakes. In return, he told her everything that had happened at school. She knew this closeness came from what they'd been through together, because friends said that trying to get a word out of *their* eleven-year-olds after school was impossible.

"I got all my math homework done," Shane said with pride. "It was really hard too — can I play Mario on Wii for half an hour before dinner?"

Vonnie was torn. She tried to limit Shane's computer game time, but tonight she didn't think she would be able to hold an intelligent conversation with her son, and he was bound to ask what was wrong. He was acutely sensitive and could pick up on anxiety easily. It was best that he didn't know how on edge his mother was because of Jennifer. Vonnie found it hard enough to think that there was a person out there who loathed her; she needed to protect Shane from that knowledge.

"Half an hour on the Wii," she agreed. "But only when you've finished all your homework."

"Yay," he said, delighted.

The town house she had bought a lifetime ago looked the best it ever had. Selling a house meant cleaning at a whole different level: making beds look perfect, putting toys away, dusting endlessly, making sure every kitchen worktop was shining before they left the house in the morning in case a viewing came up. Vonnie had thought she was verging on obsessive compulsive disorder the way she was continually sticking the vacuum cleaner nozzle into every corner to keep dust at bay.

Thank goodness the place had sold quickly.

Final contracts for both houses were being signed on the same day in three weeks' time, which gave Vonnie three weeks to pack up her life.

As soon as she came downstairs from changing into her comfortable gray sweatpants and a fleece, she checked on the slow cooker and set the table for three, then decided she might as well do a bit of sorting out. She pulled out the junk drawer. Bits of string, old batteries, a slightly melted spatula, several screwdrivers, old fuses and clothes pegs stared up at her. It was the sort of job she usually put off, but this evening it was perfect.

■ ■ ■ ■

Ryan Morrison was a big man, and when he sat in cars, he had to push the seat back the whole way.

"Daddy longlegs," Ruby liked to tease him.

He loved the teasing: it made him feel that his daughter still loved him in spite of his leaving home.

"Shorty," he'd tease her back, then hug her to show it was a joke.

Now he sat in his car outside work and it felt like a prison around him. He had a phone call to make and there was nowhere private to make it.

In the shop, his office was like a train station, with people coming in and out looking for advice, files, that paper on the new lap pool and how it compared to the old one.

The car would have to do.

He'd spent the day psyching himself up to phone Jennifer. He'd trained for an Ironman race once, and all those months cycling, running, and swimming felt like a walk in the park compared to phoning his former wife and telling her his news.

He'd tried to play down how worried he was for Vonnie's sake, but the truth was that unless Jennifer had undergone a personality transplant — a bit unlikely — she was going to explode with rage when he told her about

Poppy Lane.

Was that a normal reaction, or was it merely a Jennifer reaction?

He'd known she was fiery from the start. Had known and hadn't liked it, but she'd made him laugh and somehow a short-term thing had turned into a long-term relationship.

Whereas Ryan was the gentle giant he resembled, Jennifer liked to argue and insisted that healthy relationships needed anger and passion to survive.

"Arguing is good for couples," she'd say, face flushed after a yelling match. "Better to get all the anger out rather than repressing it."

He knew where she'd got that idea: he'd witnessed enough pyrotechnic arguments between Jennifer and her parents to understand that she'd grown up with it and was entirely comfortable with arguments as a part of family life. Once the argument was over, Jennifer would expect things to return to normal.

But Ryan couldn't cope with the endless ups and downs, the cruel things she came out with while in a rage.

"You know I didn't mean that, don't you?" she would say afterwards, wanting makeup sex once the argument was over. "I was just cross. You know what I'm like, darling."

Ryan did know what she was like, but it

seemed to him that if you said something, even in the heat of an argument, it must have some basis in truth.

They were too different ever to have been married, he thought now — now that it was too late and they had two beautiful daughters caught in the cross fire.

Jennifer was a good, if volatile, mother: the girls were beautifully looked after and the house — the big house in The Close that Ryan was paying for — was always immaculate. But she wasn't averse to using them as pawns in any battle she might have with Ryan, and it was that thought that made him dread the conversation he needed to have with her tonight.

"Hi, Jennifer, it's Ryan. Can you talk? I've something to tell you," he said in an ultra-calm voice.

"What? The shop's gone bust, nobody wants to do stupid triathlons anymore, and the plans for another shop in your great empire have gone down the drain?" she snapped.

"Since that would wreck not just my plans but *all* our financial security, happily, no. The shop's doing fine," he said, anger shifting him out of his enforced calm. How did she *do* that to him after all these years?

"What is it, then? I'm cooking dinner."

Ryan took a deep breath. There was no easy way to do this — he had to leap in and get it over with.

"This is big news, Jen, and I don't want to hurt you, but Vonnie and I are moving in together in three weeks. We've bought a house on Poppy Lane, the one by the old train tracks into —"

"I know where it is," Jennifer hissed. "How. Could. You? This is my town, my place — how dare you move in with that bloody woman here! She's not even from around here."

The ridiculousness of this instantly annoyed him. It was as if Vonnie's nationality was what mattered most to Jennifer: not the fact that he was starting over, moving in with her, but the fact that she was from abroad.

"What's that got to do with it?" he demanded. "*I* grew up here. Bridgeport isn't your personal domain. I'm a local too. I know it's going to be hard for you, but I want to be closer to Ruby and Shelby. I want somewhere they can have their own rooms instead of bunking in with each other, and" — he knew he shouldn't say this, that it would only stoke the fire of her rage, but he said it anyway — "Vonnie's business is here and I want to be with Vonnie."

"Rub it in, why don't you? She's a businesswoman and I'm nothing but a housewife who bored you. Say it, go on, say it!"

Ryan leaned over and put his head in his big hands. He was losing already.

"That's not why we broke up and you know it."

"Oh yes, I know why we broke up — because you ran away. And now you want to act all happy families again," sneered Jennifer, seething rage in every syllable. "Someone should tell the businesswoman of the year that a man who runs away from a woman will go on doing it."

The counselor he'd seen a couple of times immediately after he left Jennifer had attempted to give Ryan what he termed emotional tools to help deal with his wife's anger. But advice given in a calm office years ago seemed futile in the face of her rage. Still, Ryan tried to remember the counselor's words: *A lot of anger comes out of fear. Concentrate on that.*

"Jennifer, I know this is scary, but we all deserve a second start. You and I need to be adult about this. We have two beautiful girls —"

"Who are going to be supplanted by Vonnie's son! Is that it — I couldn't give you a boy?"

Ryan was glad he'd told Vonnie he'd make the phone call somewhere else. Jennifer's changes of direction had always been dizzying.

"Shane is a lovely boy, but you know well that I never wanted a son for the sake of it. I

212

wanted healthy children, which is what we've got."

"And a wife," Jennifer shrieked. "You have a wife too."

They still weren't divorced. Not a day went by that Ryan didn't curse the archaic Irish law that forced him to wait another year before the marriage could officially be terminated. He ought to get a calendar and mark off the days.

Jennifer changed tack again. "Do Ruby and Shelby know about this?"

Ryan was torn between lying and having Jennifer interrogate their daughters anyway, which he knew she did regularly.

"Ruby does, but don't drag her into our fight," he said tightly. "This is about us, not them."

"That's what all you bastards say, isn't it?" she hissed down the phone at him. " 'It's not about the children.' Well, it IS. Don't tell me it isn't. I'm the one who comforts Shelby when she cries for her daddy at night, not you."

Ryan had no answer for that. He never did. It was Jennifer's final and most powerful trump card. Ruby insisted that Shelby didn't cry in the night but he could never be sure about this. His heart bled at the thought of his smaller daughter in pain. He could imagine tears on her sweetly plump little-girl cheeks and he wondered, as he always did, if he should have stuck it out with Jennifer for his daughters' sake. He was in love with Vonnie, but perhaps he didn't deserve the joy of that because his leaving had hurt the girls so much.

He blinked back tears. Was he the worst father in the world for putting Ruby and Shelby through this? Was it too much to expect that one day Jennifer would be able to put the past behind them and let go of the bitterness?

This was no good. He'd have to hang up. Yet again Jennifer had pierced his armor and made a series of direct hits.

"I'll talk to you again," he said, reverting with huge difficulty to ultra-calm.

For the first time he wondered whether he'd be able to go through with it all.

Jennifer slammed down the phone so loudly that she was sure she heard some part of the receiver crack. Damn bloody Ryan, damn him. Just when she thought she was feeling a bit better, he came along with another piece of bad news. How was she supposed to feel when he moved in with that woman and they were everywhere in Bridgeport? She might bump into them in the supermarket, probably at the holding-hand stage as they dithered over washing powders. And how dare Ryan say she was dragging the girls into this! She didn't want them to be hurt either. Not like she'd been hurt. No, damn Ryan and his insensitivity. Jennifer burst into tears. She'd meant to tell him about the school phoning about Ruby but she'd forgotten.

Number 4, The Close was a big house, with a cobblelock drive, no grass, and an uncontrollable shaggy leylandii hedge giving it an enclosed air. A cul-de-sac lined with imposing five-bedroomed houses, The Close had once been one of the most desirable addresses in Bridgeport, but that was before a gated community of large McMansions had been built in the town at the tail end of the property bubble. Ruby knew that the only reason they could afford a big, swanky house was because Dad's business was going so well and he'd gotten all the important franchises for bike and running stuff.

When they'd first moved there, Mum had loved it. Lately, though, she seemed to hate everything The Close stood for, particularly the neighbors, who were all still married and had stopped inviting her to parties and dinners as soon as Dad left.

"Women hate single women," she'd said crossly. "Afraid they'll steal their husbands."

Ruby wished her mum had girlfriends. She didn't know what she'd do without Andi, her closest friend since they'd started school. But Mum wasn't one for close friends.

"I don't want to go to any of their parties

anyway," she said airily.

Because of what her mother had told her, the normally sweet Ruby glared at the neighbors now whenever she met them. She hated them for not being proper friends to her mum, for looking down on her and Mum and Shelby, giving them fake smiles while inside they were thinking, *Poor things, the father left home, the mother's never gotten over it. She's highly strung. All a bit of a disaster . . .* Jennifer had failed to mention to Ruby that she'd brushed off all attempts at help, seeing pity in the neighbors' gestures of friendship.

Ruby unlocked the front door and drew a deep breath to ready herself. In her head she knew how hard all of this was for her mum, but in her heart she was tired of the constant sniping. You'd think they were the only separated family in Bridgeport the way Mum went on. In reality, there were at least fifteen kids in her year at school with divorced or separated parents, and most of them seemed to have figured out how to get through it without being at war all the time.

One of Ruby's closest friends, Eloise, had been to her mother's second wedding the previous year and was godmother to her baby half sister, Coco.

"Isn't she adorable?" Eloise had sighed, showing them pictures of the christening on her phone.

Ruby had stared at shots of her friend holding a frankly mutinous-looking Coco dressed in white robes, but what had fascinated her most were the photos of Eloise's mum and her new husband. They looked so happy, no taut lines around their mouths.

Ruby's dad looked a lot happier since he'd met Vonnie. If only Mum could find someone else, Ruby was convinced life would be much easier for everyone. All the anger and rage would stop. Only how could she meet someone else when she sat at home all the time brooding?

That appeared to be the key: for both parents to find new love. Eloise's parents hugged like friends whenever they met. They showed up with their new partners at sports day or the school play, and everyone sat together and chatted as if it was the most natural thing in the world. Ruby would have liked to go over and ask them how they'd done it, but she was sure they'd only smile at her and say something annoyingly grown-up like *Time, lovey, it takes time.* That was all well and good, but it didn't help her any. How much time, precisely? Nobody ever seemed to have an answer to that. Her parents had been apart nearly four years now; surely that was time enough?

When Dad had come along to Shelby's Christmas play last year, Mum had ostentatiously moved seats because he'd sat in the same row as her and Ruby.

"Come on, Ruby," she'd hissed so loudly that all the other parents had stared at them and then quickly looked away, having figured it out in an instant.

"No!" Ruby had whispered fiercely. "You move if you want, I'm staying."

As a result, her mother hadn't spoken to her for the rest of the day.

Ruby wondered what her mother would do if Vonnie got pregnant like Eloise's mum. A vision popped into her head of her mother marching around to Poppy Lane with a baseball bat to whack Vonnie over the head.

That was the problem with Mum: she overdid everything. She could never be mildly angry: she went from calm to enraged in three seconds. If she got home and found the chicken she'd just bought was past its sell-by, she wouldn't quietly return it to the supermarket, oh no. She'd storm back to the shop as if the whole supermarket industry was against her and she'd have to do battle to get her money back.

It was so exhausting.

Ruby hung her school coat in the closet in the hall, then tried to creep upstairs quietly with her school bag. She could do without dinner. Better to spend the evening in the peace of her bedroom, doing her homework.

But her mother had ears like a bat and Ruby had only made it as far as the second stair when the kitchen door was wrenched open.

"Ruby!"

"Yes, Mum," she sighed.

They stared at each other across the hall and Ruby could see the anger glistening in her mother's eyes. There was no escaping. Sighing, she dumped her bag at the bottom of the stairs and walked toward the kitchen.

"You're late," Jennifer snapped.

"Extra sports," fibbed Ruby.

"I've had two horrendous phone calls today," her mother announced, going over to the oven and taking out something that might have once resembled shepherd's pie. It was now burned at the edges, which was what happened to dinner in their house when the person it was for arrived home late. She served it up along with some dried-up broccoli and put the plate down on the kitchen table in Ruby's place.

All Ruby really wanted was a toasted cheese sandwich, but if her mother had made shepherd's pie, then she had to eat it. The argument if she didn't wouldn't be worth it.

"The first was from Principal Rhattigan over at the junior school, asking about Shelby. Or that's what I thought. But she was really asking about you," Jennifer said in a grim voice. "She hoped Shelby was happy and had adjusted to the separation. Then she asked after you — that's what she was really after:

finding out what's going on here. It's bad enough that the stupid form teacher has been on to me about your behavior, Ruby, without Grace Rhattigan sticking her nose in. She's like the secret service, that woman: she knows everyone and everything. What have you been saying?"

"I haven't said anything," protested Ruby, astonished. How had Principal Rhattigan become involved?

"Really? Nothing about a new house with your new stepmother — because I know, you know. Your bloody father just told me. Probably the whole of Bridgeport knows by now and I'm the last to find out, as per usual."

Ruby looked at her mother warily. They were so similar in looks, both small, with dark hair and gray eyes. There had been a time when they were both slim, but since Dad left, Mum had taken to buying frozen desserts and eating them late at night when no one else was around. She thought Ruby didn't know, but she did; she saw all the New York cheesecake and chocolate roulade packaging stuffed at the back of the recycling bin.

"I don't want to talk about it, Mum," she said stubbornly. "I'm tired. It's all different for me too. None of it's my fault."

"Oh, so it's *my* fault, is it? I'm the one who's messed things up by not playing the game when your father split our family up. It's all down to me." She stopped marching up and down the kitchen and leaned over Ruby to hiss: "Your father has you brainwashed to think it's not his fault, Ruby, but it is!"

"Yeah, whatever," said Ruby glumly, staring down at her plate.

"I suppose Shelby knows all about the new house too?"

That was enough for Ruby.

"Don't you dare take it out on Shelby! She's just a kid," she yelled.

In an instant, Jennifer's eyes filled with tears. As ever, faced with her mother's pain, Ruby felt torn between anger and guilt and pity.

Mum couldn't help the way she was. Granny and Grandad had spoiled her rotten; she'd been an only child, so there were no brothers or sisters to share with, she'd never had to learn to compromise. Whenever things weren't going her way, she threw a tantrum — as if then she'd get what she wanted, like when she was little with her parents doting on her.

"Sorry, Mum," Ruby said, the instinct to make everything all right overwhelming her the way it always did. Ruby the fixer. "I love you, you know that. Don't worry, it'll be all right. You've got me and Shelby. Let Dad go off and do what he wants."

Even saying it made her feel guilty, because she adored her father and she didn't want to have to play this game, but sometimes it was the only way. Mum needed her. Shelby needed her. Ruby had to be the grown-up, however much it hurt her to say these things she didn't really believe in.

"I know, honey." Mum was crying as she put her arms around Ruby and hugged her.

Mum didn't hug much anymore — she was so conscious of her extra weight that she didn't like people to touch her in case they felt the rolls of flesh. She used to wear trendy jeans and nice fitted tops, but now she bought unflattering extra-large sweatshirts in the supermarket and wore them over baggy tracksuit bottoms, trying to conceal any bulges.

"It's not easy, accepting someone else forcing their way into your life. Your father doesn't understand: this woman is a stranger, and just because he's chosen to be with her, there's no reason why you should have to see her."

If Ruby and Shelby hated this Vonnie, things would be so simple. Ryan loved his girls, he'd do anything for them, and if they wanted nothing to do with Vonnie, he would have to drop her. The thought gave Jennifer hope. With Vonnie off the scene, there would be no competition. Not that Jennifer was convinced he'd come back, but still, they could live apart, without other people, and eventually . . . maybe he'd remember why they fell in love in the first place.

Vonnie was the fly in the ointment. And Ruby and Shelby needed to see that.

Ruby stilled in her mother's embrace. Vonnie was nice. Lovely, even. She managed to be kind and motherly without acting as if she was trying to be Ruby's mother or her friend. She treated Ruby like someone whose opinion mattered, and she seemed to know without being told that sometimes Ruby needed to see her dad alone.

"Vonnie isn't the problem," Ruby said tiredly. It came out in a whisper, and she wasn't sure her mother had heard, because she didn't reply.

Mum let go and went to the fridge, where she uncorked an already open bottle of wine. She took a big glass, filled it, and drank deeply.

"Eat up," she said. "That pie's a bit overcooked but it's good for you, full of vitamins. I was thinking, you and I could do something on our own this weekend. What do you think?"

"What about Shelby?" asked Ruby.

"She can stay with Granny Lulu. We could go shopping in the city, I could buy you new clothes."

Ruby thought of the conversations she'd overheard between her father and Vonnie about money. Both of them worked so hard with their own businesses, but even so it wasn't going to be easy to pay their mortgage as well as the mortgage on The Close. It would mean cutting back on luxuries like holidays and new things for the house, but they were determined to manage.

Her mother was looking at her eagerly.

"Yeah, Mum, whatever," she said, too exhausted to resist.

The other classic response for kids of separated parents: *Whatever.* It covered every eventuality and said nothing.

Ruby waited until her mother had left the room and then scraped her dinner from the plate into the trash before covering it up with some newspaper to hide the fact that she'd dumped it.

Whatever.

It was midnight, and Vonnie was arranging her clothes in the half-light from her bedside lamp, which she'd unplugged from beside the bed and brought over to the closet. Ryan was a heavy sleeper and never minded her reading while he slept, so the light wouldn't wake him.

She simply couldn't lie in bed any longer. She was far too stressed to sleep.

Kneeling on the floor in front of the small sliding-door wardrobe, she was methodically folding clothes and arranging them into piles ready for the move.

Vonnie had never had a lot of clothes.

"No shopaholic tendencies for you," Ryan had said admiringly when he'd seen her bedroom in the town house for the first time and looked into the perfectly organized single wardrobe.

"I could never afford that." Vonnie had shrugged. "What with setting up the business in the early days, there wasn't a penny to spare. After Joe died, I didn't want to shop. I didn't buy a single thing for at least a year."

She'd had some money from Joe's insurance and could have bought clothes after he died, but she hadn't wanted anything in the house that he hadn't seen or touched. She'd worn his T-shirts in bed, and the one he'd worn the last night he'd spent with her she kept underneath her pillow, holding on to it until his scent was totally gone.

She still had it in the box of things she kept for Shane: his father's watch, cuff links from their wedding, old school reports, and their wedding album.

Even now, Vonnie wasn't much of a consumer. Things no longer seemed important. She'd learned the hard way that it was people that mattered, not how many pairs of designer shoes a person had.

Her clothes, laid out on the floor, were testament to that. All simple, none expensive. Comfortable slim-leg sweatpants and tops that grazed her hips formed one perfect pile. Pajamas, like the fleecy ones she was wear-

225

ing, were in another pile. The third was made up of the small selection of good tops she wore with tailored trousers or skirts for work: several blue-hued ones because they suited her pale coloring, the remainder in shades of gray.

She'd already organized her lingerie, folding everything perfectly, but had yet to do the pantyhose. They were hardest: she hated throwing out pantyhose before they got too old to wear, years of having to make do ingrained into her. Thrift had been part of growing up because her mother didn't believe in wasting money.

On an impulse, she got silently to her feet and looked at Ryan sleeping soundly in her bed. He was a miracle, a miracle sent into her life to make it whole in a way she'd never dreamed it could be again. In sleep, you could see that he was handsome, but sleep hid the broad smile that never seemed to leave his face.

They'd made love earlier, his strong arms supporting his body as he stared down at her, telling her she was beautiful, that they'd be so happy together, and that the house on Poppy Lane would make it all perfect.

She understood why he'd wanted to make love — he'd come in looking shattered after talking to Jennifer.

"It didn't go too well," was all he'd say.

Vonnie knew he'd tell her what had happened when he was able to; there was no need to push him. He was obviously traumatized enough without her adding to the stress.

They'd gone to bed early and he'd turned to her with passion, holding her face in his big hands and saying: "I love you so much, Vonnie. Nothing, *nothing* is going to change that. I'm so lucky to have found you finally, and no one is going to take it away."

Making love was his way of reminding himself of what he and Vonnie had.

"Shane loves that bedroom over the garage at Poppy Lane," he'd said afterwards, leaning back on the pillow. "He said he'd like it painted blue and I told him he can have whatever he wants. You don't think Ruby will mind that he got first pick? He will be living there full-time . . ."

"If she wants it, we can talk about it," Vonnie said.

The logistics were going to be trickier, no doubt about it, now that she and Ryan were moving in together properly instead of him staying over occasionally. Shelby would be thrilled with the bedroom nearest theirs. She was like a gentle kitten: happy to curl up with whoever was taking care of her. It would be different for Ruby, seventeen going on thirty.

Ruby . . . the poor kid had a lot on her plate. She tried to hide what was going on in her head, but Vonnie could see how torn she was about their move to the house on Poppy

Lane. On the one hand she dreaded it because it would make her mother angry, but at the same time she loved being with her father — with Vonnie and Shane too, but first and foremost it was her dad she needed. Vonnie tried so hard to make sure that Ruby had time with him on his own; she knew how important the bond between father and child was.

But what good did it do, Vonnie going out of her way to make sure the girls' weekend visits were as normal and stress-free as possible, when Jennifer tried to make them feel guilty about having enjoyed themselves?

And now Jennifer had behaved exactly as Vonnie had predicted, flying into a rage about their move to Poppy Lane.

You knew it wasn't going to be simple, Vonnie told herself. Take a broken marriage and add children, and you had the perfect recipe for guilt.

Ryan had plenty of guilt and Jennifer knew how to stir it. One day she might stir so successfully that Ryan wouldn't be able to take it and would leave Vonnie.

It was so unfair. Vonnie hadn't stolen Ryan; he'd been on his own for two years when they'd met, and Jennifer, according to Ryan, wouldn't have him back even if he came with a winning lottery ticket. So why was she making it so hard for Vonnie to live with him? It didn't make sense. But then Vonnie knew that often there was nothing about life and human emotions that did.

EIGHT

If I keep a green bough in my heart,
the singing bird will come.

CHINESE PROVERB

Leila remembered once sitting in on a press
conference with a onetime hell-raising movie
star, and after all the questions about precisely what drugs had gone through his
system, and how the heck he was still alive
having taken them all, he'd managed to make
everyone smile by saying that *once a year,
you should see the sun rise.*

Leila had been up since five thirty, and for
the first time in a very long time she'd seen
the dawn arrive, its soft, heady crimson rinsed
through with a wash of palest golden yellow.
She'd stared out of the kitchen window in
her mother's house, feeling awe at the beauty
of the sky, suddenly aware of what she'd been
missing by not seeing this every day of her
life.

Joyous birdsong flooded into the room
along with the light, and Leila stepped

outside with her mug of coffee, wanting to be a part of this magical world she hadn't seen for years. At home, she was so flattened with tiredness from work that she got up and went to bed on the timetable of her office.

As the sun rose, she breathed in the scent of the sea, her ears attuning to the cries of the seagulls circling the hills around Bridgeport. Next door's cat was treading a delicate path along the fence between the houses: a sleek gray creature with a bottle-brush tail held aloft as it balanced, clever eyes looking for sleepy birds.

Leila grinned. "You can't be Tom," she murmured. "Nine lives or not. He was here when I was little."

The cat eyed her with interest.

"Pixie's not here, it's safe to come in," Leila said.

But the gray cat flicked its tail and continued on its way.

Eclipse's offices had arrangements of flowers sent in every week. Reception often had odd flowers arranged architecturally on the reception desk. Devlin had a large tree in a container in his office which was still living thanks, Leila was sure, only to tender ministrations by the flower company. But here, despite the earliness of the year, her mother's camellias bloomed along one wall: perfect blossoms from three plants with their glossy viridian leaves.

Leila touched them, then on impulse went into the kitchen to get a pair of scissors and snipped a blossom for her office desk.

The joy of the dawn stayed with her as she drove to Dublin, stopping for a takeaway tea and a croissant. No guilt, she told herself, biting into the flaky richness of the pastry as she sat in her car. She needed the energy, and besides, she was already overdosing on guilt about leaving her mother in the first place.

But she'd promised Devlin she'd work Thursday and Friday, and she wasn't about to let him down. So she reckoned she deserved a treat. Why deny yourself the odd little pleasure? Life had enough damn denial as it was. She'd had her fill of it, especially after the last couple of days, spent desperately trying to deny that there was anything wrong with her mother aside from the bruises and broken bones.

Last night, when she'd left the hospital, she'd had the strangest feeling that there was something her mother wasn't telling her. Something important. Perhaps Mum was worried about money and too embarrassed to mention it. Leila hoped it was that; money she could help with.

Susie refused to acknowledge that there was anything amiss. When Leila had rung her last night, her sister had sounded entirely irritable. "Leila, Mum's in the hospital recovering from surgery — of course she's going to be stressed. And Jack has a chest infection and he's home from school, so I can't work."

Leila waited for the next line: *We don't all have fabulous careers where we can take time off when we want,* but it never came.

She finished her tea and set off into the traffic again. She'd been slimmer when she'd been with Tynan. Much slimmer. Most women put on weight when they were married, apparently, because they ate more as they sat blissfully with their beloved, curled up on the couch eating takeaway. Leila, though, had lost weight.

You never saw exquisitely voluptuous girls in the music industry. Thin was the standard. She'd thought that if she stayed slim, Tynan would never leave her, and look how well that had turned out. A pastry should simply be a sweet treat, not a symbol of confused emotions about weight and societal expectations.

She flicked the radio from a talk show to music. She barely listened to music of any kind these days. It only brought back memories of Tynan.

Blast him, she thought crossly. He was gone; it was about time she stopped thinking about him. There must be a book or a CD out there, something in the self-help line: *Ex-husband Begone,* maybe?

■ ■ ■ ■

Ilona almost threw herself on Leila when her boss finally arrived in the office.

"How's your mother?" she asked anxiously.

"Recovering, but it's going to be slow," Leila said, mentally filing her personal problems neatly away. Compartmentalize; that was the secret. "Thank you for asking, Ilona," she added, closing the door on the subject.

"Right, what's up? Devlin phoned me the other day and he didn't sound like himself at all. Clearly there's something wrong. Have you heard anything?"

Ilona shook her head. "No. The director of *Odessa 2* is coming into Dublin and wants a premiere in aid of his LA charity."

Leila groaned. "First, it's a dreadful film, and second, we can't do charity events unless they're local charities or international charities with an office here. Who's supposed to organize it all? No, don't tell me — we are. The answer's no."

"That's what Devlin said."

"Good." It sounded as if he was back to normal. "I'll go and see him now."

"Is he in?" Leila asked Devlin's assistant Eleanor, a twenty-something business school graduate who had a blunt way about her that Leila liked.

"Yes."

"Good mood?"

Eleanor laughed. "You could say that. He's on the phone to some mate of his and they're talking women."

Leila grinned. "Still doesn't realize those glass bricks aren't soundproof when he's talking loudly?"

"Still doesn't," agreed Eleanor. "Whoever his woman is, he's discussing organizing a home-cooked meal for her because he thinks it's the only way she'll take him seriously. She doesn't know he exists. He's never asked her out or anything."

"I didn't know he could cook," Leila commented, privately thinking that there could hardly be a woman on the planet who wasn't aware that Eamonn Devlin existed. But then she stopped dead. She really ought to tell Devlin to keep his voice down when he was discussing private matters; after all, she was an executive in the business. One of his close team. And it wasn't right to talk about him behind his back.

"Forget we had this conversation," she told Eleanor.

"What conversation?" asked the PA, turning back to her computer screen.

Leila knocked on the door and went in.

Devlin had his feet up on the desk and was leaning back in his swivel chair, testing its capabilities with his six-foot frame and two hundred pounds of solid muscle. He was grinning into the receiver and the grin widened as soon as he saw her, although he swung his feet off the desk.

"Gotta go, Richie," he said. "Leila, great to see you."

Must have been some conversation, Leila decided, because Devlin looked in a very good mood.

He was wearing a gray suit with a silvery gray shirt and no tie: utterly gorgeous, she thought absently, and then realized she must be really tired because that was no way to think about your boss. Still, she felt a hint of envy for the lucky lady for whom he was planning to cook.

"I feel I ought to tell you that sometimes what you say can be heard outside this office," she said, not looking at him.

"What? What did you hear?" He leapt to his feet, looking anxious.

"Nothing. But the odd word can be made out when you're having a particularly loud conversation," Leila said diplomatically.

"But did you hear anything?"

Leila was too emotionally worn out to lie.

"Honestly, Devlin, I don't care about your girlfriends — you can have millions of them for all I care. I just thought you should know that sound carries."

"Right. Thank you for that." His face had darkened. He sank back into his chair, dragged it close to the desk, and began drumming on the wood with one strong hand. He only did that when he was annoyed.

"Sorry, that came out wrong," she said. "I only meant that your private life is your business."

"Glad to hear it," he said crisply, still drumming.

Leila groaned inwardly. Somehow she'd managed to annoy him within minutes of setting foot in the door. Probably because she hadn't told him about the noise issue before.

"What do we need to talk about?" she said flatly, sitting down opposite him.

He'd begun studying the column of figures on the paper in front of him and didn't look up when he began to speak.

For the remainder of the meeting he seemed uncharacteristically offhand with her.

"We'll talk later," she said at the end, getting up.

Should she say sorry? Heck, no. Devlin had probably already forgotten about it all. But as his eyes met hers, his face was still dark, his expression unreadable.

That was all she needed, Leila thought as she left: Devlin deciding that she was no longer the best publicity director in the business.

It was eight o'clock by the time Leila got back to her apartment that evening. Feeling tired and hungry, she lit all the lamps to make the place brighter, changed into her pajamas, and ate toast and jam in front of the TV. She was shattered and didn't feel like talking to anyone, but she phoned the hospital for an update, then rang her mother's cell phone to see how she was.

"I'm fine, lovey," Dolores said weakly. "They're so good to me here. The physiotherapist is the sweetest man. You'd like him. He's single . . ."

Just what she needed — her mother setting up her love life.

"Mum, I don't have time for that sort of carry-on," she said, trying to inject cheerfulness into her voice. "I'm a career girl now. I'll be back on Saturday."

There was nothing she wanted to watch, so she flicked on her iPad and did what Katy was always telling her not to do: she went on to Facebook.

First she clicked on to Katy's page and saw lots of lovely messages of congratulations. She'd had the same sort of messages when she had become engaged.

When she and Tynan had been together, Facebook had been fun. Their walls had been decorated with pictures of them at music festivals, parties, weddings, and barbecues. Looking at her status and seeing the words "Married to Tynan" had felt as real as her wedding and engagement rings.

In love, Facebook had been a gilded mirror reflecting a happy life back at her, linking her with hundreds of other happy people.

But with Tynan gone, it hurt to look at her own or anyone else's page. She'd changed the privacy settings so nobody could see her page, as if they might spot her crying there too, as in real life.

Apart from checking in with Katy, there was only one page she liked to visit now: Tynan's.

I'm like a drug addict, always needing just one more hit, she thought to herself as she clicked to his page. Just one more glimpse and she'd stop, forever . . .

On paper, theirs had been a match made in hell. Leila liked order, organization, and knowing precisely where she was going to be at any given time. Tynan Flynn wore old band T-shirts with ripped jeans, could rarely lay his hands on any of his possessions apart from his cell phone, iPod, and Beats by Dre headphones, and when asked where he might be that night for dinner and whether Leila should get Indian from the takeaway was likely to say: "It's hard to pin down an exact time, honey. I've got to recon that new band at Whelans, and Universal is interested. Once the money men come sniffing around, I'm history. I need to get in there, sell them the whole company image, and lock them down."

A former musician hired as an artists and repertoire man for the small independent record label Steel Rivets, Tynan was never off the phone, lived for music, and was entirely unreliable.

Leila had loved him at first sight.

"He's not your type," Katy had whispered to her in the ladies' the night she and Michael met Tynan.

The venue had been specifically picked by Leila so that Tynan would like it — he dismissed many places as "bourgeois" and "overpriced" — but also so that they stood a chance of hearing each other speaking. If Tynan had been given his way, he'd have opted for a bar with live music and indiscriminate food, and nobody would have been able to hear a thing.

"I don't have a type," argued Leila, bending down and swooshing her hair with her hands to get some body into it. She didn't know why, but she always put more volume in her hair when she was with Tynan. She dressed differently too: the suits she wore at work were ditched for tight jeans and form-fitting jackets. Makeup was dialed up a notch too: more eyeliner and darker lipstick.

Once, she'd allowed herself to think about it and had come to the conclusion that the way she looked mattered to Tynan, and it mattered to her that he appreciated her. He wasn't the sort of guy who'd turn a blind eye when a woman started wearing her sloppy old leggings around the house or couldn't be bothered keeping up with the waxing.

"When Susie went out with that actor-cum-waiter guy years ago, you hated him," Katy reminded her. "Too much interest in himself and not enough interest in Susie, you said. Tynan's the same. He's sexy, sure, but it's all about him."

There was nothing Katy couldn't say to her; they'd been friends too long. They'd never had secrets from each other and never felt they had to hold back an honest opinion for fear of giving offense. If Susie had said the exact same thing, Leila would have been upset with her, but she didn't mind it coming from Katy. Somehow she felt more like a sister than her real sister because Susie was always so easily hurt, so quick to cry. But no matter what Leila felt about Katy, she didn't have to agree with her opinions, especially where Tynan was concerned.

"Susie has always picked bad men," she said, unperturbed. "Case in point: Jack's father — zero child support and no contact. You can't get much worse than that. I, on the other hand, am not bad at picking men. Tynan's fabulous," she continued, determinedly upbeat. "He has a great job too. OK, we might be oil and water, but he's ambitious and fun. And I need fun."

Katy stopped applying lipstick in the mirror. "Is he kind? If he is, I take it all back. Go for him. But fun's not enough. I don't want to see you get hurt."

"I won't," said Leila, grinning at her friend's reflection. How many times had they stood like this — shoulder to shoulder in bathrooms at parties, dinners, nightclubs? Sisters under the skin. One petite and dark-haired, one a shade taller and blonde, clear gray eyes surveying the world with enthusiasm.

Later, when Leila and Tynan's relationship had become more serious, Katy had asked her again:

"Are you sure, Leila? He's a bit — well, wild. Reckless. Like he'd do anything for a dare."

"What's wrong with being wild and doing something for a dare?" demanded Leila, a woman who used cruise control on her car rather than risk going over the speed limit.

"OK, wrong words," Katy said. "He seems like the sort of guy who's used to breaking women's hearts."

"That's just because he hadn't met the right woman — until now," Leila replied, beaming with happiness and able to ignore her best friend's warnings because this was love, she knew it. Tynan was the missing part of her; he made her feel alive in a way she'd never felt alive. With him, she was the Leila she'd dreamed of being: free, happy, in love, joyous. What could be wrong about any of that?

Only it turned out Katy had been right about Tynan.

She'd never once said *I told you so,* but Leila acknowledged the fact every time she remembered the day he'd walked out of their apartment, telling her he was moving to London for a new job, and that the woman he'd been seeing would be joining him there.

"I meant to be out before you got home," he'd said as Leila stood in their bedroom, still wearing her work clothes, her keys in her hand, watching as he hastily packed his belongings. "I was going to leave you a note."

"A note?" Leila sat on the edge of the bed and felt her entire body begin to shake. Where had this come from? Last night they'd made love. This morning he'd made her coffee as usual. How could you fake all of that?

"Leila, babes, it hasn't been working for a long time," Tynan said, not even looking at her as he swept all his aftershaves off his side of the dressing table into a smaller bag. "Diane's coming with me. It's better this way. Me and her out of your hair."

"Diane?"

Diane was a marketing manager in his office: younger than them both, scarily modern, with cropped platinum hair and endless legs so she never needed heels but wore them anyway. Like Tynan — who'd gone back to cigarettes despite Leila's begging him not to — she was a smoker; Leila had often seen them standing outside venues, sharing a cigarette, laughing. But they were smoking buddies, nothing else. Or so she'd told herself.

"Diane?" she said again.

Tynan was thirty, just a year older than her. Diane was a kid, still in her early twenties: at that age, everyone over twenty-five seemed elderly. What was he talking about Diane for?

"Come on, Leila," Tynan said. "You knew all along. Stop pretending. That time we went to Berlin and I never made it back to our hotel room — you knew."

"I didn't. I love you, I thought everything was perfect."

"*Of course you didn't!* Stop pretending."

She'd barely slept that night in Berlin, lying alone in their hotel bedroom after leaving him with the band in a nightclub. But he'd been so plausible the next day: the band wanted to party and he'd crashed in their suite. It was the music world, he'd shrugged. She hadn't wanted to moan; she wasn't his keeper, after all. He was allowed to do crazy things once in a while . . . that was how marriage worked, right? It was all about trust.

She watched him move around, trying to focus in her head. Yesterday, all week, things had been fine. She'd have *noticed,* surely?

He was in the en suite bathroom now. Tynan was so practiced at packing for impromptu trips, he had it down to a fine art.

Within minutes he was ready to depart.

"I didn't know," she said, feeling a great wash of fear and loneliness inside her at the thought of his leaving. "Please don't go, Tynan. We can work this out. I love you, and I know you love me too. What about last night?"

They'd made love after staying up late watching a movie, and Leila had felt the raw love and thankfulness she always felt in bed with Tynan. He wasn't a tall man, but his lean, toned body molded perfectly to hers and no man had ever made her feel the way he did. He seemed to know exactly where to touch her, what to say to bring her closer to orgasm. She'd forced herself not to dwell on the fact that he'd learned all this expertise from other women by telling herself that he was with *her,* he'd chosen her over the rest of them.

"How could you do that and then leave?" she asked, the pain clear on her face.

For a brief moment Tynan stared at her, and she recognized pity in his eyes.

Men were different, he seemed to be saying. They could love and then leave; didn't she understand that?

"Don't go."

In desperation, she'd grabbed his arm and tried to kiss him. He'd shoved her away, muttering: "Leila, stop, for God's sake. It's over, right?"

She thought of blocking the door, making him come to his senses, but instead she slumped on the bed and began to cry.

Katy was the only person Leila had told all of this to, right down to the shaming details of her reaction. Instead of raging at Tynan, or throwing his belongings out of the apartment window like the feisty woman everyone seemed to think she was, she'd sat on the couch and sobbed her heart out, begging him not to leave.

But he'd left anyway.

Six months and five days ago. Not that she was counting.

Tynan's Facebook photo was no longer the one Leila had taken of him on holiday outside the famous Sun Studios in Memphis. He'd removed it within days of walking out and replaced it with one she guessed Diane had taken: it showed him wearing aviator sunglasses and standing against the backdrop of what appeared to be a giant stage. Definitely a music festival.

Leila had followed his progress these last six months through his Facebook albums. The most recent one featured him and Diane on their New Year skiing holiday. Even dressed in a cumbersome ski suit, Diane looked skinny, long-legged, and effortlessly cool.

Leila scanned for new pictures, promising

herself that this would be the last time. It was ridiculous: Tynan had left her. She had not been good enough for the man she loved. There was nothing more definitive than that. Their marriage was over and she was torturing herself by trying to see what he was up to. It hurt every single time: frequency had not made her immune to the pain.

And then her gaze landed on his status. *Single.*

NINE

Lean on each other's strengths.
Forgive each other's weaknesses.

ANON

La Vie en Rose was Bridgeport's fanciest restaurant, bar none. From the plain modern entrance to the bar with its hint of art deco to the restaurant proper, where the high-ceilinged room was decorated with discreet restraint, the whole place spoke of elegance and menus with astronomical prices.

Grace had been there before with Katy's family, and once, what felt like a million years ago, with Stephen before they'd split up.

She thought of this as she parked in a spot near the door and checked her makeup in the visor mirror. She and Stephen had argued, she remembered, because she'd been so horrified by the ridiculous prices.

Not bad for an old broad, she told herself, putting lipstick on her still-full lips and surveying the lines surrounding them with compassion. She was fifty-four: lines were part of the deal.

She'd gone to the hairdresser on the way home from school, a rare event, and had enjoyed a cup of tea and a flick through the sort of magazine she'd never normally buy while the stylist blow-dried her dark shoulder-length hair into lovely loose curls that framed her face beautifully.

Dad's coming but not Julia, Michael had texted while she was in the hairdresser's.

Tell Howard so he can change the booking, Grace had texted back, without adding, *That is SO typical of your father.* Stephen never appeared to realize that it was rude to leave it until the very last minute to tell people whether he was coming.

"It really suits you curled like that, Mrs. Rhattigan," said the stylist as they both examined the result in the mirror. "You going somewhere special, then?"

"My son just got engaged, so we're having an engagement celebratory dinner tonight," Grace said.

She'd rather rip off her own leg than admit that the venue was La Vie en Rose. The stylist's sons had both attended her school, and it had never been any secret that their father spent most of his money in the pub. The cost of a night out at La Vie en Rose would be a month's rent for this woman.

"Lovely," sighed the stylist. "At least the whole wedding palaver doesn't cost you when it's your son. With a daughter, you need to have saved up, don't you?"

"Yes," said Grace, managing a smile as she thought of Fiona. No saving required there. Grace didn't want Fiona married off for the sake of it — she could live in a tree house and have a pagan ceremony in a tree grove if that was what she wanted — so long as she was happily settled with someone she loved.

Stephen hit the motorway at least twenty minutes too late and immediately found himself snagged up in the Friday-evening rush hour.

He'd driven down this road often enough to know he'd be late to the dinner, which would result in Grace glaring at him. In fairness, she didn't glare that much; even during their divorce she'd kept the black looks to a minimum. Grace was one of those people who felt that people had a duty to be grownups and take responsibility for themselves — divorcing parents in particular.

Almost nobody in his present circle of friends could believe that he and Grace had parted so well, discussed their children so agreeably, and remained friends.

"You're saying this to make me jealous," one colleague had accused him. Louise was a senior copywriter who was in the throes of a separation that made the Trojan War look like a pillow fight. "Exactly how do you manage to do it that way — unless you kill them and somehow get away with it?"

Stephen had been about to say that a lot of it was down to Grace, who was fair-minded and honest to a fault, but he'd been beaten to it by one of the partners, who'd always had a bit of a *tendre* for Grace.

"Stephen's ex-wife is one of the most incredible, decent" — the partner sneaked a look at Stephen — "gorgeous women you'll ever meet. She's a class act."

"What about Julia?" demanded Louise, who knew only Stephen's current partner.

"Julia's fabulous," Stephen had said pointedly.

"Which proves that some bastards get lucky twice," the partner went on.

Julia did a good job of glaring at Stephen. But she wasn't going to be at the dinner tonight, so the only hard looks he'd get would be from his ex-wife. Grace would no doubt suspect that his lateness was due to a subconscious desire to annoy the hell out of Howard. In fact, there was probably some truth in that, Stephen acknowledged as the traffic inched slowly toward the Waterford exit.

Howard had a control complex, an out-of-control control complex. At previous dinners over the years — and thankfully these had been few and far between — he had even tried to take charge of what everyone was eating.

"The beef's fantastic here. You've got to try it, you've just got to," he'd announce. "I'll order it for all of us, shall I?"

Stephen's hands tightened around the steering wheel and he decided to turn off the news program he was listening to and put on the classical music station. Grace would kill him if he lost his temper with Howard tonight, no matter how overbearing the old windbag was being.

The strains of Schubert's Trout Quintet filled the car and Stephen felt some of the stress of the day ebb away. His mood lifted even more when he reminded himself of the reason he was willing to endure Howard's company. It wasn't often he got to spend an evening with his beloved Fiona and Michael, and darling Katy, who was a wonderful girl. And, of course, Grace.

He wished he could tell Grace that he had the strangest feeling that the wedding was creating friction between him and Julia. Nothing he could put into words, but it was there. Julia didn't understand what it all meant to him.

Despite her brilliance, she'd never understood how linked he was to Grace and their children, linked *forever,* Stephen thought grimly. It was truly the most annoying thing about her. She seemed to think that, once he'd divorced Grace, he'd divorced himself from the life they'd had together. But when

you had children and had known each other
for more than thirty years, it was never going
to be over. Not totally. You shared a history,
family, and things that couldn't be put into
words. Things that mattered.

It was just as well she wasn't here tonight.
Just as well he'd somehow managed to imply
that it would be boring and she'd hate it.

Birdie stared into her wardrobe and wished
she was one of those women who instinctively
knew what to wear. Her mother had been like
that: always in the right outfit no matter what
the occasion. Of course, it was easier then.
Day dresses or evening dresses or perhaps a
little suit to a lunch. There wasn't anything in
between.

Birdie had gardening clothes, some of
which she picked up in Oxfam or the Vincent
de Paul shop, although she'd never tell
Howard that because he'd be apoplectic at
the notion of his wife buying her clothes in a
charity shop. She had white blouses, comfy
sweaters, and colored jeans she got at Marks
and Sparks for during the day, and good coats
to wear over the M&S ensembles for Masses
or funerals. She liked catalogue shopping too
— loved sitting up in bed with Thumper at
her feet, marking pages and deciding which
blouse might be nicest, which colorway made
the most sense. But when it came to clothes
for nights out . . . She looked at her four good

outfits and chose the lilac suit, which Howard had recently been very critical about. "Lilac is too pale, too old-fashioned. And how old is that thing? It's the sort of rig-out my mother could wear. Why don't you wear any modern clothes, Birdie? Being fifty-nine is different nowadays. You don't have to wear long black dresses and flat shoes and tie your hair up like a nun. Live a little."

But Birdie hated shopping because it made her feel so inadequate. Not that she didn't feel inadequate anyway in the face of Howard's disapproval. He thought she'd let herself go, she could tell he did.

Once, he'd liked the fact that she wasn't high maintenance, but not anymore. When a woman was young, not being high maintenance was amusing, it gave off a sense of *joie de vivre*. But for a woman over fifty, it was a sign that she'd abandoned all hope and simply given up.

Almost without thinking, she pulled on the lilac number. It did make her look older and Howard wouldn't be pleased, but Birdie had so much on her mind, she didn't care. After the wedding, which was to be held here and needed to meet Howard's exacting standards, Katy and Michael would be taking a year out to travel the world, and the very idea made Birdie sick. Her thoughts invariably ran to the catastrophic end of the spectrum, a long-worn path. You only had to open the papers to see what could happen.

In the face of such worries, Howard's irritation almost paled into insignificance.

Outside, in the black car from the limousine service Bridgeport Woolen Mills always used, Howard got the driver to honk the horn a second time.

"What the hell is she doing?" he groaned.

The driver, Tom, who'd driven Mr. Desmond many times before, had seen the great man in many of his moods. Bonhomie when he was escorting an important contact to lunch, wild irritation when he was alone in the car and on the phone to the office over some disaster, and occasionally, quiet affection in those calls he took when he gazed fixedly out of the window as a signal to the driver that he was not to listen in.

For a clever man, Mr. Desmond could be stupid, Tom thought. Looking out of the window didn't stop Tom from being able to hear what he was saying.

Mr. Desmond had to be in his early sixties for sure, but he didn't look it — that streaky mane of hair and the permanent tan made him look years younger, and the clothes helped. All expensive things some woman brought him every six months from London.

Tom had gone to Dublin to pick up both the clothes and the young woman, and she'd been worth the trip by herself — like something from a fashion magazine, he'd told his wife. Mad clothes, strange shoes, and hair like a blackbird's wing, cut short to show off a neck like a ballerina's, and red lipstick on those indecently large lips — something he never told his wife.

She must've had something injected in them to make them that size, Tom decided. Did they take the injectable stuff from your body, or was it some other sort of product? His wife would probably know, but he daren't ask else she'd want to know why he was paying so much attention to another woman's lips.

She never stayed long. She'd get Tom to carry the clothes into the house, and then he'd park outside until she emerged a few hours later with a couple of bags to return. She'd talk on the phone on her way back to Dublin, setting up meetings with other people and telling them that the gray Armani had worked a treat, as she knew it would.

"He has the shoulders for it, great physique," she'd said once, almost proudly.

She was a stylist, Tom knew, because he'd heard her say it on the phone once, but why on earth a man of Mr. Desmond's age needed a stylist was a question Tom had never been able to answer.

Mrs. Desmond hurried down the front steps, a neat little figure in a nice pale purple suit, with her silvery hair tied up in its usual knot.

"Hello, Tom, how are you?" she said, slipping into the backseat next to her enraged husband. "How're Marjorie and the children? This is an exam year for your son, isn't it?"

"Yes, Mrs. Desmond," said Tom.

He loved Mrs. Desmond, all the drivers in the firm did. She remembered their names and asked about their families, gave presents of lovely Bridgeport products for special birthdays, anniversaries, or weddings.

But it was Mr. Desmond who paid the bills and chose the car company, so Tom kept his eyes on the road and his mouth firmly closed, hoping there would be no more conversation, because he knew all too well that Mr. Desmond preferred his drivers silent as the grave, in every sense.

"We'll be late," said Howard, holding his fire because of the driver. Normally he treated drivers as if they weren't there, but when Birdie made such a point of talking to them, it was harder to do so.

Birdie could feel him looking at the lilac suit with disapproval. He didn't have to speak for her to hear the reproach: *Birdie, this is a special occasion and you're dressed in that dreadful thing again! You could have made an effort.* But tonight she didn't care. The combination of joy over Katy's engagement and fear over her and Michael's forthcoming trip had thrown her so much that, for once, she didn't give a toss about Howard and his opinions.

Grace was the first one at the table. She liked being early. It gave her a chance to settle into her surroundings and feel comfortable before everyone else arrived. When they'd been a couple, Stephen had made them almost miss every flight they ever took, insisting that it would only take *x* amount of time to get to the airport and that nobody expected people to be there hours early, did they?

Another difference. Lately, she kept coming up with the differences between them in her head. She suspected that subconsciously she was reminding herself that they'd been better off splitting up. It had to be the thought of Michael getting married that was causing it. Nothing made a person reexamine their life so thoroughly as the prospect of their child marrying and entering the next stage of adulthood. *Did we do it all wrong? What did we get right?*

Grace knew enough to be certain that she'd been a good mother. She'd loved Fiona and Michael unconditionally, given them a home where they both felt free to speak their mind, knowing they'd be loved no matter what they said or did. Her goal had been to provide them with the security and confidence to go out and face the world, and she felt she'd achieved that.

But there was always a *what if?* That element of doubt.

There had been plenty of pain along the way: Christmases when the children went to stay with Stephen, Julia, and his parents. And the holidays with their father, after which they'd come home, eyes sparkling, telling of places she hadn't been:

"We learned to surf!! Dad has a video of it and he'll send it to you."

"Mum — the Uffizi Gallery, you'd love it!"

And she would have loved it, but she hadn't been there. Stephen and Julia had been there instead, watching her beloved children while she sat at home fine-tuning her planning for the second half of the school year for other people's kids.

She'd never cried in front of the children, never let them see how the choices she and Stephen had made had hurt her. Never let them see that sometimes she questioned those choices.

"A drink, madam, before the other guests arrive?" asked the waiter. "Mr. Desmond has ordered champagne for everyone, but I think we must wait until he gets here . . ." He sounded anxious, as though the whole staff were on tenterhooks because Howard Desmond must have exactly what he wanted. It

259

wasn't too far-fetched a notion: Howard was the richest man in town and made sure everyone knew it.

Inwardly Grace was seething. Bloody Howard. Already taking over and ordering champagne for everyone. Premier cru, she'd bet. Stephen was right: he was an alpha control freak. She'd always wondered whether he served the best champagne only at the start of his parties, decanting cheaper stuff into the bottles as soon as everyone was sozzled and couldn't tell the difference. She wouldn't put it past him.

How he'd fathered a wonderful girl like Katy was astonishing, really.

Grace beamed up at the waiter. "Mr. Desmond knows I love champagne, so I'll have a glass now," she said — which was a fib, as she was hardly a drinker, and even if she were, Howard wouldn't have paid any attention to her likes and dislikes. But tonight Grace felt a little wild. Not herself.

A glass of Howard's champagne before he got there and announced they were having it would be a childish way to get even, but even grown-ups were allowed to be childish sometimes.

"I love you, do you know that?" Michael said, sitting in the back of the taxi and inhaling the sweet scent of Katy's hair. She smelled of coconut and perfume and something else, something just Katy.

"I love you too," she murmured in reply, wondering how they could be so lucky.

Nobody else knew what love was, nobody, just them.

Howard rushed into the restaurant ahead of Birdie, aware that he was late and annoyed by it.

"Grace," he said, embracing her tightly. "I am so sorry. Beautiful women shouldn't have to drink alone."

He clicked his fingers imperiously at the waiter and shouted, "Champagne!" and both Grace and Birdie shrank a little bit.

"Birdie," said Grace, leaving Howard quickly to go over and hug Birdie. Grace knew she was puce from both Howard's treatment of the waiter and his comment about "beautiful women," but as she looked at Birdie's small face, incredibly pretty despite not a shred of makeup, she saw that Birdie hadn't flushed at all.

After so many years of being married to Howard, she must be used to his behavior, and so too must the waiters at La Vie.

"Hello, Grace, you look so lovely, as always," said Birdie, almost shyly. "You got your hair done. I should have had mine done too."

She put a guilty hand up to the tousled knot that Howard had already commented unfavorably on, and Grace said: "Nonsense. I love your hair. It suits you — and you look lovely too."

"Thank you," said Birdie, so gratefully that Grace knew for sure nobody had said such a thing to her in a long time.

Grace thought that Birdie had undoubtedly been very beautiful in her youth — it was all there in the delicate bones of her face — but years of Howard had almost worn it out of her. Through Michael, she knew that Katy was always trying to get her mother to have beauty treatments and get her hair dyed, but Birdie refused.

"She's such a lovely person, it doesn't matter how she looks," Michael said. "Her spirit is what matters," and Grace had felt a surge of pride in her beloved son that he automatically thought in such a way.

Howard was busily organizing who would sit where when Fiona, Katy, and Michael walked in together.

"Greetings, oh young people!" said Howard loudly, and Fiona shot him a horrified look before slipping into the seat next to her mother.

And then everyone was chatting, admiring Katy's ring, and if Grace sensed a look of mild disapproval on Howard's face at the size of the gemstones, for once he had the sense to say nothing.

They were all sad that because Leila was in

Dublin she couldn't make it, but what with her poor mum in the hospital, she was under huge stress.

Birdie had dropped into the hospital to see Dolores.

"Thanks, Mum," said Katy, reaching over to squeeze her mother's hand. "How is she?"

"Shaken," said Birdie sadly. "I think the shock of the accident has really shattered her confidence."

"It's not about falling off the horse, it's about how you get back on," said Howard loftily.

Grace and Michael found each other's eyes across the table.

"I think it's a little different when you're involved in a serious car accident, Howard," said Grace gently, wanting to ward off any arguments. Michael had that look in his eyes: the look that said he was annoyed but hiding it.

They were on to the first course before Stephen arrived. He went around the table saying hello, giving Howard an almighty and manly slap on the back that made Howard bang into the table and cough.

"Birdie, you light up the room, as always," he said, kissing her hand.

Stephen certainly did, Grace found herself thinking. At fifty-eight, he was still as handsome as ever, and more debonair now — a man who gave the impression that he must have been born in an Italian hand-stitched suit. His dark hair was heavily greyed at the temples and his face was lined, but he looked like what he was: a kind and definitely charming man with a heart of gold.

"Darling daughter, will you let me sit in your place beside your old mother?" he said, kissing Fiona on the top of her head.

"Less of the old," said Grace in mock outrage.

Fiona moved.

"Your legs!" Stephen said to his daughter, pretending shock. "They're out without jeans. You're wearing a skirt. I may need my medication."

"I do dress up for work, Dad," Fiona complained. "I don't live in jeans."

"She's wearing a dress for our wedding, aren't you, Fi?" said Katy from across the table. "We have ages, though, five months; no rush to get started on the dresses just yet."

"We need to," said Birdie. "You have to allow at least four months for a bride's dress."

Katy beamed. "I can't wait to start looking," she said.

"You'll look like a princess, darling," said Michael, "but no denim bridesmaids' dresses, Fi," he teased affectionately. "Or those damn motorcycle boots."

A good-humored argument started up about what Fiona considered suitable bridesmaid wear.

"A black dress, perhaps?" she suggested, putting on her most innocent expression.

Stephen slipped into the chair beside Grace, kissed her on the cheek, then whispered into her ear: "I've got a plan to cook Howard's goose — I'm going to steal his enormously large wallet, report all his cards stolen, then sit back and enjoy it as he tries to pay the bill later."

Grace made a noise that she just knew sounded like the hysterical giggles of some of the smaller girls in school.

"Don't you dare!"

"Don't you dare what?" asked Michael.

"Nothing," said Grace cheerfully, thinking of Birdie's sad little face earlier and how grateful she'd been to be given a compliment. Perhaps Howard's wallet should be appropriated after all. Punishment for his treatment of his poor wife.

Grace finished her starter and Stephen ate bread with too much butter while they talked. Grace thought he shouldn't have butter — at his age, heart and cholesterol problems were a worry. But then it wasn't her job to worry about him: that was Julia's role.

"How's Julia?" she asked.

"Fine," he said, which was his stock response.

You can talk to me about her, you know, Grace wanted to say in exasperation. *I won't disappear in a puff of sulphur and brimstone.*

But she said nothing of the sort.

In their effort to change the subject, they somehow landed on a similar one, and found themselves talking about couples they knew who'd broken up. Always people you'd never have expected to separate. Like Harry and Megan, who'd seemed to fit together like a complex jigsaw — until they'd split up the year before.

"He was boring me to death," a chain-smoking Megan had explained to Grace when they met for a drink one evening. Megan hadn't smoked since teacher training college and Grace was stunned in every sense of the word.

"But —" It was out of her mouth before she'd been able to stop it.

"I know," said Megan bitterly. "*But* he was lovely and everyone thought we were the perfect couple. If I hear that once more, I will scream. Nobody, I mean *nobody,* has any idea what goes on in other people's marriages. You should know that, Grace."

Grace held her tongue after that and listened to a litany of Harry's failings, none of which sounded too awful to her, but then she hadn't been living with them for thirty years.

Besides, she'd probably been like that when she and Stephen had split up — although only to Nora, her closest confidante; she'd have never ranted about him to anyone else.

He's obsessed with work . . . He's never there

for me and the children . . . His career comes first and he's determined to move to Dublin, even though we're all perfectly happy here.

Some of it had been the need to let off steam, to tell someone how annoying he was, but it wasn't entirely fair, and Grace had known that even at the time.

"I'm astonished about Harry and Megan," said Stephen. "They always seemed so . . . together."

He went on to tell her that Ed and Cara had split up too.

"Now *I'm* shocked," Grace said. But then if she thought about it, she hadn't seen them for years, so it was no wonder she'd missed the transition from deeply-in-love to clearly-on-the-verge-of-murdering-each-other. They were one of the couples Stephen had somehow won in the divorce without trying. It seemed impossible to share friends once you'd split up. The friends took sides, and many, Grace knew to her cost, chose the husband, because a single man was still welcome at any party whereas a middle-aged woman with a failed marriage behind her was both difficult to partner up and something of a specter at the feast.

"It's as if divorce is a communicable disease," she'd told a friend, "and they'll catch it if they hang around with me."

Howard was loudly announcing that he wanted a toast and more champagne would be needed.

"He'll be plastered soon," Stephen whispered. "Just the time to steal the wallet . . ."

Grace shot him a look.

"To our beautiful children, Katy and Michael, and the most fabulous wedding of the year," Howard said, raising his champagne flute.

Fiona raised her glass and wondered if Howard knew he was a class-A moron.

Birdie looked at her darling daughter and thought about after the wedding and the terrifying year of backpacking. How would she endure it? She would say nothing, of course. Katy and Michael had to live their own lives . . .

Grace thought how proud she was of Michael and Fiona. She and Stephen must have done an all-right job of raising them.

Stephen caught her eye and grinned at her.

Katy and Michael stared at each other, marveling at how wonderful life was.

And Howard drank deeply, thinking of how he was going to organize the perfect wedding, the most amazing one Bridgeport had ever seen. Then he raised a hand to summon a waiter, did that clicking thing with his fingers that he'd found worked a treat, and demanded more champagne.

"Start as we mean to go on!" he boomed.

Grace mentally noted a few things for her

nightly gratitude list: having such a wonderful night with her family would certainly be on it. Having Howard around, even if he was paying for it all, would not.

Early on Saturday morning, Leila drove out of Dublin feeling cranky and out of sorts. Devlin had been weird with her all Thursday and Friday — something that wouldn't normally have bothered her because he had moments of wild impatience with everyone. He always apologized afterwards, which went a long way to explaining why he was a popular boss. But the past couple of days it wasn't that he'd been impatient with Leila, more that he seemed to be avoiding her. And when he did speak to her, the tone was very different from his merely being irritated.

"Genius at work," murmured Dave, Eclipse's director of marketing and the only other staff member at Leila's level, when Friday's boardroom meeting to run through the week's business had been overwhelmed by Devlin's dark mood. The elegant suit had been replaced by a black shirt, black jeans, stubble — which added to the pirate look — and a grim face.

First the coffee was too weak.

"Is it too much to get someone in to fix the machine so we're not drinking this pale brown slop?" Devlin demanded.

"Cranky level one," said Dave quietly to

Leila, who had to smother a grin.

Then the blinds could not be adjusted to keep the low winter sunlight from shining into his eyes.

"I don't know," Dave said jokily. "It gives you a halo effect. Angelic . . ."

Instead of grinning back as he normally would, Devlin glowered. "Funny, is it?" he snarled. "If comedy hour's over, let's look at the week's numbers."

Dave and Leila didn't look at each other, but surprise radiated between them. Devlin was never rude.

At least, Leila tried to console herself as the meeting progressed, it wasn't just her. Something else was bothering him. Maybe the woman he wanted to cook dinner for had said no. Although why? If Leila allowed herself for one moment to think of Devlin in that way, she knew that no woman in her right mind would say no to him.

Still, the aftereffects of his bad temper lingered as she drove to Bridgeport, and no amount of pulse-quickening music — nor coffee and a cinnamon muffin in a small café en route — could lift her spirits. She could trace her boss's bad mood to when she'd called in to see him first thing on Thursday.

Never assume it's about you, an old mentor had once told her. Pre-Tynan, she'd practiced this motto with ease. Post-Tynan, emotionally fragile and blaming herself for everything, she tended to assume the fault must be hers.

Therefore she was possibly in the worst state of mind to arrive at her mother's house to be greeted by an exhausted Susie, who had clearly been waiting for somebody to blame for all her problems.

"Jack woke up at five. Five! It's sleeping in a different bedroom, having a chest infection — *and* the fact that Mum is in the hospital. Kids are so sensitive to all that. I brought him into my bed but he wouldn't go back to sleep. I'm exhausted — I need to lie down for an hour. You'll have to take over."

Leila, who was still standing in the hall and hadn't gotten so much as a hello into the conversation, stared at her sister. Susie looked positively unhinged, white-faced and stressed.

"Well, sure —"

"Great."

With that, Susie turned and marched upstairs.

"Where's Jack?" called Leila after her sister's departing back.

"In the kitchen, making 'buns' from flour, salt, and water," said Susie, still in the same high-pitched, stressed-to-the-tonsils voice. "It's a disaster area in there. Flour all over the place and the dog in the middle of it."

Leila winced, picturing the kitchen she'd scrubbed to within an inch of its life earlier that week. But the mention of Jack made her smile. She felt a stab of guilt at the thought of Susie coping with him on her own all this time, but willed herself to put on a cheerful face as she headed into the kitchen.

Pixie was on the floor, wriggling happily like a seal in the flour. Despite herself, Leila grinned.

"I'm making buns, Leelu," said Jack proudly, showing his aunt a muffin tray half filled with little lumps of dough with faces made of raisins and squiggly dough worms.

Leila grabbed him, flour and all, and hugged him. His small body was solid and warm, the sweet little face full of love and happiness, and Leila thought that no matter how grumpy Susie was with her, she was clearly doing a very good job of raising her beloved son.

He was so gorgeous: that olive skin and the dark eyes of his long-gone father, all so different from Susie and Leila's coloring. He'd be handsome when he was grown-up, but for now, he was adorably six and a bit. The *bit* was important, apparently.

"When will those yummy buns be ready?" said Leila. "I am SO hungry."

Jack untangled himself and went back to the serious business of squiggle rolling.

"Not until I finish them all," he explained gravely. "You can help." He shoved a lump of dough at her. "I'll show you how to do them."

Pixie leapt up at Leila, covering her with flour.

"Pixie can't help," said Jack. "She sneezed all the flour."

Leila laughed at the thought.

"Look," commanded Jack. "You get a bit, make it into a sausage, then roll it into a caterpillar. Mum calls them worms, but I wouldn't like to eat a worm," he confided.

"Caterpillars would be nicer to eat?" asked Leila, dividing her dough into several sections so she'd have enough for the face.

"Yeuch. Gunge might splodge out. Green gunge!" Jack looked delighted at this notion. "But it wouldn't taste nice."

Leila shook her head. "No," she agreed.

"Leelu, you say funny things," said Jack happily. "I love you."

"I love you too, munchkin," said Leila, feeling as if she might burst into tears.

Nobody else called her Leelu, but Jack had been too little to get her name right when he'd started talking, so she'd become and stayed Leelu.

Nobody else said *I love you* to her either.

She knew her mother loved her, knew that Susie did too, somewhere in there. Katy loved her, as did Michael in a brotherly way. But the words didn't often emerge. They had become the exclusive property of romantic love, something that was totally missing from her life.

The purest, most frequently enunciated love came from Jack. Little Jack, whom she hadn't seen since before Christmas.

"I'm sorry I wasn't with you at Christmas, Jack," she said in a rush. "I should have been there. Sometimes grown-ups can be selfish, and I was selfish."

"Can you come this Christmas?" Jack asked, head bent over a particularly tricky bun face. "This is a king," he explained. "Crowns are hard to do."

"I will come this Christmas," vowed Leila. She reached out her smallest finger for his smallest one. "Pinkie promise."

"Can Pixie eat the buns?" asked Jack suddenly.

"Well, they might make her tummy sick. Why?"

Jack's gaze shifted under the table, where Pixie had settled with her paws around a giant lump of gray splodge, which she was consuming with zeal.

Leila didn't even want to think about what uncooked dough would do to Pixie's intestines and where it would all end up ultimately, so she lunged under the table.

"Pixie!" she yelled.

But she was grabbing at thin air: Pixie and her bun had legged it.

Delighted at the mayhem, Jack threw back his head and roared with laughter.

Two hours had passed when Leila brought a cup of tea and some biscuits upstairs to her sister. Jack, worn out after an energetic game of hide-and-seek in the garden with Pixie and Leila, threw himself on to the bed beside his mother.

"Mum!" he cried. "Me and Leelu had so much fun. Pixie had to be washed, and me too. I got bun in my hair."

Leila had had to bite the bullet and bathe both Jack and Pixie — thankfully not at the same time — in order to clean them up. She figured that if Susie hadn't been woken by Jack's roars when water got in his eyes, her sister must have been truly exhausted.

Jack snuggled in beside his mother, telling her everything.

"Pixie was shaking in the bath, but I kept giving her biscuits. The small ones Granny gives her. She liked that. I had one too. They're nice."

"Aren't you wonderful," Susie crooned sleepily, holding her son close. "Were you good for Auntie Leelu?"

"I was," he announced. "Wasn't I?"

"Very good," said Leila, smiling. She hadn't taken care of Jack for so long and had forgotten both how much fun it could be and how tiring it was. "I'm sorry for waking you now,

Suze, but I ought to visit Mum this afternoon. You should go to bed early tonight and I'll take care of Jack."

"No," said her sister. "We'll be heading home. I told Mum I'd go as soon as you were here. Thank you for taking over. I'm OK now."

"All right," said Leila, trying to fight down the feeling that she'd been snubbed. Susie was running away again. What would have stopped her from staying another night so that the three of them could be together?

She'd promised Jack they'd take Pixie for a walk and they could look for beetles. Jack had said he liked beetles and had a library book with pictures of them. "Mum is scared of creepies," he'd said. "I knew you wouldn't be."

Leila had felt ten feet tall. Now Susie was dashing it all.

"And I'm leaving the dog with you," Susie added. "There are numbers for some local kennels beside the phone in the hall."

"Fine," said Leila tightly.

She leaned in to drop a kiss on Jack's forehead and felt ludicrously like wanting to cry. "See you soon, darling boy."

The hospital was busy with people there for Saturday visiting.

Leila had the flowers she'd brought from Dublin, a sweet bouquet made up of yellow and white spring flowers, along with a bag containing some clean nightclothes. She walked slowly toward the ward, and in the corridor outside saw a man talking to what appeared to be a doctor.

A doctor! He looked younger than Leila, but he had the white coat and the stethoscope, and the harried expression of someone who probably worked too many hours a week. Hoping he would be able to talk to her about Mum, she stationed herself at a discreet distance and waited.

Finally the other visitor walked away and into her mother's ward, and Leila buttonholed the young doctor.

"Dr. . . ." She peered at his badge. "Whelan. I'm Leila Martin — Dolores Martin is my mother. I've been trying to talk to a doctor since she was admitted and I haven't managed it, but I'd love a word with you. Are you part of her team?"

She said *team* because she hoped it wasn't just him; he was too young, surely.

"Hello," he said. "Dolores, yes, I'm familiar with her case. I understand she's going to need nursing home care afterwards because she lives on her own. The team thinks the main problem is how she's coping with this latest flare-up."

"Flare-up?" said Leila, realizing they must be at cross-purposes. "My mother's Dolores Martin, sixty-three years old, bed four inside the door, car crash, broken hip . . . ?"

"Yes, Mrs. Martin. I mean flare-up of her rheumatoid arthritis — RA can floor a person emotionally," the doctor said, shrugging. "Perhaps that's what's happened here. It's obviously been difficult for your mother, especially living on her own. As far as I can remember from her chart, she's been on painkillers and steroids for a while, but in view of the damage to her hip, her rheumatologist is most likely going to have to discuss other options with her."

"Her rheumatologist?" Leila didn't think she could have heard him properly. "When was she diagnosed with rheumatoid arthritis? This is the first I've heard of it."

"Ah," said the doctor, face closing.

"With all respect, please don't *ah* me," said Leila. "My father is dead, my sister and I are my mother's next of kin. She's stressed and I don't know why; I arrived here a few days ago to find her house in a terrible mess — and she's always been a woman who kept the place as neat as a pin. Something is wrong and I need to know about it. I thought . . ." She hadn't been able to bring herself to say the word that had been preying on her mind, but now she forced it out: "I thought she had dementia."

"You should talk to her about it," the doctor said.

"I want to talk to you about it!" Leila said loudly.

"I understand, but — it's possible she doesn't want you to know."

"Of course," said Leila grimly, with a look on her face that Devlin would have recognized and steered clear of. "Obviously my motives are utterly suspect. Me and my sister want to take advantage of my mother to rob her blind now that she's ill. Those plates we collected with the supermarket stamps are worth a fortune. And the dog who's not toilet trained might be pedigree. We'll make a killing selling off her things while she's in here out of the way. All I need you to do is tell me how sick she is."

He gave her a sad look. "Talk to your mother, and if she's agreeable, then we can discuss this again. Unfortunately, I have seen patients fall victim to that kind of asset stripping. You see it all in this job. Some people only care about whether the will's in their favor."

Leila was shocked out of her rage.

"Really?"

"I had a lovely patient here last year: she was eighty-five, fractured both wrists in a fall. Poor old dear was perfect mentally — as sharp as you or me — but she had no close family. Suddenly a distant nephew rolls up saying he and his wife could look after her, but I could tell he just wanted to get his hands on the inheritance. I put the lady on to Nora Hummingbird — she runs the Hummingbird Nursing Home in Bridgeport — and she sold her home to pay for her care and moved in there. She's still happy there, as far as I know. That put an end to the nephew with the euro signs in his eyes. You might want to consider the Hummingbird place for your mother until her hip is healed. And no," he grinned. "I do not get a cut. But if it were my mother, that's where I'd send her."

"So Mum's really ill?"

"No, but she won't be able to go back to living on her own until her hip is healed and she can get about with a stick. After that, well, RA can be limiting, it needs monitoring, drug treatments, and special care. People need to manage their pain and be aware of what they can and cannot do."

He looked at his watch.

"I have to go. Talk to your mother."

And he turned neatly and walked off in the other direction.

Leila watched him go. Did they teach doctors that in college: how to cleanly send people freewheeling off into space once they had nothing else to say?

"Mum!" Leila managed a smile for her mother, who was sitting up in bed doing the newspaper crossword. "You look so much better."

"Really?" asked Dolores tremulously, eyes brimming at the sight of her daughter.

"Really. I just had a chat with the doctor and he told me you had rheumatoid arthritis. Mum, why didn't you tell us? And how long have you had it?" Leila's eyes were as wet as her mother's.

"I didn't want to worry you," said Dolores, and the tears began flowing down her face. "You were so distraught after Tynan leaving you, and I'm afraid poor Susie isn't coping at all well with being on her own — not that she'd tell anyone. I worry so much about both of you and I simply couldn't bother you with my problems in the middle of all that."

Leila handed her mother a tissue and then took one herself.

"How could you even think," she said, wiping away her tears, "that Susie and I would not want to know what's going on with you?"

She didn't even acknowledge the statement about her mother worrying over them both. She was fine — lonely but fine. And Susie . . . Susie was different: sadder, lonelier, and Leila had added to it . . . No, she pushed that thought away.

"When were you diagnosed, Mum?"

"Last year," her mother said. "I knew there was something wrong for ages. I thought it was normal arthritis and then I began to realize it was worse, but I kept putting off going to the doctor." She bit her lip. "A bit like Pixie when she knows she's done something wrong. She hides her head — thinks that will make it go away. It's funny when a dog does it and denial when an adult does it. I thought if nobody said there was something wrong, then there wasn't."

They both sat quietly for a moment.

Denial was clearly in the air, thought Leila sadly. Some part of her kept hoping Tynan would come back and tell her he loved her, even though it was totally obvious that no such thing would happen.

She understood denial all right.

"I've been on painkillers, although they're hard on my stomach so I have to have stomach stuff, and steroidal injections when it gets bad. But the last month it's been awful. The pain was horrific. Sometimes it's as much as I can do to get to the bathroom, and poor Pixie never gets out and the poor little love makes a mess in the house."

Her mother began to cry again, and Leila felt a wave of guilt at how she'd grudgingly cleaned up after the dog.

"I know the house is a mess and I hate it, I hate it. You know how tidy I am. I felt so low and everything kept piling up."

"Why didn't you phone me?" Leila begged. "I just don't understand why you didn't. You can't go through this on your own, Mum."

When Dolores looked up, her blue eyes appeared even bluer against the reddened lids.

"You grew up with your father an invalid — I couldn't put you through that again. You need to live your life, not look after me. I know what being a carer can do to you. I want you two girls to have good lives and freedom. Roots and wings, remember? It's what parents are supposed to give their children. I want you to have that, both of you."

"Oh, Mum." Leila leaned down till her head was on the pillow beside her mother's and held her as gently as she could. "You don't have to go through this on your own anymore, I promise. I'm here now."

Even as she said it, she wasn't sure how she'd sort everything out, but one thing was certain: she would be there in every way she could.

"Where's Pixie now?" asked her mother after a while.

"At home," said Leila. "She's had a great day. She helped Jack make flour-and-water buns, ate a fair amount of the mix herself, had a bath —"

"You bathed her?" Dolores was astonished.

"Yes," said Leila. "Susie was exhausted when I got there, so she went to bed and I took care of Jack and Pixie. We baked, then played in the garden, and then I gave up hoping the gunge would just fall off the pair of them, so I washed them. Pixie was very good really. I didn't know which shampoo to use, so I used that coconut one. Jack fed her dog biscuits nonstop while she was in the bath, and had one himself."

Her mother laughed. "He loves those biscuits no matter how often I tell him they're doggy ones, not human ones. I checked the label — it's all harmless stuff. Won't do him harm to have the odd one. Has Pixie had her walk yet?"

"Well . . . we played in the garden with her," Leila said.

"No, she needs a walk," Dolores said, distressed.

Leila clamped her mouth shut. Now was not the time to tell her mother that Susie was threatening to refuse to look after Pixie anymore and had suggested kennels.

"I'll walk her," she promised.

"As soon as you get home?" Dolores asked. "I feel so guilty about the poor thing. It's not right, getting a dog and then not being able to take care of her. I love her and I don't know what I'd do without her." Her eyes were filling with tears again.

At that moment, Leila made a decision. She couldn't spend every moment with her mother, but she could certainly cope with dizzy little Pixie for a few weeks. It would be her way of making up for all Dolores's lonely pain.

"I'm going to look after Pixie, Mum. She'll have a lovely bed in my bedroom but I'll have to get the hang of walking her and feeding her. So far, she's professed a fondness for Jack's uncooked dough worms."

This had the desired effect, and for the first time in ages, Dolores smiled. She put a hand on her daughter's, eyes wet again.

"Where do you walk her?" Leila asked.

"You go down the road in the direction of Katy's house, take the laneway on the right at the Mastersons', and go into the parkland behind. I let her off the leash there."

Leila brought two cappuccinos up from the canteen, plus a lemon muffin for her mother, along with more magazines, and they talked for a couple of hours, both deliberately staying away from the subject of rheumatoid arthritis.

"Can we discuss it tomorrow?" Leila asked before she left. "I don't really know anything about RA and I'll need to. I'll be on Dr. Google tonight, and by tomorrow I'll be an expert."

Dolores nodded, then gripped Leila's hand with her own unbandaged one. Despite the fact that her hand was misshapen and swollen, her grip was surprisingly tight.

"You can help, but you are not giving up your life to take care of me," she said fiercely. "I can't bear to think about all those years caring for your father and then for something similar to happen to me." Her blues eyes glittered at her daughter. "I can manage and I will. You need a life and a family, Leila."

"You're my family, Mum."

"No, I meant a husband and children. You're good with Jack, you always were."

Leila felt the pang of guilt she'd tried so hard to suppress: Susie and Jack. She'd let them down so much, it hurt to even think about it.

"Men are out of the picture for me," she said jokily. "I haven't made a very good stab at that so far."

"It wasn't your fault, lovey. Tynan was no good for you," her mother said.

"I thought you liked him." Leila was shocked. Tynan had made a huge effort to charm Dolores, although once he'd marked his territory, he hadn't wanted to visit Bridgeport again.

"He was very charming, for sure, but he wasn't the one."

Laughter burst loudly out of Leila. "*The One*. Why does everyone talk about The One? There are seven billion people on the planet and we are supposed to find the perfect partner out of the very small pool of our friends and acquaintances. How can anyone be The One? It's a crazy notion set to addle women's brains."

"You'll find him," her mother said with total assurance. "A treasure like you, you'll find him. I know you will."

"You know more than me, then," Leila said, leaning down to kiss her mother good-bye.

"You will, I'm telling you," Dolores insisted. "Remember what I told you about rain and rainbows?"

"You have to have rain to get the rainbow?" Leila's childhood had been full of sweet sayings from her mother. *When life gives you lemons, you make lemonade.*

What was the point of rainbows anyhow? thought Leila. They led to nothing — no gold, no contentment. Just a combination of precipitation and physics.

But her mother appeared pleased with the idea.

"That's it," Dolores said happily. "The Martin girls will have their rainbow, darling, I promise you. We deserve it."

Putting all thoughts of true love and rainbows out of her mind, Leila walked briskly to the parking lot. Mum was certainly looking brighter, as if a huge weight had been lifted now that her secret was finally out.

If positive talk helped, then Leila could go along with that. She didn't have to believe in it, though.

It was drizzling, and she realized that, once back on Poppy Lane, she'd have to set out in the rain to walk Pixie. But it was the least she could do, despite how shattered she felt.

Pixie barked hysterically when Leila arrived home, and nothing Leila could do would stop her.

"Shush, Pixie, I'm here," she said, and bent down to the little dog, who was whirling crazily, her long caramel fur flying. "Shush."

Finally the wild barking ceased and Pixie quivered with delight instead as Leila petted her.

"You are a sweet little thing, aren't you?" Leila said when Pixie's cold nose was thrust into her palm and those dark doggy eyes were shining up at her with adoration. Leila had been happy, although surprised, when her mother had gotten Pixie just over a year ago — they'd never had a dog growing up because Leila's father had been allergic to dog fur. But the decision made more sense now that she knew about the RA diagnosis: the puppy had been a way of staving off the fear and loneliness.

She petted Pixie gently. "I'll just grab a cup of tea, and then we'll have a walk."

At the word "walk," the hysterical barking started again. There was nothing for it, Leila decided: it would be easier to take the dog out now and leave the cup of tea until later.

She found a raincoat under the stairs, along with Wellington boots. A red nylon leash hung from another hook, with a pouch filled with what looked like tiny flesh-colored plastic bags. Nappy bags, according to the label.

Leila stared sternly at the dog.

"Do not do anything I have to pick up," she warned.

Still Pixie gazed up adoringly. *As if I would,* she seemed to be saying. *I am a nice lady dog.*

Leila wasn't entirely convinced. "You do understand, don't you?"

As they walked along Poppy Lane, Pixie weaved back and forth across the path sniffing out interesting smells.

Katy's mum had always had a dog, and as teenagers Katy and Leila had used the pooch shamelessly. "Walking the dog" was code for going down to the playing fields on the off chance that Michael and his pals would be hanging around. Often Leila would end up walking the dog around the fields on her own while Michael and Katy kissed. Eventually she'd told them they could walk him themselves.

"Walk *and* kiss," she'd said cheerfully.

Today, she decided that it wasn't so bad, this dog-walking thing. It reminded her strangely of the morning she'd watched the dawn come up and had gone outside to be a part of this glorious event. The sight of the woods nearby, the scent of earth drenched by rain made her feel relaxed and happy. Grounded, in fact. She was a part of this planet, yet she never noticed her surroundings, just rushed blindly from one place to the next.

Pixie was so obedient that Leila felt guilty for trying to get out of taking care of her. After all, this little bundle of furry love was her mother's sole companion. If Mum had to go into a nursing home to recover from the accident, then taking care of Pixie would be the least Leila could do — although she'd need to figure out how she was going to combine it with long days in the office.

There were bigger problems to worry about, though. When she got home, she would have to google "rheumatoid arthritis" and find out all she could about it. How limiting an illness was it? It was so unfair that her mother, who'd spent much of her life taking care of her husband, should be struck down by illness at a point when she should have been able to relax and enjoy her retirement.

Finally they came to the laneway by the Mastersons,' which Leila remembered well from her teenage days. The drizzle was easing off and a hint of winter sun was peeking out from behind the clouds. There was nobody in the parkland and she bent down and unclipped Pixie's leash.

"Just a quick run," she said.

Pixie licked her hand gratefully, then set off like a steeplechaser. For a small dog, she could really go, Leila thought in surprise as Pixie belted toward the goalposts halfway down the field. When she reached what looked like the middle of one of the pitches, she squatted down.

"Sh—" Leila stopped herself. "Sugar," she said instead, and felt in her pockets for the nappy bags.

Finished, Pixie bestowed a winning doggy smile on Leila and raced off again.

Leila looked down with distaste. This type of thing was why she'd never wanted a dog.

It took four bags, because Leila had to double-bag her hands before touching the dog feces. When she eventually straightened up, she looked around for both the dog and the poo bins; there was no sign of Pixie, but she spotted a red bin at the other end of the field and set off toward it.

"Pixie!" she roared. "Come on, walk with me, Pixie!"

There was no response.

She felt a surge of panic combined with irritation. Where the hell was the damn animal?

The Wellingtons were too big and were flapping around her legs, making it difficult to stalk through the damp grass to the last place she'd seen Pixie.

To her left was the disused railway line that had once linked Bridgeport with Waterford. All that remained was a section of track and the ruins of a tiny station where generations of local teenagers had hung out at night. If Pixie was there, she'd be in danger of having her paws sliced by broken glass, Leila thought with mounting horror. The teenagers inevitably brought beer bottles and packs of cigarettes, so that the ruins resembled the aftermath of a music festival. The Tidy Towns people had never made it as far as the train station, even when Leila was young.

"Pixie!" she roared. "Come here!" She started to run.

When she reached the ruins, she found a smashed vodka bottle, many cigarette butts, and Pixie cavorting with a large black-and-white dog. It was clearly a love affair, as Pixie was coquettishly sniffing the bigger dog's ears while his plumy tale wagged in delight.

"Please tell me you haven't been doing naughty things with this lovely boy?" Leila said, petting the black-and-white dog's head and then grabbing Pixie by the collar. "We do not want a litter of puplets and I have no idea if you've been spayed or not," she said.

The lovelorn Pixie wriggled free simply by pulling her narrow head through her collar.

"Oh," said Leila, staring at a happy sex-starved spaniel flinging herself at her boyfriend in a way that implied she had a feminine itch and he might scratch it. A delirious and clearly excited Romeo made few efforts to be lover-like.

"Pixie, at least play hard to get," yelled Leila, running after her. "He won't respect you in the morning."

But Pixie hadn't read The Rules, and

neither had Romeo.

"Somebody should have told me you were in heat," Leila panted, Wellingtons flapping, as she tried to catch them.

It took ten minutes, a lot of sweat, and plenty of shouting before Pixie was once again firmly on her leash. Leila dragged her away and the other dog followed happily.

"I hope he's your boyfriend and not a one-day hookup," she said as Pixie trotted beside her, the model of good behavior again. Nobody would think she'd been totally ignoring Leila's roars for the past ten minutes. "If he is your boyfriend, well done — at least one of us has a man. Not that I want a man, just so you know."

The two dogs looked up at her, panting and happy.

"Yeah, the second sign of madness is talking about your love life to dogs," Leila told them. "This can be our little secret, right?"

The rain began to pelt down, and the three of them started to run toward the lane.

"He is not coming home with us, Pixie," Leila informed her. "It's all I can do to look after you. We are operating a one-dog-only household."

By the time they'd made it down Poppy Lane, Leila and the two dogs were soaking wet, but Leila knew she couldn't relent and let Romeo in, even though he looked at her with anguished black eyes as she slipped through the front gate with Pixie and shut it firmly behind her, leaving him outside.

"No, Romeo, go home. We'll be out again tomorrow and you can smooch then. Smooching only, no lurve. We don't want any surprises in . . . well, however long doggy gestation time is."

In the utility room, Leila stripped off the now-soaking raincoat. Pixie stood waiting beside the radiator, where an old towel was hanging. She looked meaningfully at the towel and then back at Leila.

"You get dried with that? Fine."

Being dried was clearly one of Pixie's favorite things, and she wriggled luxuriously as Leila used the towel to rub her coat. Once she was dry, she scampered into the kitchen and sat expectantly beside her water bowl.

"Dinner, right?" said Leila.

She found dried dog food and some un-opened cans in a cupboard and gave Pixie what she hoped was a suitably sized portion. Pixie gulped it down at high speed, and when Leila had changed out of her wet clothes and made herself an omelette for dinner, the dog sat hopefully beside her, eyes moving in time with Leila's fork.

Afterwards, Leila lit the fire in the living room, flicked on the TV, and curled up with a cup of tea and some biscuits. Pixie leapt on to the couch beside her, snuggled in close, and studied the biscuits with the zeal of an undercover policeman watching a suspect.

Leila laughed and hugged the small dog closer to her.

"You're a little sweetie, do you know that? I can see why Mum got you. It's a long time since I had anyone to watch telly with, Pixie. I could get used to having you around."

Nora Hummingbird always sang as she did her rounds at the nursing home. Sometimes she hummed under her breath, shimmying to the tune as she walked, beautifully light on her feet for a woman who'd been on those same feet since dawn.

Occasionally she found herself humming when she showed new people around the home, scared, anxious people who were looking for somewhere their loved one could receive the care they could no longer get at home.

"We do our best to make the Hummingbird as much like home as we can," she said on her introductory tours. "None of the residents are restrained here, either chemically or physically. We take care of them."

First, there was the music. Miss Polka, as everyone called her, came four times a week with her bells, triangles, small drums, and little sound system. She wasn't called Miss Polka really, but when she'd first arrived, a few people had had trouble with the Russian name Ekaterina, so Miss Polka had stuck. It suited her too: small, dainty, with gray hair worn in a knot, a colorful scarf always tied just so around her neck, and bright clothes like a flower, Miss Polka seemed shy until she was behind the Hummingbird's piano, when she blossomed like the flowers she resembled, and sang till everyone did their best to join in.

It did a person's heart good to see Miss Polka in the downstairs living room on Mondays, Wednesdays, Thursdays, and Saturdays, spending a happy hour with her listeners, who could often be moved by music when they'd long since ceased to understand anything said to them.

"Music touch us when all else is gone," Miss Polka said to Nora in her heavily accented English.

"True," agreed Nora.

Ger, who led the exercise classes, brought people for gentle walks around the large walled garden, where there were plenty of seats and a tiny pond where several loud frogs obediently sang as soon as human beings went near. Ger had child-sized water bottles half filled with rice for people who could manage a bit of arm-lifting.

"It helps with the muscle wastage," he explained to the families of the residents. "And if the bottles get dropped, nobody gets hurt, unlike with real weights."

He organized gentle movement classes

twice a week, when the chairs were moved from the center of the big sitting room to the walls, and people could follow him doing steps to the right and left, and making pointy toes and upwards toes. Nora knew that new families walking around were often surprised to see a magazine-handsome gym instructor leading a group of people who were generally all following their own regime, moving happily in different directions.

"His granny was a resident for five years," she explained. "He likes coming here."

It was, as with everything in Bridgeport, a little more complicated than that. But Nora was good with people's private business.

Leila Martin, for example, didn't know that Nora was best friends with Grace Rhattigan and already had a mental picture of Dolores Martin's life, including how she'd superbly cared for her husband for so many years.

"She lives on her own, and my sister and I want her to be fully recovered from her hip injury before she has to go home," Leila said, with the slightly tearful anxiety that Nora saw in some people when they came to the Hummingbird for the first time. "Plus, she has rheumatoid arthritis and —"

At this point Leila burst into tears. "I didn't know," she sobbed. "I should have noticed. How could I not have noticed?"

"How could you, when you work in a different city?" Nora said softly, no reproach in her voice. "Your mother must have had her reasons for keeping it to herself. Now that you know, you can help."

Leila nodded as if she agreed, but her eyes told a different story. "I feel so conflicted about this," she blurted out. "I should be taking care of my mother, the way she looked after Dad."

"We can't always do what we'd like to," Nora said, pouring tea. "Life is rarely that simple."

Nora was used to people coming to the Hummingbird Nursing Home scared and guilty about bringing a loved one there to stay. It seemed so final, like saying, *I have to give up, I can no longer look after this person who nurtured and cared for me for so long.*

It was one of the dilemmas of the modern age. In a world where generations no longer lived under the same roof, who would take care of the parents and grandparents? She always tried to tell people that in an ideal world families would live in big houses, or in lots of smaller interconnected houses, where everyone was taken care of, be they old, infirm, whatever. But this was not an ideal world.

The reality was that sometimes people reached a point where they were no longer able to look after their relative, where their mother or father or grandparent needed twenty-four-hour care from somebody else.

As Leila Martin sat in her office, hands clasped together, eyes big in her pretty face, Nora could tell exactly what was running through her mind: *I should be taking care of my mother, I should be looking after her until she's totally back on her feet. I should somehow move my life so that I'm with her, so that she's no longer lonely or anxious or worried about her hip or wrist or rheumatoid arthritis . . .*

"There's something you'll find here that will make you feel a lot better," Nora explained. "The carers who will look after your mother have boundless energy and kindness and love. You'll sometimes look at them and think, *Why can't* I *do that? Why do I get annoyed when she can't do such and such?*"

She could see Leila's eyes brimming.

"The reality is that someone who's paid to come in here and take care of people can go home at the end of the day. Yes, they do become emotionally involved with the people they care for, because that's the sort of nursing home I run. Nobody works here if they're not made for the job, trust me. But at the same time, they're emotionally removed because they're not a relative. It is their job — a vocation, but nonetheless a job. It's different for the families. Perhaps this won't be the case with you, Leila, because your mother will get better and go home. But some of our patients have dementia or other illnesses from which they won't recover, and their families are torn in two about leaving them here. They go home feeling guilty, asking themselves, *Why can't I give them the care they need? There must be something wrong with me; if I were a better son or daughter I'd love them enough to look after them.*

"But they *do* love them enough. The Hummingbird is a place where we care for people, but we do not have thirty or forty years' love for that person behind us, and that makes a difference. It makes it easier for us and harder for relatives like you."

Leila started to cry in earnest now, and Nora slid a box of tissues across to her.

"That's *just* what I'm thinking," said Leila, mopping up her tears. "*I* should be doing this. My mother looked after my father — he was bedridden with a back problem, and she gave up years of her life to him. I feel ashamed because I can't do the same for her. My sister lives nearer, but she's all on her own with a small son to take care of. I have to do this."

When Leila had rung her sister to tell her about the Hummingbird and suggest they go to look around it together, Susie had cut her off.

"You organize it, Leila," she said. "You go see what it's like."

"But you should come —"

"I trust you to make the decision," Susie said fiercely. "I'll take time off when she

300

needs to move into the nursing home. She might have to go by ambulance, but if not, I'll drive her."

Even though Leila was mindful of the fact that Susie, being older, had helped out more with her father's care, and that it was all she could do to cope with her own life and Jack's, her attitude seemed harsh, as if she was washing her hands of her mother. It had taken till now for Leila to understand that what Susie was really saying was that it was her turn to step up to the plate.

Nora patted her hand gently. "Leila, you have to make peace with your decision and understand that your mother needs the type of care that you can't give her. Full stop. She will get that here; she will be loved and taken care of. She will make friends among the other residents and she will enjoy her time here. I promise you," she added, grinning, "she'll want to come back and visit."

Leila managed a weak smile.

Nora got to her feet. "Let's go have a look around then, shall we?"

The Hummingbird Nursing Home was nothing like Leila had imagined. Parts of it were new, like the lovely reception area and the big octagonal sitting room with huge glass windows overlooking a fabulous garden. Other parts were old, but everything was spotlessly clean. Leila had looked up the things to watch out for: an overpowering scent of urine, or worse, for example, and she was on the alert, but there was no smell like that at the Hummingbird. Cleaning products, yes, but overall an amazing rose scent.

"What a lovely smell," she said. "Where's it coming from?"

"It's my special secret," said Nora. "I have these very nice rose candles that are made locally using a strong natural aroma. I light them for maybe ten minutes in the morning — keeping an eye on them, because you can never be too careful with candles. The scent is so pure it lasts for the rest of the day. It's nice for people to be able to smell the outside when they can't get out. Of course, plenty of the residents *can* get out, and they enjoy making use of the garden."

She led the way through the sitting room, where all manner and ages of people were sitting, some accompanied by visitors, others chatting to each other. Nobody looked sad or lonely, as if they'd been confined to a chair and ignored. There was music on the radio, staff in yellow-striped outfits moving between the patients, plenty of cheerful talk and laughter.

Nora showed Leila the type of room her mother would have: a pretty bedroom with a big window looking out at a raised bed filled with primroses and a wooden garden seat where two elderly ladies were sitting bundled up in warm clothes, chatting. There was an en suite bathroom equipped with emergency buttons and cords, and a television and radio.

Finally Leila relaxed. She and Nora got chatting and discovered that they had connections in common: Leila's best friend, Katy Desmond, was marrying the son of Nora's best friend, Grace Rhattigan.

"Isn't that incredible!" said Leila, looking happier.

"I always tell people that this entire country is one big village," said Nora. "Isn't it lovely the way we all know each other? Sure, you can't walk up a street in Dublin without finding someone who was at school with your mother or danced with your father at a party sometime."

She put a hand on Leila's.

"It will work out fine," she said, her eyes wise.

"Thank you," said Leila, breathing deeply. "I think it will."

Ten

Love is composed of a single soul
inhabiting two bodies.

ARISTOTLE

From: Katy&Michaelwedding@gmail
.com
To: Leila Martin

Hi Leila,

Don't you love the new email address? I
figured it was easier to keep track of the
wedding stuff this way. You know how I
love to organize . . . Am trying to keep it
out of work time!

First, how's your mum? I'm going to be
home over the weekend, so will go in and
see her in the hospital.

My mum's been in already and says Dolores is so much happier now that she's
talked to you, so stop worrying — the
nursing home is the right thing after she
gets out of the hospital. She has a broken

hip — you can't take care of that. The Hummingbird is supposed to be brilliant. Just do what you can, right?

OK: wedding. I have been buying wedding magazines and going on wedding websites. Michael loves the magazines and keeps turning down the pages to mark ones with dresses he likes. He fancies those Scarlett O'Hara ones with tight bodices and laces down the back.

I did stop laughing eventually. Apparently Grace watches *Gone with the Wind* every Christmas and loves it. It's gotten into Michael by osmosis. I would never have thought she'd like that type of thing. She's a headmistress! But then I'm convinced that Fiona's a secret romantic under all that androgynous chic.

Back to the wedding — apparently, I need to decide on a color scheme. Yes, this was news to me too. Did Siobhan have a color scheme at her wedding? I honestly didn't notice.

Michael says I am not to ask Fiona's opinion on this as she'll say indigo or black. What do you think? I love violet and it suits me, but you? I don't know. So we — well, you and Fiona — have to try on some bridesmaids' dresses to figure out what works. The color scheme affects everything from invitations to flowers to what color Dad is going to have the outdoor pavilion painted.

He wants pale blue. You know Dad.

Finally, before we do the whole searching for bridesmaids' dresses thing, I need to get you to think about Susie. Will she be upset if she's not asked to be a bridesmaid? She seems so busy with Jack these days. I know she must have lots of friends who have children and they have more in common than we do now, but what do you think? She never has time to meet for lunch or anything anymore. I did wonder if she's struggling with money, but you know Susie, she'd never say. And the wedding will be fun — we could do a spa day for the hen night?

OK, enough about the wedding. I promise not to turn into one of those crazy Bridezilla people. Kill me if I do.

Work is mad. The new product line has to be ready in a month. Mum's terribly nervous I haven't sorted out a dress yet, but I have to sign off on the product line first!

Love Katy

From: Katy&Michaelwedding@gmail
.com
To: Stephen Rhattigan

Hi Dad, just to keep you up-to-date with all the wedding stuff. Katy got this email for us — cool, isn't it? Emails to this go to *both of us,* OK?

So far, we have decided nothing except for the date: second Thursday in June. Fridays and Saturdays are all booked out already. Wedding season, huh. As soon as we figure out what the invitations have to look like — color is important in this, Katy says — we will send one to you and Julia.

Hope you're well.

Love M

From: stephenrhattiganHHR&RAd@
  ireland.com
To: Mrhattigan7@gmail.com

Yes, Michael — I get it totally. Do not diss your future father-in-law on the group email. Got it. I adore Katy, by the way. She is a wonderful woman, and so is Birdie, I just do not know how they can be part of the same family as Howard, who is a horse's ass, if you'll forgive my French.

I am delighted about the date. Just give me the details and I'll be there.

Dad xx

From: stephenrhattiganHHR&RAd@
ireland.com
To: Katy&Michaelwedding@gmail.com

Katy and Michael,
That's fabulous news. I have saved the
date. I wouldn't miss it for the world.
Shall I wear my gownless evening strap,
or is it formal?

Love Dad/Stephen

To: Katy&Michaelwedding@gmail.com
From: Leila.Martin@EclipseFilms.com

Katy, thank you for saying that about
Mum, and yes, I know Hummingbird is
supposed to be the most amazing place,
but I feel SO GUILTY. Mum dedicated
her life to looking after Dad and I'm not
looking after her now. I can't take any
more time off work, though — this is such
a busy time for us. Don't say that Susie
should do more of it: living close to Mum,
she's always had to be the one who was
there. Plus she works full-time as well as
having Jack. It should be my turn.
Re: Susie and being a bridesmaid. I have
no idea. I phoned her last night and she
bit my head off. I feel guilty — I did
abandon her when I married He Who
Shall Not Be Named. Yes, she probably
has tons of new mummy pals and we bore

the hell out of her. I guess . . . ? Or maybe she is just tired and this could be a lovely treat for her? I wish I knew.

Tell me when you want me to be there for bridesmaid dress shopping. Your mother is right — choose the dress soon. I think they like you to pick it out about two years in advance. Hyper-organization and lots of bridey hissy fits are key, you know!

I will wear anything to make you happy, but tell Michael there will be no bodices or laces at my end either. The way things are going weight-wise, an eyelet might burst out of the dress, ping off danger-ously, and blind somebody. I read a bit about a blood sugar diet in the paper and clearly am killing myself with muffins. But post-breakup pain needs sugar, doesn't it?

Walking Pixie should be helping but it isn't. I drop her off in doggy day care dur-ing the week and walk her at night. I like having her around, but it's costing me a fortune.

I have to go to Rome for a conference sometime next month. It'll mean putting Pixie into kennels because Susie refuses to look after her.

L xx

From: Katy&Michaelwedding@gmail
.com
To: Howard.Desmond@Bridgeport
woolenmills.com

Dad,

Sorry missed you at the office earlier —
but please don't order blue paint for the
pavilion. Michael and I haven't decided
on colors yet, OK? You will be the first to
know. I need a color that Mum likes too.
I was thinking of one color but I suddenly
remembered how she loves the color of
the old roses near the back door. Wouldn't
that be nice?

I will tell you when we have decided.
And no, we don't want a wedding planner. Michael says thank you for offering
so generously to pay for one, but we'd
like to do this bit ourselves.

Thank you, Dad.

Hugs, Katy

From: Katy&Michaelwedding@gmail
.com
To: SusieB@indigo.ie

Susie,

I wanted to ask you personally but your
phone is off — will you be one of my
bridesmaids when Michael and I marry
in June? I know you're so busy with Jack

310

and everything, but I'd love it. It will be you, Leila, and Fiona. I know Fiona's not one of the Three Musketeers, but she's lovely. Addicted to jeans and biker boots, though, so when we go shopping — which we need to do soon — you'll have to help me get her into something girlie.

Do tell me what you think,
Love Katy

From: Katy&Michaelwedding@gmail.com
To: BridgeportNaturalCakes@gmail.com

Hello,
We're getting married in June and we wanted to make an appointment to talk to someone about getting our wedding cake made.

Our friends Sinead and Kevin had the most wonderful cake from you with one layer made up of chocolate biscuit cake and it was *delicious.* Could we come in for an appointment on a Friday evening or Saturday morning, anytime over the next month or so? The wedding will be in Bridgeport.

Thank you,
Katy and Michael

From: Katy&Michaelwedding@gmail
.com
To: FionaRhattigan@TechMetrics.ie

Fi, we have a problem. Where can I seat Julia at the wedding? Katy and I have been making a list of guests and then it hit me. Normally if your parents are divorced and remarried you seat all the new husbands and wives together at a table. (I know: totally asking for trouble if they hate each other.) But Mum hasn't a husband so we can't simply stick Julia at some random table or we'll upset her. What are we going to do? I told Katy I'd deal with it, but I don't know how to. Help! Unless you happen to be thinking of asking someone fabulous she could sit with . . . ? You're good at sorting out that type of thing.

M x

From: FionaRhattigan@TechMetrics.ie
To: Katy&Michaelwedding@gmail.com

Michael, for the last time, I have not decided who I am bringing to the wedding. I wish everyone would stop trying to pair me off. It's a pain! Put Julia beside Howard. If she's upset, nobody will notice because he'll be loudly cheering her up telling her how beautiful she is. Plus, I am not dancing with him even if I am supposed to according to all the etiquette books.

Fi

From: JuliaMcCann@DdW&Xadvertising .com
To:
   Rosalynch@McGovernpartnersinc.com
Subject: Personal

Rosa, I have turned into the stepmother from hell: it's official. Last night, Michael phoned and said he wanted to discuss wedding seating and that above all else he wanted me to be happy.

You know what that means — *you are not going to be happy.*

This whole wedding thing is a nightmare. Stephen's been so caught up in it there's no talking to him. I didn't want to put a damper on all the excitement by raising the thorny issue of the seating plan, but it turns out that since Grace doesn't have a hot stud muffin to invite, they don't know what to do with me. You'd think the Internet would have a segment on this — ex-wives with no new man — but apparently not. Michael rang because he has a list of places where I could sit and he's emailing it for me to look at.

Thing is, I snapped at him that I didn't care where I bloody sat.

I don't know why he and Katy don't just carry on living together. It's worked perfectly well for his father and me.

So you see: bitch stepmother from hell — that's me.

Aaagh.

Julia x

From: Rosalynch@McGovernpartnersinc .com

To: JuliaMcCann@DdW&Xadvertising .com

Subject: Personal

You are not a bitch stepmother. You have always been amazing — I don't know how you do it, to be honest. I couldn't.

Weddings are a cause of major stress not to mention a ridiculous waste of money — you wouldn't believe the number of intelligent people who come to us with a huge dent in their finances and blithely say *Well, that was my daughter's wedding,* as if it's money well spent. At least Howard's paying for all the madness. Count yourself lucky. When Fiona gets hitched, you and Stephen will be shelling out for that. Sorry! If I were you,

I'd start telling her that barefoot on a beach somewhere is the way to go. Fly a few people out, pay for cocktails, and the thing is done. Result.

Michael and Katy's wedding is just a day, Julia. In six months, it will all be over and things will get back to normal. You should plan a nice getaway for you and Stephen for when they're on honeymoon. Give yourself something to focus on. You never did that St. Petersburg cruise, did you?

Organize that, and trust me, Stephen will be thrilled. A little of that family/wedding thing goes a long way.

Rosa xx

From: NoraHummingbird@humming birdnursinghome.ie
To: GraceRhattiganBridgeportSchool@ eircom.net

Grace,
How are you, honey? I always know that when you don't get back to me, something's up. Wedding, work, life, the universe and everything? I know it's not a coven weekend, but himself is busy with his barbershop guys on Friday evening. They got a paying gig. I love those guys. I told him they're *his* coven and he got all insulted until he thought about it.

You can only call women's nights out a coven, he says.

I could do with a night out, a glass of wine, and a mindless movie starring a nice man who takes his shirt off a few times. They're all out of Bruce Willis movies in the cinema right now — *why?* I love him. The newer movie stars are so young — but we could find something in the listings. What do you think? I'll book the taxi?

Tell me if you're too tired.

Love
Nora

From: GraceRhattiganBridgeportSchool@
  eircom.net
To: NoraHummingbird@humming
  birdnursinghome.ie

Nora,

I'd love to go to the movies on Friday night. *Thank you.* I've been working late all week — there's a head teachers' conference next weekend and I'm trying to read all the advance notes, plus we're practically over budget again — so I'm tired and fed up with my own company. Shall we have dinner before or afterwards? I've got a ton of things to tell you, and yes, the wedding is on the list. Howard has had to be almost physically restrained from booking a wedding planner because he wants it done "properly." I may yet have to bail Michael out of jail for punching him. I don't know how poor Birdie puts up with it. The woman's a saint.

Fiona says Michael's driving her mad worrying about where to put Julia at the wedding. I told him she can sit beside his father if it makes him feel better. I don't care, honestly.

I am thinking of going online and renting an escort for the next six months and then everyone will be happy. What do you reckon? I'm thinking someone younger, called Dirk or Brad, with fabulous muscles. Then everyone can stop worrying about seating placements — they'll be too busy worrying if he's after me for my money. Ha! (Nobody will think he's after me for my body, because apparently I am too old for that kind of thing. Fiona said the other day that it was ridiculous for anyone to expect me to have a date at the wedding!)

How can you simultaneously be too old for a boyfriend and too young to go to your son's wedding without one?

You pick the movie and tell me the time, honey.

Grace xxxxx

From: Katy.Desmond@Bridgeportwoolen mills.com
To: Leila Martin

L — *can you pick up the phone? Please????* Not sure if you got my text, and not sure of your whereabouts — whether you've gone to Italy yet — but Michael's away for some work conference and I was looking through my diary and — I think I might be pregnant! Not that I don't want to be at some point, but *now?* Googled the symptoms and I need someone to talk to! Please phone.

Katy xxxxxxxx

ELEVEN

Life's greatest happiness is to be
convinced that we are loved.
VICTOR HUGO

Leila was sitting on her couch, Pixie curled up beside her, and she was Facebooking. Or rather breaking and entering, which was what it felt like when she crept onto Tynan's Facebook page and looked at his wall.

His status was still tantalizingly single, but for how long?

Recent pictures included many of him at after-event parties with women all over the place, plus one thirtieth birthday party of a "close mate" she'd never heard of before.

Clearly a close London mate, a six-month-old mate.

How close could you get in that short a time?

But then Tynan was good with people: he could swoop to the head of the express line of the supermarket and beg to go next because he only had milk/a six-pack of beer/

whatever.

"Of course, love, you go on — I'll be here for ages," would come the response from little old ladies with bent backs and dodgy knees who were bone tired of waiting, while Tynan, whose back could bend entirely in the opposite direction when he was doing tequila shots, raced past, entirely unappreciative of these gestures of kindness.

He did a nice job of pretending to care, Leila thought. So why did she miss him still?

Diane was hooked up again. Living in a house in Clapham with a gang, including her current "main man"; it was party central according to both the description and the photos. Bet the neighbors love that, Leila thought grimly.

She fled from Diane's page and swooped through some of her old schoolmates, all of whom appeared to be living the dream with fabulous holidays, fabulous friends, and fabulous parties.

Why wasn't there a Facebook for people who sat at home and knew the TV schedule intimately? People who could make a bath last two hours because that way the evening seemed shorter; who had begun making complicated dishes for dinner simply so they'd have some semblance of a life instead of eating microwave meals in front of the box.

When Leila's work BlackBerry pinged with an incoming email, she was tempted not to look at it — for at least a quarter of a second.

Pixie opened one sleepy eye, already tired after day care and her evening walk, and looked at Leila with eyes shining with love.

Leila stroked her gently. Having her mother's dog in the apartment wasn't perfect, because it was hardly a dog-friendly spot, but taking Pixie out to do her business at least gave Leila something to do in the evenings aside from Facebook-stalking Tynan. And having a creature to love — that was precious, she'd discovered.

She reached over for her BlackBerry, grumbling about late work emails, then saw it was from Katy. Some news about the wedding, no doubt . . . Oh, wow! Not the wedding at all. She looked at her phone and saw the battery was dead. Not even bothering to plug it in, she dialed Katy on the landline.

Katy answered on the first ring.

"Sorry, Katy, sorry, my iPhone battery's dead — I didn't get your text. But — oh my God! It's good news, you know. You're with the man you love, so what's wrong with getting pregnant?" Leila said, launching straight in.

"Nothing," wailed Katy. "Nothing. It's just, the wedding, and my chance to walk down the aisle in a fitted dress."

"With corset ties," Leila reminded her.

"I'll be in a maternity tent," Katy said. "Oh, Leila, I wanted to talk it over with someone,

321

but . . . well, I'd sound like a complete cow if I told Michael I didn't want to be pregnant for our wedding and that I'd planned for us to have a baby-free year at least so we could travel . . ."

"Get a test done," Leila said.

She paused.

"Do you want a baby?"

"Yes!" said Katy. "It's our baby."

"Right, do a test and if you're pregnant, the answer's simple: move the wedding forward a couple of months so you can still wear the fitted dress. As for backpacking . . . well, that's another story."

"But the wedding date's set!" said Katy.

Leila laughed. "You're an organizer par excellence, babe. Nothing is ever set in stone until you've put the cash on the table. You've talked to the church, sure, but you haven't sent a single invitation, you haven't tried on so much as one dress, and you have managed to stop your father painting the pavilion a hideous blue. Get married in March instead of June."

"But I love June," said Katy, sounding so tearful and unlike herself that Leila figured she *must* be pregnant and hormonal. No test required.

"March will be lovely too," said Leila gently. "Perfect for that old-rose color you've been saying your mum likes."

"I'll be . . ." There was a pause for calculations. "Four months pregnant by then."

"We could go the Jane Austen route, get empire-line dresses to hide your bump and my comfort-eating belly. You can be Elizabeth Bennet and Michael can be Darcy, stomping around looking proud and thrilled with his manly duty done."

Finally Katy laughed. "I haven't even peed on the stick yet. Haven't got a stick to pee on."

"Phone Michael," urged Leila. "Think of it as an early wedding present."

"He'll be so happy." Katy was wistful. "I am too, honestly. I only needed to talk it over with someone who wouldn't judge. I never expected it, you see. Not yet."

"Life is what happens when you're making other plans," quoted Leila.

"We could have that printed on the church ceremony missalettes," said Katy, sounding more cheerful by the minute.

"Good plan. Go on, phone Michael. He needs to know he might be a daddy very soon so he can practice his fainting technique in the delivery room."

Katy laughed. "He'd better be in there with me. If there's going to be screaming, I want to be holding his hand so I can squeeze it black and blue."

For a second, Leila stilled, taken back in time to when Jack was born. She had been her sister's birthing partner. The labor had taken nine hours. By the end, Leila had been shaking so much she'd almost felt unable to hold the seven-pound six-ounce baby in her arms in case she dropped him.

Being at his birth had been such a privilege. And for the first few months of his life, Leila had taken a lot of time off to help Susie deal with looking after a tiny baby on her own. But around that time her own job had gotten busier; to further her career she found she was working weekends, so she couldn't drive home as often; and then . . . then Tynan had come along. Tynan, who'd consumed her to the extent that she'd thought of nothing but him.

She'd seen Jack and her sister so much less since then.

No wonder Susie was full of resentment.

Leila's ever-present feelings of guilt about her sister melted away, to be replaced by a sense of huge love and sorrow for not having been there when she was needed. Like a sister ought to be.

She reached out to pet Pixie, who was always ready for affection, and who instantly rolled onto her back so her speckled belly could be rubbed.

" 'Course Michael will be there," she said, managing to sound upbeat for Katy. "He adores you. Tell him if he wants to prove it, he'd better be there to hold your hand when you break the news to your dad."

Katy gasped. "I just remembered something Susie told me after she had Jack — the pain of childbirth is supposed to be like breaking nine bones in the body simultaneously. Or is it eleven?"

Leila winced.

"Ah no, you're making that up."

"No, it's on the Internet. Makes you wonder how the human race has survived at all," Katy said.

"Drugs," said Leila.

Birdie was on her own in Vineyard Manor, watching television with Thumper squashed up against her on the couch. It was a rerun of a period drama, full of dramatic tension, secrets, sternly romantic men, and fabulous bosom-enhancing dresses. Birdie loved period dramas because she found it somehow reassuring that life seemed just as complicated then as it was now.

Previous generations had had to endure the anxiety of wars taking adult children away, the threat of illness, the powerlessness of women at a time when life was far from equal . . . Seeing all this made her feel as if her own worries weren't abnormal. Just because Howard didn't understand her fears, it didn't mean she was crazy. Other people worried too; that was the way it had always been.

The house phone rang and both Birdie and

Thumper jumped at the unexpected noise.

It was probably Howard, telling her how well his meeting had gone in London and what he was up to for dinner. He always told her what he was doing, which was nice. Of course, he knew what she'd be doing because it was what she always did: sitting at home with Thumper.

But it wasn't Howard. It was Katy.

"Mum," said Katy, "I've got good news —"

"You're pregnant," breathed Birdie. She had no idea where it came from, but the words flew out of her mouth.

"Yes! How did you know?"

"Your voice," Birdie said, eyes wet, heart soaring. "You sounded different, softer. My baby having her own baby. Oh, Katy, I'm so happy. But when?"

"The doctor says I'm about seven weeks," said Katy, "and we're scared about telling people so early, but we'll have to because of the wedding. Are you pleased?"

"Pleased?" breathed Birdie into the phone. "Pleased doesn't even go halfway to expressing how happy I am right now."

Birdie was eager for details and Katy filled her in, including the possibility of moving the wedding forward.

Birdie, worrier extraordinaire, was totally unfazed. "When it takes place is neither here nor there," she said blithely. "Vineyard Manor isn't going anywhere. It's only a matter of rearranging the details."

"The dress is a bit more than a detail," said Katy. "I was thinking it might be nice to go all Jane Austen-ish, you know, something flowing and empire line."

"Fine, we can start looking next weekend," said Birdie. "Now, as soon as you hang up on me, I want you to call your dad. He's in London for a business dinner, but he won't mind if you drag him out of it. He'd blow the biggest business meeting for you, darling. He'll be so thrilled." Birdie wasn't sure about the last part. Howard might not be too thrilled at the disruption to his plans, but he'd soon come around: anything involving his daughter got his full attention. She didn't even reflect that Howard didn't give *her* his full attention.

She never expected it in the first place.

"London?" On the other end of the phone, Katy stilled. Her father was in Kildare; he'd told her the other day that he was taking a bit of time off to play golf with some pals. There'd been no mention of a business meeting in London, she was sure of it.

"What's wrong?" Michael mouthed at her, seeing the confusion flicker across her face.

Katy shook her head and, utilizing the "fake it till you make it" mantra, smiled broadly into the receiver. "I'll give him a buzz now, Mum," she said.

"Love you both," said Birdie.

"Love you, Mum," said Katy before putting the phone down.

With a groan she uncurled herself from the corner of the couch where she seemed to be spending all her spare time lately. At least now she knew why she was permanently tired. Exhaustion seemed to have permeated her very bones, so that lying down on squashy cushions was the only thing she could bear after a day at the office.

As she headed into the kitchen, Michael got up to follow.

"What is it?" he asked.

"This is going to sound crazy." Katy reached the cupboard with the herbal teas. The chamomile one with spiced apple was nice. And a banana. She wanted a banana so badly. A banana sandwich on white bread, with sugar on the banana.

You want that too, baba, don't you? she telepathically asked the tiny being inside her.

"What's going to sound crazy?"

"Dad lied to Mum about where he is," said Katy, reaching over to flick the kettle switch. "I don't understand it."

She looked up at her husband-to-be and was stunned to see that his face didn't show confusion at all. His eyes met hers steadily, but he was hiding something from her, she was sure of it.

"What?"

Michael shrugged. "Must be a misunderstanding," he said easily. "You lie down and I'll make the tea."

"Don't. Do. That." Katy glared at him. "You know something, don't you?"

"Katy, I love you and you love your father. I don't want to fight over him. Please," he begged.

"But you know something," she said.

"I don't know anything, I promise," Michael said, sighing heavily. "But if you were to ask me whether he tells your mother the truth about where he is all the time, I'd have to say no."

"How do you know this?" she demanded.

"I can see it," Michael said, exasperated. "Katy, let's not get into this —"

"We're in it!"

"Listen, this is a conversation that can't end well. I love you, I don't want to start our married life with you thinking I don't like your father."

"It doesn't sound like you do!"

"See? It's not ending well," he groaned, "and we've only just started. Let's forget it. Your father is wonderful, we get along fine. It's a misunderstanding."

"But —"

"No buts, honey." He enfolded her in his arms. "Pregnant women need no stress in their lives," he murmured into the cloud of her hair.

"Dad can be tricky, I know that," Katy said.

"But he's a good man."

" 'Course he is — how else could he have had you?" Michael asked.

Katy laughed gently. There was no point continuing. She'd always known there was mild friction between Dad and Michael, but then there was friction between Dad and lots of people. He was the best dad in the world, but not everyone understood his little ways. When they were married and Michael was properly part of the family, things would be better.

And Mum probably got things mixed up. She was inclined to live in her own little world, as Dad often said.

It would all be fine. She was reading too much into a mix-up.

Dad had told her he'd be in Kildare playing golf and Mum had thought he'd said London. Simple.

Michael leaned into his fiancée and thought of all the notions that had passed through his head about her father's golfing holidays and business trips. For some time he had suspected that Howard had female company on his various jaunts. Not that he had a shred of proof. He'd never seen him with another woman, but all the same he had a gut instinct about his future father-in-law. An instinct that told him Howard Desmond was not the most faithful of men.

Still, it was none of his business. Best to steer clear, keep out of it. Because if what Howard was up to ever came to light, it definitely wouldn't end well.

"Michael, darling!" Grace cradled the portable phone in her shoulder and continued stirring her soup with the other hand. "How are you and Katy? How are the wedding plans coming along?"

"Well . . ."

Michael's hesitation threw her. She knew immediately that something was wrong. Turning off the gas, she pulled out a kitchen chair and sat down.

"What is it — what's happened?"

"Nothing," said Michael and this time she heard him with total clarity: the only wrongness was in her interpretation. "I've got good news, in fact."

Grace held her breath.

"Katy's pregnant. You're going to be a granny."

"Oh, Michael," she said, and she didn't know where the tears had come from — or why, for that matter — but they were there, streaming down her cheeks. "That's the most wonderful news in the world, darling. I am so happy for both of you — so happy for me!" she added joyfully. "I'm dying to be a granny."

"You never said," Michael pointed out, with the faintest hint of irritation.

"What sort of madwoman would you both think I was if I started demanding grandchildren?" she laughed. "You have to make your own choices."

"Sorry, yes," he agreed. "But you're going to be a granny now in . . ." He was counting. "Late August."

"Michael, it's wonderful," Grace breathed again. "The most wonderful news ever. Late August. So Katy will be seven months pregnant at the wedding."

"That's the thing," Michael went on. "We're going to move the wedding forward to March. Katy has her heart set on walking down the aisle in a slinky sort of dress, and they don't do them in maternity sizes, apparently."

Grace laughed loudly again. It felt glorious to be laughing with sheer joy.

"Katy will look fabulous even if she walks down the aisle in a trash bag!" she told him. "But I can see her point."

"We've decided on six weeks' time or thereabouts," Michael said. "It will probably be early in the week, because there's no way we'll get a church on a Thursday or Friday now, or we might go for register office, but think six weeks. I know it won't suit term-wise, Mum, but we can't get a weekend wedding at this stage."

"Right," said Grace. "I shall start the mother-of-the-groom dress search right away. Tell me," she joked, "am I to wear the gigantic flying saucer hat, or is that Birdie's job?"

"Oh hell, neither of you, please," he begged. "No teasing."

A thought occurred to Grace.

"What does Howard say about this change to his great plans? I heard he was going to have the garden totally renovated for the occasion, even though Birdie has worked tirelessly on it for years and you couldn't find a more beautiful spot in Bridgeport. There won't be time for all that with a six-week turnaround."

"He never told Katy he was doing that," Michael said, an edge to his voice. "She specifically said that she didn't want her mum's garden touched."

"You know Howard."

"I sure do. We haven't told him yet."

"Right."

Grace kept her voice neutral. It was on the tip of her tongue to warn him to expect fireworks, but she knew that Michael already had the measure of Howard. Plus she was mindful that interference, no matter how well meaning, was the kiss of death to families joined by marriage. If Michael were to let on to Katy that Grace had said something negative about her father, it might cause her to feel very differently about her future mother-in-law. She'd managed to hold her tongue all the years they'd been going out, and she wasn't about to slip now. Blood was thicker than marriage vows.

"Is Katy there? Can I talk to her?"

"She's lying down — she's really tired, keeps having to flop on the couch," Michael said.

"It's called growing a little person inside you," his mother informed him, "and it can be exhausting. Get her to give me a buzz when she's up to it — I want to tell her how thrilled I am."

Howard was in the car on his way home. He was tired. Sometimes it was tough being all things to all people, he thought wearily. People expected him to be immune to exhaustion, but he was only human — he just didn't show it. No, never let them see the fear or any sign of weakness: that was his motto.

The driver had tuned the radio to a classical music station. Howard liked classical music. Birdie had turned him into a fan; she was a mine of information when it came to symphonies and overtures and the composers who wrote them. She was the one who'd told him about the fabled Ninth Symphony Syndrome, listing all the famous composers who'd died after their ninth symphony. And it had been Birdie who told him how you had to imagine a little boy running in between the legs of the elephants in Handel's "Arrival of the Queen of Sheba." It was the sort of knowledge Howard had never had time to learn in his fierce quest for success.

But he liked to know it all the same.

His phone rang and his gaze shifted listlessly toward it, wondering whether he could be bothered to answer.

The moment he saw Katy's name on caller ID, his energy was magically restored. "Hello, love."

The driver, eyes fixed on the road, face expressionless, had driven Howard Desmond often enough to know that the caller could only be his daughter. There was a gentleness and fondness in his voice that was reserved for Katy alone.

"Dad," said Katy. "I've got some news."

"Work, honey?" Howard asked, straightening up in his seat and reaching into his jacket for a pen and the small notepad he carried everywhere. Gadgets and technology were fine, but you couldn't beat the feel of paper and pen; it helped the ideas to flow better.

"No, Dad, not work," said Katy, and he could hear excitement bubbling in her voice. "Big news. I know you might think you're too young to be a grandfather, but you're going to be one all the same."

She got no further.

"Darling! A baby! Oh . . ."

Michael, standing beside Katy, strained to hear what Howard was saying, but there was no more conversation. Just a muffled noise.

"Dad, are you all right?" asked Katy.

"Yes," said Howard.

Katy looked at her fiancé in astonishment.

"He's crying," she whispered.

"So wonderful," croaked Howard, barely able to speak.

In the front, the driver kept his eyes on the road, but he couldn't wait to tell his mates. Howard Desmond, scourge of all who served under him, a hard man if ever there was one, reduced to tears at the news of a grandchild.

Maybe he wasn't such a tartar after all.

Julia knew she'd always remember the moment Stephen told her he was going to be a grandfather. They'd arrived home from work at the same time and she had opened the front door of their apartment feeling as she always did that it was such a lovely haven away from the hustle and bustle of their working lives. With no children's footprints to worry about anymore, she had carpeted the whole place in a soft cream, which was highly impractical but felt wonderful when she took off her ballet flats and let her feet sink into the soft pile.

"I'll just put these in the kitchen," Stephen said, slipping past her, his arms full of grocery bags.

She was surprised, as she was sure they had cold chicken in the fridge and she'd planned to make a speedy salad to go with it.

The blond wood table sat to one side of the huge window that looked out over Dún Laoghaire harbor, so they could sip a glass of wine, talk about their days and relax with the exquisite view in the background.

"What did you buy?" she called as she went into the bedroom, dropped her jacket and handbag on the bed, and ran a brush through her short blonde hair before spiking it up in front of the mirror with her fingers. There was a fine line between artfully tousled and windblown. A lipstick was lying on the Gustavian dressing table, and she slicked it over her lips, turning her face to examine the effect. She still looked good, she thought, although it took longer to achieve the effect these days. Careful makeup and good hair helped.

"Champagne!" Stephen yelled from the kitchen. "And a fabulous dinner."

Put the chicken in the freezer, Julia reminded herself.

"Did you get another client?" She was on her way out of the bedroom and met Stephen coming in, two champagne flutes in his hands.

He wore a smile from ear to ear. Before Julia had time to wonder what was making him so happy, he handed her a glass and announced, "Katy's pregnant! I'm going to be a grandfather!"

Julia's mouth formed a perfect O.

"I know — I can barely believe it myself," he went on, beaming and clinking his glass with hers. "They weren't planning on this, but it's wonderful all the same. I think Michael is shell-shocked, but as I told him, it will settle him down and he'll love it. Isn't it wonderful?"

"Gosh," said Julia, which sounded very stupid but was all she could come up with. "That's — incredible."

"Yes, isn't it!" he said delightedly.

Putting down his champagne flute, he slid his arms around her and gave her a hug. "It really is incredible. I never thought of what it would be like to be a grandfather — and I know it's early days and everything, but just imagine, me, a grandad! Oh, Julia, I hope we get to mind the baby. You'd be up for that, wouldn't you?"

Somehow, Julia managed to nod. "Of course," she said, "of course I'd be up for it."

"You'll be a step-granny!" he said, grinning at her before draining the rest of his champagne. "We could get a car seat for my car and have a travel cot here, just in case. I want to be involved. That's something Grace used to say years ago and it drove me mad — that I wasn't involved enough with the kids. But things were different then. I was out at work. I didn't have the same hours she had. It was difficult. This time around, though, it's all going to be different. Drink up, it's good champagne. I thought we needed to splash out."

Julia drank deeply, but the champagne tasted like bitter lemons in her mouth. Despite not being their mother, she'd been great with Michael and Fiona when they were younger, without trying to be their mother. That was Grace's job.

When it came to having children of their own, it had all been decided in the early days, when they wanted to be truthful with each other, with no gaps in their understanding.

"I couldn't do it again — have children," Stephen had said, being up front with her. "I want to say this to you so you know, so you have the chance to walk away now, because I know it's important to women, and you're eight years younger than me, and I'm not going to stop you. I'm just saying that I don't want to go down that road."

"I don't have the time," Julia had said, because she honestly hadn't wanted to go down that road either. Then.

She'd rarely spoken about it because people seemed to find it strange — a woman who didn't want children? She'd have to be an unnatural being.

She'd always been annoyed by the assumption that there must be something wrong with a woman who didn't want children, but right now she felt as if maybe she *did* have something wrong with her. Why hadn't she and

Stephen had children? When they'd first met, she'd come out of a horrendous relationship in which she'd decided that bringing children into the world was wrong.

But now she could see that this had been her previous partner's view more than her own. Now, with hideous pain, she realized that she'd fooled herself about not wanting to be a mother. Katy's pregnancy had ripped her heart open.

Worse by far, though, was Stephen's sheer joy at the news. It struck her that she'd never seen him that happy before, not even when they'd met first and been lost in those glorious days of courtship when the rest of the world hadn't mattered. Not even when they went on marvelous holidays and woke up in luxurious beds in foreign countries on the first day of their trip, lounging in sumptuous sheets with nothing to do but enjoy themselves, enjoy each other.

His son was going to be a father. His son. No matter what Julia gave him she could never give him that.

Things had been tricky between them lately. She wasn't sure why, but she could date it to precisely one thing — Michael's engagement. The link to his family, which Julia had expected to stretch with each passing year until it was so fine as to be almost invisible, had proved to be as strong as ever, pulling him back into the fold the moment he heard the news. He'd been so excited. And suddenly distant. She could tell he didn't want her to go with him to the big engagement dinner: she'd been hurt by that, but had said nothing. Over the years she'd learned that sometimes she came second and there was nothing she could do but adapt to it.

She had done her best, really she had. But now this . . .

This excitement over the baby seemed to herald a new phase. What would happen when Stephen had his precious grandchild? Perhaps he'd want her involved, but then again, perhaps he wouldn't.

Perhaps it would be like the engagement dinner in Bridgeport; the grandchild would be deemed something that she, as a non-mother, wouldn't want any part of. She'd be back to coming second, or even third.

Julia sipped her champagne and felt as if her heart would break.

TWELVE

The course of true love
never did run smooth.

WILLIAM SHAKESPEARE

In the car on the way to the Golden Vanilla Cake Shop, Katy was fretting.

"I don't know if you can get a wedding cake made that fast," she said anxiously. "It's like getting a wedding dress made quickly. You have to pay a fortune extra. Of course I know Dad can pay a fortune extra, but what if she says no? Because the whole plan was that we wanted a really special cake and they might not be able to organize one at such short notice . . ."

Sitting calmly beside her in the driver's seat, Michael reached over and put a comforting hand on hers. There was no doubt that the pregnancy hormones were having a strange effect on Katy. She had never been highly strung, but lately she seemed to go from totally exhausted to wildly excited and full of energy with a bit of anxiety thrown in for good measure.

"We shouldn't have told people I was pregnant so early," she fretted. "I must have been mad, completely mad. Most people don't tell until three months and I told everyone immediately."

Michael had tried pointing out that because her pregnancy was going to have a big effect on the wedding, they'd had no alternative.

"But what if not everyone can come to the wedding, all the people we want to come?" was Katy's tearful response.

"All the people who are important to us will be there," Michael had said.

He managed to get a parking space outside the cake shop. Katy had passed the premises many times as she walked around the town, but they'd chosen it chiefly because they'd tasted the chocolate biscuit cake at their friends' wedding and it had been simply magnificent. Beautifully decorated, utterly original, and delicious.

The exterior of the shop was just as magnificent: two bow windows painted cream, with a cream and old gold sign shaped like a five-tier bridal cake hanging over the door.

The window displays were straight out of a fairy tale: cakes sitting on gold-and-white domed cake stands, an old birdcage painted antique gold with little white doves hanging off it, peering down at a curlicued cake with crimson flowers trailing down like a bride's bouquet. A modern cake made like an A-frame handbag and decorated with red lips, along with displays of scores of tiny, perfectly decorated cupcakes, showed the other side of the company's design scope.

A tinkling bell announced their arrival, and Katy clutched her fiancé's arm in delight. "I love it," she whispered. "It's so romantic."

Vonnie was at her desk, staring at the recent messages on her phone.

Ryan had texted telling her that he loved her so much and everything would be fine.

He clearly felt as shattered as Vonnie did about the three phone calls he'd had yesterday from Jennifer. He'd spoken to her the first time, but after that, he'd let the phone go to the answering service.

"There's no talking to her when she's like this," he'd said wearily. "She doesn't listen: she just rants."

Maura, who clearly had some psychic ability when it came to Vonnie being stressed, had texted hello and added that she'd be in Bridgeport the next day and could they meet for a quick coffee?

Love you too. It will all be OK, Vonnie had then texted to Ryan.

But would it?

She just didn't understand Jennifer. Was this refusal to accept that her husband had left her a religious thing? she wondered in exasperation. Was Jennifer one of those conservative people who viewed divorce and separation as wild, ungodly insanity?

But why stay with someone if it was over? Whom precisely did that serve, because it didn't help the poor children of the shrieking, arguing parents, and it didn't help the parents.

Quick coffee at two tomorrow? she texted to Maura.

She knew what Maura would say, because she'd said it before: "Joe's great-aunt Lizzie is divorced — and she's eighty-five and a regular Mass-goer. It's nothing to do with devoutness."

Vonnie wished she could send Jennifer to Great-Aunt Lizzie's for a month and let her work her magic. But then Vonnie was so fed up with it all that she had her own brand of magic she'd quite like to try on Jennifer: *Grow up and get a life.* Yeah, that would do.

The shop bell made her click her phone to silent, and she got up.

A tall, blonde lady came forward to meet Katy and Michael.

"Hello," she said, with the softest U.S. accent. "I'm Vonnie. You must be Katy Desmond and Michael Rhattigan."

"I love this place," Katy burst out. "It's magical. The cakes in the window . . . And that chocolate and ruby-red flower one in the

345

old gold birdcage — I just love it. They look like real flowers."

"I love flowers," Vonnie said, face lighting up so that Katy could see that she was truly beautiful: like a flower that needed sunlight or kindness to show it off. "Baking saved my life. Crafting flowers, making delicate petals . . . it's such a joy. Those flowers on the chocolate cake in the window are peonies, and I think of their scents as I make them and find the right colors."

"I knew we were right to come here," Katy said, pleased. "I didn't want any old cake from a production line. I wanted special, and this is special. You're an artist."

Vonnie beamed at them. "Come this way and I hope I can show you even more special cakes."

She led them through to another room, where there were comfortable seats arranged around a large desk already set with a cafetière of coffee and a teapot.

"Please sit down," Vonnie said.

Katy began to explain, as she already had on the phone, that her pregnancy had pushed all their wedding plans forward.

"I do hope you can help us," she said.

"Of course we can," Vonnie said with a smile. "Pregnant ladies get what they want."

"Hopefully I'll get a wedding dress to fit," Katy added wryly.

"You're a pixie," Vonnie said. "Pixies R Us

should sort you out."

Katy giggled.

"That's what I've told her," Michael said. "She's afraid she'll go down the aisle like a cruise liner decked out in white silk."

"You'll go down the aisle with the start of your family nestled inside you," said Vonnie. "Much more precious. And I doubt if you'll need the cruise liner look. So, we'll have a cup of coffee or herbal tea, and I'll show you samples of our work to give a sense of what we can do."

She rang through to the kitchen, and one of the girls came in bearing the platters of miniature wedding cakes.

Katy gasped out loud at the selection. "Oh my goodness!" she said, looking at the various chocolate and fruit and sponge cakes with interesting designs somehow *in* them, some covered with beautiful white icing and delicate flowers of every variety.

"Wow," said Michael in admiration, "this is pretty amazing."

Katy chose fruit tea, so Vonnie poured hot water into a minuscule china teapot for Katy, and coffee for herself and Michael, and then she went through her usual explanation as to what sort of cakes could be made and showed them various designs on the computer.

"You're very good," Katy said at one point, "taking us on with so little time to spare. I know it's —"

Vonnie stopped her: "It's fine, really, this happens every once in a while. Sometimes we can't accommodate people on short notice simply because we're so busy — our cakes take a lot of handcrafting — but this isn't our busiest time of the year, so we're delighted to be able to help."

Katy and Michael looked at each other and beamed. Their hands found each other and Vonnie smiled with them. Such happiness was infectious.

When they left the cinema in Waterford, Grace and Nora were still laughing over the movie. They'd failed to find anything with Bruce Willis or anyone else taking their top off, and had gone instead to a chick flick that had made them laugh, chat, and generally enjoy themselves.

"I guess they don't ask Bruce Willis to take his top off much anymore," Nora said wistfully as they got out of Grace's car and walked toward Pedro's wine bar.

"No," said Grace. "Like ourselves, he's probably considered a bit old for that sort of carry-on. The people who take their tops off now are all in their twenties — thirties max — with washboard stomachs. I bet they never eat bread."

"Wow," said Nora, horrified. "Imagine never eating bread."

"That's what you have to do," Grace revealed. "Katy's friend Leila, who works in the movie industry, says it's tough out there. She was taking care of some fabulous young actor in Paris recently and he told her that if he has to do a big scene or a photo shoot, he won't eat bread for two days. Carbs, that's what they call them. That's not even taking into account that he works out two hours a day."

"Wow," said Nora again, then a twinkle came into her eye and she added, "Let's have some carbs, shall we?"

Pedro's, situated on a small side street in Bridgeport, was no longer a wine bar, but that was what Grace and Nora still called it. In the past two decades it had been transformed from a gloriously darkened establishment with fat wine bottles holding dripping candles atop clichéd red-checkered tablecloths into a fabulously modern steel-and-glass place that Grace and Nora hadn't liked. Its current incarnation, which they did like, was a much cozier affair, with nice squashy seats and low tables where you could have coffee and buns in the morning and beautiful meals in the evening, all with the fire roaring in one corner and music low enough so you could talk and actually hear each other.

They were led to a corner table, and as they sat, Grace could see Nora craning her head, listening in to the people all around her. Nora always did that — she was an inveterate eavesdropper. Grace looked at her friend and grinned. The couple beside them were actually quite easy to overhear; the woman, who looked to be in her thirties, was talking heatedly. "I am not having your mother to stay," she huffed, "and that's final. It's not even *our* child's eighteenth birthday. She didn't stay with your brother when Sean made his first Holy Communion last year; oh no, she stayed in a hotel on that occasion. So she can stay in a hotel now. You know all she'll do is criticize me, so forget it. I have enough stress in my life as it is."

The man looked gloomily down at his plate.

"I'll be the mother-in-law soon," said Grace, wincing.

"Oh, hush," said Nora. "You're never going to be that sort of mother-in-law. Katy and Michael are both blessed in the mother-in-law department: Katy's got you, and you're fabulous, and Michael's got Birdie, who seems such a sweet woman, the sort of person who wouldn't say boo to a mouse."

"I think that's the problem," Grace said with a sigh. "Howard walks all over the poor woman — now more than ever. You can see the tension in her. The night we all went out to dinner, he almost totally ignored her, while gushing to me about how wonderful I looked. Then he started in on the same old spiel with Fiona, who looked at him as if she'd never heard anything like it in her life. All wildly inappropriate. I felt sorry for Birdie." Grace shook her head. "I suppose marriages can look strange on the outside and work perfectly well on the inside."

Nora wrinkled her nose. "We both know that if it looks like a duck, quacks like a duck: it's a duck."

They both fell silent.

"Quack," said Nora finally. "You can't fix the whole planet, Grace. Enough about Howard — I want to hear all about the baby and Katy and what's going to happen with the wedding."

For a moment Grace looked anxious, which wasn't like her, Nora thought.

"I'm a bit jittery, and will be until she passes the three-month stage," she admitted. "I know they have to tell people because they're moving the wedding forward, and I suppose you have to give a reason why, but there's a lot to be said for waiting till the first three months are up . . ."

Nora laid her hand over Grace's. "It will be fine," she said. "Tell me, is Stephen delighted?"

"Overjoyed," Grace said. "You have no idea. He's rung me at least three times to talk about it, wanting to know whether he should give them a baby stroller as a present, should he get a travel cot for his and Julia's place in case they stay over, what sort of baby seat should he buy for the car. I think he believes *he*'s having the baby."

A waitress came over, asked if they wanted anything to drink and delivered menus, which they both looked at hungrily.

"Steak sandwich for me," said Nora. "Plus chips." She smiled up at the waitress. "I need my carbs."

"I'm going to be boring and have what I always have," said Grace. "Goat cheese salad and bread rolls. I can't have her killing herself with carbs on her own," she said to the waitress.

She waited until they were alone again before saying in a low voice: "I know you'll tell me not to stick my nose in here either, but I can't help wondering about Stephen and Julia. It's not that anyone's said anything — more a case of what hasn't been said. Stephen was quite reticent about her at the engagement dinner. Not that he's ever talked that much about her with me. I guess he feels it might hurt my feelings, which is sweet, but still. I'm a grown-up. We're divorced and he lives with someone else . . ."

"Go on," said Nora. "This is your ex, you *are* involved."

"OK, well, I wouldn't have given it a second thought, except Michael told me that when he rang Julia over the seating for the wedding, she snapped his head off. Julia and I may be oil and water, but she's a nice woman and she's always been good to the children.

It was completely out of character for her."

"Could be all this happy families wedding stuff is getting to her?" Nora suggested.

"I think you're right," Grace agreed. "I suppose what makes it worse for her is that Stephen's been talking about the past, when we were together and the kids were young, like it was all some fantasy world. I don't understand it. It's as if he wants all that back again," she said finally.

Nora studied her friend. She was constantly amazed that Grace seemed oblivious to what a fascinating, vibrant, and wonderful woman she was. In her simple blue cardigan and jeans, with her dark hair tied back in a ponytail, she looked so pretty. Somehow her boundless energy and force of personality had kept her youthful, and she seemed years younger than her real age. Many men looked at Grace Rhattigan with interest — and not just Principal Derek McGurk — but Grace rarely seemed to notice. It was as if she'd closed off that part of her life in the past few years.

"Maybe he *does* want all that back again," Nora said gently. "It's not beyond the realm of possibility that he's still in love with you, that he wishes you hadn't split up."

"Don't be ridiculous!" said Grace in astonishment. "If he was . . ." She faltered. "If he was, he wouldn't have gone off with Julia and stayed with her, would he? No." She shook her head decisively, flicking her ponytail. "It's just wishful thinking about the past, when we were a family, and he can't go back in time: Michael and Fiona are grown-up, they don't live at home, so there's nothing to go back to."

"Grace," said Nora calmly, "he could go back to you."

"Oh, Nora, stop. We've been apart almost fifteen years, we're divorced, it's a crazy idea."

"And you've never thought about it?" Nora asked.

"Don't be daft," Grace said, laughing it off. "He left me, remember? Fine friend you are if you think he was an eejit then and possible date material now."

"I was just saying —" began Nora.

"No. Don't say anything. What would I want with a man in my life, specifically one I divorced a long time ago? Now that *really* would be a triumph of hope over experience. Now, tell me all about the Hummingbird."

Nora studied her friend, wondering whether to go along with the change of topic. In the end she decided to let it go; Grace needed to come to a conclusion herself. Of all the divorced couples Nora had ever met, Grace and Stephen got along the best. They didn't fight or shriek at each other, and any pain Grace had felt in the early days of Stephen being with Julia had been carefully hidden.

Nora began to talk about a staffing problem

but her mind was far from her beloved nursing home. Grace *had* thought about Stephen in that way, she was sure of it.

The house on Poppy Lane was looking a lot better than it had the first time they saw it, Vonnie and Ryan agreed as they parked outside on a stormy Saturday morning a week before the final moving-in.

A two-story with attic conversion, it sat at the end of a small cul-de-sac and had been owned by an elderly lady who'd clearly adored flowers but hadn't had anyone help her with general maintenance for a long, long time. The little old lady had died and an executor's sale had progressed slowly, so that by the time the house came up for viewing, the once-beloved garden was a tangle of weeds.

The house was built of sandstone that was dirty with age, and Vonnie guessed that the last time a window cleaner had been on the premises, bell-bottom jeans had been fashionable. But the wisteria that soared up the front of the house looked loved and strong. The wisteria had sold the place to Vonnie, its branches enfolding the porch as though to shelter any visitors from rain and wind.

"I love wisteria," she'd told Ryan. She and Joe had once nearly bought a pretty Edwardian house with cream shutters and a veranda covered with wisteria, but they hadn't been able to stump up quite enough money.

"It was just a house," Vonnie had said stoically when they'd lost it to a higher offer.

"One day," Joe had kissed her on the temple, so as not to wake Shane, who lay asleep in her arms, "we'll have a house with wisteria."

The house on Poppy Lane was it, Vonnie knew. Her past and her future coming together.

Ryan's hand found hers and squeezed it gently.

She smiled up at him. She didn't know how he knew, but he always knew and she loved him for it.

Inside were elderly carpets smelling of cat. They'd need to be ripped up, Vonnie knew. The floors would have to be sanded, rooms painted, and the kitchen — which was the newest bit of the entire premises — probably needed the attention of a steam cleaner for a week in order to get rid of the grime.

"It's old and dirty, yes," she said to Ryan, "but it just needs hard work and elbow grease, and it's not as if I don't have plenty of experience with that. Isn't the hall lovely — you can just see a Christmas tree here, can't you? And the kitchen, look — they knocked down a wall so we can have a cozy sitting room part here, and there's space for a table between the two rooms where the kids can do their homework."

"Yes," said Ryan, "I see it all too."

He was gazing around at their prospective new home with a contented air, seeing walls painted and floors sanded, imagining their three children working happily at the table while he and Vonnie chatted about their day in the kitchen. Again Vonnie sent grateful prayers up to whoever had given her this wonderful man.

Let me have some of his certainty of happiness, she prayed.

Shane, Maura, and Tom had taken to the house too.

"Ah yes, there's a bit of work to be done here," said Tom, examining the walls with the intensity of a man who'd spent years doing DIY and had the collection of screwdrivers and rawl plugs to prove it, "but the plumbing, the electric, and the structure are all grand, aren't they? So it's only a bit of dolling up. Wait till me and Ryan get at it, Vonnie love, we'll do the work of four men." He reached out and put an arm around her shoulders.

"What about me?" demanded Maura.

"You're on steamer duty," said Tom. "It's a great contraption, Ryan. You don't need chemicals or anything. It boils the dirt out."

"Does it do carpets?" asked Shane, looking doubtfully at the various dark and murky patches underfoot.

"It's not magic, Shane lad," laughed Tom. "I think those carpets have long since died. But Maura might give you a go of her steam cleaner if you ask nicely. She's very possessive about it."

"Besides, Shane, you and me are going to paint your bedroom," Ryan added.

"Blue!" said Shane excitedly.

"I told you, any color you want," said Ryan. Shane beamed at him.

Vonnie had insisted that Ryan take his daughters to see the house on their own.

"So it's their house too," she said. "If they see it first with me and Shane, it will be like we've already been there and they come second. You take them for their first tour."

"How do you know this stuff?" Ryan said.

"It just makes sense," Vonnie explained.

Shelby wanted her room pink.

"This pink," she'd told her father the previous weekend, holding up a hair clip with dusty pink flowers on it.

"Righto," said Ryan gravely. "I will get that exact pink. And you, Ruby?"

Ruby had spent a long time in the room she was to have every second weekend. "It's fine the way it is," she'd said.

"Ah, now, Ruby," her father said, putting an arm around her shoulders. "That wallpaper is so old, the museum people have been on asking can they have a bit for an exhibit.

We're going to strip it off and paint the room. We're a bit too broke to stump up for wall-paper, but we can do paint. You like apple green, don't you, like at home?"

If Vonnie had been there, she might have seen something flicker in Ruby's eyes, but Ryan was so anxious for all of this to go well that he didn't see anything.

"Yeah, green then," said Ruby.

Ruby hauled her gym bag into the girls' changing rooms and inhaled the usual scent of perfume, highly chemical body sprays, and the subtle whiff of cigarettes. The changing rooms in the technical school in Bridgeport were as old as the rest of the place, and you walked barefoot to the showers at your peril. Athlete's foot would be the least of your worries if you did that.

"Anyone got any tampons? I've got my period," wailed Lizette, eleventh-grade hypo-chondriac.

"You had your period last week for gym," said Maria, their grade's queen bee, currently dating Seamus Delaney, twelfth-grade uber-jock, a student who got a D-minus in most of his subjects but made up for it by his prow-ess on the football pitch.

"No, I didn't," insisted Lizette.

"Did," retorted Maria.

"Yeah, you did," chorused the bee-ettes, Maria's gang.

"Like you care if she has her period every week?" Ruby snapped, handing a tampon to Lizette, who huffed and marched off to the bathrooms.

Ruby belonged to a nice group in school: not with the nerds, not with the nymphets, and not with Maria's gang either. She lived in the netherworld of ordinary girls who were neither cool nor brilliant nor stunningly beautiful nor athletic. The ordinaries could roam all the various groups without ever being a part of any of them. Ruby pretended not to mind being an ordinary. She pretended not to care that she wasn't beautiful, even though Vonnie, her sort-of-stepmother, insisted she was. That was part of Vonnie's shtick — she told people they were beautiful, fabulous, talented all the time, the way she did with Shane.

Ruby found it both astonishing and quite sweet, because she could never remember her own mother saying *You're fabulous, you're beautiful, Ruby.* Jennifer just wasn't that sort of mum. She was funny, for sure. She had a wicked sense of humor and she never cared what people thought of her. *Boring old farts* was her favorite thing to say when she was driving badly and somebody beeped at her.

She'd been less funny lately. Since the news of the new house had broken, Mum was in an officially bad mood. She'd stopped watching comedy on the telly and was watching

360

old chick flicks or true life movies on cable, ones where men were mean and women suffered because of it.

Ruby didn't think it was good to watch those sort of movies on a loop.

Her mother was very different from Vonnie, Ruby knew, and she could see why her easygoing father would love Vonnie, because she was so calm. Sometimes, just sometimes, Ruby wondered if she could talk to Vonnie honestly about it all. About her mum and how awful things were. Because they *were* awful these days, and being able to decorate a stupid bedroom any way you wanted couldn't make up for that.

She couldn't talk to Granny Lulu, because she'd just shout at Mum and then everything would be worse.

She couldn't tell Dad, because she could see the way his face practically froze when he had anything to do with Mum. Which left Vonnie.

Vonnie might understand that Mum was sad and lonely, that Dad's new happiness was making it worse but that Ruby didn't know how to fix Mum. Or if she was even fixable.

And nobody seemed to think about what it was like for Ruby.

Someone in the changing room had chocolate biscuits and was handing them out. The athletic girls were taking them because they knew they'd burn off the calories soon — not that they thought about calories. For them, biscuits were simple nourishment to keep them going through running, swimming, and hockey. The nerds gobbled up the biscuits, delighted to be asked. The beautiful people said no, aghast at the very idea. Processed sugar and chocolate — like, hello?

Normally Ruby would have taken a biscuit. She was really hungry, because Mum had been so awful that all she could think about was getting out of the house, so she'd skipped breakfast and forgotten to bring a packed lunch. But suddenly, in one inspired instant, she decided she liked the pangs of hunger in her stomach. She was hungry but she wouldn't eat. She could say no to food, no to something. That was very powerful. Like the light streaming down from the clouds in one of those biblical paintings they'd studied in Miss Maguire's deathly dull art class. Rays of wisdom and knowledge shone through the clouds into Ruby's head: she wouldn't eat. There, she felt strong — in control.

And maybe if she got thinner, somebody might notice that something was wrong and ask what they could do to help. Because Ruby couldn't keep going with things the way they were, and she didn't know what to do about it.

THIRTEEN

It is not a lack of love but a
lack of friendship that makes
an unhappy marriage.
FRIEDRICH NIETZSCHE

Birdie nursed her breakfast coffee, staring out the window at the glass bird feeder on the kitchen window, where a robin was nibbling some seeds and staring cheekily in at her.

She loved robins, loved their fondness for humans. This particular one, *her* robin, liked to perch near her in the garden and angle his little head, bright beady eye watching her with interest. Even Thumper didn't try to chase him anymore, and Birdie talked to both of them as she worked.

"We should have the best spare room redone for Mother's visit," Howard announced, putting down the newspaper with intent.

Birdie put down her own cup. Oh Lord, Doris.

Even the robin flew off. Clever bird.

Howard's mother was a definite threat to wildlife. She defiantly wore fur and had an old turban made of such glorious feathers that Birdie winced every time she saw it, knowing that several poor birds must have been killed to make it.

Doris had been on the phone a lot lately. She'd raged, predictably, at the notion of her granddaughter being pregnant before she got married, and had threatened to boycott the wedding.

Birdie had stayed at a distance as Howard talked to his mother, but even so, she could hear Doris's loud tones from several feet away.

"The shame . . . in my day . . . no grand-daughter of mine . . ."

It had all been bluster, of course. Doris wouldn't let nuclear war keep her away from a wedding and the chance to wear her mink capelet and the diamond earrings she'd been promising to give Birdie for thirty years.

Howard had sternly reminded her that it was the twenty-first century and "things are different now," following it up with "It wouldn't be a wedding without you, Mam." Doris had been placated.

Clearly, the need to further butter up his mother had become a major feature of his grand plan, hence this sudden notion to redecorate the room she always stayed in.

As the wedding was only four weeks away and she had more than enough to contend with as it was, Birdie felt the fear rise within her at the thought of clearing the room, having decorators in, and then putting everything back. She hated having work done at the best of times; invariably she'd spend her days at the beck and call of the workmen, making them tea and biscuits, praising their handiwork, and then Howard would return and jackboot around the place finding fault with it all.

She flushed at the memory of Howard refusing to pay the decorators who'd put up the Chinese floral wallpaper, because he claimed they'd made such a poor job of it they'd ruined the ultra-expensive paper and the entire job would have to be redone.

"Howard, it's not ruined," Birdie had pleaded, mortified by the fuss he was making as the two decorators stood casting mutinous looks at him. "It's lovely."

"You can see the joins in two places on that wall!" Howard had ranted. "There are gaps. There should be no gaps."

Everyone had peered at the allegedly obvious joins. If she squinted hard, Birdie could make out a tiny sliver of wall. Just in one place, not two. Nobody else would have noticed it — but nothing escaped Howard's scrutiny.

"I never thought it would look so nice, and

that's a flaw in the paper itself, I think," she began, trying to placate.

"I'm not paying!" bellowed Howard.

"Fine. I'll take you to court," roared the decorator.

The very thought made her feel weak. There were already men in the garden — Howard had overridden Birdie's gardening expertise and hired a designer to come in and jazz the place up specially for the wedding — and a team of contract cleaners were arriving in a week to do a proper clean, since the combined efforts of Birdie and Morag, who came in twice a week, were obviously not up to the task.

Somehow, and Birdie had no idea how, Howard had found a woman who made houses look more beautiful "with flowers and subtle work," and she was due to make her first visit the day after the cleaners.

"She's reputed to be the best," Howard said, almost preening. "She's from Dublin, I got her name from a friend. Now, Mother's bedroom. Yellow is her favorite color; let's go for that."

And then he was off to the office, leaving Birdie with Thumper, the robin long gone, and a sinking feeling in her heart. Weddings were supposed to be lovely, happy experiences, but apart from her joy over the marriage itself, and darling Katy's pregnancy, everything else was riddled with stress.

Doris was a dreadful rip who put the fear of God into all who came across her. Argumentative and with a mouth set permanently like a steel trap, at the age of eighty-nine she approved of almost nothing — except her beloved Howard, out of whom she thought the sun shone.

Birdie lived in fear of her visits because Doris, though allegedly fragile and required to use a walking aid, could nevertheless belt around the place finding cobwebs in distant corners, out-of-date packets of flour in the kitchen, and trails of dust on furniture Birdie was sure she'd dusted the day before.

"Look at the state of this" was her rallying cry, and Birdie would leap up from whatever she was doing and follow the howl of outrage to locate Doris at the scene of her latest crime.

"You could kill Howard if you gave him this, you know that, don't you?" had been her most recent hobby horse when she'd gone through the cupboards like a malevolent Miss Marple searching out evil.

The healthy nuts and dried fruit Birdie kept for Howard's morning porridge — part of a recent health kick to slim down his belly — had been declared positively lethal because Birdie wasn't rotating things in the cupboards properly.

"In my day, we put new things at the back and the old ones at the front so you weren't in danger of eating out-of-date foods. You have no system, Birdie. No system at all. No wonder poor Howard is wasting away. He'll be skin and bone by the time you finish with him."

There was no point in Birdie protesting that Howard's new diet was his own invention and that he'd been pushing away her cheesy potatoes and fish pies lately and demanding salads, polyunsaturated spreads, and grilled chicken cooked without oil.

The dog was another cause for concern. Doris had no time for animals in the house.

"That animal should be outside!" she'd shriek every time she spotted Thumper's solid golden body. Thumper was not, Birdie thought, a clever dog, but he had plenty of sense when it came to Doris, and he hid under the kitchen table, out of reach of her walking aid, whenever she marched in. His other hiding spot was in Birdie and Howard's room, where he lay on the bed, sad face on his paws.

Woe betide them all if Doris ever spotted this, Birdie knew.

Thumper was her darling companion and she adored him. She'd always had a dog, going back to the days when she was a child and the only peace she'd known was when she was in Miss Cottontail's basket in the kitchen, letting the fighting flow over her as she buried her face in the little white terrier's soft coat. Fifty years had passed and not much had changed, she decided miserably.

When Howard had gone, Birdie decided she'd phone Katy. It was early enough and she knew Katy wouldn't have left for work yet. It was only Howard's mania for being first to arrive everywhere that made him get to the office at the crack of dawn.

"Hi, Mum," her daughter answered cheerfully.

"You sound good, darling," said Birdie. "The morning sickness getting better?" she asked hopefully.

"I feel really good," Katy said. "Incredible actually. Michael keeps saying it's some kind of miracle because up until now I've been sick as a pig every day, but this morning I feel quite normal."

"That's good, darling," her mother said. "I do worry about you."

"Mum, I'm absolutely fine," Katy said firmly. "I'm pregnant, not sick. OK, morning sickness isn't much fun, but if that's over — and I'm crossing my fingers here — things will be wonderful. Anyway, how are you, Mum?"

"Oh, fine, fine," her mother said, entirely untruthfully.

"What's wrong?" asked Katy.

"It's your father," said Birdie, caving in. "He was talking about your granny coming to stay and how we needed to decorate her room and paint it yellow, and I just got into a bit of a tizzy. You know what he's like when we have decorators in, and he's already obsessed with having some sort of house styling expert come to redo the place. Actually, she's not going to redecorate so much as reorganize: move things around and put big plant pots and gorgeous antiques in places where we never had them before."

"He's just trying to make it look nice," Katy said, pleased at the thought.

"I know, I know," said Birdie, "but we don't need to do any of that. The house is nice enough as it is. It makes me feel as if I haven't done anything right, ever. Besides, the tent is the important thing."

"Tell him that," said Katy. "Honestly, Mum, I don't know why you don't say these things to Dad."

It all seemed perfectly simple to Katy: if you had something to say, you said it. That was the way she handled her father, and he respected her for it.

On the other end of the phone, Birdie felt the rebuke.

"Of course," she said, forcing a cheerful note into her voice. "You're absolutely right. I should say those sorts of things. I should say, 'Howard, the spare bedroom is perfect for your mother, and really, what would we need to do with it, it's completely lovely.' "

"Granny will be fine. I know she can be a

370

bit of an old grumpy boots," said Katy, "probably because she thinks Dad is the most perfect human being on the planet and the rest of us are just hanging on to his coattails, but you need to stand up to her too."

"Yes," agreed Birdie. She could tell her daughter was eager to end the call and head off to work. "I will. Anyway, have a lovely day, darling. I'll talk to you this evening or tomorrow about the date for the bridesmaid shopping. I know you said Leila was busy at the moment."

"She's off on another business trip this weekend," said Katy. "I know it's work, but still. Rome sounds more glamorous than Bridgeport. I'll talk to her about finalizing a date for the bridesmaids' dresses. Talk later, bye."

Birdie was left holding the phone. Her daughter was right: she should stand up to Howard more. Tell him she didn't really want a complete stranger rearranging her furniture, which implied it was all in the wrong place and that she was hopeless at organizing things. Somehow when Katy said it, it all sounded perfectly reasonable, but Birdie knew that if she tried to use those same words to Howard's stern face, she'd falter and stammer until it came out sounding like complete gibberish. She just didn't have the strength to oppose him.

Howard liked things his own way and it was

easier to let him have free rein.

"Here are your e-tickets to Rome. I've printed two itineraries and put the phone number of the person organizing it all on top of both of them."

Ilona handed Leila a small folder.

"I asked about dress codes because of the big dinner . . ." For the first time, Ilona looked anxious, the ultra-organized assistant demeanor slipping. "Was that the right thing to do? I wouldn't have known what to wear, so I just emailed to ask and then I thought you'd probably know and I'd made you look stupid . . ."

"Don't be silly," Leila said. "It's handy having a dress code. Some people don't change after the day's meetings and turn up in their suits; others roll up at dinner trying to live up to the glamorous image of the industry. What did they say?"

"Smart dress," said Ilona, relieved. Leila was such a decent boss; she knew she was lucky to have her.

"Which means they want us to change out of our suits. Oh well," Leila said, "I'd better bring a bigger suitcase. It's so easy for the men. They can just change their shirts and abandon the ties and they're good to go. I bet you a tenner that Devlin will only have carry-on baggage. Plus he'll glare at me if we have to wait ages at the carousel. Tough bananas," she added with a smile. "Italian women are so glamorous — I'm going to bring half my wardrobe."

In the mad whirl of organization and packing, it wasn't until she reached the airport lounge that she had a free moment to phone her mother.

"Can't stop, Leila," said Dolores, with an energy in her voice that made Leila smile. "I've got to get to physiotherapy. Ger says I'm doing really well — though I must admit, I find stairs tricky. It's hilarious how they help you remember which leg to use to go up and down. *Up to heaven and down to hell,* Ger says, which means you use your bad leg and hip first on the way down — hell; and the good leg and hip first on the way up — heaven! You can't help remembering that!"

"I'm sorry I won't be there this weekend," Leila began.

"Don't worry," Dolores said. "I'm fine, honestly. I'm on the road to recovery. Do you think Pixie will be OK, though?"

It turned out that the lady who ran the doggy day care boarded small dogs in her home. She only ever took a few at a time and they slept in her kitchen.

"Pixie loves AnnaLouise," said Leila. "Adores her. When I dropped her off this morning, she barely bothered to say goodbye to me — just pushed off snuffling around the kitchen, saying hello to AnnaLouise's dog

Rufus and checking out the toys. She'll have a ball."

"Thank you," Dolores said. "You are so good to me and Pixie, Leila. I don't know what I'd have done without you."

"Oh, stop, Mum," said Leila. "What else would I do? Talk later, love you, bye."

Never joke about luggage carousels, Leila thought grimly as she stood in a sea of people at carousel four in Rome's da Vinci airport and watched a lone plastic-wrapped suitcase travel round and round. At first she'd thought nothing was amiss when there was no sign of her black case, because forty minutes after landing there were still so many people clustering around looking for their bags.

Then Devlin, who'd been on his phone, strolled up and pointed out that the jostling crowd was from another flight.

"The luggage from ours is long gone. Nobody here" — he gestured around — "was on our flight. They've all gone. These are from a more recent flight."

"My bag's lost," Leila realized with dismay.

"You'll get it back. Eventually," said Devlin, holding on to her elbow and leading her in the direction of the lost luggage department. "That's why I only bring cabin baggage."

Enraged, Leila searched his face for a sign of smugness. He might be her boss, but if he so much as hinted that this was her fault, she would clobber him with her handbag — and since it contained her iPad, makeup, phone, and purse, and a fat notebook, it would deliver a satisfying wallop. She could just imagine it . . .

"I'm sorry," he said in a different tone. "I've had my suitcase vanish plenty of times on long haul, but it's easier for guys — we just buy a shaving kit, a shirt, and a few other essentials and we're good to go until we get it back."

They were at the lost luggage now, at the end of a line. Devlin put a strong arm around her and squeezed sympathetically.

Leila blinked in shock at the gesture. *Devlin* comforting her?

"It'll be fine, Leila. We're insured against this sort of thing — let's sort out your suitcase, hit the hotel, and you can go shopping. I can't have my right-hand woman with nothing to wear."

It was the way he said it: as though she mattered to him, as though he cared. And the way he was holding on to her — Leila felt tears spring to her eyes.

She couldn't let him see. What sort of person would he think she was if losing her darn bags had her bursting into tears? Leila Martin was supposed to be unflappable, a superwoman who sorted out every crisis a publicity manager could be confronted with, from a famous elderly movie star being too tanked out on greenroom wine to appear on a TV chat show, to that time an actress's heavily pregnant sister had her water break in the limo on the way to a charity premiere. A woman who could handle such things with aplomb did not sob.

She broke free and, without looking at Devlin, summoned up all her acting skills to call cheerily: "I'm just running to the loo. Will you wait in the line for me?"

By the time she got back, they were next in line.

Leila's bags would be tracked down, an exquisite brunette with bedroom eyes told her at the desk, all the while gazing up at Devlin as if he was a bowl of delicious zabaglione she wanted to sink her very white teeth into. Beneath the brunette's gaze, Leila felt wildly underdressed in her crisp white shirt and dark trouser suit. What passed for efficient and businesslike in Dublin appeared very boring by Italian standards.

Which phone number would she take? More flirtatious gazing was required for this question, Leila noticed with irritation.

"My number," said Leila crisply, and she gave the other woman a look that said: *And I've got your number, honey.*

"We will call," the brunette said, tossing back luxuriant hair. *"Ciao,"* she added for Devlin's benefit.

"Don't know what she's doing on the blinking lost luggage desk," muttered Leila, marching out to the arrivals hall. "If she keeps flicking her hair back like that, she'll get whiplash."

Devlin laughed so loudly that Leila felt even more outraged.

"And you were encouraging her!"

Realizing what she'd said and what it sounded like — wild jealousy — she backtracked. "I want my luggage to get to the right place, not get you a date."

"Sure," agreed Devlin, not even bothering to hide his grin.

On the way to the hotel, Leila sat as far apart from Devlin as the spacious backseat of the limo would allow, and talked nothing but business. Anything to dispel the notion that she might have been jealous. She must be tired. She'd better try to sneak to bed early tonight so as to ready herself for the nonstop work of the conference.

After some hair-raising driving on the *autostrada*, the driver launched himself into Rome's traffic with a vengeance. Devlin appeared to zone out as they zipped up and down narrow streets, whizzing perilously past taxis and pedestrians, then suddenly he sat up straight.

"Leila, that's a good shop," he said with enthusiasm. "Look."

He was pointing to a boutique with elegant Italian evening gowns in subtle jewel colors in the window. One was almost entirely backless, and Leila tried to work out whether the person wearing it would be able to get away with underwear. How did he know about evening-wear shops in Rome? Besides, she certainly wasn't the type of woman to wear slinky dresses which, scandalously, didn't allow for underwear.

"A bit dressy for me," she said, knowing she sounded like a sourpuss.

They sped past Zara, which had nothing backless or too sexy in the window.

"I'll come back here," Leila said loudly.

"Whatever you like," Devlin said in a different voice.

No doubt the backless-gown shop had outfits priced in the stratosphere. Presumably at some point in Devlin's life he'd taken a girlfriend shopping in there. A disquieting image of her boss lounging like a maharajah while his girlfriend preened in front of him in a succession of skimpy outfits flashed into Leila's mind. Irritated with herself, she took out her phone and began to look at her messages. What was wrong with her? Perhaps it was this city, with its air of eternal romance, making her more acutely aware than usual that she had nobody in her life.

The hotel was a glorious sea of luxury, and Leila wished that she were here for a holiday instead of a conference. When people said things like *Your job is so exciting, you get to see so many fabulous places,* she always wanted to tell them that all she ever got to see was the inside of her room, the hotel lobby, the inevitable conference room, and the lounge in the airport.

". . . and of course, there is the spa," said the charming woman checking her in, chatting away in perfect English.

"Grazie," said Leila, which was almost the only Italian she knew. To her shame, she could manage to say thank you in many languages, but not much else. Katy had studied languages at college and was fluent in Italian and French. Howard liked to say he could speak English and profane, which was just the rudest thing ever. Birdie, for all that he never missed an opportunity to put her down, spoke flawless French and Spanish.

Poor Birdie, Leila found herself thinking. For all her own moping, she'd prefer to be a spinster the rest of her days if the alternative was being stuck with a boor like Howard.

Now that she was checked in, she turned to see Devlin chatting away to the hotel receptionist. Probably learned Italian from the same girlfriend with whom he'd gone to the backless-dress shop, Leila thought crossly.

"I'm going up to my room," she announced, and flounced off. He could flirt in privacy now, she decided.

In her hotel room — a deluxe double with a balcony and a large bath with a vast container of lemon bath salts placed enticingly beside it — Leila took control. Clearly stress was turning her into a crosspatch and making her hypersensitive where Devlin was concerned. She was so worried about her mother that any sort of kindness made her well up with tears. She'd read that people under great stress acted in odd ways, and it was proving to be true. What else could explain the urge to fall into Devlin's arms and sob out the whole story about how utterly responsible she felt for her mother, with no one to turn to, no one to share the burden. What else could explain how very cross she felt when glamorous women chatted him up?

She opened the minibar, gulped down some sparkling water, then checked her emails to remind herself that she was Leila Martin, career woman. When that was done, she removed the heavy gadgetry from her handbag, applied fresh lipstick, and marched out of her room.

The concierge was helpful but said apologetically that the store in the hotel itself was geared to holiday wear rather than business attire.

"You go this way, *signora,*" he said, drawing lines on a small map of the city, "and you will find many shops."

Leila followed the map, walking briskly

until she came to a small department store. At home, suits for working women tended to be in dark, neutral shades, but here, even in February, there were suits in jewel colors and in far more luxurious fabrics than Leila normally wore.

She stroked a velvet fitted jacket in a dark ruby and winced at the price. Damn missing luggage. She had a perfectly nice navy jacket not unlike this at home, but not in velvet and not with a heart-attack-inducing price tag.

No, Leila, she told herself. After a lifetime of not wasting money, of watching the pennies, reckless indulgence was alien to her. She shopped the sales and budgeted down to the last cent — with the mortgage to pay by herself, she couldn't afford to do otherwise. She had to rely on accessorizing with jewelry, shoes, and scarves to make the same old pieces look different.

She wandered over to the evening wear, hoping to find a little glam camisole she could wear under the jacket she'd traveled in. With a bit of shiny red lip gloss . . .

Then she saw it: an evening dress on a mannequin in a shimmering pewter color, a sliver of bias-cut silk like an exquisite nightgown turned into a dress. It wasn't backless, but the embroidered spaghetti straps crisscrossed at the back meant a bra was out of the question. Wordlessly Leila touched the dress, and a shop assistant materialized by her side as if from nowhere.

The assistant began speaking in Italian and when Leila shook her head apologetically and said, "English, signora . . . ?" she switched effortlessly to English.

"Can I help you?"

Without knowing what she was doing, and even more importantly, without checking the price, Leila asked if they had one in her size.

In the luxurious dressing room, she shimmied into the dress. Skintight clothing had never been her thing. She'd occasionally worn the black bandage dress Tynan had encouraged her to buy, but only to please him. Instead of feeling sexy, she'd felt self-conscious in it, sure that only a sleek, tanned, six-foot, hundred-pound Amazon would look good in such a dress — not a five-foot-two midget with pale skin and definite curves.

But this . . . this dress managed to reveal and conceal at the same time, clinging perfectly to her breasts, skimming over her belly and flaring out beautifully over her hips. It came to a halt just above the thinnest part of her ankle, making her look gloriously delicate.

She took off the big masculine watch she wore. Without it, her wrists looked delicate too.

How could one dress do such a thing?

"You like?" asked the assistant outside the curtain. "It is good dress, yes?"

"It's a miracle dress," breathed Leila, turning every which way and finding out that she looked better than she ever had from every angle. "I hate shopping normally. Do you have ten more like it?"

"I have more from that designer," the assistant said. "He is Italian, he understands women's bodies. He is not expensive, not yet. For now he is not discovered by the world — but he will be."

In her handbag, Leila found her darker lipstick and slicked some on, then ruffled up her hair with her hands. She looked wildly sexy, different — and she liked it.

"Here." The assistant drew back the curtain and held out an armful of clothes. "Try these."

On the final night, Leila took the pewter silk dress from the wardrobe and looked critically at it. She hadn't tried it on since she returned from her shopping expedition. Now that she'd bought it, and several more of the same brand — too much money, stuck on her credit card — she'd convinced herself that she must have been in a strange trance, overwhelmed by the clothes, the ambience of the department store, tricked into imagining she was someone she was not. It was Devlin and that blasted evening-dress shop. She'd been caught in a stupid fantasy about him and her, and hell — she must have been mad.

Stress had a lot to answer for.

Her suitcase had still not turned up. Each time she called to check, the airline could only offer apologies. Eventually Leila had told them that if it turned up, they should send it on to the Eclipse offices in Dublin. She'd bought several T-shirts, a couple of blouses, a plain black skirt, and underwear, and now had enough to last until she flew home. At least the compensation from the airline would help pay for her new suitcase and some of her new clothes. She had hair products, bought in the hotel, to tame her hair into sleekness.

What she didn't have was an alternative outfit for the dinner, other than a variation on the suit-and-elegant-top combo. But everyone else would be in evening wear, and the dress was the only evening item she had. Fresh from the bath, with her hair still wild and untamed, she held it up to herself and stood in front of the mirror.

There was something about the light in either Rome or the hotel room: something seductive and soothing, something that gilded every beam with enough warmth to make what would seem outrageous at home appear perfectly normal here.

She'd wear it. She'd try something different with her hair too, she decided recklessly. When in Rome . . .

Devlin was having a pre-dinner drink with

his opposite number from France in the hotel bar just across from the restaurant. They were comparing figures, discussing forthcoming films and generally shooting the breeze when, in the distance, Devlin saw the small figure with the mass of rippling blonde hair. The low lighting in the bar made it look as if the woman was dressed in molten metal, metal that clung its way around the most incredibly sexy figure.

"I must compliment you on your choice of female staff," murmured the French CEO, Georges, following his gaze.

"What?" said Devlin, confused.

"Your Mademoiselle Martin — beautiful and efficient, the perfect combination, *non*?"

Devlin had stopped listening after hearing the name. The molten-metal woman with the liquid curves and the Botticelli angel curls was Leila?

She was walking toward them.

Eamonn Devlin, who'd grown up with self-confidence, self-assurance, and all the other selves necessary to progress in both the world of business and that of women, felt entirely and unexpectedly thrown.

"Leila!"

Georges had risen to his feet and was greeting her in honeyed tones with an unmistakable hint of flirtation, leaning forward and kissing her hand.

Devlin grinned to himself. Leila wouldn't

like that.

But no. She was smiling at Georges, seemingly enjoying it all.

"Thank you, Georges," she was saying, her own voice verging on the husky now that he thought about it. "My suitcase went missing and I was clothes-less."

"I'd like to say what an interesting picture that makes," purred Georges, "but I am aware of the zero-tolerance policy Eclipse has when it comes to what is called sexual harassment."

Leila, who had lectured everyone who'd ever worked under her about how firmly the zero-tolerance policy was enforced in the Irish office, beamed at him.

The Georgeses of this world never harassed; they were too instinctive in their flirting. If the minute signals of reciprocation were not there, they would immediately withdraw discreetly. For a brief moment, Leila gloried in her new self in the confidence-boosting magical dress and flirted back.

After listening to them for about a minute, Devlin could take it no longer.

"Leila," he said abruptly, "I'm sorry to break this up, but we must talk about an email I had from the office."

It was the best he could do on short notice, and Leila managed to drag her gaze away from Georges to look at him.

"Fine," she said.

"Later," Georges said, eyes sweeping up and down her figure yet again.

"See you inside," Devlin said stiffly to the Frenchman, then got to his feet and led Leila away to a free table, where he sat and took out his smartphone in search of some suitable email to discuss.

Leila sat opposite him, still looking incredible in that amazing dress.

Devlin, who'd thought he had it all under control, had to say something.

"Don't fall for Georges's schmoozing," he finally muttered.

"It wasn't schmoozing," said Leila crisply. "He was being charming."

"He's charmingly married," Devlin informed her.

"Oh." Jolted, Leila sat back in her seat. "I didn't know."

"Well, now you do. Unless that doesn't bother you," he added nastily, and then instantly wished he hadn't.

Leila was silent, but her face was angry. How dare Devlin say that to her?

"It would bother me," she said, each word enunciated perfectly. Pity it hadn't bothered Diane. "Was that why you called me away?" she asked. "To tell me that?"

Devlin didn't blink. "Yes," he said, taking the high ground.

"Thank you, but you needn't have bothered," she said coolly. "I'm here to work, and if Georges was being a little complimentary, I can assure you it was going nowhere. I don't flirt wildly with everyone I see — not like some," she added, thinking of the girl at the lost luggage and the hotel receptionist. "I'll see you inside at the dinner."

She got up and swept past him regally, but the moment she knew she was out of sight, she swerved in the direction of the ladies' room. Her mascara hadn't started to run yet, but it would have if she hadn't stuck tissues under each eye instantly to catch the brimming tears. What was wrong with her? And what was wrong with Devlin, if it came to that?

He was normally the most convivial of bosses — to her, anyway. What had changed him?

The ballroom of the hotel was full of people Leila had known for years. She was glad of her pewter dress, because it gave her a confidence she wouldn't have had otherwise — Devlin had managed to rip that away from her. She felt so . . . hurt, that was it. Which made no sense at all.

But there was no time to work out why her boss's reaction had made her feel like that, because she had to swing into work mode.

As she moved through the room, exchanging hugs or handshakes or kisses with colleagues from all over Europe and America, many of them told her how fabulous she looked.

Jokingly, she brushed the compliments aside. "You mean I didn't look fabulous before?" she'd tease, and then follow it up with, "But you look wonderful too. Are you still running? It really suits you."

At least here she didn't have to put up with the endless questions about Tynan.

The first time she'd met up with the London team after Tynan had walked out, she'd spent the day grinding her teeth and trying not to cry when people casually asked how her husband was. There really was no right way to say *He dumped me for a younger, thinner woman.*

Eventually, she tracked down her table and saw that she'd been placed next to Devlin. The other guests — including someone she'd met already from LA, and the Spanish MD — were already there, so after a flurry of hellos, she realized she couldn't possibly switch the place cards. At best it would look odd; at worst it would be interpreted as a sign that she and her boss were not getting along.

The people from Eclipse were the best and the brightest and they noticed everything. So she sat, smiling fixedly as she pulled her gilt chair as far away from his as possible.

By the time Devlin rolled up, she was ostentatiously talking to her left-hand neighbor, a slim, handsome San Franciscan named

Greg, who was drinking bottled water and waving away the baffled wine waiters with their vintage red and white while intently discussing one of the studio's smaller movies, which was based on a Flannery O'Connor short story and was a film he felt could do well at the Sundance festival.

"It's hard to say if it will make any money," he said. "There's always the alternative of upping the marketing budget and pushing it into the Oscar box with dollars, but I just don't think they're going to do it with this one. Which is a pity. It's got real heart, real character . . ."

Craning her neck, Leila was surreptitiously checking out what Devlin was up to. His next-door neighbor was a chic fifty-something Spanish woman clad in what could only be Carolina Herrera. Unlike the women he had met with Leila so far on their trip, she gave off the distinct vibe of *you can look but do not touch.* Ha! Leila thought. Serves you right, Devlin.

The night seemed to drag on forever. There were speeches, lovely food, as much wine as you could drink if you wanted it. But after one glass, Leila wisely said no. She was flying home at nine the following morning and she needed to be up at six thirty at the latest if she wanted to be ready.

Partying too hard at conferences was a mistake only newcomers made.

Finally the meal and the speeches were over and a local band, much applauded, came on-stage to play.

"I wonder, would it be OK to leave now?" Greg asked her, looking around. "I'm still a bit jet-lagged and I'm flying to Tokyo tomor-row. I'm going to pop a melatonin and try to crash."

"I'm sure you're absolutely fine to leave," Leila said. "Go on, the lights are down, nobody's looking. Just pretend you're walk-ing off to the restroom and never come back."

It was a trick she'd used many a time in the past. That night with Tynan in Berlin came to mind. She'd been so tired, but she didn't want to stop Tynan having the evening of his life with his beloved band on their first European tour. He was the only person she'd said good-bye to before she slipped back to their hotel room. With hindsight, that hadn't been a very bright thing to do, but then if Tynan was going to cheat, he was going to cheat.

The realization hit her like a haymaker punch to the heart.

She hadn't *let* him cheat. It hadn't hap-pened simply because she'd given him the opportunity. It wasn't her fault for stepping aside and allowing Diane to get her claws into him. No, Tynan had decided he wanted something else, and he'd gone and got it.

It was as inevitable as a coke addict seizing

the opportunity to set out a line of white powder. It made no difference how much their wife, best friend, or mother begged them not to. They were hooked on the thrill, and regardless of what anyone said, whatever promises they made, they would not be deterred.

It was their choice.

Leila hadn't failed in her marriage. Her husband had failed at being a husband. Her only fault had been trusting him in the first place.

She smiled at dear, sweet Greg, realizing he'd no idea that he'd just helped her come to a new understanding.

"Greg, leave now. You need the sleep," she said calmly. "Go get it. There are no extra points for staying late and then being too shattered to accomplish what you've got to do in Tokyo tomorrow, right?"

"Right." Greg kissed her lightly on both cheeks. "You should come work for me — I need someone with your smarts."

"Oh, I'm happy where I am," Leila said, smiling. "For the moment, anyhow."

With her neighbor gone, she saw Devlin dragging his chair closer to hers. He was obviously tired of conversing with the Spanish MD and she wondered whether he'd overheard Greg saying she should come and work in California.

"So," he said gruffly, "enjoying yourself?"

"Yes, it's been lovely. And you?" she asked politely.

They were like a pair of dowager duchesses meeting at a ball.

"Fine, fine," he said.

The band started up. They were good, a tight unit — the years with Tynan, when he'd go through an entire band, player by player, working out if they were good or mediocre, posturing or possessing the magic, had taught Leila how to judge. They were playing some sort of Europop, which she liked. Tynan would have hated it, she thought with a grin. He'd have stomped out at the first chord, protesting that he wasn't going to poison himself by listening to this rubbish.

People were dancing now — not in couples, just people in little groups. She might dance, let her hair down a little, just move for the fun of it, because there was no Tynan to tell her that Europop was rubbish and she had no soul if she listened to the wrong sort of music. She'd listen to what she wanted. She, Leila Martin, was free in many, many ways.

"I'm going to dance," she said to Devlin, getting to her feet.

In an instant Devlin was beside her, towering over her.

"I'll come too," he said.

She looked at him in astonishment.

"If you like," she said, shrugging.

She shouldn't have lost her temper earlier.

It had been crazy and irrational. He was her boss, after all, and it was stupid to let her emotions get the better of her. Having little tantrums because Devlin liked flirting with women was incredibly stupid. He was nothing to her except her boss — and a good boss at that, she told herself firmly.

Leila didn't want to become one of those women who needed a man at all times. She was on her own, she was doing fine.

Together they moved onto the dance floor. Even though she didn't know the music, it was such an energetic beat that Leila found herself dancing wildly, twirling around in her pewter dress. Devlin leaned down close to her.

"Have you been drinking?" he asked, and she laughed in his face, giggling uproariously.

"No," she yelled back over the music. "I just want to feel free and unfettered for a change — and what better way to do that than to dance?"

He grinned at her, looking like the 'old Devlin. "Can't argue with that," he shouted.

There were plenty of other people with the same idea, and the dance floor was soon full of people laughing and gyrating, letting their hair down after a few days of tough work.

Devlin seemed to be letting go too, but he was watching her at the same time, and Leila was aware of a heat between them that had nothing to do with the energetic dancing. No matter which way she moved, those dark eyes were on her. Admiring her, perhaps?

No, she had to let that idea go. Just because Devlin was handsome and sexy, and she was manless, was no reason to fantasize.

Dance, Leila, she told herself. *Just dance.*

Finally, feeling worn out, she peeked at her watch. Eleven thirty. Time to go. Long after time to go, in fact.

"I'm going to go to bed," she said loudly.

"Good idea," he said, and followed her off the dance floor.

Leila hadn't expected that, but she collected her bag and they walked out the doors, along the labyrinth of corridors, past hidden niches and seating areas until they reached the elevators. It didn't seem late at all; there were plenty of people milling about, Muzak drifting through the lobby.

The elevator came and they got in. Both of them reached for the same floor at the same time, their fingers touching.

"Sorry." Leila pulled back as if she'd been burned.

"Same floor, huh?" said Devlin, and she realized he was slightly at a loss for words too.

It was just the two of them in the elevator now, both warm and energized from dancing. Both aware of what had gone on earlier, some strange shift in their relationship where he'd been jealous and she'd cared.

Don't go there, Leila, she warned herself.

You were imagining him watching you on the dance floor. Just because a devastatingly attractive man dances with you, it doesn't have to mean anything. Stop behaving like a woman who can only function if a man fancies her. Stop it!

"I've got a nine a.m. flight," she said, for want of something to say. "I've stayed up too late already."

"At least we won't have hangovers, unlike some of them," Devlin remarked. "The wine was flowing freely, wasn't it?"

He was trying to make conversation too.

The elevator glided to a halt and the doors opened smoothly. He let her go first and she opened her handbag to find her room key, trying to figure out which way to go. The corridors were so confusing; whether you turned left or right when you emerged depended on which elevator you had taken. She tried to orientate herself, staring at the signs pointing to rooms and suites in different directions.

"What number are you?" Devlin asked.

"I'm in 403," she said.

"That's just down the hall from me — same direction. Come on, I'll walk you. Don't want you abducted by aliens, do we?"

"Yes," she said drily. "I hear the risk of being abducted by aliens is quite high in this hotel."

He laughed, and for a moment he sounded

like the old Devlin.

"You're so smart, Leila Martin," he said.

They came to her room and he stopped. Stopped with intent. She'd been about to use her electronic key to get in, but the way Devlin stood there instead of carrying on down the corridor to his room startled her a little.

"About earlier . . ." he said. "I'm sorry. I shouldn't have interfered with you and Georges. It's your business what you do. But . . ."

He looked down at her, and this time she knew she hadn't imagined him watching her earlier.

"I felt jealous."

Shocked, Leila gazed at him without speaking.

He stepped back suddenly. "Sorry, sorry, I shouldn't have said that. It was completely inappropriate and I apologize. I really shouldn't have said —"

"No," she interrupted him, holding up one hand in a gesture of understanding. Slowly, deliberately, Devlin moved closer, and that one hand was no longer in the air, it was on his chest, touching the soft cotton of his shirt, feeling his hot skin underneath.

She was shocked at this intimacy. They'd been close before, shaken hands, stood beside each other a million times, but they'd never touched like this.

Her breath caught in her throat. She knew

Devlin had been jealous of Georges and that had made her angry, because he had no right. But she wanted him to be jealous. And she didn't want this moment between them to stop.

Very slowly, one of Devlin's hands molded itself to the back of her dress, caressing the curve at the base of her spine where the silk clung to her skin.

Leila breathed again, a long, shuddering breath. This felt so right.

"I understand," she whispered. "At least, I think I understand. You were jealous." She looked up at him, face flushed. "I like what that means. You being jealous."

"I couldn't help it," he murmured.

He was so close to her; she could feel the heat, the scent of cologne rising off his skin, the maleness of him.

This was right . . . but it was wrong too. He was her boss. Yet she couldn't pull herself away.

"I never imagined you thought of me that way, Devlin. You always have women running around you, too many to count — and you'd been flirting with that damn woman at the lost luggage office."

A hint of a grin lifted the corner of his mouth, making him look more piratical than ever.

"I could tell that annoyed you," he said.

"Then why did you do it?" she demanded.

"She was flirting with me," he protested. "It was nothing to do with me."

"You were enjoying it."

"OK, I was sort of enjoying it. I'm a man, it's hard not to. But it was wrong. It was wrong . . . in front of you. There."

It was out in the open.

They both stared at each other, Leila in her highest heels looking up into the dark face with those unreadable eyes.

"I should regret this," he said, "but I'm not going to because I've been promising myself that one day I'd kiss you. Properly . . ." and then he leaned forward and cradled her face in his big hands.

It was the opposite of what she'd expected, this gentle kiss as his mouth covered hers. Then her hands were on his shoulders, sliding inside his jacket, pulling him closer.

Devlin — how could she ever have seen anyone else? How had she spent so long with him and yet never seen this incredible man, *seen* him properly?

He was pulling her closer to him now and their bodies were pressed against each other, Leila melting into him in her molten dress, their tongues intertwining as they kissed more passionately. The gentleness was over; he was fierce as he kissed her and she matched him in ferocity.

It had never been like this with Tynan, she thought suddenly. Not this white-hot heat.

This sense of rightness.

Don't let it end, she wished. *Come in with me now. Into my bed, please . . . It's crazy and we might regret it in the morning, but what the hell . . .*

The words were in her mind and almost on her lips — and then he pulled away, breathing heavily, something in his eyes she didn't recognize.

"I'm sorry, Leila. I'm really sorry, I've no excuse. You work for me. That was wrong."

Leila stood, face flushed, strap pushed off one heated shoulder, mouth open from his kisses.

"Sorry," he said, and he strode down the corridor and was gone, leaving her alone outside her room, clutching her key card and her handbag, with her pulse racing.

Shakily she slid the key card into the slot and went inside.

In the mirror in the hallway she could see herself: hair tousled, eyes dark from all the mascara and eyeliner, her lips flushed a dark pink from his kisses. She touched her neck and head again the way he had touched her and wished she'd said the words, that she'd made him come in.

Who cared about what happened next? Nobody said they couldn't be together. Was that a company rule? She was sure it wasn't. Right now she wanted him in her room, in her bed, tenderly holding her and telling her how crazy he was for her, because she'd seen it in his eyes. And now, finally, Leila felt the same way. But something had chased him off.

Early the next morning, Leila pulled her new suitcase toward the door. Her hair was slicked back in a ponytail; she wore her suit and a stern expression. The siren of the night before had gone. No amount of Clinique could hide the dark shadows under her eyes and she might as well have sat up all night with the party animals for all the sleep she'd got. On the floor just inside the door was an envelope addressed to her in Devlin's distinctive scrawl.

Leila,
About last night — I apologize formally for what happened.
I'm flying to London today. I'll see you in the office during the week.

Regards,
Devlin

Regards? She read the note with mounting shock, which moved swiftly into anger.

Had she been mistaken in what had happened? Had he merely used her? Had he been desperate and she'd been the only available woman?

By the time she reached the airport, Leila

had rewritten the script entirely. They weren't two people who'd finally realized what they felt for each other. No. She might have felt that way, but Devlin obviously hadn't.

He clearly had more notches on his bedpost than a carved medieval four-poster. Obviously he'd briefly thought of making her another of his conquests but had stopped himself just in time because bonking underlings was a mistake and Eamonn Devlin didn't make mistakes.

She'd been taken in because she was vulnerable, that was all. She would never be vulnerable again. No man would ever breach her defenses; she'd set up a force field around her that repelled men as effectively as a "Danger" sign.

She stomped through da Vinci, ignoring all the lovely duty-free shops with their delicious scents and silken scarves. Men — she had had enough of them for a lifetime. No, for several lifetimes.

A male flight attendant welcomed her onto the Aer Lingus flight with a smile.

"How are you today, Ms. Martin?" he said after a quick glance at her ticket.

"Fine." She glared at him.

Not fair to the poor man, she knew, but she didn't care. All men had better watch out from now on.

FOURTEEN

Life without love is like a tree without
blossoms or fruit.

KHALIL GIBRAN

Tynan's flat in Islington was a far cry from
the lovely place he'd lived in with Leila. He
thought this every morning when he woke up
lying on his left side and found himself staring at the old second-floor sash windows,
which must have boasted at least ten layers
of white paint with a few insects and a generous helping of dust painted in for good
measure. Black damp was ingrained in the
corners, a spreading fungal-looking thing that
was ugly to look at and certainly detracted
from the cool man-about-town image he
liked the flat to project.

It didn't matter how many Eames chairs,
rare vinyl covers, or Lichtenstein knockoffs
you could boast; clean mattered.

He must ask Greta to scrub it off next time
she came. Or leave a note or something. He
wasn't sure she could read English, though.

She always ignored his notes and cleaned the same things she always did. Plus she'd boil-washed his new cashmere sweater till it was the size of a large sock, but when he'd pointed it out to her, she'd just shrugged and hadn't even said *I sorry.*

Leila had been brilliant with laundry. She did actual hand-washing once a week and hung the fresh-smelling clothes on a dinky little hanging thing which she left in the spare bedroom till it all dried. He'd never needed a Greta when he lived with Leila.

He shared Greta with the guy in the flat opposite. She came in every week and moved the dust around, ironed anything that needed ironing — not a big job — and half cleaned the bathroom and kitchen.

There wasn't much to do in the kitchen — Tynan felt like that fashion-mad woman in the series Leila had liked watching, *Sex and the City,* the one who kept her sweaters in the oven. He could have kept anything in the oven and it would have been safe. The only bit of the kitchen he used was the microwave, and the gas stove to light cigarettes if he'd lost his lighter. He ate out so much, drank out so much too. It was all part of the job: going to venues to see new bands, traveling around the country to the middle of nowhere to hear someone who'd sent in a demo or put a song up on YouTube. He was so desperate to find someone fabulous, he'd go to any lengths.

Tynan had been whisked off to London by MegaRec because he'd discovered Lizard, the hottest band to come out of Ireland in years, but an A&R man was only as good as his last signing. Lizard were terrific, but they weren't selling any records. *That* was what counted — not how many drooling reviews they were getting in the serious music press. The money men ran MegaRec, and if Tynan wasn't bringing in bands who made money, then he'd be out just as quickly as he'd been hired.

It was eight thirty and he had to be in the office by ten. He sat up and lit a cigarette. He'd stopped while he was with Leila. She hated smoking, said it was a deal-breaker.

"It's me or the cigarettes, Tynan," she'd told him, looking all stern the way she did at press conferences with troublesome stars. He'd have said yes to anything to get her to marry him.

Once they were married, he sneaked smokes when he was out without her, figuring that if he didn't smoke in front of her, there was nothing she could do about it.

They'd been at a wedding — a musician friend's — when he'd proposed. It had been an unconventional affair, in a field with tents for the guests to party in and several bands lined up to play on the small stage that evening.

Leila had loved everything about the wedding, especially its originality and quirky charm. Votive candles sat in old jam jars with wild flowers in mismatched vases on gingham tablecloths. There was a keg of beer and snipes of champagne with straws. And because he loved her, and loved her enthusiasm and childlike delight, he'd imagined how wonderful it would be if they were the ones getting hitched. On the spur of the moment he'd asked her.

"She's got you hook, line, and sinker, Ty," his father had said, poking him in the ribs in a jokey way when Tynan had announced he was getting married. "I never thought anyone'd catch you, kid," he'd added. "Your ma and I didn't think you were the marrying kind."

Tynan hadn't thought he was the marrying kind either, but somehow Leila Martin had bewitched him.

They should never have been attracted, let alone married. Neither was the other one's type — hell, her rich girlfriend Katy had told him so up front. "You're not her type, but for some reason she can't see that. I can, though, and I'm warning you now: if you hurt her, I'll kill you," Katy had said, with a menace in her voice that totally shocked him.

You had to hand it to Katy: for all the money and being Daddy's little princess, she could be tough when she wanted. He suspected it wasn't just talk either: it was entirely possible she would kill for Leila. Or get that giant of a boyfriend to kill him for her.

"Hey, it's cool, I love her," Tynan had said. "I love her with all my heart. I want to marry her, right? I just asked her."

"I know," Katy answered. "I still don't trust you."

"OK, but seeing as you're her best friend and I'm going to be her husband, we better get along," Tynan said.

And he *had* loved Leila. She was passionate, loyal, beautiful — once you got her out of those corporate suits — and good.

Incredibly, that quality of goodness was the thing that had finally felled man-about-town Tynan. Nobody in his life had ever been as good to him or as concerned about his welfare. She had a huge, generous heart and it was all his. She made him chicken soup when he had colds and washed his clothes instead of demanding, "Do I look like a laundress?" which was what his mother used to say.

When he left Leila for Diane, he found Diane couldn't cook and had no plans to learn how to do so.

"Cooking's for losers," she'd said scornfully one day. "My future is not in the kitchen. I make reservations for dinner."

She'd heard that line somewhere, Tynan knew. Diane might be young and beautiful but she didn't have the money for reservations — she veered from eating almost nothing to gorging on takeaways or curry chips, which was strange, given her etiolated limbs and nonexistent belly.

But the flat they'd shared in Shoreditch saw less and less of Diane until, eventually, she just moved her stuff out.

"See ya," she'd said blithely when she took the final box.

"See ya," he'd replied cheerfully.

London was full of Dianes.

But it wasn't full of Leilas. As time went on, he found he missed Leila far more than he'd thought he would: her sense of fun, her passion, the way she was so grateful for the coffee he made her in the morning. And her love. He missed that. Being adored was addictive, it turned out.

He'd had that and he'd thrown it away.

He wondered what she was doing now and if she'd like to do it in London. Leila would love it here. And he'd love to have her back in his life.

He'd never meant to break her heart. He'd been bored, found marriage somewhat stultifying — "You're married?" people would say to him in astonishment.

Plus, monogamy was a bitch.

He'd do better the second time around. He'd been stupid. Now he understood how good Leila had been for him, how much she meant to him. He looked again at her number on his cell phone, thinking . . .

Julia had kept putting it off: the talk about the wedding, where she'd sit, whether she should discuss outfits with Grace. Whether she would actually be going, because Stephen hadn't actually mentioned that at all and she was far too proud and too hurt to ask.

These days she felt more and more like an interloper in the Rhattigan family fairy tale.

Then, last night, entirely out of the blue, Stephen had told her he was going to Bridgeport next weekend to pick out his suit with Michael because the bridesmaids were all choosing their gowns. Katy, her mother, and her best friend Leila had planned a day's shopping of their own for Katy's wedding dress, but the groomsmen and bridesmaids event was apparently a major one in the bridal calendar.

It was all going to be boring, he said, and she'd known he didn't want her coming.

"I'm going to stay over," he added casually. "We'll probably all go out to dinner afterwards to finish the day off — you know the sort of thing."

Julia wondered was she imagining mysteries where there were none, so she risked asking, "Should I come?"

"No," he said easily, "you'd be bored. All that bridesmaid stuff. It'll probably just be the kids' friends."

And Grace, Julia thought. *And Grace.*

"Fine," she said, doing her best to hide the tautness in her voice.

She hadn't slept all night, turning it all over in her head.

She was being cut out. Neatly, surgically, in a way she'd never been before. She wasn't sure if Stephen even knew he was doing it, but he was separating them: his first family, the important one, from his second family, her.

She'd resolved to say something over breakfast, but when she came downstairs he was already finishing his coffee and looking at his watch as if he was late for the office.

"Talk later," he said, grabbing his briefcase and racing from the kitchen.

Julia stood motionless at the table. He hadn't kissed her, hadn't touched her as he left.

He rarely did anymore. Little details, but they mattered so much.

"Tell me everything."

Julia's longtime friend Rosa posed the question as they sat in the café that afternoon, two well-dressed women in their late forties with coffees, no cakes, a briefcase at Rosa's feet.

Julia, slim and chic in skinny jeans, white shirt, leather jacket, and gray Converse high-

tops, looked like someone who worked in a
creative industry, while Rosa was more
traditionally dressed in a smart charcoal dress
befitting a partner in an accountancy firm.

Nobody would have guessed that their late-
afternoon coffee was no chance meeting
between friends but an emergency summit.

"Can you meet me, please? It's urgent. I —
I don't know what to do," Julia had said on
the phone first thing.

Rosa didn't even ask what it was about. She
didn't have to. She knew.

"I'll see you at Café Santina at four thirty
— it's the earliest I can get away," she said in
her brisk work voice.

"Thank you, thank you."

Julia had hung up and gone out to the fire
escape of DdW&X, the advertising agency
where she'd been creative director for the
past nine years. One of the office juniors was
out there, a pretty blonde girl in a parka,
smoking as if her life depended on it.

Seeing Julia, she began to stub the cigarette
out.

"Sorry, I thought we could smoke here . . ."

"We can," said Julia flatly. "Can I bum one
of yours?"

"I didn't know you smoked," said the girl
as she offered the packet.

*I haven't, not for years, but I am in such pain
that it seemed like an option,* said the voice
inside Julia's head. "I have the odd one," she

said instead. "Sorry for pinching a cigarette — I owe you."

The girl shook her head. "No, really, it's cool."

She handed over her lighter and Julia turned away to light her cigarette, not wanting the girl to see how much her hands were shaking.

"Thanks," she said, once it was lit, then she busied herself pretending to check her messages on her phone. She might curse the phone with its never-ending connection to the office, but it was the perfect excuse not to have to speak to anyone.

She wouldn't think, she decided. She'd do some Internet surfing, maybe go on one of those designer clothes sites and look at outfits she couldn't afford. Anything to keep her mind occupied till four thirty, when Rosa might make sense of it all for her.

Rosa had been there for her the last twenty-five years, all through the disastrous relationship to the perennially resting actor Tony. And then through the years with Stephen.

Julia had been there for Rosa when the man Rosa had been engaged to had suddenly ended their relationship after ten years, married someone else within six months, and swiftly had two children — despite all those years of telling Rosa that there was no rush, they'd have kids when they'd traveled enough and enjoyed their youth. Years when she'd tried to convince herself that she agreed with him, that there was plenty of time to settle down in the future.

"My bloody ovaries have dried up waiting for him and now he's playing happy families!" she had roared, inconsolable in her grief.

In a way, their friendship was more like marriage than Julia's actual marriage and thirteen-year relationship with Stephen. The two friends understood each other perfectly; there were no silences, no sulks, no misunderstandings, no things you wanted to say but couldn't because of whatever chasm it might open up.

Julia was the one who'd gone to Rosa's flat to pick her naked body up off the floor when Rosa had fallen and hurt her back in the shower and there had been nobody else she could ask. Rosa had sat in the hospital with Julia the time she'd had to have X-rays of her ankle after twisting it on the stairs at work. Tony, her then boyfriend, had responded to Julia's tearful phone call by saying that he couldn't come right now because he had an audition in Belfast but as soon as he was finished he'd catch the next train home.

Their friendship had turned out to be more for-better-or-worse than most marriages, Rosa liked to say whenever they shared a bottle of wine — only the one — in their favorite Greek restaurant.

"So, is it over?" Rosa asked.

Julia stared down at her cup. She'd ordered a latte and now she realized she felt sick to her stomach and couldn't face all that milk.

"I don't know," she said finally, looking up to face Rosa. "I don't know how I feel anymore — not like me, is it?"

"Not like you at all," agreed Rosa. "Isn't that enough for you, Julia? That you're behaving like someone else, all because of Stephen and his bloody family? You shouldn't have to come second, you should come first. This wedding carry-on is a symptom of it. You're somehow the also-ran, and that's not what you need or deserve in life."

"Don't," said Julia. "I know, I know all of this, Rosa. I signed up for it. Once," she added weakly.

"You should have insisted that you get married," Rosa went on, into her stride now. "Then it would be different. You'd have rights . . ."

"We said we weren't the marrying type of women," Julia said with a lame smile, remembering the days when they'd believed feminism and marriage were mutually exclusive.

"It matters."

"It doesn't, actually," Julia said. "Not after yesterday."

"What happened yesterday?"

"He told me he'd be going back to Bridgeport this weekend for the big finding-the-bridesmaids'-and-groomsmen's-outfits palaver. He's staying overnight and he doesn't want me there. It's all part of the same thing, part of the wedding, the pregnancy. Do you know, Rosa, when Stephen told me about the baby, I realized I'd never heard him so happy. Ever. That was when I knew. I've been hiding it, avoiding it, but it's there and it's not going away."

"You're kidding, right? About the never-sounding-so-happy."

"No, not kidding. Nothing — not that holiday in Venice, not the best sex ever — has ever made him sound the way he sounded when he got the news. I kept saying, 'That's great, Stephen,' but inside I felt like I'd died."

Julia made herself drink some of her coffee and it tasted strange. Everything did today. Her mouth felt tinny, dry, as if her body had ingested a slow-acting poison and it was gradually working its way through her, doing its damage.

After the thirteen years she'd spent with Stephen, she'd thought she knew him inside out. Or as inside out as you could know any person, as Rosa liked to add. Rosa had trust issues.

But Julia hadn't, not with Stephen. He was utterly straight with her, never lied, even by omission.

Except the wedding had changed every-thing. Her straight-talking, urbane, and charming partner had undergone a transformation. It had been so subtle at first: phone calls to his son, long chats with his daughter, calls to Grace.

Perfect Grace, as Rosa dubbed her.

He'd seemed withdrawn as a result, wanting to go to the cinema instead of dinner, preferring to sit in silence and stare at the screen instead of facing her across a table, where he'd have to look into her eyes and talk.

Julia had known what it was, had recognized it with horror: his son's marriage had made him think about what family meant, had made him reconsider his choices. And because Grace was still sitting there unmarried, unattached, he had the opportunity of a second chance at marriage and happy families. Despite all he'd said about how he and Grace had agreed to split up, had wanted to, Julia could see that fifteen years later, Stephen actually believed he'd made a mistake.

He wanted to be back in the bosom of his family, picking up where he'd left off with his ex-wife and children, playing father of the groom, grandfather of the newborn, the whole enchilada.

There wasn't any cruelty or unkindness intended. She wasn't sure that Stephen even recognized what was happening, but *she* did. Without lifting a finger, his ex-wife and children had ensnared him, lured him away from her. The prospect of becoming a grandfather had sealed the deal.

All last night, she'd lain in bed examining the evidence, seeing the truth. She couldn't stay.

"I've tried so hard to understand over the years," she said sadly. "When they were young, we took Michael and Fiona everywhere with us. I cared for them and did all I could, but somehow, despite all that, I am not part of his family." She paused before she said finally, "I love them but there isn't enough room for me."

Julia couldn't go back to work after her conversation with Rosa. Instead she went home, where she sat on the balcony with a cup of coffee and the packet of cigarettes she'd bought after leaving the café. She didn't know why she was smoking: it was stupid, really. Like being a kid and doing something self-destructive to get back at your parents. But years ago, like many in the advertising industry, her creative process had been fueled with coffee and cigarettes; it was all part of working late into the night, tossing ideas around. Smoking now was her way of going back to the way her mind used to work pre-Stephen. Because that was the reality. She needed to return to thinking of herself in a pre-Stephen sort of way — or even in a post-Stephen sort of way. For it was over. She'd known that for a while, but only now was she ready to face up to it.

There was no question of Stephen walking out on her. He was too honorable for that. And he loved her, she knew he did. But he loved the family he'd left behind even more. It was hard to say whether it was Grace or his children or the memory of the life he'd once had, but something was pulling him inexorably toward Bridgeport, and there was no space for Julia there. If she was to hold on to her self-respect and live an honest life, then she had to end it.

Don't do anything crazy, Rosa had said.

Me, crazy? Julia had replied wryly.

There was no scent of cooking when Stephen arrived back in the apartment, even though it was one of Julia's days to cook dinner. Maybe it was a salad, he thought miserably. He liked salads in the summer, but not in the winter or spring. The good thing about Julia was that she wouldn't be offended if he said he'd rustle up something a bit warmer. He wasn't a bad cook these days. He hadn't cooked much in the days when he had been married and the children had been young. He felt guilty about that now; he felt guilty about lots of things. The past seemed to be haunting him lately.

It wasn't fair to Julia. He knew she was upset about not going to Bridgeport with him, and she had every right to be; there was no reason he couldn't take her along. Except he wanted to go alone.

"I'm out here," she called, and he followed her voice out to the balcony. She was sitting with a blanket wrapped around her; cafetière, coffee, and an ashtray on the table by her side. There were several cigarette butts in the ashtray, smoked right down.

"You're smoking?" he said in astonishment.

"I just felt like it," she said and looked at him. It was then that he saw her reddened eyes and pale face, the smears where her makeup had been washed away by tears.

"What's wrong, Julia?" He sat beside her, grabbing her hand.

"We've got to talk," she said quietly, and he realized how much he hated those words, the clichéd words from films and television where people looked into each other's eyes and announced dramatic things.

He couldn't do dramatic things, not anymore. And then it occurred to him: she might be sick. He'd been working on a cancer campaign last year and it still hit him in the deep of the night. His heart gave a lurch of pity. *Oh Lord, no, poor Julia.*

"Are you OK? Have you found something? A lump?"

She laughed then and shook her head. "No. No lump, Stephen, nothing like that, thankfully. Well, maybe there's a lump, but it's in my heart." She looked into his eyes. "I think it's over between you and me."

He drew back, let her hand drop. "What?"

"Come on, Stephen," she said. "You don't need me to spell it out. It really isn't me, it's you — funny though that sounds. We could use it in a slogan. Ever since Michael got engaged, you've been different."

He could see her eyes tear up again and she felt blindly for another cigarette.

"Don't," he said, reaching out to still her hand. "You're going to kill yourself."

"Let me kill myself if I want to," she said, shaking his hand off. "I'm an adult."

With trembling fingers she lit the cigarette, and he watched her through narrowed eyes as a spiral of smoke rose lazily into the air.

"You want to go back to Grace and Fiona and Michael and have it all back again. I know, I can tell. I don't think you've actually figured it out yet, but I have — you're like someone who's made a vow to stay with me forever but in his heart he wants to be elsewhere. I don't want to be second best, Stephen."

She stared at him through the trails of smoke. "I *won't* be second best. I deserve better."

He reached out for her hand again and this time she let him take it. Now there were tears in his eyes too.

"But I love you, I won't leave you. We've got a great life here." He waved a hand, gesturing around futilely.

"Oh, Stephen," she said wearily. "Yes, we've a great life here, but I'm not going to live a lie. You want to be somewhere else — I can see it. I can't come second anymore. Let's leave it at that."

"But . . ." Stephen swept out a hand, indicating their apartment, the home they'd made together.

"But nothing," Julia said, trying not to cry. "None of this means a thing when the real love is gone. I don't want a man who's staying with me because he's kind. I want more than that. I'd like you to move out, and if you think about it, I dare say you'd like to move out too."

With that, she got to her feet and went inside.

Stephen sat outside on the balcony and let the cold swirl around him. He wanted to go and comfort Julia, tell her she was wrong and what they had was still strong, but he didn't. Because she was right.

The Madison and Fitzgerald nuptials were taking place on Friday, and Lizzie Fitzgerald phoned to ask if she might drop into the Golden Vanilla Cake Shop briefly with her two daughters who had arrived from Dublin and London respectively and wanted to inspect the cake for what they were calling their mother's "ridiculous wedding."

"They never said that, surely?" said Vonnie on the phone.

She could be coolly remote with clients when it was required, but to people like dear, sweet Lizzie, for whom life had obviously been hard until unexpectedly love had come along, she was kindness itself. What sort of daughters, she asked herself, could be so cruel?

"I shouldn't be telling you this because you'll think I'm an awful eejit, Vonnie, but they think Charlie's marrying me for my money," Lizzie blurted out.

An image came into Vonnie's mind of the couple on the wrong side of sixty who'd entered her premises months earlier, holding hands as they giggled over cakes like a couple of twenty-somethings. Neither of them looked as if they were exactly overburdened with cash. Charlie Madison had two electrical repair shops and Lizzie was retired from an executive assistant job.

They'd met two years previously at a rock'n'roll night at the Palace Hotel and had been going there ever since. Charlie wasn't able to twirl Lizzie as much as he'd like — a tricky lumbar disc had put paid to that — but in every other respect they were having a ball.

Charlie had never been married before, Lizzie explained. Her daughters saw this as a sign that he was not fit for marriage in the first instance and was only marrying Lizzie to get his paws on her money. Or, as they saw it, their long-dead father's money and, when it came down to brass tacks, *their* inheritance.

"Is there a lot of money?" asked Vonnie, abandoning all recommended business practices.

"No," said Lizzie. "That's the thing. Charlie has his business, but I've only got the house — and the roof needs doing or else the rain's going to start coming in with the next big storm. We were going to tackle it when we got back from our honeymoon. We're going to Capri for a week."

It was the way she said it: *honeymoon*. A voice that spoke of a woman who'd been alone for a long time.

"Maybe you think I'm mad too," she finished sadly.

"No," Vonnie said with great firmness. "I think you're the sanest woman I know. I think you need some of my angel cake right now, in fact. But before we organize that, tell me, when do the girls want to come in? Give me an exact time."

Lorraine lit candles in the inner room and put on the 1950s music the couple liked.

"If you could wait with the camera and a bottle of cava for when things improve, that would be great," Vonnie said.

"What happens if things turn nasty?" asked

Lorraine mischievously.

"They won't," said Vonnie firmly.

At the prescribed time, Lizzie turned up with Marta, who had a prestigious job in London, and Tina, who'd married well and lived in Dublin. Marta wore a cashmere coat and carried a handbag that cost as much as a small car. Tina wore designer jeans, a designer polo shirt, and pink Wellingtons, as if leaving the capital city inevitably implied trudging through muddy fields and being attacked by herds of rampant cows. And yet they had both been born in Bridgeport, Vonnie knew. Clearly they had been keen to wash its dirt from their feet.

Still, she'd expected this and was prepared.

She had taken the trouble to blow-dry her flaxen hair, which she rarely did, and it hung in salon-perfect ripples over slender shoulders clad in sky-blue silk — her one and only dress. Two could play that game, she thought when she saw the surprise in Lizzie's daughters' eyes.

She hugged Lizzie, shook hands with the daughters and welcomed them in.

"A lot of our work comes from second marriages," she said, smiling but with eyes glittering like diamond chips. "It's one of the joys of working here. Seeing people of all ages seizing another chance at happiness after divorce or the tragedy of widowhood. We're so pleased that your mother and Charles came to Golden Vanilla. Their joy is infectious. I know your mother was on her own for ten years — isn't it lovely that she's found love again?"

Marta, who physically resembled Lizzie but with none of her sweetness, didn't look as if she thought it was lovely at all. Neither did Tina.

In the background, Lizzie stood with hands clasped, an eager smile on her rounded face, hopeful that at some point her daughters might share her joy.

"Your mother's cake is still being finished, but here" — Vonnie clicked a key on her computer — "is what it will look like."

Lizzie and Charlie had chosen a simple two-tier off-white cake decorated with a red bow and a spray of red roses modeled on an old floribunda bloom. Very hard to make, but exquisite-looking when done correctly.

"Dad would have hated it," snapped Marta, barely glancing at the screen.

Vonnie summoned up a smile. "It sounds like your father was a lovely man," she said. "Lizzie and Charles were talking about him the other day. As a widow myself, I understand how important it is to remember past happiness when one is getting married again."

Marta and Tina stared at her, thrown by the information that this coolly glamorous blonde was a widow.

"Tell me," Vonnie changed tack swiftly.

425

"You live in London, Marta? Do you get to come back to Bridgeport often to see your mother?"

Marta flushed, sensing the barb. "No, I travel a lot for work."

"And you, Tina? Dublin's only up the road." Vonnie's eyes were like steel.

"I work, and the children . . . you know," Tina faltered.

Vonnie nodded sagely. "It must be a great comfort then to both of you to know that your mother has her own life here with Charles. It's hard for other people to understand what widowhood is like, isn't it, Lizzie?" She reached out to Lizzie, who nodded. "People expect you to get on with life totally alone, which is so unfair."

From the direction of the kitchen, she thought she heard a snigger. Lorraine, listening in. Cheeky brat! Nevertheless, she soldiered on.

"That's why I personally love second weddings."

Beside her, Lizzie beamed.

The shop doorbell rang and Charlie arrived, as previously arranged.

"Trust me," Vonnie had said to an uncertain Lizzie as they ate angel cake.

"Charles!" Vonnie went to greet him as if he were a returning king. Charlie, whom nobody had called Charles since his First Communion, faltered for a moment, but then smiled bravely at his surly soon-to-be step-daughters.

"How lovely of you to drop by," Vonnie said. "We're all so excited here about the wedding. I do hope I can pop into the reception myself briefly."

Charlie, a red-faced man with just as much kindness as his wife-to-be, grinned at her.

"I hope so too, Vonnie love. All the effort that's gone into the cake, well, we'd love to have you, pet."

In front of Vonnie, there was no way Marta and Tina could be as rude as they might have wished.

"Hello, Charles," they both said formally.

"Ah, girls, call me Charlie," he beamed. "I'm so glad you're going to be here for your mum on her special day."

"A photo!" cried Vonnie, as though the idea had just hit her. "We need a photo of this lovely moment. Lorraine?"

Lorraine almost fell through the swing door with the camera.

Much palaver went on over the photos: everyone posed with everyone else. The kitchen staff arrived in their aprons and joined in. It was like the Changing of the Guard with a busload of tourists in front. Vonnie whispered to Lorraine to get the cava from the fridge. Gradually Marta and Tina's faces lifted and an air of faint celebration began to circulate.

"Charles is really quite nice," Marta, on her second glass, whispered to Vonnie.

"He's highly thought of around here," Vonnie said gravely. "As is your mother. A real lady. We're all so pleased that two such lovely people have found each other."

Listening in, Tina managed a smile. *A lady,* that was nice.

She and her sister exchanged glances. Perhaps this little hole-in-the-corner wedding they'd thought they were coming to was a grander affair altogether. Plus, Charles had a business and was clearly highly thought of in Bridgeport.

Finally it was all over.

"I can't thank you enough, Vonnie," said Charlie as he left. "Look at her: she's so happy."

"We're all happy for you," Vonnie replied. "And remind Lizzie that both of you deserve your happiness. Nobody can dictate to you when it comes to love, just because it suits them better."

"Yeah," Charlie agreed.

"I think it would be great if Lizzie and the girls booked into the Horizon Spa or Clara's beauty salon up on Dame Street tomorrow. Have the works done. Make it all the more special," Vonnie suggested.

Charlie agreed. "Lizzie and me would have never thought of that," he said in amazement.

"It'll keep the girls amused," Vonnie said

wisely. That way they wouldn't be stalking around their old home, working out the resale value of everything.

After the wedding party had departed, the kitchen staff retreated to the kitchen, leaving Vonnie alone to blow out the candles.

If only organizing her own life was as easy as organizing other people's, she thought.

FIFTEEN

Love conquers all.

VIRGIL

In one part of Leila's world, there was peace. The lovely peace of knowing that her mother was settled in the Hummingbird Nursing Home and that Nora was looking after her wonderfully.

Every time Leila phoned or visited, Dolores was discussing some new friend or activity.

"It's like a little community, honestly, we do so many things. Nora said I might learn to play bridge, although I don't know, I always think that's sort of an older person's game, don't you?"

"Supposed to be very good for the memory but fiendishly hard to learn," said Leila. "I think you'd be marvelous at it."

"I'll think about it. In the meantime, I'm knitting again," Dolores said happily. "Miss Polka who does the music classes has a friend with a craft van and she drives in once a week with the most beautiful knitting wools and

430

beading things — oh, you'd just love it. Ginny's Glorious Craft Van it's called. I got this beautiful dark blue wool, Aran weight but soft, and I'm going to make Jack a cardigan. It's so long since I've knitted anything, I'm quite sure I've forgotten how to do it, but Nora says it'll come back to me in no time. My hands are a bit stiff, but still, I'd like to try while I still can."

She chatted on happily about the lovely trainer, Ger, who said that physical exercise was very important for people with RA, and how he'd designed a gentle program for her for when she was back to full strength.

Leila had been so delighted hearing the happy tone in her mother's voice. It was only now that Dolores was somewhere she felt safe that Leila was beginning to appreciate the stress she must have been under for so long. She said it now.

"Mum, I didn't realize how hard things were for you before. I'm so sorry you felt you couldn't tell us about the rheumatoid arthritis. You sound like a different woman now."

"I am," her mother replied. "And Nora says she'll help me to get organized so that even when I go home it's going to be OK. It's such a relief to know that I won't be a burden to you or your sister. And talking of Susie —"

Leila interrupted her. "Mum, so sorry, but I have to dash," she fibbed. "Let's talk tomorrow, OK?"

Even thinking of Susie was too painful right now. Her sister was one part of her life that Leila felt she'd completely messed up on. It had been easy to forget the wedge between them before, but since Mum's accident, that was no longer the case.

Leila had barely spoken to her sister these last few weeks. The few phone conversations they had had were terse and strained, and Susie managed to visit their mother in Bridgeport at times when she knew Leila wouldn't be around.

To Leila's surprise, Susie had agreed to be a bridesmaid at the wedding, though as soon as she heard that Katy was coming to Bridgeport to look for bridesmaids' dresses with Leila, Birdie, and Fiona, she'd made her excuses.

"Mollsie can't look after Jack that day," she'd told Katy. "Just buy what you want in my size."

"You phone her," Katy had suggested to Leila that night on the phone. "There's no point me doing it. This is between you and her."

"How can I fix it?" replied Leila crossly.

"Don't ask me. I'm an only child," Katy said, almost cheerfully. "You'll figure it out. You and Susie have to sort out this crisis."

Leila promised to phone, but she knew Katy was wrong. Susie wasn't having a crisis. She was hurt and angry.

Summoning all her energy, she called her sister.

"It's great you can be a bridesmaid," she said cheerily. "Katy says you can't make it to the fittings because of Jack, but perhaps he could come with us?"

"Don't be ridiculous!" snapped Susie. "He would be bored within ten minutes. You and Katy go and choose the dresses. You don't need me."

Guilt smothering her, Leila said good-bye and hung up. The thing was, she did need Susie. But would Susie ever forgive her?

"I'm sorry," Leila said later on the phone to Katy, "but she won't budge. Just talking to me seems to annoy her."

"It's me too," said Katy. "Michael pointed out that things haven't exactly been easy for Susie, and neither of us have been there for her the last couple of years."

"Michael said that?"

"Yeah. He's got a point too. Says we both have exciting lives and she's stuck in a job she hates with nobody to turn to. He made me feel very guilty," Katy admitted.

Leila rubbed the bridge of her nose. It ached these days; she had a constant headache. She wasn't sleeping either. Too much thinking about Susie — and bloody Devlin.

"Michael's right," she said. "But I don't know what to do about it. I mean, how do I

433

mend bridges if Susie doesn't want to?"

"Write her a letter telling her how sorry you are?" suggested Katy. "You pushed her away when she told you Tynan was wrong for you."

"Well, wouldn't you push someone away if they said Michael was the wrong man for you?" demanded Leila.

"Oh, Leila, totally different story," Katy said. "I gave Tynan a hard time too, remember. And you *were* different when you were with him. You weren't you. Susie was only pointing out the truth."

"The truth is a pain in the butt," Leila muttered. "Bet nobody will ever put that on a Hallmark card."

That was two letters she had to write now: an "I'm sorry I was a hopeless sister when you were only looking out for me" one to Susie, and an "I ought to leave the job because it's so uncomfortable working with you after what happened in Rome" one to Devlin.

"I thought you were supposed to write difficult letters and *not* send them?" she said, thinking it through.

"That's when you're angry at people and you'll never sort it out," Katy tutted. "This is different. This is fixable. Honestly, have you learned nothing from *Cosmo*?"

Fixable, thought Leila. Ha! She hadn't told Katy anything about Rome. Now *that* was entirely unfixable, no matter how brilliant the writers in *Cosmopolitan* were.

The following morning, showered and with a just-walked Pixie looking up at her adoringly, Leila stared into her closet and tried to figure out exactly what to wear. It was still only seven thirty; she'd been up since six, what with walking Pixie, grabbing some toast and coffee, showering, and blow-drying her hair, and now she had ten minutes to get dressed and hit the road. It was going to be a very busy day. A three-times-Oscar-nominated movie star was in town to promote her latest film, and a long day of press interviews had been scheduled, with Leila sitting in. The actress, Dara Car, was incredibly beautiful and had a reputation for quiet professionalism and intelligence. She was not one of the people who demanded champagne and white furnishings and muslin curtains. Her requirements had been simple: a hotel suite on a high floor so she wouldn't be too disturbed by city noise, because when she wasn't working, she lived on a remote farm in Arizona.

Yes, she had dietary requirements, but then few people in the movie business turned up these days without them. Lactose-free, wheat-free, dairy-free — you name it. The top hotels knew how to cater for every possible diet, and nobody in one restaurant they'd booked had so much as blinked when a movie star had her assistant produce a set of scales in order to weigh her food and calculate the precise portion she should eat.

Dara, with the bare minimum of requests and no demands, was going to be a joy to work with — several of Leila's friends in the company's U.S. offices had told her so.

However, there was no doubt that when you were going to be sitting in a room all day with an incredibly famous, charismatic, and beautiful woman who spent her life being photographed, it made you ultra-careful about what you were going to wear and critical of how you looked in it. It was one of those rare and difficult-to-explain downsides of the job, Leila grinned to herself.

That aside, possibly the most tricky aspect of the day would be steering the reporters away from questions about Dara's personal life. Like most A-list stars, Dara understood that people who paid at the box office wanted to know everything about you; when promoting a film, it was often impossible to avoid the questions about your life outside the movies. But certainly, from all the interviews Leila had studied, Dara was an expert at gently deflecting such questions rather than playing the diva and insisting that the offending reporter be ejected from the room forthwith.

Devlin was already at the Four Seasons when Leila arrived, clad in her current favorite and most flattering outfit: the beautiful velvet blazer she'd bought in Rome and a pair of perfectly fitting black jeans that made her legs look as long as it was possible for a five-foot-two woman's legs to look. He was having coffee with Dara's manager in one of the two suites set aside for interviews. Dara was in a third suite, farther along the corridor, being made up and having her hair done.

"Good morning," Leila said. "Hope you slept well, Mr. Davis."

"I told you to call me Poppa," Dara's manager replied genially. "Yes, I slept fantastically."

Leila couldn't help but smile. There was something about Poppa Davis's soft, honeyed accent that conjured up sunshine and oranges, blue skies and holidays.

"And how are you, Leila?" Devlin asked, studying her curiously. "You look well today," he added.

Leila was beginning to think it was a mercy that she didn't blush easily, but somehow she still felt the heat rise in her neck every time Devlin said something nice to her. It had been the same ever since Rome and there was nothing she could do about it. It was unfinished business and uncomfortable — half curious, half something she couldn't quite put her finger on.

Their relationship had definitely changed. He didn't talk to her the way he used to, didn't come into her office late in the evening to put his feet up on her desk and chew over the day, ask her opinion, tell her what had gone wrong or right in his world. She missed it, she missed their easy camaraderie. But Rome had put an end to all that, as if some dreadful line had been crossed and they could never go back to how they used to be.

Stupid, stupid, Leila had told herself so many times. Why had she done it? She kept toying with the idea of changing jobs, leaving the company, but she knew she was being ridiculous.

Even so, she was still thinking about it four hours later when it was time to break for lunch after the sixth interview of the morning had ended. Dara said good-bye to the journalist as warmly and kindly as if their talk had been the most enjoyable she'd ever had, then Leila showed him out and shut the door. When she turned back to Dara, the actress seemed to visibly shrink in front of her eyes. Even though it was a phenomenon Leila had witnessed before, it still astonished her how stars could fill up a room with their screen or stage persona, then revert to their real selves again, almost physically diminishing, when showtime was finished.

"Are you all right, Dara?" she said.

"I'm doing just fine," Dara said, smiling at her, a tired, genuine smile. "This part's more exhausting than the acting, you know. On set, you can fly. Here, you have to keep your feet on the ground. Everyone wants to know when I am going to get married again. Do I think I'm going to have any more children now that Joshua's fourteen? I mean, come on," Dara said, "look at me, I'm forty-five."

Leila looked at her, taking in the small, elegant figure, the rippling black hair, the exquisite face, the marvelous bone structure, and those expressive dark eyes.

"You look amazing," she said frankly, "and plenty of people in their forties have babies . . . I'm sorry, I shouldn't have said that." She shuddered. "I apologize. It was far too personal . . ."

"No, I asked you," Dara said, shrugging. "It's hard enough trying to raise a teenager on your own, never mind throw a baby into the mix. The rest of the world thinks actors have such a different life. I mean, being a woman is tough, right, whatever end of the spectrum you're at."

Leila kept staring at her.

Dara slipped off the terrifically high Manolo Blahniks she'd been wearing all morning and sank into the couch, leaning her head back and rubbing her temples.

"Oh Lordy, I'm so tired," she said. "If one more person asks me about men and why I can't seem to make up my mind, I think I will just shove their digital recorder down their throat. It's the men who can't make up their minds, not me. Do you know how many men can cope with a woman in my position?"

Leila shook her head.

"None," said Dara, "absolutely none. They're either in the business — in which case their ego, their job, their career is *way* more important than yours, and y'know, God forbid you get any more column inches or better reviews than they do — or they're incredibly rich megalomaniac businessmen who think they own the world and want a movie star wife to add to their trophy collection. All they want is the kudos of a wife with an Oscar nomination, not a real-live person. I've gone out with those sorta guys, Lord help me, and let me tell you, it's a lot more fun hanging out with the horses on my ranch."

It was rare for someone of Dara's caliber to be so open with a publicist. Leila was mindful of the fact that people had a tendency to overshare when they were tired and emotional, and Dara might regret it later, but at the same time she sensed that the actress needed someone to talk to, not just to listen, so she blurted out: "It's going to sound stupid, but I always thought it was just ordinary people like me who had man problems."

Dara laughed, a deep, dirty laugh. "I'm sorry, honey," she said, "I've been talking all about me — it's clear we should have been talking about you! Tell me your story."

Leila hesitated for a second, but the request was obviously genuine and deserved an honest response. "I was married for a year, then one day I came home to find my husband packing up his stuff. Said he'd been seeing someone else and surely I must've known? How could I not have seen that it was all going downhill? Then it was *hasta la vista, baby* and he was gone."

"You poor kid," said Dara, genuine warmth in her voice. "How are you doing now?"

Leila thought about it. "If you'd asked me that question a month ago, the answer would've been 'broken.' I thought about him every minute of every day, beating myself up for having failed. Now, though . . . I don't feel that way anymore. A lot of stuff has happened: my mum hasn't been well and . . ." She could hardly fill Dara Car in on *everything,* so she let it go at: "I feel different, as if I've got things in perspective and I . . . I might be ready for another relationship."

She exhaled as she finished speaking. It was out there — she'd said it out loud. It sounded crazy: it *was* crazy. Things between her and Devlin were so distant; she longed for the easy familiarity they used to share.

"And who's the new guy?" said Dara.

Leila knew she was blushing this time. "Nobody you'd know," she said.

Dara looked at her, one eyebrow on that

exquisite famous face rising in a question mark.

"Really," she said, making the word several syllables long. "My advice — for what it's worth — is to grab it with both hands. Life's tough when you're on your own. I'm lucky, I have my son. I love him to pieces and he's everything to me, but one day he'll be off with his own life and I'll have to adjust to being alone. When I was a kid, everyone said, *Oh, Dara, you're so beautiful, you'll always have men running after you.* But it doesn't work like that. You have to grab what you want and hold on to it."

Leila felt almost tearful. This was hard-won advice and she was grateful.

"Thank you," she said earnestly. "After my husband, I didn't trust anyone — or myself, for that matter. Now, though, I think you're right . . ."

"You're welcome." Dara got to her feet fluidly. "I think I'm going to go into my suite for a light lunch and a few stretches before the next tranche of interviews — which start at . . . ?"

"Two forty-five," Leila replied, without having to look at the schedule. "We're doing two more print and then three TV."

"In that case I'd better get them to trowel on some more cosmetics," said Dara good-naturedly. "I'll see you at two forty-five."

Dara's premiere was the following night. There'd only been a few TV interviews scheduled that morning and Leila had been on duty again. She could see that the actress was looking more tired today, yet she was still able to turn on the magic for the cameras. Leila watched entranced as Dara became something else, the creature every eye in the room was drawn toward. You just *had* to look at her.

"That's what makes a movie star."

She turned and realized that Devlin was standing beside her.

"You can't take your eyes off her, can you?" he whispered.

"No," Leila said, feeling that strange flare of jealousy again.

Did Devlin fancy Dara? Of course he did; every man who'd ever set eyes on her fancied Dara. She had beauty, intelligence, sexiness, and vulnerability all mixed up together. She was catnip to men, and yet . . . she herself had said that getting hold of a real man was almost impossible, even for her.

"So, looking forward to the premiere tonight?" Leila asked Devlin, then cursed herself for such a stupid question. People in their business didn't exactly look forward to premieres: premieres were work — and demanding work at that. They had to make sure their stars were cared for, see to it that the media turned out in force, that the fans showed up in sufficient numbers to guarantee plenty of column inches, lots of TV time, and a deluge of online reviews and blog write-ups. Only then would Eclipse head office be assured that Dublin were doing their job properly. Sure, they got to dress up in their evening clothes, but it was purely a working gig.

"Yes, I'm looking forward to it," said Devlin, shooting her a big smile. "We're going to go out to dinner afterwards, myself and Poppa. I don't think Dara will join us, but we'll see who else from her team wants to come."

"Obviously I'm available for whatever's needed," Leila said.

"I think it's going to be sort of relaxed, actually," Devlin said. "Poppa's a great guy, he's not one of those ball-breaker managers."

"Even better," Leila said. "I could do with a night out."

Devlin looked at her curiously, but she managed to keep a slightly fixed smile on her face and turned back to watching Dara.

Ever since Rome, she'd been wishing that she could go back in time and undo what had happened so the tension would evaporate and they could return to the easy rapport they'd had before. But Dara's advice had her reconsidering: if it hadn't been for that night in Rome, she might never have realized how much Devlin meant to her; she might have gone on thinking of him merely as a boss. But he could be more — at least, she'd love him to be more.

If only she knew how he felt. Devlin had so many women on the go; he might have kissed her purely because she was there. And if that was the case, Leila would die if he had any clue about how she felt.

The premiere was set for seven, so at six, Leila was in Dara's suite in one of her favorite premiere outfits: a sparkly black on-the-knee dress with spaghetti straps and a tiny fitted jacket. Marc and Ilona were in the cinema with the security people, organizing last-minute details, phoning and texting through with requests and information.

"Hundreds here already," Ilona had told Leila. "It's a good crowd, though: no trouble and lots of press."

Marc kept her up to date on the usual issues over ID verification and people who insisted they were journalists, bloggers, and photographers but who weren't on any of the lists. Leila's team were well trained and could cope with it.

Next, a gang of beautiful people had turned up, entirely out of it on lunchtime champagne and far too drunk to be allowed in. They were creating a scene, Ilona said, marching up and down saying *Don't you know who we are?* Marc was somewhere else, what should she do?

"OK, let me sort it out. I'll talk to Devlin," Leila said, wishing she was there to defuse things. There *was* such a thing as bad publicity.

She phoned Devlin, who was having a drink in the bar with Poppa, and explained the situation.

"We need more security on tonight, ASAP," she said.

"Of course," said Devlin, "I'll get right on it. Everything OK with Dara?"

"Fine, fine," said Leila brusquely.

"And you?" Devlin asked, his voice softening. "Are you OK?"

Leila hesitated. "I'm fine," she said calmly. "Fine."

"Right," he said. "I'm looking forward to dinner, it'll be nice. I think it's just going to be the three of us."

"Good," said Leila, smiling as she hung up. For a minute he'd sounded like the old Devlin. That was good. Maybe it wasn't all ruined. Maybe her instincts were right.

Finally Dara emerged from her suite, looking startlingly beautiful in a long cream dress that hung off her slender body like a Grecian gown on a piece of sculpture.

"Wow, that dress is amazing," said Leila.

"I know, I'm sort of afraid to sit down in it

because I think when I get up it'll be covered in creases," said Dara. "It's this material, I don't know what it is."

"We could limit the photocall to on the way into the cinema, and then try to ensure the photographers only get you in groups?" Leila suggested. "I'm thinking no posed shots on your own, keep you with other people so there's less chance they'll use the shots in the fashion mags and comment on the creases . . . ? I know, impossible to be so specific with photographers, but we can manage it to a certain extent."

"We'll try it," said Dara. "Darned designers. The way they create dresses nowadays, you can only stand up in them and be photographed. You can't actually, y'know, sit or eat or anything normal. Right, let's rock'n'roll."

In the limo, they chatted.

"How many times have you seen it already?"

"Once," said Dara. "This'll be number two. Then, two days' time in Paris will be number three. Some people sneak out of their own premieres, but I've always felt that was sort of rude, 'cause the fans are going to see you leaving early and they'll think it's because the movie's so dreadful you can't stand to watch it."

"It's not a dreadful movie, it's an amazing movie," said Leila, who'd seen it the previous month.

"You're very kind," said Dara. She reached out and touched the younger woman. "Very, very kind. Don't lose that. This business can turn people tough, you know."

"I won't," said Leila. "I have my mother's dog to keep me grounded. She rolled in fox doo-dah the other weekend and I had to wash her in my mother's bath. That pretty much keeps your feet on the ground."

Dara roared with laughter and then had to try and stop. "This dress is killing me. It's not made for laughing either. No sitting, no laughing. That's good, I like the sound of that dog. Fourteen-year-old sons keep you grounded too. If my son could see me now, he'd say: *Mom, yeah, s'pose you look OK, for your age and everything . . .*

They both laughed.

"You need something to remind you that this business is a business and all the dressing up is just fantasy. Grounded is good."

"It is," agreed Leila.

Somehow, all the events of the past few months — her mother's accident, Katy's pregnancy, even the problems with Susie — had left her feeling grounded in a way she never had before.

Life wasn't to be thought about — it was to be grabbed.

Sixteen

Marriage is our last, best chance
to grow up.

JOSEPH BARTH

Ruby sat at the back of the eleventh grade classroom and listened to Miss Redmond droning on about some ancient battle. There were times when she was sorry she'd ever decided to study history, and this was definitely one of those times. The course was huge and Miss Redmond was not one of those teachers with the charisma to make you want to listen. No matter what great event in history she was describing, she always spoke as if she was giving evidence at an inquiry into the loss of a box of paper clips. Drone, drone, drone.

Ruby shot a sideways glance at her friend Andi, who was paying attention and making notes. Once upon a time Ruby used to pay attention and make notes, but she didn't have the energy anymore. Or the heart, for that matter. She felt tired a lot of the time; a tiredness that was interspersed with moments of great vitality, normally around mealtimes. She was doing her best to eat as little as possible, but it was difficult.

She spent hours fantasizing about chocolate, or cheese on toast — white bread, of course, with red cheddar dripping down the sides. Then she'd feel angry with herself for becoming so obsessed — it was only food, and despite all her efforts, *nobody was noticing.*

Not her mother, not her father, not even Vonnie. Nobody.

If only she could stick it out a bit longer, then someone would see and everything would be better, surely? They'd realize that she was in pain then, and all of them — Mum, Dad, Vonnie — would see that she was trapped in the middle of this adult battle and she couldn't take it anymore.

But so far — nothing. They were all too caught up in their own dramas to notice her.

What would it take to make them sit up? she wondered. She'd thought about running away, but she knew Shelby would be devastated. The whole point about shocking them by losing weight was that it didn't involve Shelby. She wouldn't even have to know, let alone get worried about it. That was part of its brilliance.

If it ever worked.

The mornings were easiest not to eat, when

her resolve was high. No matter how hungry she felt in the morning, she flattened down the feelings, buried them deep inside her, and grabbed an apple or occasionally a low-fat yogurt from the fridge. It required no effort to fool her mother. Mum rarely noticed anything anymore. She was cooking a huge amount, doing her best mother impersonation and serving up cordon-bleu delights every night to Ruby and Shelby, but she took amazingly little notice of whether they ate it or not. Ruby had become adept at pushing things around her plate, then moving swiftly to the bin the moment her mother's back was turned. She'd empty her plate, cover up the discarded food with a paper towel and be loading the plate into the dishwasher by the time her mother noticed.

"Fabulous food," she'd say blithely, giving her mother a brief hug as she walked past. "Must go up and study."

Studying was the most amazing excuse for everything. It stopped her mother in her tracks when she was about to get into her stride complaining about Ruby's father and *that woman,* as she called Vonnie. It stopped her noticing what Ruby put into her packed lunch. And it made Ruby look like a perfectly behaved teenager. In reality, she'd be staring out the window, messing around on her phone, reading, or just lying on her bed in a semi-doze, because she felt tired and was thinking about food.

Some nights, she gave in and ran down to the fridge, where she stood in the darkened kitchen gorging herself on whatever she could find. Cheese, cold chicken, a bowl of leftover apple crumble. *Anything.*

As soon as she finished, the guilt and shame would overwhelm her.

How could she have given in? Nobody would ever notice if she kept pigging out this way.

She'd tried throwing up but she couldn't do it. Ever since she was little, she'd had a phobia about being sick, and no matter how many times she tried, she couldn't.

Finally, exhausted, red-eyed, and full of self-anger at her inability to control even one aspect of her life, she'd fall into bed and sleep heavily, to wake shattered in the morning.

She was almost on the verge of giving up, because nobody paid any attention whatsoever. And then one day, somebody did notice: Maria, the queen bee of her year.

"Ruby, you look fabulous," Maria had said as they were changing for sport. "What are you doing — South Beach, the Dukan?"

Ruby had responded with a speculative look. Maria could be an absolute bitch if crossed, but thus far she'd never given Ruby any trouble. Even so, it gave her great pleasure to shrug her slender shoulders and say:

"Nothing really, Maria. I'm just naturally slim."

Maria's eyes glittered. Ruby knew exactly how hard Maria worked to keep her slim figure, so it was the ultimate irritation to discover someone who achieved the same effect with no effort.

"Oh well," said Maria, still not quite able to diss Ruby, because, after all, she was looking totally amazing, "whatever it is, you look good."

Ruby had felt triumph flood through her. Somebody had noticed! It wouldn't be long now, surely? Vonnie would see, Ruby knew she would, and Vonnie would tell Dad and it would all stop. Somebody would think about her and Shelby and see how horrible life had become for them. Mum would have to stop thinking about herself long enough to realize she had two daughters to consider. The bitching, the anger, the grand inquisition about the house on Poppy Lane: all of it would stop.

Beside her in history class, Andi reached out and poked Ruby in the arm.

"Earth to Planet Ruby," she whispered. "You're supposed to be writing this down."

"Oh, er, thanks, Andi," muttered Ruby, and stared up at the blackboard, where Miss Redmond was laboriously writing something in handwriting just as boring as her tone of voice.

That had been a near miss. Ruby was

forever getting into trouble with teachers these days because she kept zoning out in class and slipping into dreamland. What was the point of school anyway? It was all so useless, so utterly hopeless. It didn't help you deal with real life and people who were messing up their lives and yours. School was full of people telling you what to do. Ruby was sick of people telling her what to do, what to think, what to feel.

"When I think of what your father has done to this family . . . we should all totally ignore him and we should never have to see him again."

Her mother had been halfway through a bottle of wine when she said this, but no one was likely to call her up and question her about her behavior. Whereas Ruby got hassled all the time over the stupidest things. Only the day before, Miss Lynott, the eleventh grade form mistress, had pulled her aside to let her know yet another teacher had complained that she wasn't paying attention and her homework was substandard.

Since earlier in the term, when Miss Lynott had rung Mum about Ruby not doing enough work, she'd been making a bit of an effort. Not that Mum was too concerned; she'd been more upset about the school giving out than she had about Ruby doing badly.

"You're so clever — and look at all the riffraff they let in!" her mother had said crossly. "How dare they phone me about you? I gave that woman a piece of my mind, I can tell you!"

Ruby could have told Miss Lynott that her mother was not an easy person to tackle. Ruby could have told Miss Lynott a lot of things, but what was the point? The first person Miss Lynott would tell was Mum, and life was bad enough without Mum going ballistic because Ruby was washing their dirty linen in public.

Ruby knew exactly what she'd say: "How dare you tell people that you're stressed because I hate that bitch your father has moved in with! It's all your father's fault, not mine! I've done nothing!"

And then she would cry, which was the other thing she did a lot of these days. Rage and cry.

"I'm sorry, Ruby, I love you, it's just . . ." and she would sob again because she didn't seem to be able to say what *it* was.

Mum, Ruby knew, wasn't able to see anything these days.

It wasn't the same at school. Yesterday Miss Lynott had told her: "Ruby, I'm worried about you. We all are. Your grades have slipped this year and it's not like you. I know you say nothing's wrong, but clearly something is. Please help me to help you."

Ruby had stared past Miss Lynott's kind, well-meaning face and said, "Nothing's wrong, I'm fine. Really, thanks." Then she'd walked off, leaving Miss Lynott standing there. She'd felt sorry at first, because Miss Lynott was one of the nice teachers who had always been kind to her. But she was sick of all the wrong people wondering what the matter was. Sick of it.

She wanted Dad to see how difficult things were, she wanted Mum to see. But they were so caught up in their own lives that they didn't.

When the bell rang signaling that forty leaden minutes of history was over, everyone groaned with relief. It was lunchtime, time to chill out, eat something, forget about work for an hour. Ruby had a yogurt in her bag, but she wasn't sure she'd eat it. Half of it, maybe. Yes, she'd have half. The great thing about yogurts was that they didn't talk back.

Stephen said it was only right that he and his son go suit shopping while the women were off looking for their dresses.

"See if Robbie's up for it," he said on the phone to Michael a few days before. "And perhaps a pint or two."

"Robbie's up for everything," said Michael of his best man. "But he can't come out in the evenings now, with the new baby."

"If that's the case," said Stephen idly, "perhaps I might take you, Katy, Fiona, and your mother out to dinner in Bridgeport. Seeing as I'll be down there."

"Cracking plan, Dad," said his son. "Just you, or Julia too? I haven't seen her for ages. Work busy, huh?"

"Yeah, very busy," said Stephen slowly. "I'll phone your mum and ask her."

Julia. The ache in his chest was back. What he'd done to her and how he'd never meant to hurt her.

All those years ago, Julia had seemed like the perfect antidote to what was wrong between him and Grace. She was child-free, in the same business, sexy, and fun. There were never conversations about babysitting or getting one of the kids picked up from football/dancing/whatever. After the arguments he'd had with Grace about moving to Dublin for his career, this new life was seductive.

It was like being young and single again, something he'd found very heady. He and Julia could go away for weekends easily, hop on a plane at the drop of a hat, or go to a concert if the mood took them. He was there for Fiona and Michael when he was supposed to be, but when they were with Grace, he was a free agent, and he'd loved it.

And then his darling daughter-in-law-to-be had become pregnant, and suddenly, being the dashing advertising man around town had palled.

Everything Stephen thought he'd been

happy to live without had exploded into living color and he'd realized he'd been kidding himself all along. He'd had the family without the really hard stuff, the day-to-day hard stuff. Grace had done all of that.

Grace. The woman he was beginning to wonder if he'd ever really stopped loving.

He'd never realized that before. Julia had seen it before he had. Poor, lovely Julia. She'd seen how he longed to be part of his old family again when he hadn't had a clue.

Stephen wished he could turn back the clock for Julia, make it all like it had been, but he couldn't and they both knew it. The big question for him now was what was he going to do about it?

He caught Grace on her cell at the end of a long day devoted to her least favorite part of the job: dealing with all manner of financial matters including the school insurance — the policy price had gone up again.

"Dinner on Saturday?" she'd said, phone tucked between her chin and shoulder as she organized the papers on her desk. "That would be lovely — just not anywhere fancy . . ." Then a thought occurred to her: "Why don't I cook for us all?"

"I don't want you to go to any trouble, Grace," said Stephen. "I wanted to treat you all and make the weekend special. It's not as if we're paying for any part of the wedding;

it's the least I could do."

"No," said Grace, enthused over the idea. "I'd love it. I can't tell you the last time I cooked a feast. It'll be a pleasure."

"Well, I'll bring the wine and mineral water," said her ex-husband. "You're not to spend a ha'penny on drink. I can bring dessert too. There's a bakery near me that does a nice pavlova, and I could bring berries and cream."

"No," said Grace decisively. "I'll make Queen of Puddings. Katy loves it — assuming she's up to eating it, what with the morning sickness. Lord, I don't know the last time I made that . . ."

In Dublin, when Stephen finally hung up, he was smiling to himself at the thought of the lovely Saturday night ahead of him. Grace was a fabulous cook. Her roast beef and gravy was a thing of glory, and when she did that slow-cooked Moroccan lamb with pomegranates . . . He could feel his saliva glands going into overdrive at the thought.

And that was all it was: dinner, he promised himself.

In her office in the school, Grace hummed as she tidied up. How gorgeous it would be to have everyone together again. Lovely big family dinners were one of the many things she missed about being married and having the children living with her. Those family dinners she'd once taken for granted were among the happiest moments of her life, she'd realized when they were a thing of the past.

No pressure, just family around the table enjoying food and conversation. There was usually some mild argument over sports (Michael and Stephen), music (Michael and Fiona), and how nobody kept any part of the house tidy (Stephen and both kids), but they were good-humored arguments.

She could recall Michael trying to slope off without doing his share of the tidying in order to phone or text Katy. Fiona had always been wonderful about helping out, as had Stephen, and often he'd insist she sat down with the remains of her glass of wine and relax while he and Fiona tidied up.

Then Fiona would wander off and Stephen would sit with Grace. She'd have her shoes off and her feet up on another of the chairs with the red cushions. They'd talk for ages, discussing life, the children, work, that funny thing someone in his office had done, how a new mother with a child in preschool was still arriving at school in the morning in three-inch heels and a tight skirt because she desperately fancied the gym teacher, who in turn had sat in Grace's office insisting he hadn't spoken more than a word to her and what if his fiancée found out or people thought he was *that* sort of man?

She might look for some nice spring lamb,

she decided. Stephen and Michael had always adored her lamb, and she'd do some jeweled couscous and salads too, in case Katy — who wasn't a great meat-eater — was still off red meat with her morning sickness. And her favorite pudding. She left the office with a spring in her step.

She had something nice for her gratitude diary: the wonderful relationship she had with her ex-husband. How many people had that?

"Please come on Saturday," Katy said to Susie on the phone. "We need you, we're the Three Musketeers after all."

She'd rung as late as she dared, when she knew Susie would have settled Jack into bed and would probably be hurrying around the apartment organizing his clothes and his packed lunch for school.

Susie was a brilliant cook now, which Katy admired. She'd been hopeless once; Leila had been the chef in the Martin house, for all that she said she lived off ready-meals now. But Susie had changed once she'd had Jack.

"Proper food is so important," she'd said, diligently puréeing carrots while Leila and Katy played with baby Jack.

"Oh, Katy," Susie said now, tiredness in every syllable. "You don't need me, honestly. Just get a dress in my size —"

"No," said Katy decisively. "You need some time to have silly, girlie fun with no responsi-

461

bilities. It will be great. You need shoes, underwear, a necklace . . . Doesn't that all sound nice? Michael's mother is making a dinner for us, which will be gorgeous, and if you think Jack is too small to stay up late with all of us, then Morag, who works for Mum, you've met her, will mind him in her house and let him snooze until you pick him up. She has three kids under ten and a house full of Thomas the Tank Engine stuff. I don't know why I didn't think of it before. She's the perfect babysitter, Jack will love her, and . . ." she paused, "you need to spend some time with Leila."

There was silence.

"You love each other to bits, and all this rubbish about who said what about Tynan is crazy. She was a daft cow to marry him and we both know that."

Susie laughed. "Gee, you need to stop beating around the bush, Katy."

"I've said it to her face, Susie," Katy pointed out. "I'm not going behind her back with this. Leila knows exactly what I feel about Tynan. But she needs us now. And yes, I know being with Tynan meant she wasn't really there for you, but life is a bit of a learning curve. I think she knows it now. Plus, *I* need you. Who else is going to tell me how to be a modern mother? The books make it all sound so easy and I know it's not: I want the real deal, the real story of giving birth, the pain, everything . . ."

This time Susie's laughter was deeper, more real.

"I could always check with Mollsie if she could mind Jack for that Saturday morning," she admitted. "It might be nice to go shopping . . ."

"Yay! Fun, here we come," said Katy happily.

On the morning of the great bridesmaid dress hunt, Katy and Birdie were the first to reach Milady's Salon, the bridal boutique Katy had most liked the sound of after an Internet trawl.

They'd walked slowly arm in arm toward it, chatting happily about pregnancy and feeling tired, how it was the most incredible feeling in the world, and yet morning sickness: why?

"I threw up every morning religiously for three months when I was carrying you," Birdie said as they walked.

"I never knew that," Katy said, shocked. "You poor thing. It's awful, isn't it? I'm not too bad, not every morning, but sometimes in the afternoon it hits me and I have to munch on something."

"Ginger biscuits."

"Yes! Ginger biscuits. I hate ginger normally. Especially Gran's sticky gingerbread cake."

"Me too," said Birdie, "but I have to eat it. She might whack me with her walking aid otherwise."

The two women laughed conspiratorially.

"Gran can be a bit of a tyrant," Katy agreed. "Was she helpful when you were pregnant, seeing as your own mum wasn't around?"

It was a risky question, one that Katy had never thought to ask before. Her maternal grandmother had been long dead when Birdie was pregnant, and it was only now that Katy could appreciate how hard that must have been. Nobody but your own mother could possibly have that intense interest in every aspect, but Birdie had been denied that. Her parents were dead, her two brothers living abroad — leaving her to be subsumed into the Desmond family like a veritable orphan.

"Your gran was great," said Birdie, which wasn't true at all, but she had always tried to make sure that Katy had a good relationship with her one surviving grandparent.

"It's better to have your own mum, though," said Katy, squeezing her mother's arm happily.

Milady's Salon saw brides by appointment, and the proprietress, Madeleine, a smiling, chic woman in her fifties, let them in. Katy, Birdie, and Leila had already been to see her about Katy's dress. Today she was going to have her first fitting, which was exciting. But really the focus was on Leila, Susie, and Fiona.

"We have three bridesmaids coming," Katy explained.

"Three is a nice number," said Madeleine, who had happily told a bride only the previous day that one was the ideal number. People got worried at weddings and calming them down was part and parcel of her job.

"Do you think so?" said Katy. "There's Leila, who you met before, and who can wear any color. But Fiona — well, she's not a dressy kind of girl."

"It will be no problem," Madeleine said cheerfully. "How are you feeling today, Katy? Up to a nice cup of tea?"

"Yes, please," said Katy.

"Tea would be lovely," agreed Birdie, sitting down and watching her beautiful daughter walking along the rails, hands out, stroking the dresses.

Nothing could be nicer than the creamy silk gown Katy had chosen: with a covering of antique-looking lace, and an empire line so that it would fall elegantly from her bust no matter how her baby bump developed, it was an exquisite dress.

Madeleine watched her for a moment, thinking that this had been an easy bride to dress, with no interfering mother: Birdie would have been happy whatever her daughter had chosen. If only all brides were as trouble-free.

Leila and Fiona shared a companionable drive from Dublin to Waterford. Through Michael and Katy they'd known each other well for at least fifteen years and were at ease in each other's company. They talked about the wedding and how lovely it was to be involved in one where the couple were so gloriously matched and happy.

"How are you doing since the cretin left?" Fiona asked the moment she got in the car, unzipping her boots and sliding her seat as far back as it could go so she could rest her feet on the dashboard.

"For a while, pretty horribly, I have to admit," said Leila, who knew there was no point in doing the "it's all fine, honestly" schtick with her current passenger. "I kept Facebooking him." No need to mention that she was no longer doing this with anything like the same interest, and was instead thinking nonstop about her boss: how it had all gone wrong in Rome and how she was hoping that perhaps, just perhaps, Devlin did like her and might say so again one day.

Did this mean she was over Tynan? She hoped so. It was like one of those toothaches where you were in agony for ages and then it lessened over time until one day it was gone and you didn't even realize it until someone asked how you were.

"Facebook — ouch," said Fiona, wincing. "Dangerous territory, that. A girl at work who'd been dumped — sorry," she added, "started a Facebook campaign where she went to all these cool parties and gigs simply so she could post the photos of herself and say how happy she was. She got every good-looking bloke she met to pose with her. It was pretty impressive, I have to say. If you didn't know she was still sobbing over the first guy, you'd think she was glad to be rid of him so she could hang out with all these other gorgeous single men."

Leila laughed. "Was she too brokenhearted to take advantage of these fabulous guys?"

"Surprisingly, no. She's going out with this incredible man from Sligo. He has a sort of Johnny Depp thing going for him, without the eyeliner and the Captain Jack necklaces, but he reeks of sex. When he's in the room, you can't take your eyes off him. I think," Fiona said thoughtfully, "that they fell for each other because she wasn't hung up about how she looked or how she was behaving or whether he liked her — all the usual stuff that holds you back. She just wanted to look as if she was having a good time — and she forgot herself and *did* have a good time. She's totally happy now." She reached down for her bag, found the chocolate bars she'd brought, and offered one to Leila.

"Thank you." Leila took it gratefully. All this talk of happy-ever-after was making her hungry in a way only chocolate could assuage. "Do you think that's it?" she asked. "Stop worrying if he's happy or if you're behaving the right way or not? Then if it's going to work, it has a better chance because you're not pressuring the hell out of yourself trying to be something you're not?"

She'd been guilty of that when she was with Tynan, Leila thought with shame. Not at first. But afterwards, when they became serious and she was truly in love with him, she'd desperately wanted it to be perfect, she'd wanted to *be* perfect. At some point, she'd stopped being Leila and had become the Leila who wanted to match Tynan's needs. She shuddered: she *hated* when women did that. How had she become one of them?

After Tynan had gone, she'd fallen apart. Perhaps she should have done what Fiona's friend at work had done and gone off to show the world that she wasn't finished just because her husband had left her. But grieving over a failed marriage felt like a necessary part of the process. She'd needed to sit in misery in order to move on; it was like grief, really. Grieving for what might have been.

And now she had moved on. Finally.

Except she'd moved on to a man she probably couldn't have and who might not have the slightest feeling for her — or did he? She

468

wished she knew.

"Are you seeing anyone?" she asked Fiona abruptly, anxious to stop thinking about Devlin.

Fiona's escapades in the dating world always made for marvelous stories. She was the exact opposite of Leila and had spent her twenty-seven years on earth having fun and not caring what anyone, boyfriend or otherwise, thought about her.

"Not right now," Fiona said. "I'm between unsuitable men."

Leila laughed out loud.

"Why is it so hard to figure out if they're unsuitable in the first place?"

"Dunno. I get carried away by the physical bits — face, nice pecs, the tough-but-I-could-tame-him look I can't resist." Fiona sighed as if this had been a long and often-fought battle. "How about you? Are you seeing anyone?"

Leila felt the blush rise up her chest and hit her face. At least she was facing ahead so Fiona couldn't see the color of her.

"No," she said blithely.

Which was true: she wasn't. One ludicrous night where she and her boss — *her boss!* — had kissed hardly counted as dating someone. Neither did the current situation in the office, where Devlin appeared to be either ignoring her or talking to her like she was a maiden aunt he was in dreadful fear of of-

469

fending. It was all so complicated.

"I brought my iPod," announced Fiona. "Do you want to listen to some music?"

"Sure."

Fiona fiddled with the iPod for a moment, and then music flooded the car.

Fiona leaned her seat back, closed her eyes, and seemed to fall asleep.

With her passenger out for the count, Leila allowed herself to relive that moment in Rome with Devlin. Time suspended, his arms around her, fantasizing about the life they might have. In this happy haze, the miles flew past.

Susie had woken at six thirty to the sound of Jack watching *Power Rangers* on the TV in their tiny living room, which was next door to the apartment's big bedroom. Why was it, she wondered, that she had to haul him from his bed on school mornings at seven thirty when on weekends he was up with the lark?

"It's ironic, isn't it?" one of the mothers had said cheerfully the previous day, when Susie had picked Jack up from school. "It's like they've got sleeping sickness on school days, and come Saturday, they're raring to go at dawn!"

Susie had kept the smile nailed to her face when the other woman went on to happily declare that tomorrow it would be her turn to have Saturday morning in bed: "Mark had a lie-in last Saturday — this one's mine!"

There was nobody with whom Susie could share the weekend mornings. Jack's father had been gone long before their son was born. Every part of his care, except when she was at work and he was at school or at darling Mollsie's, was Susie's responsibility.

She loved him so much it almost hurt, but in spite of that, there were times when the sheer weight of exhaustion and responsibility became too much for her. She had to keep healthy, earn money, and stay sane for both their sakes; there was nobody else to rely on. If she allowed herself to contemplate the things that could go wrong, how easily their precarious security could fall apart, it scared her so much that she couldn't breathe. What if she got injured or was too sick to cope — who'd look after Jack then?

Monday was the only day when Susie could do the school pickup. She carved the hours out of the rest of her working week by taking half-hour lunches and starting early, but it was worth it to see Jack's chubby little face light up in a smile when he saw her standing with the other mothers at the school gates.

Despite the years she'd been doing it, she still had the sense of not quite fitting into any of the groups of waiting parents. There were the working mothers who made it when their schedules allowed, and the mothers who didn't work outside the home who were there come rain or shine, but Susie fell awkwardly into the gap between the two groups.

Sure, there were divorced parents, including one divorced father who had an office at home, shared custody of his daughter, and picked her up every day. But Susie was the only truly single parent. And she felt the difference keenly.

For her and Jack, there was no man to put out the trash, play football with his son and sort out the fuse box in the dark. If anything needed fixing in her small two-bedroom apartment, Susie had to try and sort it herself.

"You're great," said one school father approvingly when he spotted her in the DIY store, looking high and low for picture hooks.

"I love a bit of DIY," said Susie briskly, marching off to the till. Talking to the fathers was always a mistake. Better to have them think she was standoffish than risk them assuming she was batting her eyelashes at them.

She wondered how the other mothers saw her. She didn't have Leila's obvious sex appeal or the money for expensive blonde streaks, but otherwise the sisters were very alike, with their hourglass figures and big, heavy-lashed eyes. They certainly dressed differently, though, with Susie being careful to wear outfits that projected a hardworking, almost somber mien. At work, she dressed in the dark trousers and blouses that Broadbanz-Inc insisted upon. Outside of work, she was a fan of jeans, flat shoes, and nothing that emphasized her figure. She'd learned that lesson early.

Sexy single mothers were looked down on by people who jumped to the conclusion that they had only themselves to blame for their situation. And it made her sad to think so, but some people believed that single mothers were forever on the lookout for a man.

Susie was determined to give them no cause for talk in that direction. Nobody would ever know she was lonely.

Today, there would be no time for loneliness. She was looking forward to it all: the girlish fun of discussing dresses, being with Katy and even Leila.

She'd done nothing but think about what Katy had said to her about Leila. *She needs us now.*

At nine, she dropped Jack off at Mollsie's house and set off for Milady's Salon with a spring in her step.

An hour had passed and they still hadn't decided on a color.

The three of them tried on 1930s-style dresses in Birdie's favorite old-rose shade and stood side by side in front of the big mirrors, with Katy and Birdie, now on their second cups of tea, looking on. The color suited Susie and Leila, but it made Fiona look as if she should be in the hospital on a drip.

"It's a nursing-home bed-jacket color on me," she said, not at all put out by the sight of herself in a dress that so obviously didn't suit her.

Fiona was quite amazing, Leila thought admiringly. She didn't feel that she had failed because she looked bad in an outfit — it was just the color, not her personally.

Glancing across at Susie, Leila found that she too seemed impressed.

"I'd have thought it was somehow my fault for having the wrong coloring," said Susie.

"Me too," said Leila, and for a brief moment, the sisters smiled at each other in total accord.

"You never used to be like that," Susie said quietly, moving closer to Leila.

"Life," said Leila, shrugging. "I think I lost my confidence somewhere along the way."

Susie's hand found her sister's and squeezed.

Leila squeezed back.

"I lost mine too," Susie whispered.

"I'm sorry I wasn't there to help," Leila said.

"You're here now," said Susie, because it seemed like exactly the right thing to say. No long speeches, no shouting; just the knowledge that their relationship was strong enough after all to weather this.

The two sisters retreated to the dressing room area.

"You should be yelling at me," Leila said sadly. "I left you alone with Jack — I left Mum too. All for a bloody man who was off the first time someone shoved her push-up bra at him."

"If he wanted to go, he'd have gone whatever was shoved in his face," Susie said. "Sisters and mothers don't go."

"Or nephews," said Leila. "I love Jack, he's adorable."

"He wants to know why I don't have an iPhone," said Susie, grinning. "Apparently everyone's mum has one."

"I could buy you one," Leila offered.

"Hey, not having all the expensive stuff in life didn't do us any harm, Leelu," said her sister, and they both grinned.

"Fair enough, but promise me you won't ever make him take his driving test in a car where the back doors don't open and the driver's front window is stuck at half-mast, come rain or shine?"

And then they were laughing, discussing how awful that car had been and how they'd managed never having the money to go on any of the school overnight trips.

Katy peered around the curtain and grinned at her friends.

"Fiona has a color she likes," she said innocently.

"Blue," Fiona was telling Madeleine. "I look good in blue."

"Blue, right," said Madeleine calmly.

Leila, who hadn't worn blue since ripping off their school uniform — royal blue — for the last time many years before, grimaced. "Blue?"

"Yeah, a nice blue," said Fiona, oblivious to Leila and Susie's looks of horror. She pulled out a taffeta dress with a high neck and an A-line skirt, not unlike the shape of the one they'd all had to wear for so long in school. "It's a bit geeky, but the color's nice, don't you think? You could, you know, cut the neck down a bit or something."

She turned to see Birdie smothering a laugh while Leila shook her head and made throat-cutting gestures with her hand.

"But I like it," cried Fiona.

"How could you like it? It's the school color and it suited none of us," said Leila. "I looked like a short blue Smurf."

"Smurf blue is nice," remarked Katy. "This is not Smurf blue. It's school uniform blue!"

Susie snorted.

Soon, Katy, Leila, and Susie were all giggling helplessly.

"What?" demanded Fiona.

Madeleine turned to her assistant, Leda, and whispered that it might be time to boil the kettle again.

"Let's all change back into dressing gowns and have a rethink," she announced in the voice of a woman who had seen many, many bridal parties pass through her doors, including one memorable one where nobody — *nobody* — was speaking to anyone else and it had been left to her to go from one person to the next, transmitting remarks they should have been addressing to one another.

This lot were lovely, no trouble at all really, apart from the tall one who actually would have liked a denim dress if they'd had one. But tea and a break were definitely required.

Michael's best man, Robbie, was, he told Michael and Stephen, a broken man.

"Colic," he said, heading for one of the comfy seats in the coffee bar instead of the stools, and fortifying himself with a double espresso. "Marco cries all the time. It's heartbreaking holding him because you can't do anything except rub his back and talk to him or sing. None of those remedies from the pharmacy work. Is it natural for a baby to be in pain like that?" He turned to Stephen for this question, his eyes the sunken red of someone who had only a passing acquaintance with sleep.

"All sorts of strange things are natural for babies," Stephen pointed out gently. "Nobody tells you how intense and difficult it is at first. You wonder how people get through it all, what with the lack of sleep, the crying fits, the problems feeding . . . and that's only the parents!"

Robbie managed a laugh. "I had no idea, none, what my parents went through," he said, shaking his head. "Maureen worked out that at one point my mother had five kids under the age of seven. I can tell you, I have more admiration for her now than I ever had."

"Wow," said Michael, who was quite shocked at how shattered his best man was looking, and even more shocked at this insight into how traumatic it could be caring for a first baby. He didn't remember reading any of this in the pregnancy guide he and Katy spent all their time poring over. That was full of stuff about how big the baby was now and what bits were developing. No talk of colic or near-derangement due to lack of sleep. "I didn't think it would be that bad."

"It's not that bad," said Robbie, distressed at having given the wrong impression. "It's the most incredible experience ever — but it is hard. Marco's three months now and he still doesn't sleep. Maureen and I took turns when I was on paternity leave, but since I've gone back to work, I've been doing weekends. He goes to bed at seven, then he's up at twelve, down again — if you're lucky — at one, then up again at four."

Michael was looking paler and paler as this tale was recounted.

"All Maureen's friends seem to have babies who are already sleeping through the night, and I want to kill them," Robbie said. "Sometimes I'm convinced they're just saying it to make us feel inadequate. Babies' sleeping schedules are a competitive sport, Maureen's mother says."

Stephen sat back in his chair and took another sip of his latte. "You didn't sleep for months," he told Michael, his mind drifting back to those early days of fatherhood. "Your mother did more of it than me, God love her. I'd come home from work and find you asleep on the floor, with her lying beside you."

"The floor?"

"On beanbags," his father chuckled. "Beanbags were the height of fashion then, and babies could lie in them happily and gurgle up at you."

He seemed lost in memories.

"You don't know it at the time, but they're some of the best days of your life," he said wistfully.

Madeleine was on the third hour of the Desmond/Rhattigan bridal party, which wasn't unusually long. Some brides, like that sweet but dithering girl from last month, couldn't make up their mind if their life depended upon it. Four and a half hours had been required to get her to buy the first dress she'd tried on.

Katy wasn't like that at all, Madeleine knew. She'd chosen her gown two weeks earlier and all they had to do now was keep an eye on her emerging bump. It was the bridesmaids who couldn't come to a decision. The two sisters loved coral, but Fiona didn't. Pink of any hue made her shudder.

"Fiona, it's not your blinking wedding!" said Leila crossly. She'd have worn anything if it pleased Katy. What the bridesmaids wore was not that important as long as they didn't frighten the guests or resemble giant meringues. It was all about Katy.

"I don't like girlie colors, that's all," said Fiona stubbornly.

Katy looked at Leila and shrugged.

"You don't have to be a bridesmaid if you hate the idea," she said kindly to Fiona. "I didn't know you hated dresses that much, Fi, honestly. I won't be upset. I want everyone to have a lovely day, that's all."

"Now, ladies, I think I have the answer to all our prayers," said Madeleine, emerging from the back of the shop carrying several gowns. She was followed by Leda struggling under the weight of many more.

"These are from a few seasons ago, so they're cheaper, and they might be perfect with your dress, Katy. There hasn't been anything really empire line for the past few years, but these are very Jane Austen and you girls are all slim."

"Don't tell your father they're cheaper," Birdie warned anxiously. Howard would have a fit if he thought any money had been spared for his beloved daughter's wedding.

"These," said Madeleine, managing to look both steely and shop-owner professional at the same time, "are a good choice for a spring wedding. There's navy with silver cobweb shawls you might all like." She glanced at Fiona as she said this. "Or if you're so anti-pink, how about an amber-colored dress?"

The girls took a navy and an amber dress each and went into the dressing rooms.

"Is it always this tricky?" asked Birdie.

"This is a walk in the park," confided Madeleine. "We'll get your girls sorted, I promise."

Grace's dinner party had grown as the week went on.

Susie, Leila, and Birdie were all coming too, but Howard — Grace felt guilty as she sent a silent thank-you heavenward — was going to be in France for a work thing, so couldn't be there.

She was nearly ready: all she needed were a few tidbits for nibbles and she'd be all set. And some flowers. She'd seen purple parrot tulips in the florist's just off the square, and with a bit of greenery from her own garden, they'd be perfect.

But as she set off for the town center to do her last-minute shopping, Grace was struggling to keep the tiredness at bay. Why did she have to feel so exhausted today of all days? She wondered whether it would be worth making a doctor's appointment next week for one of those vitamin B injections she'd heard about.

She had to be lacking in something, because there was no other explanation for how she was feeling. A wave of loneliness kept coming over her at the oddest times: watching a TV show featuring a happily married couple, even though she knew they were acting and heaven knew what went on in their real lives.

Grace saw enough of other people's lives secondhand through her work. People might think they could fool the world, hide the pain behind closed doors, but inevitably it would reveal itself in their children. As a headmistress, she had learned to recognize the signs: uncharacteristic behavior, loss of interest in school activities and lessons . . . She thought again of Ruby Morrison. Apparently there had been no improvement since Derek McGurk first alerted her to the problem; the form teacher had made several attempts to get Ruby to confide in her, but she kept insisting nothing was wrong.

Grace's efforts to find out more about what was going on in the Morrison family life had come to naught — so far. She'd been hoping that an old pal of hers who knew Ruby's grandmother could give her the inside scoop, but she was spending the winter with her family in Canada, putting paid to that line of inquiry. Undaunted, Grace intended to keep trying until she got to the bottom of it. Ruby was at that dangerous age when pain at home could have a devastating effect.

She hated to think of that sweet, intelligent child in pain. It was so frustrating, knowing that Ruby was suffering and yet she couldn't fix it. Any intervention had to be handled carefully, subtly, or it could do more harm than good. What was the point of being old enough to have worked out what life was all about if you couldn't act on what you knew?

Then again, how could you sort out someone else's life when you were still trying to figure out how to live your own?

She wished her mother were still alive. Vivi, funny, bright, and with an inquisitive mind to the very end, could always be relied upon to help with life's conundrums.

"It's your age, lovey," she'd said when Grace had been flung headfirst into the menopause, with hot flashes to beat the band, mood swings the like of which she'd never known, and a terrifying mental wooliness which meant she had no longer been able to do three things at once.

"You'll come out the other side," Vivi had assured her. "Look at me. Who'd think to look at me now that I was a raving lunatic for five years? Your poor father was driven to build himself a shed in the garden so he could have somewhere to hide! I swear I lost everything on a daily basis, from the keys to the car to my purse. You have to travel through it, lovey, and you'll be stronger and braver when it's over." She'd rattled her collection of colorful bangles collected on trips all over South America as proof. She'd been to South America with a girlfriend only a couple of years before, on a special trip for people who were single but had no plans to find another mate.

Vivi had been right, as usual. One day Grace realized that her body had stopped surging with heat like a straightening iron and that her mind had returned to its pre-menopausal clarity.

Walking with her shopping bags to the Delectable Deli, where they sold the fattest garlicky olives and cheeses that made her mouth water, Grace added the loss of her parents to this current and bewildering sense of uncertainty. Mum and Dad had died far too early, she felt wistfully. If only they'd been around to see the birth of their first great-grandchild. Wouldn't that have been wonderful?

Was it Michael getting married that was making her feel so bereft? No, that made no sense. Grace was overjoyed to see her son's life falling into glorious place: a woman who adored him and a baby on the way. There was nothing to be sad about there. And she was beyond excited at the prospect of being a grandmother.

So why this strange dark cloud constantly hovering over her? Could it be anxiety about Fiona? No, not that. Grace wanted her daughter to find love and happiness, but she accepted that there was nothing she could do to smooth her path for her, no matter how much she'd love to. Fiona had to find her own way; besides, she seemed truly happy with her life. Her job was keeping her extra busy, judging by how often she had to stay late at the office, but the ability to work hard was a vital part of a person's resources, Grace thought. Both her children understood this: she and Stephen had never been rich, so as soon as they were legally able, Michael and Fiona had taken summer jobs to pay for any little luxuries they wanted.

As she entered the Delectable Deli, and the heady aroma of garlic and the tang of freshly made pesto hit her, a realization crept slowly into her head — the olives she'd come to buy were for Stephen. Nobody else.

He'd always adored them, occasionally making martinis on Friday evenings when Fiona and Michael were upstairs doing their homework and he and Grace were down in the kitchen telling each other about their day as they cooked together companionably.

Stephen had always had a fondness for the cocktail: a throwback to his vision of the old days of advertising, when sharp-suited men

came up with world-beating ideas and cel-
ebrated them with a martini.

"Far from martinis we were reared," he'd
say every time he mixed them a drink, and
they'd both laugh.

Stephen's maternal grandmother had been
a tough countrywoman with a dislike of
anything modern or fancy. Getting too big
for your boots or forgetting your humble
roots were huge, soul-blackening sins in her
mind, on a par with failure to attend early
Mass on a Sunday.

"When the money's gone, you'll be back
on the land, helping with the milking and
wearing them fancy clothes to make the
silage," Grace would add, which was another
of his grandmother's lines.

They'd laugh and agree that Granny Mul-
hern was probably right and there was a very
fine line between having the money to buy
the makings of a martini and not having
enough to buy dinner for the children.

Grace stood in the deli and breathed deeply:
she was buying olives for her ex-husband with
all the happiness as if they were still married.
What was wrong with her?

"Hello, Mrs. Rhattigan," called Luka, who
ran the Delectable Deli with his wife, Berna-
dette. They'd both been pupils at Bridgeport
National School under Grace's tutelage, and
despite her constant urging, neither of them
seemed able to abandon "Mrs. Rhattigan"

and address her as Grace. "Can I help you with anything?"

"Olives, Luka," said Grace, distracted. "I was looking for those fat garlic ones." *The ones my ex-husband loves. The ones I have realized I am buying purely for him.*

"Of course — big tub, small tub? Have you tried the chilli ones? It's a very subtle kick. Care to taste one?"

With his frank, smiling face, Luka could sell ice to any number of Inuit peoples, and Grace found herself tasting a chilli olive.

"See? They're lovely, aren't they?" said Luka, eager for his new product to be a success.

To knock herself out of her ridiculous longing for the past, Grace texted Stephen as she wandered around the deli with two types of olives in her basket. As usual, he hadn't mentioned whether he was bringing Julia or not.

Is Julia coming? she typed quickly, then added a little smiley face to take the edge off it, because the text did sound a bit sharp. Still, that was what she needed: the bluntness of knowing that her marriage was long since over and legally finished and that her husband had found love with a beautiful and accomplished younger woman. There was no point Grace indulging in fantasies about what might have been and what should have been and whether she had made the right decision all those years ago.

She stuck her phone deliberately at the bottom of her handbag where it would be impossible to reach, and went on shopping. It was only when she got back to the car that she allowed herself to look at the screen.

No, she can't come. Really sorry, meant to tell you.

Stephen had added a smiley face too. These emoticons were very handy, Grace thought with a grin. The perfect way to add tone to messages that had a tendency to sound remarkably toneless otherwise.

Grace hadn't specifically invited Julia, but Stephen knew that in the spirit of the Good Divorce à la Grace Rhattigan, all partners were to be treated with respect, so her inclusion was a given. She felt a frisson of irritation that it had been years since she'd had a partner to bring along to family gatherings. She could probably invite Principal Derek McGurk if she was desperate, but that would open a whole other can of worms, and she wasn't *that* desperate yet.

Or was she? Wasn't it desperation to be cheerfully buying the things her ex-husband loved to eat?

She was heading along the road out of town when she spotted a parking space outside Renee's Salon, where she got her hair done.

There was never a space outside Renee's, never. Yet here was one today.

Taking this as a sign, Grace parked, ran in and grabbed the girl on reception.

"I know it's madness," she said, "seeing as it's Saturday and you're probably full all day, but you don't happen to have a wash and blow-dry slot any —"

"Grace!" yelled Renee happily, emerging from the rear of the salon.

"Sorry, I know it's a crazy idea, but I was just wondering if you had a spare slot," began Grace.

Renee smiled. When her son was being bullied, Renee had been at her wits' end until Principal Rhattigan stepped in and sorted it out. Kevin was at college now, steady and happy. Renee would never forget that.

"For you, there's always a slot," she said.

Birdie didn't mind what she wore to Grace's. Grace never made her feel inadequate, unlike most of the women they socialized with — mainly the wives of Howard's business colleagues, who all appeared to live big lives with ladies' golf events, girls' weeks abroad in somebody's villa, appearances in the local papers at fashion shows, and grand days out for Ladies' Day at the races, where they all wore towering hats and heels that got pegged in the racecourse grass.

"Birdie, you must join us some day," Evelyn, one of the nicer ladies, had said many times. "You'd love it. I bet you have a wardrobe of fancy clothes and nice hats."

"You're so kind, Evelyn," Birdie would reply. "But I honestly haven't got a hat to my name and I'm not at home at places like that. I'm an old fuddy-duddy."

She saw the looks exchanged between the others, knew they probably regarded her as one step up from a bag lady. With her money, they'd have a different life entirely, but Birdie knew from long experience what suited her and what didn't. She knew how to dress for comfort but didn't have a clue about fashion. Trends came and went so quickly, and she hated anything that made her feel self-conscious and unnatural. When it came to shopping, she was happiest with her lovely catalogues. So much better than having to take things into a changing room and try them on while an assistant fussed over you. Katy said that ordering things on the computer was the best way to go, but you couldn't read a computer in bed and there was so much choice it was bewildering. No, she would stick to her catalogues.

She wished she had Grace's sense of style. Grace wore lovely clothes, but she was hardly a slave to fashion; she was an energetic woman with an important job who had more to do than worry over whether her sweater was high fashion or not.

Over the years, they'd slowly become friends. Typically, Grace had been the one to raise the knotty subject of what would happen to their friendship if Katy and Michael ever split up. Her solution was that they should resolve to remain friends no matter what, and simply agree never to talk about what had gone wrong between their children.

"It would be easy for one of us to take offense over this being said or that," said Grace wisely, "and like children in the playground, they'd be over it long before we would. No, if it all ends, we shall behave like intelligent mothers who would kill for our cubs but know that life must go on, right?"

"Right," agreed Birdie, in awe of Grace's wisdom and her ability to say out loud the sort of things she would fret about but never have the courage to discuss.

Grace would be a wonderful mother-in-law to Katy — already was, in reality.

Going to her house was always a treat, but tonight would be extra special. Birdie had been so busy making her special lemon torte for the dinner party because she knew everyone liked it that she barely had time to brush her long silvery hair and take off her floury smock T-shirt and replace it with a floral blouse and a cardigan with matching lavender tones.

Thumper, who'd been walked earlier in the day by the river but who was watching his mistress's preparations like a dog en route to the gallows, sat in his bed and sulked.

"You are *never* left on your own," remonstrated Birdie, giving him a big hug and a rawhide bone to chew. "It's just for one evening, remember. No eating cushions, now."

Thumper gave her a doleful look as if to say he'd be far too miserable to even think of cushion consumption.

Birdie hugged him again.

"I'm going to have a nice night out, darling," she told him gently. "We'll have extra hugs when I'm home."

After all, Thumper was the only one who gave her extra hugs these days.

Seventeen

Better a dinner of herbs where love is, than
a stalled ox and hatred within.

PROVERBS 15:17

Birdie was the first to arrive, slightly out of
breath and bearing her huge and delicious-
looking lemon tart. "I know it's Michael's
favorite," she said at the door as she handed
it to Grace.

"You're so kind," Grace said, touched as
ever by Birdie's kindness. "I'd gone to town
on everything else but I'd run out of time
when it came to dessert, so it was going to be
bought chocolate cake or else fruit and crème
fraiche. But this! You are an absolute star."

Birdie looked delighted and Grace thought
again what a wonderful person she was, and
yet so nervous and anxious. It seemed a
miracle that Birdie and Howard — strong,
forceful Howard with his dominant personality — had ever gotten together, let alone
produced a daughter like Katy, who combined the best of both parents: gentle and

kind yet super-confident.

"Goodness, Grace," said Birdie, "you're so busy with all you do, running the school, I don't know how you fit anything else in. Honestly, it was the least I could do. I should have offered in advance and I'm really sorry I didn't."

Grace waved away her apologies. "Come on in, Birdie, and sit down. Get settled, you are the first to arrive. We can have a nice chat before the others come."

Birdie loved Grace's house and walked around the cozy living room admiring cushion covers and pictures, photographs on the wall.

"It's all so elegant and yet warm," she said. "I never seem to manage that with the Vineyard. I don't know why. It's just too big and grand."

"You have a beautiful house," Grace said.

"Oh, I didn't mean to imply it's not," Birdie added, flustered. "Of course it must have sounded wrong because of the money and I'd never want anyone to think I was complaining, because we're so lucky to have money when some people don't. It's just that so many of the things are . . . Howard chose them and . . . It's just so pretty here." Her voice faded away, as if she was ashamed to have said anything against her husband.

This time Grace felt more than a pang for Birdie. She might have all the money in the world, but something wasn't right in that beautiful big house, and it had never taken long in Howard's company for Grace to identify the source of the problem.

Stephen arrived next with an enormous bouquet of beautiful white flowers interspersed with greenery — roses, just-opening lilies, magnolia blossoms. He held them up to his face at the door so at first all that Grace could see was her ex-husband's body and a huge bunch of flowers.

"Oh, a Triffid has come to dinner," she said, trying to joke in order to hide how jolted she was. It had been a very long time since Stephen had brought her flowers.

"I know you like white flowers," he said casually, "and you're being so good to have this wonderful dinner for everyone, I felt it was the least I could do. I brought wine too. Here, you take these while I go and get it from the car."

He handed her the flowers and gave her a kiss on the cheek. Grace felt a quiver of something, a long-buried feeling rising to the surface, despite her best efforts. She hoped he hadn't noticed. What was wrong with her?

But he was already gone, apparently not noticing anything in his hurry to retrieve two supermarket carriers of wine and beer and sparkling water.

"Now," he said, returning with his load, "we've got a bit of everything: sparkling nonalcoholic drinks for anyone who's driving or is pregnant; some white; that Beaujolais you used to like . . ."

"Fantastic," Grace said, still entirely thrown. She'd got used to Stephen being polite and friendly, but not quite this enthusiastic. He was just being nice to her, that was all, but even so, his grace and confidence was such a contrast to sweet, anxious Birdie, who was sitting inside at this moment, worried she'd said the wrong thing by criticizing Howard, albeit in the mildest of ways.

"Birdie's inside," whispered Grace as Stephen followed her into the hall. "She's a bit nervy tonight so I've settled her down with a big glass of wine, which she didn't entirely want, but I thought — and I know it's the wrong thing to do — I thought I'd give her a little relaxation in a bottle. We'll order a taxi to take her home. I know she's not a drinker, so one glass should be quite enough. Go in and be nice to her, the poor darling. I don't think anyone really is, apart from Katy and Michael."

"How I dislike that husband of hers," said Stephen with disdain. "He doesn't deserve either of them, Birdie or Katy — it's the one flaw in this whole marriage, having him as part of the family. I tell you, I love to think of Birdie minding the baby, but Howard?" He shuddered. "What a horrible prospect. If it's a boy, I can just see him at football matches bellowing from the sidelines if the child does something wrong, or roaring, 'That's my boy!' as if he deserves the credit when the kid does anything right. Those sort of people just make me sick."

"OK," said Grace firmly, steering him toward the room where Birdie was. "Now that you've got that out of your system, put the wine away and be nice."

She busied herself in the kitchen arranging the flowers, burying her nose in them. They were gorgeous, just the kind she would never treat herself to. It was nice to be spoiled sometimes. She fiddled with the oven, checked that everything was OK, and poured herself a drink. Like Birdie, Grace wasn't much of a drinker, but she'd always been fond of a tiny schooner of sherry. She brought it into the living room, where Stephen was making Birdie laugh. He was wonderful at that, Grace thought fondly. He was a good man, a kind man. She knew exactly why he didn't like Howard: because he could see that Howard was the sort of man who'd be rude to waiters and his wife, and charming to complete strangers if he thought they were necessary to his advancement. Stephen would never be so shallow, and he would never dream of trampling over other people's feelings.

As she gazed around her lovely cozy room with the lamps lit, the fire casting warmth

497

over the beautiful cinnamon-colored rug, Grace thought how lucky she'd been to have had a good man in her life. For a brief moment she wished she had him back, but quashed the thought immediately.

Katy and Michael were arguing. They'd started before they'd even got into the car and they were still at it fifteen minutes later. "I don't know what your problem is with my father," Katy was saying, her face set, as they drove through the night. "Just because he has something on a Saturday night doesn't mean he's deliberately not coming to your mum's dinner party."

Michael tried to breathe deeply.

"All I said was that he could have changed his plans. This is a special weekend, what with the girls finally getting their dresses and everyone together for once. My mother has gone to a lot of trouble to make this dinner party for all of us, and he can't —"

"He works hard," Katy cut in.

"Yeah," said Michael shortly.

"What do you mean, *yeah*?" Katy demanded.

"Just that. Yeah," said Michael. "He works hard — lots of people work hard. It doesn't mean he has to be away on a Saturday night."

"What are you implying?" Katy bit back angrily.

"I'm not implying anything," Michael

sighed. "I just wish you'd take off your rose-tinted glasses when it comes to your father. He might be Mr. Super Entrepreneur, sure, but in real life, he's far from Superman. You can see his flaws when it comes to business — you seem to argue enough in the office — but you just can't see them otherwise. Doting dad or not, he's not so lovely to your poor mother — and he certainly isn't being very nice to *my* mother or me or any of us by missing tonight."

"Well, it was all arranged so suddenly," said Katy.

"Not that suddenly," Michael said doggedly.

He was annoyed about Howard not being there tonight. He didn't know why, but things had changed between him and Howard the last few weeks. Actually, if he thought about it, he *did* know why. It was Katy being pregnant that had brought about this shift in his relationship with her father.

Because Michael had met Katy when they were so young, it had never occurred to him to question Howard's role as the alpha male in her life. In truth, he'd been overawed by his wealth, his name-dropping, his fancy cars and gadgets. Howard took delivery of a new BMW every January, as if making do with the old one was somehow beneath him. He had the latest in technology long before anyone else, even if he still preferred to write in the notebook he carried everywhere.

He had always been cavalier in his treatment of his poor wife and hideously rude to anyone he considered beneath him in the pecking order while fawning on those above him. Michael, while secretly appalled, had put it down to Howard being Howard, and left it at that. It was, after all, none of his business how Katy's father conducted himself.

But now that Katy was carrying Michael's child and they were going to be a family in their own right, he had begun to see Howard's behavior in a new light. He didn't want his son or daughter to witness their beloved grandmother being ridiculed and humiliated, or waiters and tradesmen treated as if they were a lesser species. Michael had been brought up to treat everyone with respect and courtesy, and he wanted the same for his child.

He wondered how Katy had managed to avoid picking up her father's ways. It was almost as if she was blind to that side of his personality.

While he realized this might not be the best moment to persuade her to open her eyes to Howard's flaws — tonight's dinner party was supposed to be a happy occasion — he found he couldn't let the subject go. Perhaps it was because they were both so tired. Every day when they came home from work there'd be some sort of wedding-related chore to tackle, and on top of that they'd both been waking up very early because of Katy's morning sickness. This afternoon she'd arrived home exhausted because of the length of time it had taken to find the dresses. Apparently Fiona had been the fly in the ointment, fussing endlessly about the choice of colors and styles.

That had started the argument. The whole time they were getting dressed for dinner she'd moaned about his sister, wanting to know why Fiona was being so difficult when it wasn't as if she cared about dresses in the first place.

Somehow, once they were in the car, the argument had moved on to Howard's absence.

"Look, let's call a truce on this," Michael said as he drove up his mother's road.

"I don't want to call a truce," said Katy, a hint of petulance in her voice.

Michael tried to think of what his father or his mother might say if he were to ask for their advice. He was pretty sure the answer would be: *Howard's going to be your father-in-law come what may. Say nothing.*

He hadn't asked their advice, though. Partly because he was afraid he would blurt out his suspicion that the reason Howard took so many "business" trips was because he had a girlfriend. Michael had absolutely no proof of this, just a feeling in his gut that a man like Howard would want *every* executive toy, including a mistress. The feeling in his gut also told him that Howard was missing Grace's dinner party not because he had a business engagement but because he was off with his fancy woman. And *that* made Michael Rhattigan mad.

He glanced at Katy in the seat beside him. She was staring straight ahead, her face rigid with tension. Michael sighed. He shouldn't have said anything. Arguing was bad for Katy and the baby.

He took a hand off the gearshift, reached over, and entwined his fingers with Katy's.

"I'm sorry, darling, I didn't mean to upset you. I'm sure your dad has a good reason for not being here tonight. I'm just stressed, that's all."

He hated lying to Katy but sometimes lies were more palatable than the truth.

"It upsets me to hear you say those things. I look up to my dad. He's an amazing businessman and I want you to like him; I want you to *love* him," said Katy.

"Of course. I understand," said Michael, neatly sidestepping the issue. There was absolutely no way he was going to say he loved Howard — no way, ever.

Stephen stared at the huge bouquet of flowers that Grace had arranged beautifully in a

502

vase. When had he bought Julia flowers like that? He couldn't remember.

No matter what he did, he still felt like a heel.

Because he was an idiot, he'd messed up two relationships. But watching Grace rush around, tending to poor Birdie and checking on dinner, he could only feel longing. Was it so very bad to want her and their life again?

Probably was. Grace didn't feel the same way, it was obvious. She had her busy life, the life he'd walked out of. There really was no fool like an old fool.

When Grace opened the door to Michael and Katy, she could see instantly that they'd been arguing. Katy was tight-lipped and white-faced, and Michael's jaw was set in the particular way it always was when he got angry.

"How lovely to see you both," she said, hugging them, her voice extra cheery. To her relief, the cavalry arrived behind them in the guise of Leila, with Pixie dancing happily on her leash, and Susie, who had been persuaded to come because Birdie's beloved cleaner Morag was going to babysit Jack for the evening. When they'd arrived at Morag's, Jack had taken one look at her son playing with his Thomas the Tank Engine, smelled the pizza, and run into the house with barely a backward glance at his mother.

"You are so good to let me bring Pixie, Grace," Leila said, coming up the drive with an orchid in a pot, a bottle of wine, and what looked like several large blankets and towels under her arm. "I just feel bad because I was out all day picking the dresses and going to see Mum, and poor Pixie's been on her own the whole time. Thank you, thank you for letting her come."

"Nonsense," said Grace, "I'm delighted to have her here. She's your dear mum's little pet, so of course she's welcome." Grace thought privately that the dog was a welcome diversion from Birdie's anxiety and whatever simmering argument had been going on in Michael and Katy's car.

"Susie, how lovely to see you! It's been too long, darling. I hope you've got photos of that beautiful son of yours."

Susie, who'd been nervous about coming, relaxed.

"He wanted to come here until he got to Morag's. I doubt I'll ever get him out: they have all sorts of computer stuff, and Morag rented a new movie for them."

"They always want their mum at the end of the day," Grace said, smiling. "Now, come on in."

She ushered Katy and Michael on through to the living room as Pixie had her feet wiped on one of Leila's many towels. "You don't need to do that," Grace said.

"No, really," said Leila, looking up through her tangle of hair. "Her paws get so dirty, and you're not a doggy household, so I thought it would be better if I was careful."

"Nonsense! I may not be a doggy household, but it's hardly a precious sort of house," said Grace briskly. "You know carpets can be vacuumed," she added with a twinkle in her eye as she took Leila's coat and turned to take Susie's. "Now tell me, girls, how's Dolores?"

"She's settling into the Hummingbird home really well," said Susie.

"Nora really is the most amazing person. I didn't know you two were friends," Leila added.

"For many years," said Grace, "and I would trust her with my life, so your mum's in very safe hands."

"You can tell the minute you meet her, can't you?" Susie said.

"Yes." Grace nodded enthusiastically. "You feel this instant sense of calm. She knows everything about everyone, but she'd never tell; she's very discreet."

Grace, Leila, and Susie followed Katy and Michael into the living room, where Pixie was already running around sniffing everywhere. She made a beeline for Birdie, who clearly smelled of dog and was delighted to have another pet to hug and love.

"Aren't you beautiful?" said Birdie, who'd

505

relaxed an awful lot after being cheered up by Stephen and drinking nearly three-quarters of a glass of wine. Now there was this lovely dog who seemed to want to get on the couch beside her. This was turning out to be her ideal dinner party. "Katy darling, and Michael!" she said, getting to her feet.

Katy and Michael glanced at each other quickly.

"Mum," said Katy, hugging her mother.

"You look wonderful," Birdie told her. "I'm so sorry your dad's not here, but you can tell him all about it when you see him at work on Monday. You know how he is about the business." She smiled. "He really is married to it."

Behind his fiancée, Michael stood with one eyebrow raised, but kept his mouth firmly closed.

The doorbell rang, announcing Fiona's arrival, and Grace excused herself, saying she needed to start serving dinner as she'd promised they wouldn't have a late evening.

"You never know when you want to go to bed when you're pregnant," she said fondly, smiling at Katy.

"You used to come in from school and go straight upstairs to bed when you were having Michael," Stephen reminded her.

"I had to eat chocolate from about one thirty onwards to keep me awake," Grace recalled, laughing. "No wonder I put on so much weight."

They smiled at each other, then Grace hurried off. This was ridiculous, she thought. Could you go through menopause a second time? It was the only answer, because her mind was so addled. All this smiling at her ex-husband had to stop.

By dessert, everyone was laughing and chatting, all arguments were forgotten, and Katy's feet were on Michael's lap as he rubbed her toes.

"I couldn't eat another thing, Grace," said Leila, who was sitting on Katy's other side discussing all things weddingy with her friend and Susie, who was opposite.

"Pixie could," said Birdie, and they all laughed.

Pixie had set herself up between Birdie and Leila and was doing her ravenous dog impersonation.

"Don't mind her," said Susie. "She always looks like that. I'm nominating her for an Oscar. When she stayed with Jack and me, she looked half starved the minute I'd fed her. Jack kept giving her doggy biscuits because he said she looked hungry."

"Thumper's like that," Birdie said. "There's not enough food in the world for him."

Grace looked at the clock. It was nearly ten thirty, early by most standards, but she was concerned it shouldn't be a late night for her future daughter-in-law. Plus, Susie had to leave to pick up Jack. The evening was coming to an end. She wondered where Stephen would be spending the night. He must have organized to stay with Michael and Katy.

"Thank you for the flowers," she said to him now, across the table. She was incredibly touched that he'd gone out of his way to bring such a beautiful bouquet — and remembered that white flowers were her favorite.

"You're so good to have us all to dinner," he replied.

"It's nothing," she said.

"It feels like old times, doesn't it?"

Grace sighed. "Yes, it does," she said softly. "I was just thinking that myself. There's something very comforting about dinner at home. Much better than being in a fancy restaurant . . ." She lowered her voice even more till it was almost a whisper. "With Howard pushing his weight around." She grinned at Stephen.

"You never liked that restaurant anyway," Stephen teased her.

"I liked it," Grace protested, "but it was so blasted expensive. I suppose it comes of seeing so many of the kids at school living in difficult circumstances — every time a plate was put down in front of me, I couldn't help thinking you could feed an entire family for the price of that one portion."

She paused. It was difficult to work in education and see families struggling to cope with money issues. It had always affected her greatly — and she and the board had done their best to make sure that whenever there were cases of genuine hardship, funds were made available for the family in question. No child was ever made to feel uncomfortable in Bridgeport National School.

"It's one of the things I like about you," Stephen said suddenly.

"Only one?" teased Grace. But a voice inside her was warning that this conversation was becoming too personal. No good could come of it. Stephen was only being nostalgic, nothing more. It was up to her to ward him off at the pass.

"So," she said brightly, "tell me about Julia. I haven't seen her for ages. We should probably talk on the phone and discuss our wedding outfits — not that I have a clue what I'm going to be wearing. All I know is that I don't think I can do the hat thing. I'm not tall enough," she added lightly.

A fleeting look of sadness crossed her ex-husband's face.

"Well," he said slowly, "I've been meaning to talk to you about it, but there just hasn't been a good time."

Before she could respond, he got up and began to clear away the dessert dishes.

"No, don't move, anybody," he ordered.

"Let me do this, since Grace did all the hard work."

Grace got up too and collected the dishes on her side of the table, then followed Stephen into the kitchen. The rest of the party continued chattering happily.

She set her dishes down on top of the dishwasher and stared at him, shocked to see the pain etched on his face. "Stephen, what is it?"

"We've . . . we've split up."

"Oh," said Grace, stunned. She hadn't been expecting this. "I'm sorry," she added. "I don't really know what to say, Stephen. You don't have to tell me anything — it's your business, yours and Julia's."

She could see it all now: he and Julia were finished, and he'd come looking for the comfort of his ex-wife, which would be a huge mistake for both of them.

"No. I want to tell you . . ." And he looked at her, the sort of look he used to give her all those years ago when they were married. Long, intense looks that had some hidden meaning.

Let's go to bed.

Aren't we lucky?

And then, the ominous *We have to talk.*

Grace could feel everything slowing down around them. It was as if the noise from the dining room had suddenly faded and it was just the two of them in the house.

Somehow she had to remain calm and removed.

"I'm really sorry for you both," she said, willing him not to say anything else. They had a good relationship and the last thing she wanted was to have it clouded by some mistaken comforting, which would bring them back to square one, when they'd first split up.

She would not go back there again. He might be able to walk away unhurt, but she wouldn't, she knew it.

"I've wanted to talk to you about this, Grace," Stephen said gravely.

"I don't think that's wise, not now, not after a few drinks and with emotions running high," she said.

"It's incredibly stupid," Stephen began, one hand fiddling with a glass, speaking as if he hadn't heard a word she'd said. "You know me — dumb about emotional things, but I have to tell you —"

Grace threw him a look. Stephen had never been dumb about anything.

"No, honestly, Grace. I didn't see what was happening, but Julia did. That's why we split. It's the past and —"

"Mum, Dad!" shouted Michael from the dining room. "You've got to sort this argument out. Fiona is telling everyone I sucked my thumb until I was nine. Please come in and defend me!"

The moment was broken and Grace said a silent prayer of thanks. She was not up to this, not now.

"Yes," she said in her brightest voice, walking past Stephen to pop her head around the dining room door. "Thumb-sucking — I could tell you all about it, but I'd have to kill you first!"

"Thanks, Mum — you're a star!" yelled Michael, while Fiona giggled and insisted she'd get the truth out there.

"I'm telling Robbie so he can use it in his speech."

"If that's the worst Robbie has for his speech, then we're doing OK," remarked Katy wryly.

There was no time to talk again. Grace managed it so that there were no private moments between her and Stephen until he was borne off by Michael to stay with him and Katy for the night. She closed her front door with a combination of relief and sadness. What else had Stephen been planning to tell her about his breakup with Julia — and why did he think she wanted to listen?

Coward, she told herself as she finally went upstairs to the comfort of her toile de Jouy bedroom, a lonely bower. She knew why. But it would be a mistake.

It was impossible to revisit a marriage once it was over, and theirs had ended fifteen years ago. It was only nostalgia and loneliness that was making them feel any different.

On Sunday evening, a much happier Leila was back in Dublin and yearning to stretch her legs after the drive from Bridgeport. Walking Pixie gave her the perfect excuse. In the glow of the streetlights, the city had a certain charm to it, she decided. She no longer felt any hint of fear when she set off in the evening, thanks to Pixie bouncing along beside her, eager to be plowing through puddles and sniffing trees already scented by other dogs.

At night, the streets had their own atmosphere, with people out walking their dogs or jogging or zipping past like Lycra-clad superheroes, heads down low over the handlebars of their bicycles.

The early-morning walks were her favorite, though, because she loved watching the trees along the canal change, the bare branches reaching bleakly into the sky becoming covered with green shoots tipped with buds.

The wedding was just weeks away, and Leila thought about it as she walked, in between smiling at Pixie's antics. She and Susie had talked twice already today, and they'd made plans for Jack and Susie to visit Dublin soon for a weekend.

Jack insisted he wanted to go to the zoo. "I like the rain, Leelu," he'd added determinedly, ruling out the possibility of his treat being ruined by the weather.

"Rain or shine," agreed Leila.

"Leelu loves the rain," teased Susie, and it had felt to Leila as if she and her sister were back where they'd always been: close.

How could she have let that bond disappear over a man?

Why did people want to search for mates anyway? It was so crazy, so doomed to failure.

Then she thought of Michael rubbing Katy's feet. There was something so luxuriously *together* about such an act, Leila thought. Would anyone ever massage her feet for her?

They never had before. Tynan hadn't been much of a man for feet; more of a breast man, to be honest. The gentle romance of caressing her toes would never have occurred to him.

Leila sighed as she walked. That was the past, she told herself: move on.

Searching for that impossible dream had nearly cost her her family.

As they walked in the dusk, Pixie had begun to tug on the leash, dragging Leila back to planet Earth. The dog had spotted Tasha and Mitzi, two of her doggy friends, in the distance.

"Don't pull, Pixie," said Leila automatically.

The special harness she'd bought had

helped, and she'd got herself a couple of dog-training books as well. When her mother went back to living at home, it would be a help to her if Pixie was walking to heel instead of her usual meandering zigzag; with a bad hip, she couldn't risk being pulled over or unbalanced. And to save her mother chasing after Pixie when she was running wild on the playing fields, Leila was planning to train her to come when called. It was such a nuisance that all the training classes she'd found seemed to be on the weekend, because Leila spent her weekends in Bridgeport, visiting her mum. In the meantime, she was trying a few lessons in the apartment with doggy-biscuit rewards, though they hadn't been having much success so far.

Leila let the extending leash out. Tasha and Mitzi were off the leash because they were beautifully trained and came when called. Their owner was one of those women who looked elegant even in Wellingtons. Leila smiled at her, thinking how funny it was that they had no idea of each other's names. It was a real dog walkers' thing. Everyone knew the dogs' names but nobody knew the people's. Quizzing a fellow dog-walker — *what's your name, what do you do, where do you live* — seemed a bit like asking someone in prison what they were in for.

"Hello," Leila said cheerfully.

"Hello," said the woman. "Lovely evening,

isn't it? I'm so glad the days are starting to get a little longer — it makes it easier when you're out walking. I do so hate walking when it's pitch dark. I'm not sure these two would be much protection against any would-be assailant."

"I doubt Pixie would be either," Leila said ruefully. "I think we probably should all have alarms or big sticks."

They both smiled at the idea, and then suddenly the other woman let out a roar: "Girls, stop!"

Leila turned in time to see the three dogs joyfully taking turns to lie on their backs and wriggle deliciously in some suspicious-looking mud. The way they were trying to coat their bodies in it made Leila think that this was no ordinary dirt.

"If that's fox shit, I'll murder you, you monkeys!" yelled the soignée woman, and Leila was momentarily more shocked at hearing her swear than learning that Pixie had rolled in the dreaded fox poo again.

She pulled the extending leash in, but it was no good, the damage was done. Pixie looked up at her, a huge grin on her face. Leila bent down and sniffed, and instantly smelled the pungent aroma that confirmed her fears.

"Oh no," she said, "what a nightmare. I can't believe I have to bring her home and wash her again."

"I've to wash two," sighed the other woman. She called the two dogs, snapped their leashes on and started giving out to them. "I can't believe you did that, you are so bold."

Neither Mitzi nor Tasha looked in the least put out by this as they panted happily up at their mistress.

"We're clearly wonderful disciplinarians," the woman said.

"Yes, clearly," said Leila gloomily. "I've never washed her at my place before."

"Really?"

"No. She's my mother's dog, and the only other time I had to wash her was at my mother's house. Unlike Mum, I don't have a bath, just a shower, and I'm really not sure how that's going to work. With the bath, I lay out lines of teeny dog biscuits for her to eat."

The other woman laughed. "I'd advise that you take pretty much all your clothes off too, because you are going to get wet and sudsy, and possibly a bit foxy if any of the nastiness comes off on you. So arm yourself with lots of towels and some sort of antiseptic stuff to get rid of the stink. Uh, good luck, that's our evening sorted," she added, and she marched off.

"I can't believe you, Pixie," Leila said as they turned in the other direction.

Pixie looked up at her mistress and finally appeared to show some repentance — but not much.

"I suppose fox poo is lovely to you, like eau de cologne for dogs."

They made it home in ten minutes, with Leila no longer thinking about her sister or her friend or foot-rubbing. Her mind was fully occupied with figuring out how the heck she was going to get Pixie into the elevator and up to the apartment without touching anything on the way. And then into the shower.

She was so busy thinking that when they reached the apartment block, she barely registered the figure standing just inside the door. She assumed that whoever it was must be waiting for someone to come down from upstairs; you had to use a code to get in, and then unless you were a resident and had a key, whoever you'd come to see would have to buzz you in or come down and open the door.

She keyed in the pin for the door, pushed it open, trying to get Pixie in without banging off doors or walls, and then suddenly stopped, because the figure leaning against the wall was Tynan.

"What are you doing here?" said Leila. Afterwards, she was glad that there'd been so much drama about the dog and the fox poo and that she'd been irritated about it all, because it meant that when she set eyes on her husband for the first time in eight months, she hadn't looked at him with longing and burst into tears.

"I'm back in town and I wanted to come and see you," said Tynan with the skill he had for making the unbelievable sound entirely plausible.

"You want to see me, why?" said Leila, standing her ground and aware that the stench of fox crap was now beginning to permeate the small hallway.

"To say that I've missed you, darling. And by the way, what is that smell, and when did you get a dog?"

"She's my mother's dog — Pixie, remember?" said Leila, desperately trying to find her self-possession.

"Oh yeah," said Tynan. "Cute, isn't she?"

The self-possession arrived just in time.

"Very cute," snapped Leila. "Now, what are you doing here?"

"Honey, I told you — I missed you. I made a mistake."

Suddenly Tynan was right beside her, and even in her messed-up state of mind, she could see that he looked good. Still lean, sexy, and with that fabulous smile and dangerous charm that made a girl think she was the only one in the world.

Except when there was another girl, called Diane.

"Oh well," she said sharply, "we all make mistakes. Again, what are you doing *here*, Tynan?"

If he was surprised that things weren't going as well as planned, he didn't show it.

"I'm here to say sorry. I should never have left you."

Somehow he was closer to her and she could smell his cologne, the scent of him, and at that moment, it smelled wrong. She couldn't put her finger on it, but while she'd once loved the scent of Tynan, right now he smelled strange — and that was in spite of the overpowering scent of fox.

"But you did leave, didn't you, and I've moved on, so bye, Tynan. I have a dog to wash."

"Please," he murmured.

"No, go away."

"I could help you wash her."

"Don't be ridiculous."

Leila still couldn't believe she was saying this. Not that long ago, she'd have begged for the chance to meet him face-to-face so that she could tell him how much she missed him, and promise that whatever she'd done wrong, she'd do better the next time. She'd change, be whatever he wanted. She'd stay up all night with him at gigs, *anything.*

But things were different now.

Even though Tynan was standing there looking as handsome and charming as ever, Leila knew something had changed since he'd been gone.

Then it hit her: *she* was different. She

could not go back to the old, clinging Leila, the one who'd begged him not to leave.

"You can't do it on your own — wash that dog in our apartment, I mean," Tynan said.

Leila glared at him, feeling a flash of anger.

"Just so you know," she said grimly, "it's not *our* apartment, it's *my* apartment. It always was. And yes, I am going to wash my dog in my apartment."

"You'll need some help," he said. "I could do it, I'm great with animals."

The thought of having someone else to give her a hand, even Tynan — *especially Tynan* — made Leila falter. "Well . . ." she began.

He took Pixie's leash from her. "Come on," he said, "I'm brilliant with dogs."

"I thought you were brilliant with girls from marketing," she said bitchily.

Tynan ignored this. "You never saw me with a dog before," he said. "I must be losing it — I don't remember this little honey at all. Aren't you lovely?" he said to Pixie. "Come on, Leila, open the door, we'll go up. It'll be done in a flash. You change, I'll do it. We can talk some."

She looked at him, clad in typical Tynan clothes: the usual cool ensemble of a battered but elegant leather jacket, jeans that molded to his lean body, a band T-shirt clinging to his chest. His slightly curly hair was long again, and he had the trademark stubble.

He was entirely irresistible, no doubt about it.

Stop it, Leila! shrieked a voice inside her head. *He left you, remember!*

Yes, he left. No phone calls afterwards, no nothing.

But it would be fun to watch him get all those fabulous clothes dirty washing fox crap off Pixie, she thought wickedly.

"Right!" she said, making her mind up. "You can come up and help. And then you're going — OK?"

"Yes, sir," he said, saluting. But he was grinning now.

"Stop with all the smiling and the flirting," she warned. "Don't forget you marched out of here and I haven't heard a word from you since. So don't think you can march back in and things are going to be fine again."

She didn't know where all this was coming from, but somehow the anger was helping.

"I just wanted to see you, Leila," he said gently, his voice a low purr. She'd forgotten how he could do that. His bed voice: the one that would make her melt as he whispered all the things he was going to do to her.

But it wasn't working properly on her anymore.

"Get the keys out, Leila," he added smoothly, "before somebody comes along and complains about the smell in the lobby. I'm sure there's something in the statutory bylaws of these apartments that says stinky, crappy dogs cannot hang around here for too long."

They went up the back stairs and Leila, who'd thought so often about their meeting again and how she might just slap him across the face, was wondering what exactly had happened to her.

For months, she'd cyber-stalked this man on Facebook and longed for him to return. Now he was here and she felt . . . distant. Unconnected to him. Strange.

She felt very self-conscious as they walked into the apartment, remembering the last time he'd been here, but that was sort of taken away by trying to steer Pixie in the direction of the bathroom.

"You haven't changed much," said Tynan looking around. "It's all pretty much the same."

It's not the same, Leila wanted to say. *It's different because you left it. You left it hollow and lonely, the way you left me.* But she didn't say those things. She might have said them a couple of months ago, but not now.

"I've got new throws and candles, and that wall" — she pointed at his damn mortuary wall — "is going to be painted next weekend." She'd do it herself. They'd always decorated their own home in Bridgeport. Only people like Tynan pretended they couldn't paint and brought decorators in. Leila was an expert with a paint roller.

Between them they got Pixie into the bathroom.

"There are doggy biscuits on the kitchen counter in an old marmalade jar; bring them in here," Leila commanded. "Get some towels from the cupboard — the dark ones."

"Those old navy ones we hate?"

"Yeah, those will do," she said, "and . . ." She stopped. She'd been about to say *Bring me my leggings and an old T-shirt to wear while I wash her,* but she could hardly strip while Tynan was around.

She didn't want him going into their bedroom either. It wasn't their bedroom anymore; it was *her* bedroom.

"That'd be great," she said.

While he was gone, she took off her coat and her boots until she was down to her T-shirt and jeans.

"Pixie, you're going to have to stay here on your own for a minute," she said.

Leaving a now confused Pixie in the bathroom, she shut the door behind her. Immediately Pixie began to howl.

"Leave her in there," Leila commanded Tynan. "She doesn't know you and I don't want her upset."

"But I told you, I'm good with dogs," he said, coming out of the kitchenette with the dog biscuits.

"I said leave her," Leila repeated in a voice

that brooked no opposition.

Tynan was good with everything of the female gender: old women, younger women, clearly even female dogs. She would not let him worm his way back into her life again. Not now.

In her bedroom, she quickly dressed in old leggings and an even older T-shirt, tied her hair in a ponytail, and was back in the bathroom within a minute. Tynan followed her in, having shed his boots and jacket.

"Now, baby, how are you?" he said, crooning gently to Pixie, who wriggled up against him, fox poo and everything.

He didn't move away, Leila had to grant him that. Clearly he was back here looking for something. She wasn't sure what it was, but the old Tynan would not have been in favor of strange dogs covered in excrement rubbing themselves against him.

Pixie was not keen on any type of washing experience, as Leila knew, so she stepped into the shower with the dog, got the showerhead down, and began talking nonsense to the dog as she grabbed the strongest shampoo she could find.

"Feed her those biscuits," she instructed Tynan.

"Yes, ma'am," he said, saluting.

It took three serious washes until finally Leila judged Pixie to be a clean, shiny, de-pooped dog. She herself was soaked through, and Tynan's T-shirt was both damp from Pixie's shaking and smudged with suspicious dark marks.

"Now," said Leila, "get the biggest of those navy towels and just wrap it around her."

"You've done this before," he said.

"Yes," she replied bluntly.

She and the shower were both filthy. "Can you take her outside and finish drying her off while I clean the bathroom and have a shower?" she said. "And don't let her on the couch — except on the bit with the big blanket on. That's where she and I sit. Actually . . ." A thought occurred to her. "Put another towel down there so she can get totally dry."

"Yes, ma'am," Tynan repeated, grinning.

Leila watched him leave, a devoted Pixie following him and the biscuits.

Hell, he even has that effect on dogs, she thought. He's got her eating out of his hand.

It didn't take her long to clean the bathroom, then she took a long shower before wrapping herself in her dressing gown. Her hair was wet too and her makeup was long gone. Better that she emerge from the bathroom like that, she told herself. Tynan would get entirely the wrong impression if she came out all made-up and scented.

He had made himself at home and was drinking red wine and watching MTV. He'd taken his T-shirt off and was wearing what looked like one of her own ancient gym T-shirts, a merchandising one from a long-ago movie.

"Terrible crap," he kept saying at the screen.

Pixie had set herself up on the couch far away from him on her own patch, and Leila felt a surge of love for the little dog. *Loyal girl,* she thought. *Clever girl too. Far cleverer than me.* Pixie wouldn't have fallen to pieces when Tynan had left — she'd never have married him in the first place.

"So," she said, taking a seat beside the dog, "what are you here for?"

"I told you: to see you and tell you I made a huge mistake." Tynan gave her his dazzling smile.

"Did Diane dump you?"

For the first time, he looked taken aback.

"No-o," he said, rather too slowly. "It was my decision. It was a mistake, leaving you."

"Really," said Leila, buying time. "Well, it's over between you and me, obviously. I didn't wait for you," she said coolly.

She *had* waited. Oh, how she'd waited, longing for his call, for his touch. Wishing she'd begged harder that morning.

"You're seeing someone else?" His eyes widened in surprise.

Leila nodded, thinking of Devlin. She wished she really was seeing him: that would give her the strength to do what she knew was right. Tynan wasn't good enough for her. He would never treat her any differently than he had that morning he walked out. He would leave again if he felt like it and come back again when the mood hit him.

She deserved more than that. Susie and Katy had been totally right on that score.

"Who?"

"Who what?" she asked.

"Who are you seeing?"

Try as she might, Leila couldn't stop herself blushing at the thought of Devlin. Even with Tynan here, wanting to be with her again, the very thought of Devlin made her skin heat up. He was more of a man than Tynan was. He was kind, good, decent, passionate . . .

"Bullshit!" Tynan said triumphantly. "You're a crap liar, Leila. Always were."

In one fluid moment he was beside her, hands trying to undo the knot on her dressing gown.

"Stop it!" she said, pushing him away. "I'm not lying. There is someone else."

They glared at each other, and then Tynan seemed to sink into the couch. She could almost sense him regrouping, trying to come at it from another angle.

"I've messed it all up, baby. I'm so sorry. Can you give me another chance? Don't we deserve that? We're married, after all."

Leila wanted to cry that she'd spent many

sad hours on this couch thinking just that and wondering where it had all gone wrong. It wasn't good enough to come here and announce that he was ready to be married again.

She stood up and then held up the hand where she'd once worn her wedding and engagement rings. It was bare.

"I'm sorry, Tynan, but I've moved on. Now please leave."

He caught the hand quickly and kissed her fingers.

"I've hurt you, baby, but we can get over this."

He got to his feet effortlessly, and Pixie growled.

"Steady, girl — steady, *girls*," he added, smiling that charming smile of his. "I love you, Leila. Always have. I just had a bit of a meltdown, midlife crisis, whatever. I will apologize any way you want, honey." He flicked a card on to the coffee table. "New number," he said. "I'll call."

"Don't call me," she said furiously. "You're months too late."

"You don't mean that."

"I do," she said. "I waited for you, you little shit, and *now* you come back? Forget it."

A gleam shimmered in Tynan's eyes, and Leila was furious with herself for telling him the truth.

"Get out!" she yelled so loudly that Pixie jumped, startled.

"Don't forget, I love you, Leila," said Tynan, and, blowing them both a kiss, he picked up his jacket and discarded T-shirt and left, shutting the apartment door firmly behind him.

Leila slammed the locks home, then looked at the still-wet Pixie, sank onto the couch, and burst into tears.

Instantly Pixie plonked herself down on her mistress and began to lick Leila's face.

"You smell lovely now," Leila told her, not caring that her dressing gown was getting wet.

And then she remembered. Tynan's scent. She used to love it, and now she didn't, not anymore. His aftershave was a heavily advertised one, all male models with fake stubble and wearing tiny bathing shorts.

It wasn't masculine at all, really. Not like Devlin's . . .

At the thought of him, she stilled. If Devlin had been here, who knew what would be happening right now. She breathed out heavily. What had she done? Fallen out of love with Tynan, who hadn't deserved her, and fallen in love with Devlin, who was definitely not the right man for her. Who barely knew she existed unless he was in a foreign hotel and desperate.

Yes, with her track record, celibacy was definitely the way forward.

EIGHTEEN

There was never any heart truly great and
generous, that was not also tender and
compassionate.

ROBERT FROST

The industrial kitchen of the Golden Vanilla
Cake Shop was still redolent of the day's baking — a scent that encompassed vanilla, the
soft hint of cinnamon from one South
American-inspired dark chocolate cake, and
the comforting aroma of lemon from the
lemon angel cake they'd made in vast quanti-
ties for a double silver wedding where two
cakes were needed.

It was nearly six thirty and everyone else
had gone home. On the board beside the
kitchen phone was the list of tasks for the
day, all neatly ticked off.

Vonnie was tired, but she had one more appointment to get through: a couple who
needed a high-speed cake for a registry office
wedding in March because they were moving
to Brussels.

Most people booked their cakes well in advance, making it difficult to slip emergency jobs into the system without disrupting the natural flow of the business. Yet when Vonnie had received the email from one-half of the couple begging for a speedy cake to be made, she'd found it hard to say no.

Making wedding cakes was such an emotive business in many ways. It was hard to turn down people getting married. She'd loved meeting that sweet young couple where the girl, Katy, was pregnant. She didn't feel that ache in her heart at the sight of people in love anymore. Ryan was responsible for that. Wonderful, kind, loving Ryan.

The couple were due in at six thirty and Vonnie had the kettle boiled and a platter of cakes ready to go. Ryan and Shane were shopping for dinner together and said they'd have it cooked when she got home.

It was their third day at Poppy Lane and it still felt exciting and new, despite all the work that had to be done.

Ryan had taken a week off and had finished Shane's bedroom, which was now blue, with a spotted pale and dark blue beanbag and a lovely desk for homework.

Next he was starting on Shelby's room, and then on Ruby's.

"Ours can wait," Vonnie had said. "Let's sort theirs out first."

She felt that it would take more than painting Ruby's bedroom to sort her problems out, but she hoped that the following weekend, the first they'd all be living together, would give her the chance to tackle the teenager properly. There was something closed down about Ruby lately. Ryan didn't see it.

"She loves you, Von," he said, misinterpreting Vonnie's anxiety. "She loves the house."

"It's not that," Vonnie said. "She's not coping and I don't know what to do about it."

"She's a teenager," Ryan reminded her.

Was that all it was? Vonnie hoped so.

Shane was beside himself with excitement at the thought of being in charge of dinner.

"Ryan says we can make pasta and stuff it with cheese," he had told her that morning at breakfast.

"Did he now?" said Vonnie, grinning over at Ryan. "Or you could make something easier like a four-course banquet including partridge pie . . ."

"Or we could see what's on offer in the supermarket," Ryan said to Shane, swatting Vonnie on the behind with the day's newspaper as she passed.

The front bell of the shop buzzed and Vonnie left the kitchen and hurried to open the door.

To her surprise, it wasn't a couple standing there but a heavyset woman of about her own age with shoulder-length dark hair, eyes clouded with too much makeup and wearing a heavy black coat against the cold.

"Er, come in," said Vonnie, unable to shake off the feeling that something was very wrong.

For a start, there was one person instead of two. And the email had given her the impression that Amanda and Larry were young, keen to marry at speed so they could be married when they arrived in Brussels, where Amanda had a high-powered job waiting for her. Yet here was this forty-something woman who seemed strangely familiar and whose accusing eyes were openly surveying Vonnie from head to toe.

"You don't look like I thought you would," said the woman slowly.

In that instant, Vonnie knew who she was.

Her face, the way she spoke, those dark eyes: she was the very image of Ruby. An older, heavier Ruby, but Ruby all the same.

This had to be Jennifer.

Vonnie had often wondered what she'd say if she and Ryan's ex-wife ever met. So many words and ideas had clouded her head, many of them hot, angry accusations about the way Jennifer was deliberately making the whole business of separation far harder than it needed to be. About how she was clearly hurting Ruby by trying to force her to take sides — the opposite of what every divorce guidebook recommended; about how Jennifer had swiftly and totally absolved herself of any responsibility for the disintegration of her marriage; how she blamed everyone but herself.

Still, faced with Jennifer — who bore almost no resemblance to the smiling, curvy woman in the old photos Ryan had of them from when Ruby was a toddler — everything changed.

Vonnie had no desire to launch into an argument. There was, she realized with sudden and absolute certainty, no point.

The woman in front of her had anger and pain in her eyes in equal measure. Her hair was unkempt, she was wearing too much makeup and it had been carelessly slapped on. Vonnie could never imagine herself arriving at a rival's business to tell her side of the story — but if she did, she knew she'd go into battle looking her best.

Jennifer was far beyond that place. She had no "best" left, only anger.

Until that moment, Vonnie hadn't grasped how hard it was for Ryan, Ruby, and little Shelby. Only now that they were face-to-face could she see the anguish; it was obvious that Jennifer Morrison was utterly lost in her own misery. Some people couldn't cope with life's pain, and clearly Jennifer was one of them. They searched for someone else to blame because it was easier than either moving on or taking responsibility.

"Would you like to sit for a moment, Jennifer?" Vonnie said kindly, leading the way into the shop. "I had a couple of clients coming, but I am assuming that *you* are Amanda and Larry, that you made all that stuff about Brussels up and nobody else is actually due because they'd be here by now . . . ?"

"Yes. How did you know who I am?"

"You look so like Ruby," Vonnie said. "You both have such beautiful eyes."

Jennifer didn't hesitate. She came in and sat on one of the floral armchairs. The showroom was still warm and she unbuttoned the coat, wriggled out of the sleeves uncomfortably and sat staring at the woman all the people in her life seemed to love.

Ryan loved her, for sure. Shelby did too, though she no longer let slip any little giveaway remarks about how nice Vonnie was — Ruby had trained it out of her. As for Ruby . . . Ruby said so little these days. But Jennifer knew that she liked Vonnie, and had from the start.

Almost greedily, she took in everything about Vonnie's appearance. The slimness was inevitable, wasn't it? Jennifer Morrison, who'd battled with her weight all her life, stared in silence at Vonnie's lean figure, the delicate ankles emphasized by flat pumps, the naturally blonde hair in a sleek ponytail, and the high, finely arched pale brows over silver-gray eyes.

"You look different from what I expected,"

she said again. "Less obvious. I thought you'd be all red lipstick and a push-up bra."

Vonnie's smile barely touched the corners of her mouth.

"A bit of a cliché, don't you think?" she said carefully.

"Clichés become clichés for a reason," Jennifer replied smartly. She would not like this woman, she wouldn't. Vonnie was ruining everything.

"Why are you here, Jennifer?" Vonnie thought she already knew the answer: Ryan's ex-wife wanted to pour out her anger and recriminations, blaming Vonnie for all the things wrong in her world. "You could have come to meet me at the house, to see where your daughters will be staying. I told Ryan that you should come, so you'd feel happy knowing where the girls will be. We could have done this the formal way. It would have been good for Ruby and Shelby to see us together —"

She got no further.

"Don't say that you know what's good for my daughters. I know what's good for Ruby and Shelby!" Jennifer said. "Me! *I'm* their mother. I know what's good for them."

She was on the verge of tears, and Vonnie felt it keenly again: that Jennifer Morrison was not the monster of her imagination. She was lost, alone, unable to fix herself and desperately trying to get other people to do it for her.

Yet that couldn't happen in the real world: as Vonnie knew, you had to fix yourself. Nor could you wreck other people in the process, people like Ruby, whom she was worried about.

She spoke bluntly, tiredness making her more brutally honest than she would have been otherwise.

"Jennifer, this isn't fair to the girls. You're trying to make them choose between you and their father. That's not good for them and you know it. They're kids, they need love and support, not to be pawns in your game of chess. If you and Ryan would try mediation, perhaps, talk to someone about how to support the children —"

"That's none of your business," hissed Jennifer.

"Of course it's my business," said Vonnie in astonishment. "They're Ryan's children, and when they're with us, I have a responsibility toward them. We, as the adults, have to help them through this. They didn't ask for your and Ryan's marriage to break up any more than they asked for me and Ryan to fall in love. We all owe it to them to manage this as best we can. I am a little anxious about Ruby, to be honest —"

"I don't want you having anything to do with my daughters! They're none of your business. You think they like you but they don't. Ruby hates you, hates you."

Real weariness mixed with anger hit Vonnie. Ruby wasn't coping and Vonnie could see it. But her own mother was oblivious to anything but her own feelings, and even though Vonnie empathized, Jennifer had to be a mother first, didn't she?

"I'm sorry," Vonnie said, "but you should go."

There was no point continuing this. Jennifer was too upset, and soon, something really dreadful would be said, something from which there was no coming back.

She rose to her feet. She was taller than Jennifer and she knew she could look imposing if she chose. Drawing herself up, she said: "If you wanted to see me, you only had to say so. This pretending to be a client so you could hijack me here is not worthy of either of us. When you" — with an effort she bit back the words *grow up enough* — "are ready to have a real conversation about your daughters and how to manage their future now that you and Ryan are no longer together, come and see us by all means. But don't try to bully me or play games, Jennifer."

Jennifer glared at her and finally Vonnie's patience ran out. This was the woman who'd made her and Ryan's lives hell for a long time. The anger kicked in.

"It's time you grew up and accepted that

what you want isn't paramount when you have children. As soon as they're born, it all changes: they come first. I'm sure you know that. I'm worried about what all of this is doing to Ruby and Shelby. Can you think about that? I have to close up now, so if you wouldn't mind leaving, please."

I've said too much, Vonnie thought suddenly. I should have held my tongue.

"Think you're in charge, don't you?" hissed Jennifer. "Bossing me around, calling all the shots. You're not. *I'm* the mother of Ryan's daughters, not you. *I'm* his first love, I'm the one he married."

The bile and pain kept rushing out of Jennifer's mouth and she couldn't stop it. She didn't care what she said as long as she could wipe the cool look off Vonnie's face. How dare Vonnie accuse her of not being a good mother, *how dare she?*

"Don't forget, he walked out on our family," Jennifer went on as Vonnie stared at her stoically. "Me and the girls he says he loves. And our relationship hadn't had any troublesome baggage either, like someone else's kid and a dead husband to contend with. He might say it doesn't matter, but I bet it does."

Vonnie's sharp intake of breath told Jennifer she'd gone too far.

"Get out," said Vonnie, holding her body so tightly she thought she might break. "Get out of my store *now.*"

"I'm going," said Jennifer, draping her coat around her like a cloak. "But you might do well to remember that men who walk out on one woman will walk out on another. It becomes a habit, apparently. They run when it all gets too tough."

She fled then, the damage done, fumbling with the door because she was so wired with anger and the adrenaline coursing through her system.

Outside on the street, Jennifer started to run. She hadn't run for a long time, but she was desperate to get away, to put some distance between her and what had just happened. Tears rolled down her face and she didn't care who saw her: a tearstained woman with her coat flying as she ran down the footpath on a cold winter's night.

As she fumbled to let herself into her car, parked outside the Copper Kettle, she looked through the window and saw relaxed, happy people chatting over coffee, people alone at tables nursing cups and laptops, two girls around Ruby's age giggling over something on a smartphone.

Ruby. Just the thought of her caused Jennifer to pull up, feeling the pang of intense hurt. She knew Ruby wasn't happy, but that wasn't her fault, was it?

Kids were strong, they got over divorces; they were so resilient. Ruby had school to go to, where she could forget, while Jennifer had nowhere to go to escape the loneliness.

The kids would get through this, but Jennifer didn't know if she would.

Vonnie put all the cakes away and tidied up the way she would have done under normal circumstances. Jennifer's rage had shocked her, so much of it wound up and directed at her.

It *had* been shocking, there was no other word for it. How could that woman mention Joe in such a way, how?

Vonnie's hands shook as she worked: stacking the unused crockery, turning on the answering machine, switching off the computer, locking up. She felt herself retreating with every moment. It was how she'd coped with Joe's death.

In front of Shane, she'd been a lioness: they would get through this, *Dad will always be here in our hearts, he loved you so much.* On the inside, she'd closed down and thought it lucky Shane was so small and didn't understand.

The grief counselor she'd finally gone to had cautioned that bottling up pain was one way of dealing with it, but that it wasn't a long-term solution.

"You can numb with drugs or alcohol, or just by retreating inside yourself," he'd explained. "There are lots of ways to lock down. This is intense pain and it's understandable that you want to deaden it all. It's just not helpful in the long term. Not for you and not for your son."

Vonnie had worked hard to stop retreating inside. She'd done her best to let herself feel the pain. But tonight, after the confrontation with Jennifer, she could feel herself withdrawing to that old place where she could bottle it all up for another day.

She drove home slowly, edged the van onto the drive on Poppy Lane, thinking of how much joy she'd felt as she'd driven home the past two evenings. Tonight, she just felt sad and numb as she looked at the devastation of the overgrown garden. With the inside needing so much work, Ryan reckoned the wasteland outside would just have to manage on its own for a while.

"Besides," he liked to joke, "we're environmentalists, aren't we? Think of what we're doing for the butterfly, bee, and insect communities with a sanctuary like that."

Vonnie had laughed along, delighted at a perspective that would never have occurred to her. She'd have worried over the overgrown grass and profusion of strange weeds, worried that the neighbors would be looking askance at the new family.

"We've just moved in," said Ryan. "Let's unpack first and then hire a man with a scythe to cut it all down."

"Or ask Uncle Tom to do it," Vonnie had said, because they hadn't enough money to hire so much as a rabbit to tackle the garden.

She barely had her key in the door when Shane wrenched it open.

"Mum! Wait till you see what we cooked!" He was so delighted with himself he was practically dancing around her with excitement. "We made pasta. Pasta!! Not in a machine, but on our own."

"You do need a machine, I think, so it might be lumpy in places," Ryan added, coming into the hall and kissing her on the lips. "Only my parts of it, though. Shane is a pasta master."

"It's the rolling," Shane said seriously. "You have to roll and roll and not let it get sticky. But some of it did . . ."

Vonnie didn't move.

"We cleaned it up," her son assured her.

"All sparkly," Ryan said.

Vonnie knew some response was required. Somewhere, she found the actress in herself, the actress every mother needed.

"Pasta," she said, smiling. "Just what I'm in the mood for." She hugged Shane, kissed Ryan on the cheek and shrugged out of her coat. "What kind of sauce are we having with it?"

Somehow, she fooled them, and the two men in her life looked at each other and grinned.

"It's a surprise," Shane said. "You have to guess."

"Dandelion?" she asked, head to one side.

Shane giggled. "No! Yeuch."

"Banana?"

They made it into the kitchen and Vonnie allowed herself to be propelled toward the saucepan where a carbonara sauce sat waiting to be heated up.

"My favorite!" she said.

"I know." Shane beamed.

The pasta, fat lines of it like overweight tagliatelle, lay ready for cooking, hung over carefully balanced wooden spoons: "In case it sticks," Shane told her seriously.

The Jamie Oliver cookbook was on the counter and nicely floured. The table was neatly laid for three with napkins, place settings, and even a flower, which must have been the only non-weed to have survived in the back garden.

"I'll just run up to the loo, then I'll be ready," Vonnie said with a great beaming smile.

She took the stairs two at a time and fled to the bathroom, where she shut and locked the door. She couldn't cry, because with her coloring it was so noticeable afterwards. Instead she tried to compose herself by taking deep breaths, the way the counselor had showed her. Breathe in to a count of six, hold, breathe slowly out again. Keep going. Trying all the while not to think that Jennifer's words had followed her home and were now swirling around the house on Poppy Lane, contaminating it with their anger: *you might do well to remember that men who walk out on one woman will walk out on another . . . They run when it all gets too tough . . .*

Jennifer was wrong, totally wrong. It wasn't the thought of Ryan walking out that scared her. He'd explained why, and meeting Jennifer in a rage, she could understand it. But this was all so hard. Could they make this blended family work? Vonnie couldn't bear to be hurt again. Losing Joe had almost destroyed her. She didn't have anything left inside to survive another cataclysmic ending.

At midnight, she lay in bed and listened to Ryan's breathing. Contented breathing. He could sleep anywhere and under any circumstances, and she envied him that.

She should be used to her sleeplessness by now, but she wasn't. She'd flirted with insomnia ever since Joe had died.

At their home in Brookline, she'd spent many nights lying with her eyes open, still on her side of the bed, still not able to reach over to his side. As if imagining him there would somehow make him *be* there, and reaching over and not finding him would make him utterly gone. Never seeing him again was too huge for her to think about.

Even now, when the miracle of her falling in love with Ryan had happened, she couldn't escape the insomnia trap. This time it wasn't sudden tragic widowhood and its violent stages of grief and fury. No, this time it was caused by Ryan's past and the fact that it could easily destroy the precious thing they shared.

Jennifer didn't seem to realize that life was so fragile, love and happiness so fragile, that you could never take any of it for granted. You had to grab it with both hands. If only she understood and could move forward and be thankful for her two healthy daughters.

Vonnie hadn't told Ryan about Jennifer's visit yet. She had to, she knew. But not in their first week in Poppy Lane. She wanted there to be nothing to take the shine off their happiness.

Jennifer's words still echoed in her head, though. *Ruby hates you.* Could that be true?

Vonnie slipped from the bed, found her slippers in the dark, and put on the pink fluffy dressing gown that Shane said made her look like a pink bear.

"A nice bear," he'd added quickly, a worried look streaking through silvery-gray eyes like hers. "Not one of the dangerous grizzlies."

Shane wasn't like any of the other eleven-year-olds in his class. He worried about his mother's feelings, always careful not to cause her pain: the behavior of a child whose father had died suddenly in a car crash and whose mother was his whole world. Last night she should have been so happy because he and Ryan had been cooking companionably together, having fun, behaving like a father and son.

The experts in the stepfamily books had warned that Shane might resent it when Ryan came into her life, mistrustful and jealous of this new male presence who wasn't his dad and was somehow usurping Shane's position.

But they'd been wrong about that.

Maybe, Vonnie thought hopefully, they'd be wrong about Jennifer too.

The kitchen was covered in splashes of sunflower-yellow paint, because Shelby loved sunflowers.

"It's so bright and shiny and lovely — could we draw sunflowers on the walls?" she'd asked Vonnie, and Vonnie had hugged her and said they would definitely see what they could do. Lorraine, with her amazing gift for sugar-craft flowers, was also a wonderful artist, and Vonnie was toying with the idea of asking her to come and paint some beautiful sunflowers on Shelby's wall.

For the kitchen, Vonnie and Ryan were leaning toward a lovely buttercup yellow that lit the room up, while another corner had a big splash of dark blue paint at Shane's request.

"I like dark blue," he said gravely. Everyone still smiled a bit when they walked into the room and saw the big patch of the color in one corner. It was very un-kitcheny, particularly with the pine cabinets that were never going to be rescued from their pine-ness unless she and Ryan painted them.

There was great mirth surrounding the kitchen redecoration and the painting of the whole house in general, with everyone joining in the fun. Except Ruby.

Vonnie and Ryan talked about it late at night in bed.

"Do you think she resents me?" Vonnie asked Ryan anxiously, Jennifer's hateful words making her question herself. "I'd understand if she did. It's just that I thought we were getting on so well up to now. But perhaps us all moving in together has been a step too far. There's a whole psychological thing about girls and their fathers, and maybe she thinks I've stolen you away from her . . . I don't know, Ryan," she said in frustration. "I wish I did. I feel as if Ruby's gone into some untouchable place and I can't reach her anymore."

Ryan merely looked haunted. "I don't know either," he said quietly. "There's something not quite right, but I don't know what it is. I thought she was just being a teenager, but she's so quiet all the time. It could be just teenagerdom but I think . . . maybe I'm wrong about this, but I think it's something to do with home and Jennifer and the pressure she's been under since we moved in together. How do we fix that?"

There was silence.

From Shelby's artless conversation, they had a pretty clear picture of the way Jennifer was forever giving out about the house on Poppy Lane.

"I don't think Mum would like to come in," Shelby said to Vonnie. "She says it's a bit of a tip from the outside and she thinks the inside must be much worse. I told her it was lovely and I'm going to have a pink bedroom with sunflowers and she says I can have sunflowers in my bedroom at home too, so I'm going to have two places with sunflowers!"

Shelby had laughed with delight at the thought, but Vonnie hadn't joined in. Didn't Jennifer understand that you couldn't play with kids that way? That when parents split up there was bound to be hurt and pain, but that hurt and pain became so much worse if children were used in the battlefield?

Jennifer's most recent trick was to insist that Shelby and Ruby come home first thing on Sunday morning because there was a family event involving Jennifer's family and they had to be there.

"What is it exactly?" Ryan had asked his

daughters, having received nothing but a text message from Jennifer on the subject.

"Granny Lulu is having a lunch party," said Shelby.

"Is that all?" Ryan directed the question to his older daughter.

"Yeah." These days Ruby tended to answer in monosyllables, if at all.

"Well, that's hardly any reason for you guys to go home early. I bring you to school on a Monday morning on your weekends with me, that's the deal."

It wasn't a deal as far as Jennifer was concerned, though. Ryan was furious and wanted to phone the lawyers to intervene, but Vonnie calmed him down.

"Look," she said, "let's work on the theory that she's very angry and stressed at the moment. Things are bound to calm down, given time. We've just moved in together. It's all so different for her."

Ryan had still looked mutinous, but Vonnie had continued to pour balm on the troubled waters. "There's no point making an issue out of it," she said. "The last thing we want is to upset Ruby by entering into a big argument with her mother, OK?"

"OK," he'd agreed.

Vonnie still hadn't told him about Jennifer's visit but she was sure Jennifer's latest plan was due to their encounter. Couldn't Jennifer see that Ruby was suffering in all of this?

Vonnie's gentle attempts to find out how the girl was doing had got nowhere. Whenever she showed an interest, asking "How's the homework going?" or "How's school?" Ruby would avoid meeting her eyes and respond with a muttered "Fine, busy, y'know."

Just enough of a conversation not to be rude, but not enough to put Vonnie's mind at ease.

Still, Vonnie thought, at least the house was improving. She and Ryan were working on it as often as they could, with Tom's assistance. He was a great man to have about the place, full of advice about paint and carpenters and how best to sand ancient floorboards. Whenever he came, he always brought beautiful homemade cakes from Maura, who'd hurt her wrist using the steam cleaner and had been ordered not to get involved in any of the cleaning, painting, sanding, or other house renovations. Maura was a fabulous cook, and when break time came, everyone leapt onto the container of cakes and buns. All except Ruby.

"I'm not hungry," she'd say, or, "I've just had an apple, and sugar's so bad for your teeth and your skin."

She always had an excuse. Vonnie couldn't be sure, because with all the weird layers Ruby and her friend Andi wore, it was difficult to tell if Ruby was losing weight, but her face seemed thinner. Since she wasn't in a position to ascertain how thin Ruby was underneath her clothes, all Vonnie could do was watch her at mealtimes and offer her food she knew she liked. Growing teenagers went through a lot of changes, so perhaps it was entirely normal that Ruby's face was losing its hint of juvenile plumpness. But the nagging doubts inside Vonnie wouldn't go away. She decided to get a second opinion: when Maura dropped in on their next weekend with the girls, she'd ask her. When you saw a lot of a person, it was hard to spot any changes because they happened so gradually, but Maura might notice.

Vonnie hoped with all her heart that she was imagining it, but she just wasn't sure.

All at once, the happiness Poppy Lane was supposed to bring seemed very fragile.

On Sunday morning, Jennifer surprised herself by going for a walk. It was a gloriously sunny morning and, astonished that she'd noticed such a thing, she searched high and low until she found her old sneakers and dragged them on.

It had been months — no, make that years — since she'd been to an exercise class. She'd liked aqua aerobics. Nobody could see you sweat.

Her mother had introduced her to the idea. As a child growing up, Lulu had tried out every exercise craze for a while, and had a library of fitness videos from Jane Fonda and Callanetics onwards. When the fad was over, she would embark on a cooking frenzy. Jennifer had learned her love of cookery from her mother, but she wasn't as keen on the fitness.

Yet today, something — OK, she admitted to herself, not *something:* Vonnie, with her annoying slenderness — had made her think about getting fit. Or thinner.

She drove down to the pier and walked along it, finding herself saying hello to people as they passed with dogs and children. There was no need to walk quickly, which was what put her off normally: the thought of people seeing how unfit she was. Here, people meandered happily or strode at pace, whatever they felt like.

She met one mother from school, and for once, she didn't feel at a disadvantage. Caroline, the other woman, was no sylph either and was checking her pace on a pedometer.

"Dratted thing. It's harder than you'd think getting up to ten thousand steps a day."

"Is that what you're supposed to do?" asked Jennifer, interested.

"Yes," panted Caroline. "This is my second week of it. I thought I walked about twenty thousand steps around the house every day picking up laundry off the floor, but it turns out I don't. Still," she grinned, "I have lost three pounds, my jeans don't threaten to rip my waist in two anymore, and I feel better."

"You sound like an advert for a gym," said Jennifer, unable to keep the cynicism out of her voice.

"It's more for my head, actually," Caroline replied candidly. "Since Dan was diagnosed, life's been all about cancer."

Shocked and embarrassed by her cynical tone, Jennifer reached out. "I'm sorry, I didn't know . . ."

"He's doing well," Caroline said, chin firm. "I thought chemo was bad, but six weeks of radiotherapy has taken it out of him. He has a scan in two weeks and I have to be strong for all of us: him, me, and the kids. Walking helps."

"I didn't mean to sound bitchy," Jennifer heard herself saying. "I'm the expert at opening my mouth and putting my foot in it. If you want a walking partner, I'm around . . . ?"

"That would be nice," said Caroline, and for a moment, she let the energetic facade fall. "It's hard motivating yourself when you're so tired."

"We could walk the whole pier again, at speed," Jennifer said, "and then go for a low-fat coffee?"

Caroline smiled. "We could do that," she said. "What speed exactly?"

Nineteen

Lovers' hearts are linked and
always beat as one.

MANDARIN PROVERB

In the end, it was Andi who noticed.

Ruby and Andi were in the changing rooms and Ruby was trying to change without actually letting anyone see that she was getting thinner. But somehow, Andi clocked it.

She grabbed her friend's arm and held it tightly.

"What's going on, Ruby?" she demanded.

"Keep your voice down," hissed Ruby.

"OK, but what's happening? You're turning into one of the skinny cows and I want to know why."

"There's no reason," whispered Ruby, but she couldn't stop the tears. Someone had noticed, but not the right people. Not Dad, not Vonnie, not even Mum.

"Oh, Rubes," said Andi. "Please tell me it's not what I think it is."

"It's not."

"It bloody is," said Andi. "Come on, let's get out of here. We're going to my place and we're going to sort this out."

"I can't!" Ruby tried to wriggle out of Andi's grasp, but her friend wasn't letting go.

"No, you're going to come with me. Screw school. School will be no good to you if you're dead."

"Don't talk like that," said Ruby, horrified.

"I will talk like that," said Andi, rage in her voice. "I love you. You're my best friend and you have been for a long time and you're doing this crap to yourself, this not eating — don't deny it. I know. You have nothing for lunch. So we're going to go to my house and I'm going to show you what happens to people who do this."

She stopped dragging her friend by the arm and turned to face her. "You're going to end up like Monica. Remember her? I'm going to show you what she's like now — and it won't be good. She was a nice girl, that's what my sister says, and now she's nothing. She's just skin and bones, going from the hospital to home and back to the hospital again, because she can't get well. I'm not going to stand by and let you get that bad."

Ruby didn't know what to say. Monica had been in their school until she'd been hospitalized for anorexia. She'd never come back after that and rumors had sprung up about where she was now. Recovered, not recovered

— nobody knew.

That wasn't what Ruby had wanted at all; she wanted to say so to Andi but she couldn't. Instead, she stood silently by her locker as Andi pulled out their stuff and shoved Ruby's coat and rucksack at her.

"We'll be killed," said Ruby.

"No, we won't," said Andi. "We'll go out the back way."

The back way meant climbing over the fence near the basketball courts. Ruby had done it before, but not for a long time. She was very tired. She hadn't eaten all day, and the gluttony in front of the fridge last night hadn't provided any sustenance. Not enough protein, she knew. There'd been no cold chicken, no cheese; just cake, a yogurt, some cream — crap like that. Nothing that would give her any energy.

Seeing her struggling, Andi grabbed both rucksacks and threw them over the fence, then hauled her over too.

"You see," said Andi between gritted teeth, "this is what not eating is doing to you."

It was freezing cold and wet, and they both pulled their hoods up and trudged through the polar wind up the back lanes and out on to the main road. It didn't take long to catch a bus. Andi's house was only eight stops away, closer than Ruby's.

They sat in silence together until Ruby said: "Will there be anyone home?"

"No, nobody home today, just you and me."

Ruby relaxed back into the seat. Perhaps Andi was the right person to tell. She couldn't go on with this much longer.

Andi's home was so very different from The Close and from Poppy Lane.

While Poppy Lane at least felt as if it was trying to be a home, however full of packing cases and old wallpaper it currently was, the house in The Close had lost all sense of that a long time ago and had turned into a mausoleum of slammed doors, with Ruby's mum stamping around the place, rattling saucepans in the kitchen as she cooked. Sometimes Mum spent hours on the phone to Granny Lulu, ranting about Ryan and Vonnie at the top of her voice, totally forgetting that Ruby was sitting in the room with her.

Ruby had learned how to tune out, more or less. It was always nice to come to Andi's place, though. It wasn't a big house; not really enough room, as Andi always said, for parents, a nineteen-year-old brother, an eighteen-year-old sister, and Andi. The plus was that Andi's sister, Clare, never minded lending her clothes. Andi was much envied among the other girls in eleventh grade for having a sister who would lend.

"I'm sure Shelby'd lend me her clothes," Ruby used to joke, "but they wouldn't fit me."

Thinking of Shelby now made her want to cry. How long had it been since she'd made a joke or laughed at anything?

The house was warm inside, the radiators on low. Andi frog-marched Ruby straight into the kitchen, threw the rucksacks down, and steered her toward the big old couch covered in cushions and cat hair. The family's two cats, Jasper and Georgie, looked up from their comfortable spaces, blinked sleepily, and then put their heads back down again.

"What do you want to eat?" Andi demanded.

"I . . . I don't know," Ruby stammered, instinctively thinking of her regime and what she could not eat. Then she let her body relax. "Toasted cheese — a toasted cheese sandwich and a cup of tea. I think about toasted cheese all the time."

"And when was the last time you had it?"

"Don't know."

Andi turned on the radio so there was music and made the food in silence, then put it in front of Ruby.

"Gimme a sec," she said.

Ruby could hear her running upstairs, the thump of her feet, and then she was back with her sister Clare's laptop.

"Won't she kill you?" said Ruby. Clare might have been good about her clothes, but a laptop was a personal thing.

"She won't kill me," said Andi. "This is important — *you're* important."

Again Ruby felt that prickling of tears in

her eyes.

Andi was brilliant on a laptop. She'd studied typing in junior high, and her fingers flew over the keys much faster than Ruby's ever did. Suddenly they were there.

"I didn't know these things were still on the Internet," Ruby said. She'd often thought about looking up a pro-anorexia website but she'd been nervous — nervous someone might check her history and figure it out . . . and then what?

Not her mother, no, but it was the sort of thing Vonnie might do if she found Ruby's laptop lying around and wondered why she wasn't eating properly. Vonnie was the kind of person who'd notice that.

For some reason this thought made Ruby even sadder. She'd done this so someone would notice her, and the person most likely to notice was her stepmother. Not her mother. That made her want to cry and never stop. Her family didn't have to be together — in fact, her parents were better separated — but she did want parents. A mother who cared.

"OK," said Andi, scanning the home page of the first site. "Gallery, I think that's where we'll start."

The gallery was shocking. They both stared at it openmouthed. There were pictures of girls proudly sucking in nonexistent stomachs to reveal the full extent of their rib cages.

People bent over in the shower showing the bony nobbles of their spine, each etiolated rib visible.

There were blogs with titles like *Can't be loved until I'm skinny,* or *Too fat.*

They both read silently. The music in the kitchen ceased to exist in their heads. There was Maria, who was racing off to buy cayenne pepper because she'd heard that cayenne pepper and lemon juice and vinegar was the most wonderful diet ever and suppressed the appetite.

A banana was the answer, somebody else said. *It keeps the potassium levels up. I know it's really fattening, but y'know.*

There were girls berating themselves for not having had the energy to exercise for three days, but determined that they would.

Another girl had eaten a thousand calories the day before, planned to eat six hundred the following day and then fast for the third day because there was a party. She'd seen a boy she liked and the girls he liked were all skinny. It had to make sense, didn't it?

Andi kept clicking up picture after picture, blog after blog relentlessly until Ruby couldn't bear to look anymore.

"I want to talk to them all and tell them they're crazy," she sobbed. So many of the girls had beautiful, innocent faces with hollow Bambi eyes looking out sadly, apparently incapable of loving themselves. "I feel so sorry for them."

"Is that what you want to be?" Andi demanded. "Because that's the path you're going down. You choose that and you know what it will lead to: hospital, then death. You can't do that to yourself — I won't let you. Tell me, what's going on?"

"Turn it off, please, I can't look at it anymore," begged Ruby. "There's so much pain, it's too dreadful."

"Fine."

Andi exited the site and soon Clare's screen saver came up: a dolphin leaping endlessly through blue waters.

"I didn't know she liked dolphins," Ruby said.

"Obsessed with them. She wants to swim with them, dance with them, kiss them — you name it. I read an article once about somebody who went on holiday and kissed a dolphin; she said its smell was very fishy — duh! What did she expect? Anyway, enough about dolphins." Andi looked her in the eye. "What's going on, Ruby?"

Ruby sat in silence and Andi decided she wouldn't press her for the moment. Instead she watched Ruby eat her sandwich, devouring it as if she hadn't eaten in a month. Halfway through, she stopped.

"Is it not nice?" Andi asked.

"I'm full," said Ruby, shamefaced.

"Really?"

"Yeah, really." Food made Ruby long to lie down, put her head on the pillow, and sleep. "Andi, can we talk tomorrow? We will talk, I promise. We can meet early, before school. It's just that I'm so tired."

"I'm not surprised, if you haven't been eating."

"Please don't be angry with me. Please. I get enough of that at home," Ruby said, her lip quivering. "I'm not anorexic, I promise. I started doing this —"

She stopped. She didn't have the energy to explain.

"Tomorrow," said Andi. "Early."

"OK."

They met the next morning at eight o'clock outside a coffee shop near school. The café was far too busy for them to talk in private, so they got takeaways. Andi watched Ruby, who'd always taken two sugars, order a black coffee and add absolutely nothing to the cup.

"Ruby," she said pointedly. "Sugar? Milk?"

Ruby flushed. "I've gotten out of the habit."

"I know sugar is the devil and all that, but put some milk in please, for me."

"Sure."

Andi didn't even bother offering to buy Ruby a bun: she knew they'd have to take this slowly. All night she'd been wondering what to do, who to tell — because she knew she couldn't deal with this on her own, it was too serious. But who to talk to?

There was no point approaching Ruby's mum, that was for sure. Andi had seen enough of Jennifer to know how self-absorbed she was. She'd been around their house when Jennifer went off on one of her rants, not even caring who saw her. If Andi told her about Ruby's problem, she would wail and cry and make a big fuss. And that wouldn't help Ruby.

If Andi told her own mother, it would send Ruby's mother into orbit with rage. Same if she told Ruby's dad. No, she needed somebody neutral, someone who would help.

Miss Lynott, their form teacher, came to mind. She'd be good. Ruby liked her. Everyone liked her. She was a kind, decent person who could actually talk to the girls and make it sound like she'd been a teenager once herself.

So that was the plan.

Andi was going to sit Ruby down and tell her they were going to skip maths and go to Miss Lynott. Finding a private place to talk in school even early in the morning was virtually impossible; Andi figured the best place was the bench beside the trees between the junior and senior schools. It wasn't a hot spot for the smokers because it was in full view of Mrs. Rhattigan's office from the junior school.

"Come on, let's sit here," she said, making

her way over to the trees.

"It's freezing," protested Ruby.

"We've got our coffee, we can hold on to that. We'll be fine. We'll just be here ten minutes. It's not that cold."

"It is," said Ruby.

"That's 'cause you're not eating," Andi said grimly. "Severe dieting makes you cold all the time."

"Enough about the severe dieting," said Ruby, looking tearful.

"I'm sorry, I didn't say it to be mean," Andi said quickly. "I just want to help. I feel like I've been a crap friend because I should have known. You're definitely skinnier — how did I miss that?"

"How could you know?" Ruby said. "I hid it, that's the whole point. You don't let anyone know."

"Yeah, but I'm with you all the time. I mean, what were you eating for lunch? Oh, wait, I know — you were eating apples and yogurts and almost nothing else. I thought it was some health kick. You kept going on about how your mother was cooking up a storm every night."

"She has been," said Ruby. "It's her way of making a point in the great battle to prove that she's a fabulous mother and Vonnie isn't. Vonnie's at work all day, therefore she cannot possibly be making fabulous nutritious meals for us when we're with Dad."

"Oh God," said Andi. "I didn't know it had gotten that bad."

"Yeah," Ruby said dully. "You've no idea; we get the whole cordon-bleu menu. The thing is, she doesn't really notice whether we eat it or not; it's just the fact that she's made it. She's so obsessed with proving how good she is at cooking, she never looks at Shelby's homework. I have to look at it for her. And then there's the constant interrogation. As soon as I get home on Monday night after a weekend with Dad and Vonnie, Mum wants to know *everything.* What we did, where we went, what films we watched. Was Shelby in bed on time? What did we eat? That's her favorite one. Or what did Vonnie wear? There's no good answer to that. It's a nightmare, Andi. I can't cope with it."

"Have you told your dad?"

"I don't want to. It's hard enough for him already. I can see the stress every time Mum rings about something. She's always so angry and he looks so upset. I know he and Vonnie are worried about money because of the mortgage, and I overheard them talking one night about how handy it would be if Mum got a job. And they're right, it would be brilliant for her, but can you imagine saying it to her?"

Andi shook her head.

"Me neither," said Ruby. "That's when I thought of the food —" She broke off. It

567

sounded so stupid telling Andi about it now. "It was just something I could be in charge of. I thought that if I got thin, someone might notice, then they'd realize how hard this is for me . . ." Her voice trailed off and she started to cry.

Andi put her arms around Ruby's slender frame and hugged her tightly.

"You utter, complete dork," she said tearfully. "I can't believe you went through all this without telling me. There's got to be a better way to let people know you're hurting."

"I'm sorry I didn't tell you," sobbed Ruby. "It's stupid, I know, but —"

"But you felt so miserable, and the self-destruct button is easier to push."

"I can see why you get As in your English essays," muttered Ruby, with a hint of her old grin.

"Nah, it's reading my mum's self-help books," said Andi. "Listen, Ruby, we're going to sort this out and there's going to be no more food-controlling crap."

Ruby said nothing; she just let the tears roll down her face, turning cold in the wind as her dear friend held her tightly.

Jennifer was getting ready for her walk with Caroline that morning when she heard the front door opening.

Burglars was her first thought.

Swiftly she looked around her bedroom for a weapon, but there was nothing except a heavy crystal vase decorated with dust. Great, she'd be found flattened in her own house and the police would be able to tell everyone she was a crap housekeeper. She grabbed the vase anyway and crept carefully on to the landing.

"I'm armed," she yelled, and began dialing the police on her cell phone.

"Yes, officer, I've got burglars," she said loudly, before the call was even answered. "Number four, The Close —"

And then she saw her burglars: Ruby and Andi. Something was definitely wrong, though. Quickly she ended the call.

"Girls, what's up? Ruby, what are you doing home at this time of day?"

By the time she got to the bottom of the stairs, she could feel the hairs standing up on the back of her neck at the sight of Ruby's white, tearstained face.

"Mrs. Morrison," said Andi coldly, "Ruby's not well and I thought she should come home."

Shocked as she was by the sight of her daughter looking so dreadful, Jennifer wasn't disconcerted enough to have missed the note of reproach in Andi's voice.

She grabbed Ruby, who looked as if she might faint, and together they helped her to the couch in the living room. Ruby lay down on it, as if she didn't have the energy to sit up. Jennifer took one of her daughter's wrists, and every instinct screamed at the frailty of it.

"What's wrong, Andi?" she snapped. "What aren't you telling me?"

"Look at her, Mrs. Morrison!" yelled Andi. "She's skin and bone. She's not eating, and it's all your bloody fault. Don't you care about her at all? If not, she can come and live with me. *I* love her." And Andi hugged her friend and burst into tears.

Jennifer watched as if from a great distance, her only connection to the tableau her grasp on her daughter's thin wrist.

All the voices she'd managed to block flooded into her head.

I'm worried about Ruby, from Vonnie.

It's our job not to let the girls get caught up in our battle, from Ryan.

Honey, you need to get out there and find a new life, a new man, from her mother. *It's not good for anyone when you stay at home feeling sorry for yourself . . .*

And she'd ignored it all, too enmeshed in her own pain to see anyone else's. The sensation of holding physical proof of her daughter's problems, and the scorn of Ruby's seventeen-year-old best friend, had achieved what nobody else had.

Jennifer sat down heavily on the floor. She

570

wanted to cry, but there was no time for that now. Besides, she'd cried enough. Selfish crying. She wanted to scream at herself over her selfishness, but she had spent enough time on herself and too little on her daughters.

"It's going to be OK, girls," she said firmly, finding strength from somewhere. "Andi, thank you. Ruby, my love . . ." She put her head close to her daughter's, noticing for the first time the purple shadows underneath Ruby's dark eyes. "It's going to be fine. I am sorry, so sorry. I'll make it better, I promise. No more fighting. New start. But let's get you to the doctor first."

She pulled her phone from her pocket and rang their local doctor for an appointment. Then she texted Caroline to say a crisis had occurred and she'd have to skip the walk.

Can I help? Caroline texted back instantly.

The guilt Jennifer was trying so hard to bury galloped back. Caroline had three kids, and a husband undergoing cancer treatment, yet she was prepared to be there for Jennifer if she should need her.

Not just guilt, but shame too. Jennifer's cheeks burned. When difficult things happened, some people stepped up to the plate; she'd whined and moaned and made everyone's life difficult. Oh, the *shame.*

No thanks. Will talk later.

"Tea and toast helps, honey," said Jennifer, holding both Ruby's hands tightly.

571

Ruby opened her eyes and smiled a little. "That would be nice, Mum," she said.

"How about you, Andi? I'm going to phone the school and explain what's happening here."

Andi's eyes rounded.

"Really explain," Jennifer said. "And I guess you should call me Jennifer."

Once the girls were installed in the kitchen with the small TV on, and tea and toast in front of them, Jennifer began to make her second round of phone calls. There would be no shirking, she told herself: the truth had to be faced.

Ryan didn't answer at first. Unsurprising, Jennifer thought, given the sort of abuse she usually heaped upon him. She texted instead.

Ryan, this is urgent. Ruby's here, she's not well. Can you call?

He phoned in seconds: "What's wrong with her?"

Jennifer paused. All the raging arguments they'd had raced in front of her eyes. The names she'd called him, the emotional blackmail she'd used. He'd told her it wasn't good for the girls, but she'd been so determined to hurt him that she hadn't cared. What sort of a mother was she?

She took a deep breath: one who was determined to change.

"It's all my fault, Ryan," she began.

Finally, she made the easiest phone call, the one to the person who wouldn't judge her: "Mum?"

"Jen?" said Lulu. "What's wrong?"

"Oh, Mum, I've messed everything up so badly. Could you come around now?"

Vonnie had been working on the accounts for about twenty minutes before she realized that her head just wasn't in the right place. You needed to be calm and focused to do accounts — not anxious and feeling as if something bad was going to happen. She put the books aside, went into the kitchen, donned an apron, washed her hands, and sat down beside Lorraine, who was painstakingly making sprays of white and lemon-yellow orchids.

Orchids were Lorraine's specialty. She'd been in since seven thirty and was already halfway through the order for the Maguire/Reynolds cake. "It's going to be absolutely beautiful," Vonnie said, admiring the younger woman's work. "You really are an artist. And thank you, by the way, for doing the sunflowers in Shelby's room this weekend. She is so thrilled."

"She's a darling kid," Lorraine said, eyes still on the sugarcraft. "She and Shane get along really well, don't they?"

"Yes, they do," Vonnie said, relieved that someone else could see it too and she wasn't just imagining it. That was the thing about trying to blend families: you spent so long agonizing about whether it was working or not that you no longer trusted your own eyes.

"I do worry about everyone getting along," she said, sighing.

"Really?" said Lorraine, pretending to sound shocked. "Gosh, there's a surprise. I never would have thought —"

"Oh, stop," Vonnie said. "Just because you're young, free, and single, madam. One day you might understand what it's like to have . . ." She paused.

To have what? she thought. To fall in love with a wonderful man and have to deal with the rage of that wonderful man's former wife? She wouldn't wish that on anybody.

"Actually," she said, "I sincerely hope that you don't have to go through what I have. If life is full of lessons, then I want to put away my schoolbooks. But thanks for the sunflowers — much appreciated, honey. Now, I'm supposed to be doing accounts, but my mind just won't settle. What else do we need to do? Something practical might help."

"Somebody has to do the peonies for next weekend."

The peonies were wonderful to look at, but making them was a whole other story. They took so long. There were endless petals to be shaped and fluted.

"Point taken," said Vonnie. "I'll start on the

574

peonies. That's exactly what I need: slow, painstaking work where you have to build up every petal."

"A metaphor for life," said Lorraine naughtily.

"Yes," said Vonnie wryly.

She was just getting organized when her cell rang. She always kept it with her in case there was a problem with Shane in school, and she slipped it out of her pocket now and looked. It was Ryan.

"Morning, love," she said, a feeling of heightened anxiety rising inside her without her quite knowing why. Ryan knew she was at work and he rarely rang her at this time.

"Vonnie — I've just had a phone call from Jennifer." The note of panic in his voice confirmed all her worst fears.

"What's wrong, has something happened to the girls?"

"Not Shelby, Ruby." Ryan sounded devastated, all his usual cheery confidence gone. "Andi brought her home and says she hasn't been eating. She wanted one of us to notice so we'd do something about it . . ." He sounded as if he could barely breathe. "It's early stages, a cry for help, but still . . ."

"Take deep breaths, darling," Vonnie commanded, "deep, deep breaths. And Jennifer rang you?"

"That's the incredible thing: she says it's her fault, really means it, if we can take that at face value. But she got Ruby an appointment with the doctor for this afternoon. I have to go."

"The doctor will know what to do. Just remember that: we love her and she will be taken care of."

"But what if it's really serious?" Ryan said.

Vonnie closed her eyes and said a quick prayer. Strange, she'd thought she'd never pray again after Joe's death, and now here she was asking for help from above. Fingering her wedding ring, she realized she had a new family now.

"We'll take care of her," she repeated.

"I love you, Vonnie," said Ryan. "I love you so much."

"I love you too."

"Thank you," he mumbled, and was gone.

She was left staring at the phone, all thoughts of peonies forgotten.

"What is it? What's wrong?" said Lorraine.

"Oh God!" Vonnie sank into a chair and buried her head in her hands. "I saw this coming, but I didn't do anything about it because I wasn't sure."

"What?"

"Jennifer's rung Ryan and it sounds as if Ruby's in the early stages of an eating disorder."

Even the words made Vonnie shudder. But surely it had to be early stages. She would have known, wouldn't she?

"I've been watching her and worrying, but I didn't do anything because I wasn't sure. I was so busy trying to tread carefully because she's my stepdaughter rather than my daughter; I didn't want to step on Jennifer's toes, even though I know she's been so caught up in herself that she hasn't been emotionally there for Ruby. So I stood back and did nothing — and now look what's happened. The poor, poor girl . . ."

Lorraine looked over at Inge and made a tea-drinking gesture. Then she found a tissue and handed it to Vonnie.

"I'm going to ring Maura, ask her to come in." In Lorraine's opinion, Aunt Maura always knew the answer to every problem.

"I have to get home," said Vonnie. "I should wait there for Ryan —"

"Then I'll let her know she can find you there."

Vonnie was about to protest, but she was in desperate need of Maura's soothing presence and gentle wisdom. How would they ever get through this? Somehow she had failed Ruby terribly. If this was what Ryan and her living together had caused, how could they possibly make Poppy Lane work?

When Ruby saw her father, she burst into tears and ran into his arms. He started crying too, holding her tightly. "I am so sorry, my darling, so sorry. Why didn't you tell me?"

"Because I couldn't, I didn't want to hurt you — it wasn't meant to hurt anyone, it was just meant to . . ." Ruby's voice trailed off. She couldn't say what it was meant to do. It sounded stupid now.

"Do you make yourself sick, honey?" he asked. "Or not eat at all?"

"No, none of that. Well, I haven't been eating much . . ." She didn't know how to explain it all. She'd only wanted to be noticed.

Jennifer stood to one side, looking very unlike herself. She hadn't been crying, but it was clear to Ryan that she was about to.

"It's my fault," she whispered. "I did this." Seeing Ryan made it all worse. They'd created this beautiful girl together, and she'd nearly destroyed it all.

But Ryan didn't scream at her or shout that she would never have custody of their daughters again. Instead he looked at her with what actually seemed to be sympathy.

"We all played a part," he said. "Now we have to make it better."

He held an arm out, and Jennifer found herself hugged into the circle of her former husband and their beloved daughter. This was family: not the way she'd wanted it, certainly, but life had moved on and if Ruby would get over this, Jennifer knew she'd need to move on too.

■ ■ ■ ■

Maura and Vonnie sat in the kitchen in Poppy Lane.

"No tea," said Vonnie. "I couldn't bear it. The number of times we've had tea when something dreadful was going on, as a sort of displacement activity. I think I hate tea now."

"No tea," agreed Maura. "It gives you something to do with your hands, that's all."

"I have a ton of peonies to make," Vonnie said absently, looking at her left hand and the finger where she and Ryan had discussed the possibility of placing an engagement ring.

But not now. How could they do this now? Jennifer would go into orbit — and what would that do to Ruby?

Maura watched her splaying out her long, slender fingers.

"I don't often do advice," she said. "You know that, Vonnie. Advice can backfire, and I love you too much to destroy our relationship."

"But . . ." began Vonnie mirthlessly.

"But," agreed Maura. "Don't back away now. Ryan loves you and you love him. What's more, Shane loves him. And I have every reason to believe that Ruby and Shelby love you."

"What if that's not enough?" said Vonnie, tears and anger mixing.

"It is," said Maura. "Life is messy and painful, Vonnie. Heaven knows, you've had enough experience of that. I won't let you sacrifice yourself on the altar of Jennifer Morrison's anger. Ryan left her, and I can understand how that would hurt desperately, but she can't wallow in it if it means hurting everyone around her. She has to face reality. She's pushed her daughter too far. Ruby comes first. You won't do those girls any favors by leaving Ryan now."

"I don't want to leave Ryan," said Vonnie.

"Right then. Jennifer needs to go off and get a job. No wonder she's going crazy, on her own in that big house day after day. I'd go mad if I had nothing to do but think that nobody loved me. Must be hell if you're overemotional like Jennifer."

"I've thought of all that myself," said Vonnie. "But how am I supposed to get this miraculous event to happen?"

"Tell Ryan to stop trying to please all the people all the time," Maura said bluntly. "Either Jennifer sorts herself out or they have to go back to court to discuss custody. Ruby can't be put at risk anymore. All this tiptoeing around for fear of upsetting Jennifer has to come to an end."

Vonnie nodded. "It won't be easy," she said.

Maura snorted. "Since when has anything worthwhile been easy?"

■ ■ ■ ■

Ruby didn't know what her mother, Granny Lulu, and Dad talked about before they left for the doctor's office, but it was serious.

Still, Mum and Dad weren't fighting, which was a miracle in itself — they were actually talking but there was no yelling.

Andi and Ruby had moved up to Ruby's bedroom and were lying on the bed chatting when Granny Lulu came in. She sat on the edge of the bed and sighed.

"You should have told me, Ruby," she said. "You know what your mother's like — she's always been tricky, but she loves you. Still, it'll all be different now. None of that feeling sorry for herself anymore. I think your parents should sell The Close. Let you girls and your mother move somewhere closer to your dad and Vonnie."

Ruby blinked. She'd never heard her granny so much as mention Vonnie's name before.

Granny Lulu caught the look. "I've heard she's a lovely woman," she said, startling Ruby even more. "I have to say sorry, love. It's my fault too. I should have seen what was happening."

Behind Granny Lulu's blue glasses, her eyes were tearing up.

"I came to say your mum's getting upset downstairs — no, not an argument," she added, seeing Ruby's anxious face. "But she's got some stuff to say to you. Andi and I can stay here and chat."

Andi glanced at her friend for confirmation. Ruby nodded.

"Just one thing." Granny Lulu grabbed Ruby's hand. "Are you anorexic? Is that what you've been aiming for, because it's a disease, pet, and once it gets you, it doesn't like letting go."

Ruby had never seen her grandmother look so distressed.

"No, Gran, I'm not anorexic. Andi showed me some anorexic sites yesterday." She couldn't hide the shudder that ran through her. "I don't want to be like that, honestly."

"Really? Well, you'd lie if you were anyway," Granny Lulu said with a sigh.

"I'm not," Ruby said fervently. "I promise."

Her grandmother made the sign of the cross and muttered a small prayer. When she was finished, she held out her arms for a hug.

"If I ever catch you messing around with this type of thing again, I'll murder you, you monkey," she said, in her normal voice.

"I won't, Gran," said Ruby, relaxing into the embrace.

Downstairs, there was no sign of Dad, but Mum was sitting on the chair in the hall beside the phone, and she'd clearly been crying.

"Oh, Ruby," she sobbed. "I am so sorry."

She hugged her daughter, then tried to hold her at arm's length as if to see how thin she'd become. "How did I not notice? It will be different from now on, I promise," she added fiercely. "You and Shelby come first. And Vonnie cares for you, I know she does."

Ruby was still for a moment. Had her mother just said Vonnie's name without hissing? Things really were going to be different, and she was going to grab this with both hands.

"She does, Mum," she said finally. "She's a nice woman and she does worry about me, I can tell. I don't want to have to choose between her and Dad and you. I don't want to."

Her mother held her even tighter. "I know," she said. "I'm sorry, Ruby. Can you forgive me? Because we need to get you well again, and that's going to take you and me working together. No skipping meals, no yogurts for lunch; proper food."

Ruby leaned into her mother. It felt lovely, all these hugs, like a normal family again after so long.

"And you'll meet Vonnie, become friends?" she added, determined to cover all bases.

Jennifer closed her eyes and wished she'd never made that deranged visit to Vonnie's cake shop. But at least it had done something: it had shown her that Ryan's new partner cared about their daughters, had seen what Jennifer herself was too blind to see. She'd always be grateful to Vonnie for that.

"You bet," she whispered into the cloud of her daughter's hair. "I'd like to meet her." *Again,* she said to herself. "We may be a strange sort of family, but we're still family, and if this is going to work, we've got to give it everything we've got."

To her astonishment, Ruby laughed.

"What's so funny? Don't you believe me?"

"I do, Mum. It's just Vonnie's not going to believe what you're like when you're giving something all you've got."

TWENTY

> To love someone deeply gives you
> strength. Being loved by someone deeply
> gives you courage.
>
> LAO TZU

Birdie heard the front door slam. Howard
had left as usual by six fifty. He would go
and swim twenty lengths in the health club
pool, as he did every morning, and be at work
by eight.

Once, Birdie had got up with him. Now he
brought her tea before he left, and let
Thumper back upstairs to heave himself up
for a morning snooze on a bed superior to
his own, snuggled up at Birdie's side.

He had always been full of energy, her
husband. Liked to get in early to steal a
march on the world, as he put it.

Bridgeport Woolen Mills had been only a
small family business before Howard had
taken the reins when his father, always
referred to as Poor Paidin, due to a fondness
for hard liquor, had suffered a major heart

attack at the races. The liquor and losing a hefty sum to the bookies had no doubt contributed to his early demise, and people had wondered what would happen to the mill then.

Howard had happened.

Twenty-three, and fresh from college, he'd been about to head to the U.S. for a masters in business studies, but canceled his plans after his father's death. He upended the business, changed everything it was possible to change — including a few things that people didn't think could be changed — and then set off to do business with huge luxury stores who'd never heard of the tiny mill on the south coast with its wools in soft peaty colors. Howard Desmond had dazzled them all.

The buyer at Saks hadn't known she'd like a range of wheaten throws in softest wools with vanilla velvet edging. The man in Tokyo had said he was only interested in a few scarves, but somehow ended up ordering a complete lifestyle package encompassing cushions, blankets, and whisper-thin wall hangings.

It was partly down to business acumen, partly down to a savvy business sense that made other people believe that Howard knew the inside track. He had a way of telling them things that implied he knew much more than he was saying, but that he was letting them in on the action because they were his friends.

The final part of the equation was the way he looked: though he had a short, stout alcoholic for a father, and a rather hard-faced mother, Howard had somehow turned out to be a shade under six feet, with a head of leonine hair and the good looks of his mother's favorite movie star, Leslie Howard.

Doris Desmond had chosen the name of her only child as an act of defiance — Paidin wanted his son called Patrick, after him. The priest had wanted a saint's name. Doris's own sister had said that a child without a saint's name was asking for trouble.

"And you have enough of that, Doris," she'd said meaningfully.

"He can be Howard Patrick. It's a lucky name," Doris said, asking her husband to go over to the priest's house with a good bottle of whiskey and hoping that he'd make it there without breaking into the bottle.

Paidin had brightened at the thought of luck. Luck ruled in the turf accountants.

Luck made Howard grow up to resemble his famous namesake, to his mother's joy. But her greatest joy was that Howard's run of good luck had continued through the years.

Doris was a tough woman, and Birdie had grown to dread her visits, but even the thought that her mother-in-law would be staying at Vineyard Manor for Katy's wedding couldn't upset her these days. There was too much to be happy about.

She looked at her watch. She had to be in the church hall at nine for a meeting with a group of women who organized events every year for local charities — ones for children, people in need, and animals.

The weather continued to be wintry, despite it being March, so the church hall would be cold as the tundra. Having already spent too long putting out bird feed and breaking the ice on the bird bath, she would have to hurry to get ready if she was going to be there on time. Not that there was much to Birdie's toilette: a shower, a quick spritz of whatever eau de cologne was at the forefront of her dressing table, then it was just a matter of slipping into her usual loose indigo cords, a floral blouse, a cardigan, and flat shoes, and pinning up her hair.

Howard was still grumbling about her clothes. It seemed to have become a sticking point for him. He'd left a glossy magazine on the coffee table, opened to show a double-page feature on successful men's wives. She knew that if she'd been included in the big group picture, she would have looked as if she'd wandered into the wrong photo shoot: anxious expression, shabbily dressed, eccentric. Her beauty seemed to have faded to nothing, perhaps because she had never believed in it. Such things were for other people, not her. But she was starting to feel anxious about finding an outfit to please

Howard at the wedding.

Shaking herself, she hurried downstairs. She'd given Thumper his breakfast, but now her blasted phone was missing again. Retrace your steps, she reminded herself.

Last night, Howard had gotten home late — some work thing — so she'd sat on the couch in the kitchen with Thumper asleep beside her and watched a documentary about the mysterious migration of whales.

Could the phone be on the couch?

Instead, Birdie found the iPhone Howard reserved for U.S. calls under the cushion of the armchair where he liked to sit at night for a Scotch and soda. Her husband was so organized, and yet he was careless with his possessions, rather in the manner of a medieval king waiting for people to return things to him.

She hoped there was nothing he'd missed, no important calls.

Thumper at her heels, she picked up the kitchen phone and rang Howard's office line. But Roberta, his executive assistant, didn't start till nine. She stuck the iPhone in her pocket, hoping that would remind her to call back later.

Abandoning all hope of finding her own cell phone, she pulled on her warm coat. As she did so, Howard's iPhone pinged with a message. Frowning, because her own phone was ancient and iPhones terrified her, she pulled it out of her pocket and slipped on her glasses to look at the screen. She could only see part of the message.

Hi sexy, loved last night. Call me if you want to meet tomorrow.

Hands shaking, she scrolled down to see the rest of it.

Love you so much and thank you for my present. N xx

Somewhere deep inside Birdie, a fierce pain took hold. Her gut, she realized in an unreal way. Her gut was reacting to the text. Her gut before her brain. She'd read that there were more nerve endings in the gut than in any other part of the body apart from the brain.

Her brain must have been asleep for a long time and was slow to register stuff. But her gut knew what this meant.

She sat down on the couch and stared at the message again. She looked, but there were no other texts in the history with N's number. All carefully erased to remove the evidence. You could wipe out entire series of messages, Katy had told her one day, showing off her new iPhone and explaining how it worked.

Handy, that.

It was like dominoes falling in a line: Howard's careful eating plan, the increase in the number of business trips he was taking, the designer clothes from Dublin — something he'd only gotten into over the last few years. When they'd first married, he hadn't noticed what he'd worn. As long as it was clean and serviceable, it would do.

Birdie had been the one who'd bought him decent shirts and suits, found ties that matched, steered him in the direction of the best shoe shops. Howard had been too fiercely involved in turning Bridgeport Woolen Mills into an empire to worry about his clothes, but eventually he saw the method in her madness.

"That gray Italian jacket went down very well in Milan," he'd told her, before reciting proudly all the shops that would now stock Bridgeport's luxury goods.

Then, a few years ago, he'd shocked her and Katy by suddenly becoming interested in fashion.

"Is that a Paul Smith shirt?" Katy had asked one night at dinner.

"Think so," said Howard, unconcerned.

Katy had giggled. "Dad, you're becoming cool in your old age," she'd teased.

Birdie had joined in the good humor: "Your dad has always been cool, Katy."

Untrue. Just Birdie sticking up for him — something he never did for her.

She left the phone on the counter and ran upstairs, Thumper happily following her. In the master bedroom, she opened her husband's wardrobe and rifled through his clothes.

The designer names mocked her: Armani and Ermenegildo Zegna suits, some Brioni ones, which Birdie had a faint idea cost thousands. Calvin Klein socks, silk boxers with French names, ties labeled with a litany of designers she'd never heard of.

These were not clothes her husband would have bought himself. These were things he'd had bought for him by the stylist, Nadine, who came twice a year and had never appeared even slightly in awe of Howard. She bossed him around, joked with him, and generally smiled, Birdie realized too late, with the confidence of a woman who was sleeping with her client.

Nadine. In her early thirties, fashionable beyond belief, possessor of short, modern hair of the type Howard hated. Or perhaps he didn't.

Birdie didn't stop to cry. She was too numb. Instead, she carefully shut the wardrobe door and went to her husband's study, his sanctum. She and Morag were forbidden to so much as vacuum in there, and once a month, Howard polished and organized it himself.

"I can leave plans out on the desk and I never lose a document that way," he'd told Birdie, who knew better than to be offended.

There were no papers on the mahogany desk now. Nothing laid out, just a faint sprinkling of dust.

With a methodical mindset that Birdie had

forgotten she possessed, she opened drawers and cabinets. In a box tucked in the bottom desk drawer were photos of Nadine gazing up at someone from a swimming pool; others of her perfect body in a bikini on a sun-lounger.

One with a man's hand on her leg, the hand of a man who wore a Patek Philippe watch, Howard's watch, in fact.

Thumper was bored at this point and hoisted himself up into his master's plaid armchair to watch the proceedings. Under normal circumstances Birdie would have shrieked at him to get off, as Howard would notice the dog hair and go mad at the thought of it clinging to his precious trousers.

But today wasn't normal. Still numb, she continued her search in a box file with *Credit Cards* written on the spine.

Howard's private credit card. Reading the list of purchases reminded her of that one occasion she'd flicked through the *Financial Times* "How to Spend It" feature.

These purchases were not trinkets. He'd bought jewels that cost thousands, a car, spa trips in glamorous hotels — the hotel bills themselves were no doubt on his business account; even while taking his girlfriend away, he was careful to arrange it so that he could write off business bills against tax.

With great effort, because her limbs felt

leaden, Birdie put all the files carefully away. Then she enticed Thumper from the room, shut the door, and headed to the couch in the kitchen where she spent so much time. She might sit there with Thumper's solid body beside her: sit and think.

She'd known for years that Howard's heart didn't leap with joy when he saw her. She'd witnessed this behavior in other couples, people they knew who still, unaccountably, seemed delighted with each other despite marriages as old as the Ark. She'd accepted that this was not her lot, and yet she had still believed that her husband loved her. Not wild, passionate, crazy love, but love all the same.

The removal of that love felt like the cornerstone of her world disintegrating.

She was *not loved* after all, not cared for.

In fact, she was barely tolerated. An object of amusement with her funny clothes and her occasional attempts to dress in an up-to-date manner from her mail-order catalogues.

She had no hatred for the fashionable Nadine, who would, no doubt, move on. But Howard had betrayed her utterly. It wasn't the sex. It was letting her go on believing that their marriage meant something.

If he'd come to her and told her it was over, she could deal with that. She could live with honesty and courage, no matter how much it hurt. But this — this facade . . . this was like an assassin's bullet.

Somewhere in the fog of her brain, Birdie heard the house phone.

"Hello, Mrs. Desmond," said Roberta, her husband's assistant. "Mr. Desmond was looking for his U.S. phone. Says he's expecting an important call."

Roberta must know what was going on, Birdie realized suddenly. She sounded anxious about the phone's whereabouts, and not because of any important international calls.

"I haven't seen it," said Birdie, who never lied.

And lying to lovely Roberta, whom she liked so much. Did *she* know where Howard was when he wasn't spending his nights with Birdie? Of course she did.

Other people knew that Birdie and Howard's life had been a lie, and stupid Birdie was the only one who hadn't.

"I'll phone and we'll see where it is," said Roberta.

"Yes," replied Birdie dully. "I'll listen out." The phone was in Howard's study, where she'd left it. Too far for Roberta to hear it over a phone line.

She stood half in the kitchen, covered the phone's receiver with her hand, and heard the distant sound of her husband's distinctive ringtone. Trumpets. *Only Howard,* people would say at dinner parties when it rang.

"No," said Birdie. "Can't hear it. He might

have left it in the office. I'll look later, Roberta, but I have to race off. I've got a meeting."

Birdie drove in the direction of the church hall but found she couldn't bring herself to go in — she might cry in front of everyone. Instead, she parked and walked blindly down the main street until she found herself outside a clothes shop with a lively coral dress on the window mannequin. The outfit looked so vivid, so alive, before she knew it she'd been drawn into the shop, enticed by the notion that the coral dress would transform its wearer into someone happy, smiling, carefree.

Feeling as if she was sleepwalking, Birdie slowly moved through the shop, running her fingers lightly along the clothes. She'd never been in here before. This was the poshest and most chic boutique in Bridgeport, the place where many of Howard's friends' wives bought their clothes. Birdie had heard them discussing the fabulous selection of dresses at dinners and parties, while she hung back, silent and invisible. If they deigned to notice her at all, it was only to dismiss her; it was obvious she had no interest in her appearance. Birdie had four evening outfits that she rotated, never deviating from them.

It wasn't as if she needed anything new.

"Mrs. Desmond, hello!" said Lucinda, the shop owner, moving forward hastily.

Everyone in town knew Birdie Desmond,

wife of the owner of the Bridgeport Woolen Mills.

"Could be a very valuable customer. Rolling in cash," as Lucinda had whispered to her assistant manager moments before, when she'd seen Birdie gazing in the window. "Don't think she's into clothes — she's never so much as set foot in here — but she certainly has the money to indulge."

"Mrs. Desmond, have you seen our new autumn looks?"

Within minutes, Birdie was in the biggest changing room, with the coral dress and a selection of other garments hanging from the hooks on the wall.

"Tell me if you need me, Mrs. Desmond," said Lucinda happily from the other side of the curtain.

Birdie whipped off her catalogue-bought sweater, wincing at the sight of her greying bra and pale skin. She'd never put on weight, had remained birdlike for sure, but time had wrought havoc in other ways. Her skin was crêped and wrinkled, her small breasts drooped. Had those wrinkles driven Howard away?

Or had it been something else? Her in general?

Once, she'd been what he wanted — or had she merely been what had suited him best at the time? Like the pinstriped suits he'd abandoned for the latest Italian designs. Was she like those old garments: surplus to requirements, destined to be left untouched in a corner of the wardrobe forever more?

"Mr. Desmond rang," said Morag when she got home.

Morag never called Howard by his given name; it was always "Mr. Desmond." Birdie wasn't sure whether Howard had demanded this; she'd been too embarrassed to ask Morag. The two women had become friends over the years; they talked, laughed, and discussed all manner of things. Birdie wouldn't have been able to cope if she'd thought Howard had been uppity with her dear Morag.

Morag's eyes widened at the sight of the Couture & Co. bags hanging from Birdie's arms.

"Jesus, Mary, and Joseph, Birdie!" she gasped. "Did you buy the shop?"

"Sort of," said Birdie miserably.

"Give us a look."

They went into the kitchen where Morag took a few of the bags and peered into them. She pulled out the coral dress in amazement. "Are you going on a trip?" she asked.

"No," said Birdie. "I just walked into the shop."

"Ah," agreed Morag knowingly. "I've heard about your woman in that shop. Once you're in, you're like a fly in the spider's web. She won't let you out the door till you've spent every ha'penny you own and some you don't. It's the wedding, isn't it? My aunt was just the same with her daughter. You get caught up in overhauling everything because you don't want to let them down, do you? These things are lovely, Birdie, but are you sure they're you?"

She was examining a little chiffon shirt designed to be worn with a tiny camisole underneath. It was a silky cream and would look lovely on Katy but was probably far too young for Birdie.

"She definitely saw you coming," Morag pronounced.

It was only seeing the little Tupperware container of buns on a kitchen counter that made Birdie remember she'd promised to visit Dolores today.

"Oh, Morag," she said anxiously, "I was supposed to go up to the Hummingbird this morning to see Dolores Martin. I'd completely forgotten."

"It's only eleven forty now," said Morag, consulting her watch. "Go early this afternoon, once they've had lunch. Or don't go at all. Have a lie-down. You look tired. One of the committee phoned, by the way, wondering where you'd gotten to this morning. I said you had a headache." She looked shrewdly at Birdie.

"I do a bit," said Birdie, wondering where

the morning had gone. "I might lie down after all." Since the horror of finding out about Howard's other life, it was as if time was melting in her head. It couldn't be only a few hours since she'd discovered the text message, could it?

"I'll make you some nice tea before you go upstairs," Morag said. It upset her to see Birdie so distressed. No doubt Bloody Howard had been on at the poor woman to smarten herself up or something equally stupid and it had sent Birdie into a spiral of worry, forgetting all her morning plans.

Morag might have called Howard "Mr. Desmond" to his face, but in her internal monologues he was always Bloody Howard.

While Morag went about her work, Birdie remained rooted to the bench in the kitchen, her thoughts veering from Howard's infidelity to the forthcoming wedding and her darling Katy. Whatever happened, she couldn't have Katy finding out about her father's affair. Or affairs? Who knew.

The urge to protect her daughter allowed Birdie to conveniently numb any thoughts of how Howard's deception was affecting her. She'd known for many years that she wasn't what he wanted. He'd married her because she'd represented a world of class and prestige — albeit a world where the money had long since run out. Her family could trace their ancestry back hundreds of years, while Howard's had never amounted to anything and had appeared to have left no trace in the Bridgeport annals. His father and grandfather had eked a living from the woolen mill, plowing any profits into horses or booze. No wonder, then, that Howard and his mother preferred to draw a line under the past. All that mattered was Howard's success now, what it meant for the family, how it had elevated them. Birdie had been a part of that, no doubt about it. And it wasn't as if he'd married her only for the background that gave him a gentility he might not otherwise have had. He'd once seen beauty in her.

But adoration, kindness, pure affection — the things she noticed in other couples — those had always been absent from her marriage. And she'd accepted it. Being the sort of shy, self-effacing person she was, she had felt lucky just to have married. Yet despite all that — despite his mother being controlling and contrary and determined to criticize everything Birdie did; despite Howard's obsession with the business and then with their beloved Katy — Birdie had somehow felt that together she and Howard were strong. As a couple, they seemed to fit pretty well, and if he grew irritated with her sometimes, she didn't think that mattered. They were a family, and that had to be enough, surely?

But this . . . this was proof that they hadn't been a real family for a long time.

Beside her, Thumper nudged her as if to say, *Look at me. Play with me. Why are you so sad?* Automatically, Birdie reached down to pet him. The warmth of his fur, the way he groaned happily at her touch should have made the tears come. Here was someone who loved her absolutely, in complete contrast to her husband. But no tears came.

Birdie had read about people who'd been betrayed; she'd seen it enacted on TV and cinema screens, always with a massive outpouring of emotion: tears, sobbing, yelling, screaming. She wondered how they could have gotten it so wrong. All she felt inside was an incredible emptiness, as if a massive hole had been gouged out inside her. And along with the emptiness had come a savage sense of loss, of feeling truly alone.

After Morag left, Birdie spent the rest of the afternoon wandering around the house in a sort of trance. She kept looking at photographs, picking them up and examining them carefully. Wondering what had really been going on in Howard's mind as he pasted on a smile and posed for the camera. That holiday they had taken with Katy when she was eighteen — had he been seeing someone then? Had he been secretly texting *Miss you darling. Boring as hell here. Wish I were there with you?*

Birdie could remember all the places they'd stayed. She loved making albums of their holidays. Howard and Katy used to tease her about them.

"It's in the past, what do you want an album for?" Howard would say dismissively, but Katy liked looking at them, and she liked showing them to Michael too. Sometimes the two of them would sit on the couch and Birdie would peek in from the kitchen to catch Katy saying: ". . . and that was when we went to the Rhône . . ."

Everything in the house seemed to have a memory attached, even the wallpaper in the dining room, the expensive Chinese wallpaper that had caused so much trouble. Howard had probably rung whoever he was seeing at the time and told them how annoying his wife was and how she was incapable of managing anything, couldn't get the decorators to put bloody wallpaper up properly, leaving him to come in and fix it all.

She was driving herself mad thinking like this when Howard rang — or rather, Roberta did. Howard didn't make his own phone calls. He didn't have the patience to dial his home number and wait for her to pick up.

"Hello, Mrs. Desmond," said Roberta. "I've got Mr. Desmond here for you."

"Yes," said Birdie faintly.

"Birdie." It was the great man himself. "A

bit of business has come up: I have to go to Dublin tonight. I realize it's a pain, and I'm sorry, dear, I'm sure you've something very nice cooked for dinner, but it can't be helped, I'm afraid."

Birdie was utterly silent, but Howard didn't appear to notice.

"Fortunately the clothes I keep in the office for these eventualities will see me through, so I don't need you to pack anything for me. In fact, there's nothing I need from home, so I'll set off from here. I should be back tomorrow evening, okey-doke?"

He paused for the expected response, but the obligatory "Of course, darling" was not forthcoming.

Birdie thought of the years she'd spent jumping to Howard's demands. Treading on eggshells. Desperate to say the right thing. But now there was quite simply nothing to say. Howard was lying to her. She knew it. Everything was a lie. Her ability to react had deserted her.

"Birdie, are you there? Are you all right?" demanded Howard.

"Fine," said Birdie. "All fine here. You go to Dublin. Must dash." And she hung up.

TWENTY-ONE

Where there is love, there is no darkness.

BURUNDI PROVERB

Devlin popped his head around the door of Leila's office to find her and Ilona having a meeting. His eyes met Leila's across her assistant's head, and before she could stop herself, she'd smiled at him, a dazzling smile that came straight from the heart.

Immediately her eyes widened and the smile vanished. What the heck had she done that for? The last couple of weeks she'd mastered the art of being cool, behaving as if they were just colleagues, as if she wasn't secretly hoping he felt something for her . . . What had she been thinking?

Devlin stared at her, and Leila was beginning to curse herself for her stupidity when he bestowed his own slow, just-as-dazzling smile on her. It was like watching his face lighting up, and at that moment, Leila knew she hadn't imagined it: she could see the warmth in his expression, the glow when he

looked at her.

She wasn't going crazy: he felt the same way, the way he'd felt in Rome. She wasn't just any port in a storm in a hotel corridor. He felt something for her and she'd allowed herself to show him that she felt the same way.

"Morning," he said in a formal voice, eyes still glinting. "Everything all right?"

"Wonderful," she said and he grinned back.

"Ilona," Devlin said, "can I have a moment with Leila?"

Leila had to stop a squeak of joy emerging. Her phone rang. Wincing, she picked it up.

"Hello," she said, professional again. "Yes, I've been trying to talk to you for a few days now . . ."

She smiled apologetically at Devlin, who shrugged and left her office.

"Coffee?" whispered Ilona.

Leila nodded. Coffee, not that she'd taste it.

Devlin had smiled at her.

It was amazing the sensations she felt at the notion that his piratical smile was for her and her alone. Blissful — that was it.

He was in meetings all morning, and whenever he looked around for her, she either had somebody with her or was on the phone. There was never a private moment, Devlin thought with irritation. This was probably why companies didn't like their employees having relationships: offices weren't the place for private moments.

Whatever, he thought, they'd work around that. He had decided to take her to lunch at one of the places he took important people to, only this time, he'd be bringing the most important person of all.

He rang Ilona. "Does Leila have a lunch appointment?" he asked, trying to get the correct note of brusqueness into his voice. "Or anything urgent after lunch, in fact?" he added.

"Er, no," said Ilona.

"Fine. I have some things to discuss with her, might have to have a lunchtime meeting. Don't say anything for the moment," he told her. "I need to organize it."

He put the phone down, a wide grin on his face. Seeing that his own assistant was not at her desk, he rang his favorite elegant restaurant and asked for a table for two. "One of those banquette ones," he said, "in the corner at the back."

"Of course, Mr. Devlin," said the person on the phone. Devlin was a good customer, spent shedloads and brought movie stars in. He could have whatever he wanted.

"Thank you," said Devlin and hung up, his grin wider than ever.

Tynan was fed up. Leila wasn't returning his

calls or his texts or his emails and she'd blocked him from her Facebook account. What was going on? Where was the lovely compliant Leila of the past? It was probably a game, he decided. A game to teach him a lesson. Well, he'd learned his lesson and he was back; surely that ought to be enough? He decided that the grand gesture was what was required. Something she wouldn't be able to resist. Something that would say to her that he loved her. And say it to everyone else into the bargain, he thought delightedly. Yes, that was it: she needed everyone else to see that he was sorry. Fine, if that was what it took, then that was what he would deliver. Red roses, he decided. An enormous amount of red roses. Or something different, maybe. He'd ask the florist. And perfume too. His eyes glinted as another thought occurred to him: he'd buy her another little French coffeepot, a reminder of the morning coffees he'd made for her, a shiny new one so she could throw the old one out — now *that* she wouldn't be able to resist.

He did, genuinely, miss her. Having thought about it, he wanted to move back to Dublin. He knew he'd been flaky and he wanted to show Leila it was worth another shot.

It was proving impossible to ask Leila to lunch. No matter how often Devlin stalked the area near her office, she was never alone.

How the bloody hell was he supposed to ask her out when they couldn't get a minute's peace?

Finally he sent her an email.

Lunch, La Belle Jardin, 1 p.m.? We'll leave at 12:45 in my car?

When the message pinged on to her screen, Leila, who was talking on the phone to a journalist, almost dropped the phone with excitement.

"Are you still there?" said the journalist, because Leila had stopped speaking mid-sentence.

"Yes, sorry, something fell off my desk," she improvised. "Now, where were we?"

Inside, she was thinking of her outfit. Was it nice enough for La Belle Jardin? If only she'd made the extra effort today, but then, if she'd thought about it beforehand, she'd never have instinctively smiled at Devlin and broken down all those barriers they both seemed to have erected since Rome. Still, at least she'd washed her hair that morning, that was good. But more lipstick was definitely required — and mascara. She needed mascara, oh gosh.

Somehow she managed to get off the phone. Grabbing her bag, she made a dash for the ladies', calling over her shoulder to Ilona, "Back in a minute." Thankfully there was nobody in there, so she was able to spray perfume and deodorant, adjust her trousers and look sideways at herself in the mirror to see if her belly was having one of its sticking-in or sticking-out days and cast a critical eye over everything to see how good she looked. Then she stopped. This was Devlin, not Tynan. She didn't have to be what she wasn't for him. He'd seen her in every situation and he liked her for what she was. There was no need for frantic puffing-up of hair or changing into shiny black leather trousers so she'd look like a rock chick. No, Devlin liked Leila Martin for being Leila Martin.

She grinned, cleaned her teeth, and put on more lipstick, thinking about how lovely it would be if it was all kissed off in Devlin's car.

At twelve forty-five, she hurried out to reception, shouting: "I'll be back later" to Ilona without pausing at her desk, because it was all she could do to stop herself breaking into the biggest grin imaginable, and if Ilona saw it she would instantly know that *something* was up.

Through the glass door of his office Devlin could see her striding toward reception. He loved the way she walked in those high heels, the way her hips swung, the way her blonde hair shimmered down her shoulders. He got up from his desk, tried without success to quell his sense of excitement, and went to the door. After all the women and all the years chasing them, this was different. Leila

Martin was the real thing. He couldn't mess this up; he wouldn't.

Why had she smiled at him today of all days? He'd been working himself up to asking her out but he was still nervous. Him, Eamonn Devlin, who had a little black book of enormous proportions, a book he had no interest in anymore.

Rome had been such a disaster. After all the time he'd been thinking about asking her out, wondering would he cook her a meal, what could he do to show her she was amazing and she should forget about that waster husband of hers, because he would take care of her forever. And then today, miracle of miracles, she'd given him that glorious smile and he'd known she felt the same way. As he paused to collect his coat, Devlin glanced out of the plate-glass window and felt a benevolence for all the people on the streets who didn't know happiness the way he was feeling it right now.

Tynan had managed to get into the building by brandishing the enormous bouquet of designer wildflowers and twigs and the gift bag.

"Delivery for Leila Martin in Eclipse," he said to the man on the desk, who made him sign in and sent him up in the elevator. Not that Tynan didn't know where to go — he'd been up to the Eclipse office many times in

611

the past — but he didn't want Leila to know that he was coming today. He wanted to surprise her. He imagined her face, the look of joy when she realized he was serious, that he was back.

And that everyone else could see it too. She'd been hurt, he knew that. Probably that was why she wasn't returning his phone calls. Her pride was dented. Flowers like this would go some way to restoring that pride, he thought confidently. Cost a blooming fortune, though. Whoever said love was free had never been in a flower shop, that was for sure.

He got out of the elevator and walked to the double glass doors of Eclipse, where he pressed the entrance button. Sinead, the receptionist, saw the big bouquet and let him in. At that exact moment, Devlin reached Leila in reception. Tynan laid the bouquet on one of the couches and saw Leila standing there, looking at her boss.

Tynan grimaced. He'd never liked Devlin. Still, he could go hang. It was lunchtime, Tynan was there for his woman, and he was going to get her. He was wearing his leather jacket, the expensive one, and new boots he'd bought in London, fiercely hip and still on the waiting list for those not in the know. He'd also covered himself with her favorite cologne, spraying it everywhere, because you never knew when you were going to get lucky.

"Hiya, honey," he said, giving her his rueful

grin. "I brought you a present."

It was hard to say who was more horrified.

Leila felt her blood chill at the sight of her ex-husband, whose phone calls, emails, and texts she'd pointedly refused to reply to. Had he not got the message yet? It was over.

But what might Devlin think? Oh no . . .

Devlin stared at Tynan, the little rat, with his giant bouquet of flowers and some gift bag with silvery tissue paper spilling out of the top; then he looked at Leila, who wasn't saying anything but was just staring at Tynan.

Devlin couldn't read the look on her face, but he heard her whisper: "Tynan, what are you doing here?"

Tynan walked toward her. "Like I said the other night, honey, I'm back," and he reached up and cupped her cheek, staring deep into her eyes. Before she could stop him, he leaned in and kissed her, the sort of slow-burn kiss that would have once turned her to mush. Right now, it turned her to rage.

Leila muttered something, but Devlin couldn't bear to watch.

"Sinead, I don't think I'll be back this afternoon," he growled, and stalked off, letting the reception doors swing shut behind him.

"Tynan, get off," shrieked Leila, pushing him away and turning around frantically, but it was too late. Devlin was gone. There was no sign of him in the lobby.

He'd either gotten straight into an elevator or he'd run down the stairs. Probably the latter, she thought, thinking of the pent-up energy that was Eamonn Devlin. The man she loved.

She turned and glared at Tynan.

"Tynan, you're a complete moron," she snapped. "I told you the other night I wasn't interested, and I'm not, OK — don't you get it? Did you really think that a big bunch of flowers and some stupid present was going to make it all better?"

"Hey, babe, I'm just trying to tell you I love you."

"You don't love me," Leila said. "You love *you*. That's the biggest love affair in your head: Tynan and Tynan. You dumped me like I was nothing, and I'm not sure why you're back, but I won't be a part of it. I told you that the other night."

She had, she knew, but she hadn't infused the words with the correct level of dismissal. Tynan's charm and the fact that he'd helped wash Pixie had made him think he was in with a chance. That would not be happening again, not ever.

She drew herself up to her full height and glared at him, thinking of all he'd put her through.

"Now get out of my sight with those bloody twigs and your stupid present, and get out of my life: I do not want to see you ever again — apart from the bit where you sign the divorce papers."

"Babe —" he began.

"Don't *babe* me!" she roared.

She left him standing there openmouthed, with quite a few members of the Eclipse staff watching openmouthed too.

"Way to go, Leila!" whooped Sinead after her departing back.

Leila took the stairs, running as fast as she could.

"Devlin!" she shouted, her voice echoing down the stairwell, but there was no reply. She reached the parking lot, ran to his space, but his car was gone and her phone was upstairs with her handbag. Shit! She ran back inside, got an elevator back up to their floor and ran into reception to find that Tynan was still there.

"Leila," he said, sounding unsure for the first time in his life. "You didn't mean that. You're just angry and, yes" — he held his hands up — "I humiliated you, so you want to humiliate me back. I get it; I get the game, but let's stop playing now."

Leila stood at the reception desk and ran her hands through her hair. It was either that or punch Tynan till his nose bled, and she thought she might break her hand if she did that.

"Do you know why I haven't returned your

phone calls or messages?" she said, deadly calm now.

He said nothing, eyes wide, the Tynan charm no longer set to stun.

"Because my lawyer told me not to," she fibbed. "I said I wanted a divorce and I didn't want to either see or talk to you again, and guess what? I don't have to. Now get out of my office before I take out a restraining order against you!"

It was worth it to see the shock in Tynan's eyes. He had no happy comeback, no sharp remark.

"But, Leila —" he began.

All the frustration of having her lunch with Devlin ruined, of what Devlin must think, hit Leila.

"GO!" she roared, and with one confused look, Tynan left, without his flowers.

"I can't believe he didn't take them so he could palm them off on some other poor cow," she snapped.

"Can I have them?" asked Sinead.

"Of course, I would be thrilled," said Leila. She looked at the space where Tynan had been. "I honestly don't know what I ever saw in him."

"Ah well, he's easy on the eye," Sinead said. "But he's a bit of a cretin, no offense."

Leila found she was fighting back tears. What had Tynan done? She found her phone and dialed Devlin's number. It went straight to voicemail. Damn. She couldn't leave a message here in reception, so she ran back into her own office, slammed the door shut, and rang again.

Again the phone went to voicemail.

"Devlin," she said, "there's nothing between me and Tynan anymore, I promise you. He came to the flat the other night and said he was back and that he wanted to start again. I threw him out. It's over. Please ring me back, please, I'd love to go to lunch. Tynan's gone. I've told him I never want to see him again. I want to see you. Please call me," and she hung up.

She should have said "I want you," she thought miserably, but she couldn't phone again immediately. All she could do was wait.

"Men: can't live with them, can't kill them," Leila muttered to Pixie as they walked along the canal bank that evening. She'd left work on the dot of five thirty, and as a result there was still a glimmer of daylight in the sky as they walked, now that it was officially spring.

Devlin hadn't returned to the office and he hadn't returned her calls either. After leaving two more voicemail messages, she'd stopped phoning him. Now she felt both foolish and heartbroken. Stupid man — why hadn't he stayed long enough to see her push Tynan away? Unless he wasn't that sure of himself, and that thought gave Leila pause: Devlin not entirely sure of himself.

The arrival of Mitzi and Tasha, bounding along the path toward her, broke into her melancholy.

"Hello, you two," she said, barely able to summon up the energy to talk to them.

Pixie danced around them delightedly, entangling their legs and Leila's with her leash. The extending leash was brilliant until she started running in and out and winding it around everything and everyone in sight. With the little dogs all wriggling around and the leash getting more and more tangled, Leila finally lost it.

"Pixie," she ordered, "stay still for one minute while I unhook you — do not run off, OK?"

She unclipped Pixie's leash from her collar and began untangling it from the dogs' legs. Finally she had it and stood up. "There, sorted."

And in that instant, Pixie, Mitzi, and Tasha belted off down the path, running like the wind, clearly in pursuit of something.

"Pixie, come back!"

Leila was wearing her sneakers, tracksuit bottoms, and a fleecy jacket, so at least she was dressed for the occasion, but one grown-up who didn't run a lot was no match for three little dogs intent on their quarry. No matter how many times she yelled the dog's name, it was to no avail.

All she could do was keep running, passing all the other dog-walkers she knew, leaping over small dogs, sidestepping big ones and doggy poo, until finally she couldn't see Pixie anymore. It was getting dark and she'd disappeared.

Mitzi and Tasha's owner appeared out of the gloom.

"Are you letting Pixie off the leash these days?" she asked cheerfully.

"No," wailed Leila, "I'm not. I just unhooked her because she was all tangled up, and now she's run off. She never comes back. I've tried letting her off in a playing field near my mum's place, but I have a terrible time getting her back — and that's in broad daylight. I would never risk it here, not when it's almost dark."

"She'll be fine," the woman said. "I'll call my pair and she'll come back with them." She held up a silent dog whistle and blew into it. "This is the trick — the whistle is what they respond to, not your voice."

"Oh, thank you," said Leila, feeling her heartbeat begin to calm down.

Suddenly two white bundles of fluff appeared, racing along the path.

"Great," said Leila as she spotted them, craning her neck in case Pixie was hidden behind them. But there was no sign of her.

"Oh gosh, that's worrying," said the woman. "Girls, where's Pixie?"

They stared up at her happily, tails wagging.

"Oh no," said Leila, her heart beginning to race again. "Where do they go when you let them off the leash?"

"They generally just run a bit farther down. Sometimes they swerve off to the side to sniff out somebody's gateway, but that's it."

"Pixie's no good on roads or gateways," said Leila, horrified. "She could have been run over. She's frightened of cars — you've seen the way she is when we have to cross the roads at the bridges!"

"Don't worry, we'll find her."

Together they walked up and down the stretch of canal bank, then the woman said she would go over the bridge to the other side of the canal while Leila backtracked along the path they'd just come along.

"Keep calling her name — and try this," the woman said, handing over the whistle. "Don't worry, she'll be absolutely fine."

She set off with Mitzi and Tasha trotting after her obediently, and Leila turned away, tears rolling down her face, cursing herself for letting Pixie off the leash. She was a puppy at heart; she had absolutely no road sense, no sense whatsoever. Goodness knows what might have happened to her. She could have run into traffic anywhere. Somebody could have taken her . . .

The tears kept coming. This had been the

most dreadful day ever, and now Pixie was gone too. Leila had grown to love the little dog, and as for poor Mum . . . She couldn't bear the thought of having to tell her mother that Pixie was lost. What was she going to do?

Her phone rang and she grabbed it frantically, thinking that perhaps someone had found Pixie. She'd taken the precaution of putting her number on the dog's ID, and now she said a quick prayer that someone was ringing to say they'd got her.

"Hello," she answered breathlessly.

"Leila . . ." It was Devlin.

"Devlin, oh God, I'm so sorry about today — I've been leaving messages trying to talk to you, but I can't talk now because Pixie's run away on me and I can't find her. I've been up and down calling her and whistling, but now it's dark and . . ."

She was so distraught she barely knew what she was saying. She had such faith in Devlin — he could do anything, fix any problem — that she was ready to plead for his help in finding the dog, even though he was angry with her, even though this wasn't the sort of problem he was accustomed to dealing with.

"Pixie — that's your mum's dog, right?"

"Yes," she said. "I walk her along the canal at night. I let her off for just one minute near the lock on Baggot Street Bridge so I could untangle her leash, and she ran after two other dogs and now she's gone. Please help."

"Stay where you are," he said. "I'll be there in ten minutes."

In the event, he was there much sooner, striding toward her in a big leather coat and jeans with a packet of biscuits in his hand. "Let's rattle these," he said. "Dogs love biscuits."

"Oh, Devlin," Leila said, and burst into tears. He pulled her into his arms as if it was something he'd been doing for years, and held her tight. Not a romantic hug but a comforting one.

She buried her head in his chest and he whispered into her hair, "It's going to be fine, Leila. It's going to be fine."

"I'm so sorry about earlier," she said. "It's all over with Tynan."

"I know," he whispered, "I know. Sinead gave me the details. Restraining order, huh? I wish I'd been there to see that." He smiled at her. "I should have stayed around longer and knocked his block off. Now, let's find this naughty little doggy, shall we?"

It felt better now that he was there, calling out for Pixie. It was fully dark by this time, but Leila didn't feel afraid. Only a very foolhardy person would take on someone Devlin's size.

Finally they'd walked both sides of the canal, two miles in each direction.

"Let's head back to your apartment," said

Devlin. "She'll know where to go. I'll ring the police and the dog pound while we're walking."

With one arm around her, he used the other to make the phone calls. Leila couldn't stop crying. All she could think of was poor Pixie out there, lost and frightened, not knowing where she was. Maybe somebody was hurting her. People did such dreadful things to dogs. Leila had seen the programs about animal cruelty and she couldn't bear to think of anyone hurting Pixie.

Devlin finished his calls and shook his head at her. Nobody had found Pixie; there was no news of her from the police, the dog pound, the ISPCA.

"She's not microchipped, is she?" he asked at one point.

Leila shook her head.

"I should have done that," she said. "I should have."

She was out of tears by the time they reached the part of the canal where she and Pixie had started their walk. They crossed the road, turned up the lane and walked toward Leila's apartment building. And suddenly she blinked, for there, sitting under the streetlight beside the entrance, was Pixie.

"Pixie!" yelled Leila, and the little dog turned and flew toward them, tail wagging frantically. She leapt ecstatically onto Leila as if she'd been waiting for her all evening and was wondering where she had been.

"Oh, Pixie, you terror, you frightened the life out of me."

She fell to her knees and began hugging and kissing the little dog, who seemed more interested in the biscuit Devlin was holding out for her.

"Hello, Pixie," said Devlin, and, seeing as how he was the great biscuit source, she began to leap all over him too. "You're a terrible scamp, you know that," he said fondly, "running off and scaring Leila."

Pixie wriggled against him joyously.

"I didn't know you liked dogs," said Leila.

He grinned at her. "There's a lot you don't know about me."

TWENTY-TWO

The man may be the head of the home,
but the wife is the heart.

KENYAN PROVERB

Devlin stopped for gas on the outskirts of Bridgeport. While he was inside paying, Leila flicked down the passenger mirror and looked at herself critically. She was glowing. There really was no other word for it. It was like she was lit up from the inside. She wanted to pinch herself, because she couldn't quite believe what was happening.

"Do you think I'm glowing?" she asked Pixie, who was sitting very happily on the back seat of Devlin's big, luxurious car.

Pixie instantly scrambled up to the front seat to give her a lick.

"So glad you agree," murmured Leila happily. "Or do you just want to lick my face cream off?"

Devlin slid back into the front seat.

"Now, Pixie," he said, "kissing her is my job."

Leila grinned. "Pixie doesn't see it that way — I'm afraid you're going to have to share."

"All right," he said with a pretend groan, reaching out to ruffle Pixie's fur. Then he leaned forward and kissed Leila on the lips with a passion that still hadn't stopped thrilling her. How had she thought Tynan could kiss, or that Tynan was sexy, for that matter?

Somehow Pixie wriggled herself in between them.

"I'm going to miss this little puplet when I have to give her back to Mum," said Leila, laughing.

"You could get your own little puplet," said Devlin, eyes glinting, "but we'd have to train it not to come between us when I want to kiss you."

Leila laughed. "I don't think you can train a dog not to do that. Besides, the gas station outside town is not the place to do proper kissing."

Devlin's face lit up with that grin that always took her breath away. "Later, then," he said. "When we get to this hotel you've booked me into."

Birdie had had her hair styled for the rehearsal dinner. She'd asked Grace where the best hairdresser was and Grace had recommended the place she went to.

"Birdie," Grace had said, thinking about it, "I keep picturing you with lovely waves. Still, ask Renee. She's an expert. She'll know what to do."

Birdie liked the rippling curls that added body to her silvery hair.

She was wearing the soft coral dress she'd seen in the window of the shop the day she'd first found out about Howard's affair. It was strange: she should have been disgusted at the very thought of the dress, but it was so beautiful and such a lovely color. Besides, rather than associating it with the betrayal, she had decided to look upon it as the first thing she'd bought after she was set free.

Not that she'd realized it at the time, no, but she realized it now.

Howard had given her a wonderful gift by cheating on her. He'd given her her freedom, and that was what she'd needed for a very long time.

"You look nice," he said, walking into the bedroom to get ready himself and stopping in astonishment at the sight of his normally drab wife dressed up in something other than one of her four going-out outfits.

She didn't reply.

"I said, you look nice," he repeated, more loudly.

"Thank you," Birdie replied, looking at him with a lot more self-possession than he'd ever seen in her eyes before. She carried on putting on lipstick to match the outfit. She had another dress for tomorrow too.

Just tonight and tomorrow, Birdie thought, doing her best to ignore her husband. That's all I have to get through.

The divorce lawyer had been so helpful.

"Decide what you want to do," she'd explained to Birdie. "We have a no-fault divorce system in this country, but you should be prepared — your husband will want to protect his assets and may do everything he can to keep them from you. Do you think that's a possibility?"

"Oh yes," said Birdie, "I'd put money on it. Thing is, I'm not after his money. That's not what this is about at all. I don't need a lot."

"That's a lovely way to think," said the lawyer charmingly. "Many clients come in with that attitude. But the old adage that you don't know a person until you meet them in the divorce courts is very true, so let's make sure you get what you deserve. *Then* you can choose what to do with it. If you want to give half of it to the animal rescue, that's up to you, but my job is to ensure that you get what you're legally entitled to."

Legal entitlement, thought Birdie, finishing with her lipstick. None of this was about legal entitlement or money or anything like that. It was about self-respect and having the sort of life she wanted to lead. She hadn't had that with Howard for a very long time. Not that it was really his fault; they'd simply been wrong for each other from the start.

The only wonderful thing from their marriage was their darling, beloved Katy. And for that reason alone she would never regret marrying Howard.

Telling Katy was going to be the most horrendous thing, and Birdie had decided she'd break the news to Michael first and let him gauge a good time. Upsetting her pregnant daughter was not what she wanted to do, but, she thought with resignation, it had to be done. There was to be no more hiding. Birdie would have the sort of life she wanted — and Thumper, sitting beside her adoringly, would be a big part of that.

Stephen was one of the first to arrive at the restaurant. He hugged Katy and Michael, who'd gotten there before anyone else.

"How are you doing, Dad?" said Michael, holding his father for longer than usual in the embrace. "Have you spoken to Julia?"

Stephen had told Fiona and Michael that he and Julia had split up.

"I'm doing fine," said Stephen. "Things are OK. I've moved out of the apartment, but I caught up with Julia a few days ago. She seems good; full of plans to walk the Camino de Santiago de Compostela with her friend Rosa. Apparently it's something she's always wanted to do, and I never knew. Amazing — you can live with someone for thirteen years and not know stuff like that."

Katy put her arm through Michael's. "We know everything about each other," she said, grinning up at him.

Stephen smiled at his daughter-in-law to be. "Yes, I think you probably do," he said.

It was knowing everything about yourself that he found tricky. Now he knew what he wanted, what he'd probably wanted for years, and it was too late to do anything about it. Yes, self-knowledge: that was the thing.

Grace knew she was late, and was furious with herself because of it. She'd spent ages trying to figure out what to wear, which was entirely ridiculous given that this was a dinner with a group of people she knew incredibly well. Her wedding outfit — a cerise-pink shift dress with a matching slim coat, hung in the spare bedroom, and the hat she was still dithering over was there too. Tonight was supposed to be casual, not at all like tomorrow.

She wondered whether she was on edge because she knew that this was the last night that Howard and Birdie would be together. By tomorrow, after the wedding, Howard would be hearing some pretty scary news.

Grace had been stunned when Birdie had come over for coffee one day and announced, almost casually, that Howard was having an affair and she was going to leave him.

"Are you sure?" Grace said, shocked out of her usual sangfroid.

630

"Yes," said Birdie, sounding most unlike herself. "If we stay together, it will be fake, and I don't want that. Not anymore, Grace. Not at my age."

Birdie didn't want anyone else to know.

"Please don't tell the others," she begged. "It's my decision, Grace, and I wanted to share it with you. You always seem to know what to do with life."

"I'm not sure about that," Grace said ruefully, thinking of Stephen. "I should warn you, Birdie, it's not always easy being on your own."

She wanted Birdie to enter into this new phase of life with her eyes open. The loneliness she herself was going through when she thought about Stephen had hurt her anew.

"I understand," said Birdie thoughtfully. "But you've never been married to a man like Howard. I won't know for sure until I do it, but I think I'll have peace to choose how I want to live the rest of my life. I'm going to tell Howard that I know about the affair and want a divorce the minute the wedding's over."

"So you're absolutely sure?" Grace had said.

"Oh yes," said Birdie, with a happy clarity in her voice that had been absent before. "I'm absolutely sure. I'm just going to wait until Katy and Michael have driven off, and that'll be it. They're going straight to the airport hotel and flying out first thing in the morning. They can have their honeymoon and come home and find out then. I hate doing this to Katy, but we have to be true to ourselves, don't we, Grace?"

"We do indeed," said Grace, thinking how surreal it was to be having this conversation with Birdie. "Yes, we have to be that."

Even though Grace liked being truthful, she knew she wasn't being truthful with Stephen. They should have had a proper conversation, come to some sort of understanding by now. He'd phoned several times since her dinner party, but somehow all their chats had been of the bland variety: *how is everyone, let's hope the weather's good for the wedding.* All very superficial.

"Perhaps I was imagining it," Grace said to Nora. "I must have been mad to think he was going to say something meaningful, or was thinking about him and me getting back together. Mad, that's me. Imagining my ex-husband still had designs on me."

"In your defense, he was certainly giving you hints in that direction," said Nora.

"No, I was clearly imagining them," Grace said, "which is wildly embarrassing. It's all this wedding stuff. It just brings the past back and makes you have regrets and get all nostalgic about what it was like years ago.

Madness, that's what it was. The past is the past."

But she wished it wasn't — except she could never say that, not even to Nora. What clock could ever be turned back?

"Okey-doke," said Nora calmly. "Have a lovely night at the rehearsal dinner and I'll see you at the wedding."

It wasn't really a rehearsal dinner, Susie thought, as she got dressed in her mother's house. More of a party, to which Jack was invited.

"He has to come," Katy had said on the phone, and Susie had felt so thrilled. Katy hadn't understood what it was like to have a child before she'd become pregnant, but now she was getting it.

Susie had teased her about it. "You just want my carrot purée recipe, I know," she'd said.

"You got me," Katy replied. "I never realized how much there was to taking care of children before."

Susie roared with laughter.

"So says the pregnant lady. Call anytime," she said. "When you have a baby, you need your girlfriends."

Now, Susie thought fondly, she'd have someone to share her mothering experience with, someone she could help.

"Mum, it's Leelu — and she's got a man

with her!" roared Jack from downstairs.

Susie admired herself in the mirror. She'd gotten her hair streaked for the wedding. She did it so rarely but she'd decided to splash out. She was so into saving money *just in case* that sometimes she forgot to live. It was like looking at her younger self now, with blonde hair and made-up eyes and lips. Like someone she'd lost a long time ago but had found again.

"Mum!" yelled Jack again. "Come on! Pixie's here!"

The tall, strong guy was a very different kettle of fish from Tynan, Susie thought, when they'd shaken hands. The first time she'd met Tynan, he'd given her the once-over as if he was sizing her up and mentally awarding marks out of ten. Devlin, on the other hand, was polite, with a genuine charm. Plus, he immediately notched up plenty of gold stars by being chatty with Jack and admiring his LEGO collection.

"Is it a diving watch?" Jack asked, attempting to take the huge watch off Devlin's enormous tanned wrist.

"It is," said Devlin, unhooking it. "Put it on and stick your hand in some cold water. It changes color. It's cool."

"Really?"

"Really. Water from the cold tap, remember — not the hot tap."

Susie and Leila exchanged glances: Susie's curious, Leila's besotted.

"Lots of nephews and nieces," explained Devlin. "Best to say cold water or he might burn himself."

Devlin sat down on the couch and Pixie flung herself on top of him. Susie couldn't imagine Tynan putting up with that either, but Devlin just shifted her so she was comfortable and petted her fondly.

Jack had gone off with the watch to the kitchen.

"He's a great kid — I've heard all about him," Devlin was saying. "Must be hard being on your own, though."

Susie felt like crying, but then an arm went around her.

"Yes," said Leila. "Damn hard, and I haven't been there for her these past few years, have I? I'm sorry, Susie. Pretty useless sister I turned out to be. But that's going to change."

Devlin got up. "I'd better see how my watch is doing in the kitchen," he announced diplomatically.

"Don't cry, you'll ruin your makeup," Leila whispered, hugging her sister.

"It's happy crying, not sad crying. Happy crying makes makeup better."

"Didn't know that," Leila said. "I'm still sorry, though. I did that dreadful thing of ignoring my sister for my man — and a crappy man at that. I don't think I realized how difficult it was for you on your own. I suppose I felt that you had it all sorted out because you had Jack and you were happy."

Susie laughed. "I *am* happy with Jack, beyond happy, but that doesn't make it easy. And I thought you had a fabulous life while I was stuck at home every night watching *Thomas the Tank Engine* reruns."

"I can watch *Thomas* when I babysit," Leila said.

"*Thomas* is so over," Susie said. "He's into *Ben 10* now."

"Right. Must keep up," Leila said. "Changing marketplace and all that."

"I like Devlin. He's got nice eyes. I've got a good feeling about him."

Leila blushed. "Me too," she said.

"Are you staying at the hotel with him tonight?" asked Susie.

Leila blushed even more. "Would you mind? I know it's Mum's first night home, it's just —"

"I wouldn't mind at all, and neither will Mum," said Susie. "Just don't stay up too late. Remember: bridesmaids on duty at eight. Now, how about we go and pick Mum up from the Hummingbird?"

Katy woke at five to six on the morning of her wedding, disoriented for a moment until she recalled where she was: in her childhood bedroom, which was still endearingly teenage — posters on the walls and cute teddy bears Michael had given her lined up on top of a chest of drawers. When she'd moved out, Mum had tried very hard to hide her tears and had kept rushing out on the pretense of making more tea in order to cry in her own room.

This would be the last time she'd lie in this bed as a single woman, Katy thought, smiling. Possibly the last time she'd lie in it as a non-parent. Next time she stayed, she'd have her baby. Katy didn't close her eyes and pray that this would be so — she wasn't like her mother, who would have said many prayers that the baby would be born safely. Mum was like that. Anxious about things, worried until they happened safely. Although she seemed calmer over the past few weeks, which was lovely.

Moving slowly so as not to set off the recently abated morning sickness, Katy sat up and stretched luxuriously. Without going near the curtains, she could tell it was a lovely morning. The weather lady on the news the night before had forecast a glorious day, and if that wasn't enough, Katy had spent enough years in this room to know that when a shaft of sunlight was shining in through the gap at the bottom of the curtains, it was a good sign.

Today your mummy and daddy are getting married, she told her bump. It was still tiny.

"First baby," the nurse in the antenatal clinic had said. "Your stomach muscles are still strong."

"Is that good or bad?" Katy wanted to know.

The nurse laughed. "Good for the first baby, because you've a neat bump for ages and can still fit into normal clothes, and a shock for any babies thereafter, because you look like you're carrying triplets in comparison and have to buy stretchy tent T-shirts and special trousers straight off."

Katy laughed too.

"You're going to do fine," the nurse said approvingly. "You're not a worrier. It does help. There's enough to worry about without finding new and unusual things to fret over."

"My mother worries for both of us," Katy said. "I'd love her to come to one of the appointments with me, but if something was up, like my blood sugar today, she'd totally panic and then I'd worry about her."

"Best to keep the anxious people at home," the nurse agreed.

In bed, Katy stretched out one arm so she could admire both her newly painted nails and the glitter of her engagement ring.

"Today is going to be a glorious day," she said aloud, stroking her bump.

Birdie slipped quietly from her side of the bed at ten past six. On his beanbag on the floor beside her, Thumper lifted his head and smiled a sleepy, doggy smile.

"Hello, Thumper sweetie," whispered Birdie, leaning down to stroke his silky ears.

Thumper knew how to be quiet in the mornings. He waited outside the bathroom while his mistress brushed her teeth and pulled on her dressing gown.

In the bed, Howard snored deeply, but Birdie still closed the bedroom door as quietly as possible before tiptoeing downstairs.

The house, resplendent and different with furniture moved and vast vases of flowers everywhere, greeted her, and she knew it looked lovely as the morning sun shone in. There was a kind of magic to the way the dark floorboards gleamed and the reflection of china and glass vases warmed up tables and alcoves. The scent of flowers mingled with the scent of the rose candles that had been lit the night before, and Birdie knew that Vineyard Manor had never looked so pretty.

She felt no sense of loss, however, when she thought that she would not be living here much longer.

This vast house was for a different life, a different woman — one who'd done what was expected of her and what she was told. On her own, she'd never have chosen the wildly expensive hand-painted kitchen Howard had insisted on — and nitpicked over endlessly while the poor kitchen installer was working on it. She much preferred Grace's neat little kitchen with the old dresser Grace had once spent a month of weekends stripping before repainting it in a matte honeyed yellow.

"Not a great job," Grace had laughed, showing Birdie her handiwork. "I shouldn't have used cheap brushes. Look . . ." She'd pointed to where a skinny black bristle was embedded in the paint. "But it was fun and I get such a sense of achievement when I look at it."

The garden had been the one place that had given Birdie a sense of achievement — until Howard had brought in his team of designers to tear out her herb bed so they could position the tent just so, leaving her queenship over the garden in tatters.

Broken, like so many things that had once mattered to her, she thought as she filled the kettle and switched it on.

Unlocking the back door and switching off the alarm, she let Thumper loose into the garden, where he raced off to snort at the tent in case any strange animals had been leaving their scent on it in the night. It was still cool despite the sun, but she left the back door open and took her tea outside to the terrace, where she sat down by one of the hired bay trees that would later, apparently, be swagged with cream ribbons.

The Child of Prague statue was sitting where Birdie had left it the night before. She picked it up and smiled. "Thank you for the weather," she said.

She'd always loved the notion that if the holy statue was put outside before a wedding, then it wouldn't rain. How many Irish houses over the years had put the Child of Prague in their gardens and yards and window boxes before weddings?

His mission finished, a satisfied Thumper returned to her side and sniffed her hand, looking for breakfast.

"In a moment, honey," she murmured, and he leaned into her and sighed with pleasure at being petted.

She needed another moment or two in peace with her tea and the quiet of what remained of her garden before she could face going inside to become Birdie again, the woman everyone expected her to be. Just one more day, just for the benefit of her beloved Katy.

And after today, it would be a whole other story. A new story.

Leila woke up in a sea-view suite at the Cliff House Hotel in Ardmore with Devlin's large body warming hers.

She'd toyed with the idea of going home after the dinner the night before, but somehow she couldn't think of anything nicer than going back to Devlin's hotel and letting him make love to her, slowly.

And after that . . . well, she'd simply wanted to curl up beside him, his body wrapped around hers, as they talked gently. She'd never known you could spend so long talking to another person. Finally they'd fallen asleep, contented.

In the gloom, she peered at her watch. Six thirty. She ought to get up and race home to spend time with Mum and make sure she was ready for the wedding.

Dolores had been so thrilled to get back to Poppy Lane yesterday evening. She'd wandered around the rooms with a delighted Pixie at her heels, saying the same thing over and over:

"It's so lovely to be back."

Nora's people had made the house ready during the week. Nora herself had given Dolores a list of printed instructions with details of the newly installed emergency buttons upstairs and downstairs.

The health nurse's phone number was on a list, Mum's next physiotherapy appointment was on Monday and there followed three names of local people who helped out by driving injured or elderly people to their appointments. Beneath the list was a lovely note from Nora:

Charity Delaney, yes, that really is her

name! She's a darling, Dolores, and I think you'll like her. She has dogs too, and can help with walking Pixie. Charity also takes a few people to the crafting morning in the St. Erconwald parish hall on Thursdays, so with your brilliance with knitting, you should definitely go. It's from ten to twelve thirty and you could help out with the newbies who are learning to knit. I've seen you with the cable needles! You'll be a fabulous help to dear Charity.

Don't get into a panic about having an emergency button — it makes sense with your rheumatoid arthritis. You don't want to be seizing up at home on your own and have nobody to call. You're not on the scrapheap yet, thank you very much. An emergency button is just sensible.

Deirdre, the health nurse, will talk to you about the home help; you know health service money's tight and I'm not sure you'll get anyone long-term, but you might get a few hours' help a week till you're totally healed.

Leila had read the note with a lump in her throat. She'd never be able to thank Nora enough. Her kindness shone through — there was no hint that Dolores Martin was a fragile woman who'd need help forever after; just the message that she needed more support these days and that this support was in the community.

With her stick, Dolores was able to get around everywhere, she'd told Leila.

"No crutches for me anymore," she said cheerfully. "I'll be able to come to the wedding for a bit too. I couldn't manage the whole day, but I'm so looking forward to seeing my girls in their bridesmaid dresses."

Leila loved seeing the glow in her mother's cheeks. The haunted, tired look was gone, and despite the stick, there was a lightness in her appearance that filled Leila with hope for the future.

Dolores had an appointment with her RA specialist in three weeks, and Leila was taking the day off to drive her there.

Pixie had sat faithfully beside her mistress ever since Leila had arrived, staring up at Dolores as if she wasn't quite sure she was real.

"I missed you so much," Dolores said, with the first sign of tears Leila had seen.

"*I'll* miss her," Leila pointed out truthfully, thinking back to how shocked she'd been at the notion of taking on her mother's dog. She'd gotten used to coming home to see Pixie in the evenings, organizing her day around the dog's routine: up early to bring Pixie for a walk, phoning the walker to make sure she'd had a good lunchtime outing, home as early as she could for another walk, and then snuggling up on the couch with the dog, watching TV, having another creature to talk to.

"You could get a dog," her mother said eagerly.

Leila shook her head. "My hours aren't fair to a dog," she said. "I had to jump through hoops as it was. Although we might get one . . ."

Her mother smiled.

"I love the way you say *we,*" she said.

"You like this we?" Leila said, smiling.

"Yes, I approve of this we and I can't wait to meet him."

"You approve without even meeting him?"

Her mother reached out her swollen hands for her daughter's.

"I can tell how he makes you feel: happy about yourself, lovey. That's the sort of man I wanted you to have. Plus, he loves Pixie, doesn't he? You have to adore a man who likes dogs."

Ruby came into the shop with Vonnie to pick up the cake for the Desmond/Rhattigan wedding.

She'd only been there once before, with Shelby, Dad, and Shane, so it felt different and somewhat special to be there with Vonnie on their own for work.

She felt so clear-headed these days, partly due to the wonderful new food plan she and Mum were on. Who knew she'd ever see her mother making vegetable soups?

But the clear-headedness was also due to the psychologist she was seeing once a week.

Mum drove her most days, but sometimes Dad did, and she liked getting into the car afterwards feeling as if she'd downloaded all the difficult things in her head.

She'd told Mum she'd quite like to train as a psychologist when she was older.

"You have plenty of material for a home case study here," Mum had said, laughing.

"We're not so crazy," Ruby had said easily. "We just hit a blip, and now —"

"We're on our way to being blip-free," finished her mother.

"Delivering the cake is one of the most exciting parts of the whole business," Vonnie explained now, unlocking the door into the kitchen.

Ruby wandered around looking at various drawings and photos of cakes, marveling that this spotlessly clean and almost sterile place was a working kitchen.

"Wow, what's this one?" she asked, peering closely at a sketch of a cake that looked like a cathedral complete with ancient clock and gargoyles.

"Two architects requested this one," said Vonnie, standing behind her to look at it. "They love Gothic buildings and we modeled it on several cathedrals. It's a little crazy, for sure, and is going to take some work, but

Lorraine loves doing it. I'm beginning to think she's wasted on flowers. The fun she had with those gargoyles!"

Right on time, Freddie and Dennis, who helped move cakes, arrived for work.

"If you two can deliver the Ryan/Fitzgerald cake to this address," said Vonnie, handing out papers, "and then the Vinci/Keyser one to the Central Hotel, we're in business. Ruby and I will deliver the Desmond/Rhattigan one because there are going to be tent people there who can help us set it up."

She turned to Ruby. "The cakes are heavy, so we need assistance sometimes," she explained.

By eight thirty, they were in the van heading in the direction of the vast and elegant Vineyard Manor.

"Fabulous place," Vonnie said as they drove in, admiring the beautiful gardens and a lawn where a huge tent was set up.

"Poppy Lane is nicer," said Ruby suddenly. "It's got heart. This place hasn't."

Vonnie felt her eyes prickle with tears. "That's a lovely thing to say, Ruby," she said.

"It's true," Ruby replied, reaching out and putting one small, cool hand over her stepmother's slender one as it rested on the gearshift.

"It will be better if we can do up your room, though," Vonnie added. "I know you didn't mean it about keeping that antique wallpaper, because it didn't matter to you at the time. Please, can we rip it down? It breaks my heart to see it. You deserve something lovely."

"Butterflies," said Ruby. "I'd love wallpaper with butterflies on it."

Vonnie thought of a chrysalis breaking open to reveal something truly lovely — the way their family had had to crack open in order to be truly whole.

"Butterflies it is," she said.

Fiona stood patiently while Susie hooked up her dress.

"Done?" she asked.

Susie clicked the final hook in place.

"Done," she said. "No danger of you falling out of it now."

"Who'd be looking even if I did?" said Fiona, with a hint of gloom.

Katy, her hair in rollers, her lovely face made up, and dressed in a soft, fleecy dressing gown, gave her a cheeky pinch as she walked past.

"My wedding will be full of handsome men, you minx," she said. "Loads of lovely men."

"Really?" said Susie.

"Oh, I have a special one in mind for you," Katy told Susie. "He's a friend of Michael's and he's lovely. Decent, kind —"

"Probably gay but hasn't come out, lives with his mother, and has his sock drawer color-coded," said Fiona.

Katy delivered another pinch.

"Ouch. I'll be the same color as the dress if you keep this up," protested Fiona. "I'm just warning her."

"He's not gay. He's been living in Australia for a while and he's back now," Katy said. "I'm going to introduce you to him, Susie. You'll love him. I told him all about you."

"He'll run when he hears I'm a mum," Susie said.

"That's where you're wrong," Katy said triumphantly. "He has a son from a previous relationship. Ha!"

"Oh," said Susie, pleased.

"Does anyone else want more coffee?" asked Leila. "I'm a bit tired."

Susie smiled at her but said nothing.

Birdie came into the room with Morag, carrying a tray of tea, coffee, and sandwiches. Jack, who now adored Morag, followed bearing a tin of small cakes.

"The yellow ones are the nicest," he said to his aunt, proffering the tin.

"Should I buy yellow ones like this when you come to stay with me in Dublin?" Leila asked him.

"Yellow and purple," he said, adding conspiratorially: "But don't tell anyone that I like purple ones, OK? It's not a boy color."

"Secret," agreed Leila, deciding that she'd mention that there was no such things as boy or girl colors when she had the chance.

"I've got the camera," said Morag. "On the bed, the lot of you, so I can get a photo."

They all sat beside each other, with Jack perching half on his mother and half on his aunt, an arm around each one.

"Say cheese," said Morag, and Leila, Susie, Katy, Fiona, Jack, and Birdie all said cheese.

The speeches were almost Grace's undoing. She'd been fine for so much of it. She'd cried of course when Michael and Katy had walked into the tent to a round of applause; she'd never seen either of them look so gloriously happy. There was no fear for the future for this marriage, no threat of splits or divorces down the road.

They knew each other so well. Michael, as the son of divorced parents, was not precisely anti-divorce, but he believed marriage was for life. He'd told her that once.

"Mum, I'm not trying to upset you or anything; it's just that I do want to stay married to Katy forever. Do you think that's possible?"

"Of course it is," his mother had said fondly. "You know each other so well, you're older than Dad and I were when we got married. Things are different now and you've seen where we went wrong. It's not easy, of course, but I think you'll manage it."

All this flooded into her head now as she watched them, and she had to reach again

650

for the quite sodden hanky in her handbag. Sensibly, she had an entire packet of paper handkerchiefs, but she was beginning to think she'd get through them all.

The wedding breakfast had been glorious, fun, joyous. People were enjoying themselves, the music was low and beautiful, the tent exquisitely decorated, and the scent of flowers rising up into the air mingled with the perfume of the ladies.

Many times Grace had looked across at Stephen and caught his eye, and he'd smiled back at her, an incredulous smile that seemed to say, *Look — look what we've done. We've created this amazing young man and he's getting married today.*

I know, she wanted to beam back.

And then came the speeches.

Robbie, Michael's best man, had judged his speech to perfection. There had been no below-the-belt references or embarrassing revelations. No jokes about bridesmaids or how everyone thought Katy was a fine thing. Instead he had spoken with huge fondness of his great pal, he'd told funny stories that reflected well on Michael, and he'd praised Katy and said she was perfect for Michael.

"She's also the only person who can get him up in the morning — I should know, I've been on holidays with him."

He had concluded by praising the bridesmaids, the food, the bride and groom's parents, everyone he could think of.

But it had been Michael's speech that had her fumbling in her bag for her tissues yet again.

At first he had followed the traditional route, thanking all around and name-checking everyone.

"Everyone who knows us said they could tell we were going to be married from the first day we met," he said, looking around at the sea of smiling faces urging him on. "They thought we were boring, to be honest." His face took on a look of surprise, as if astonished at such a notion. "While everyone else was talking about going to parties and meeting complete strangers and having fabulous relationships, there we were, always the two of us together. Well, it might have looked boring — but it wasn't."

He glanced down at Katy, his gaze shot through with so much love that Grace had to hold her breath to stop herself crying. This was her son; this decent, strong, loving, wonderful man was her son. How proud she felt.

"But I knew that what we had was better than what any of them had," Michael went on. "I had the most wonderful woman in the world, and I knew this from when I was exactly sixteen and three-quarters. That was the day you agreed to go out with me —

though your father wasn't keen, it has to be said."

Howard looked delighted at this proof that he had been doing his fatherly duty.

"I've never wanted another woman since. There's never been anyone else for me — how could there be, compared to Katy? She's beautiful on the outside but she's even more beautiful on the inside, and that's what I fell in love with. This woman, who could be strong and feisty, no doubt about it, but loving and kind and good. And she loved me."

Grace could barely hear. She felt so emotional, so happy for her darling son. She prayed he'd never know any pain in his life. If only Fiona could find such happiness too.

She tuned in again.

"That's what I could never quite understand, that she loved me. And as the years went by, I knew I was the luckiest man in the world. But earlier this year, when we went to Paris, I was still nervous."

A few of his friends let out roars and "Ah, now, c'mon, Michael" noises.

"No, really," he said. "I was nervous. I had the ring. I knew what I wanted to do. I wanted to bring her to the top of the Eiffel Tower and ask her if she would marry me. I wanted it to be memorable. But there was a moment of fear that she might say no.

"I sort of wanted to ask my dad about it, because that's where he and my mother had gotten engaged."

Grace bit her lip and squeezed her nails into her hand. The tears were going to run down her face now, there was no doubt about it.

"My parents got engaged on the Eiffel Tower. And I want to pay tribute to my mum and dad here, because it's the example they gave me — the strength of their love, the way they loved us even when they weren't together anymore — that made me what I am today. I saw what family and love meant. Life never stopped them being friends or putting us first or being the most amazing parents ever. Maybe it's the Eiffel Tower effect."

The tears were rolling down Grace's face now; she couldn't look at Stephen, she couldn't look anywhere.

Robbie leaned over and squeezed her hand.

"I'm fine," Grace muttered, "I'm fine."

But she wasn't. So few people knew about the Eiffel Tower. She and Stephen had had no money in those days, and the flights had nearly bankrupted them. She'd had absolutely no idea of what was going to happen. She could see it all now: the crowds pushing forward, and Stephen, taller and stronger, protecting her against the people in the elevator, muttering how they were all intent on being first to see everything.

"And that's why I wanted to bring Katy there. Because I want her to have love all her life and to have the best of me, and that love is entwined with the Eiffel Tower. She is my heart, my true love, and as all of you know, she's carrying our little baby right now, which makes me the happiest man on the planet."

Grace knew her makeup must be running desperately and she probably looked like some deranged panda with mascara circles down her face, but she didn't care. She dared a glance over at Stephen, and he was looking at her with something close to anguish.

Are you all right? his eyes were saying, because Grace could read his face like a book after so many years. She nodded and managed to smile, and turned back to look at her beautiful son.

She knew it was a tribute to his darling Katy, but her heart felt swollen with love at how much of a tribute it was to her and Stephen too.

There had been pain and sacrifice, years when Grace had felt alone, but it was worth it to know that Michael had always felt loved the way she had wanted him to.

When Katy stood and kissed her new husband, everyone cheered and Robbie gave Grace a huge hug.

"Don't fall over on me now, Mrs. R," he teased. "I've got to keep you standing till our dance."

"I won't," said Grace. "I'm just so moved."

"Ah, weddings," Robbie said. "Tearjerkers every time."

Dolores loved Devlin.

She watched Leila dancing with him, saw the way he looked at her as if she were something precious.

Jack sat on his granny's lap, shattered and ready to go home soon. Meanwhile, his mother was dancing with a very nice man who apparently also had a little boy who was also into *Ben 10*. Dolores watched them both.

"That's it," she said happily to a sleepy Jack. "The Martin girls will have their rainbow, darling, I promise you. About time too! They deserve it."

Howard was a little tipsy. He never really got drunk; he liked to remain in control.

"Control," he would inform Birdie in his booming voice, "is vitally important in a captain of industry."

Birdie waited for him to say it now. They were standing side by side as the lights of the car carrying Katy and Michael faded into the distance. All the twinkling fairy lights in the trees seemed to gild the place so that it really did resemble something out of Disneyland. Disneyland crossed with *Alice in Wonderland*. The organizer had done a marvelous job, Birdie had to admit. It had been so beautiful — beautiful and precious.

"Back to normality now," said Howard, sighing. "Oh well, I'm going to go in and have a proper drink."

"Howard," Birdie said, "there's something I need to mention to you."

"Can't it wait until morning? I'm exhausted. All this organizing and —"

"I know," she interrupted him.

Howard looked surprised. Birdie did not do interrupting.

"I know about you and Nadine. I'm not upset. Well, I was in the beginning, but actually you've done me a favor. *She's* done me a favor. I'd never have had the courage to leave, or rather to ask you to leave, without Nadine — so do send a kiss from me or something. I'm sure that shouldn't be too hard."

Howard was watching her in utter amazement. His mouth was slack.

"Na-Nadine . . . what are you talking about?" he said, some of his old bluster returning.

"I'm talking about your girlfriend, the woman who's been choosing your clothes for the last few years, the woman you bought the car for, the mews house, the jewels. The house sounds particularly lovely — I did toy with the idea of driving to Dublin to have a look at it, but you know that's not my sort of thing," Birdie said earnestly. "I'm not a fighter, not an arguer. I'm a gentle sort of person and I don't want our divorce to change that. I want to remain me, without any nastiness or viciousness, so let's try to be kind to each other. The lawyer says I should really clean you out, but that's not me either, is it?"

Howard's face was even slacker.

"Nadine? You're imagining it, you're mad. She's just a friend. I sometimes stay in Dublin near her. Who's been telling you this?"

"Nobody told me anything, Howard," Birdie said. "I figured it out. Your American phone. Goodness, Howard, stop denying it. Let's have a bit of dignity and separate like intelligent adults. You and I aren't suited. You're not what I want and I'm certainly not what you want."

"Who said you're not what I want?" demanded Howard, sweat glistening on his brow.

He tried to pull her away into the house, where there was no chance of anyone overhearing. Gently, Birdie disentangled herself.

"Howard, don't try and deny this. I know the truth and it's over. I've known for quite some time. I put off saying anything because I didn't want to ruin Katy and Michael's day — so let's not mention this to them if they phone us from the honeymoon. We can tell them when they come back, when they're full of the excitement of the pregnancy and the honeymoon and being married. I don't think they'll be that surprised, to be honest. I'm pretty sure Michael has some idea, and Katy would have found out eventually."

"Michael knows?" shrieked Howard.

"He will soon enough, but I reckon he's had his suspicions. I've told Grace, by the way. I needed to confide in someone, and she's such a good person to talk to about these matters. Look, let's not argue. I got Morag to make up the bed in the spare room, the one closest to your mother. If you wake up early, you can go in and chat with her. I think we should sell Vineyard Manor. I'd quite like somewhere smaller myself, and of course I'll be taking Thumper."

"Birdie, I can't believe you're behaving like this over something so silly."

Birdie turned and looked at him with a combination of fraternal love and pity.

"Howard, my dear, it's not silly. It's one of the most serious things in the world. I think you broke my heart a long time ago, but it's only now that I have the courage to walk away. You weren't a bad husband, just not the right one for me. So let's cut our losses and we can go off with our broken hearts and fix them. You can't have been happy either."

She turned away for good this time, and she didn't feel tearful or anxious. She wanted to find Grace and grab her by both hands and tell her, *I did it, I did it!* Because Grace would understand.

Howard groped his way to the stone wall

and sat down. He realized he was shaking. This was not how he'd planned to spend the evening. By now, he should be back in the tent with his cronies, breaking out more cigars and opening bottles of Armagnac. Instead, he felt utterly alone.

"Do you remember our engagement?" Stephen asked Grace, his voice low.

They were standing outside, looking up at the moon and the stars, marveling at how clear a night it was. They'd seen their son leave with his bride, Katy and Michael beaming and waving as the wedding car flew down the drive, and now it was so strangely mild and clear that they'd stayed outside, looking at the fairy lights decorating the trees. Away to the side, the wedding party continued, people laughing and talking.

"Yes," said Grace softly.

"Let's tell nobody tonight," she'd said all those years ago after Stephen had asked her to marry him. "Let it be just us for now."

They'd headed back to the Eiffel Tower elevator and squashed in again, with him against the wall and her leaning against him.

"I love you," he whispered, bending close to her ear so that nobody heard.

In reply, she twisted her head and mouthed *"Je t'aime,"* which wasn't the only French she knew, but were the words she liked best.

"There's been a lot of water under the

bridge since then, Grace," Stephen said as they stood watching until the lights of their son and new daughter-in-law's wedding car disappeared from view. "Is it too much, too long?"

Grace considered this.

"I don't know," she said honestly. "We're very different now, both of us. I don't want to set us up for disaster or pain, or get the kids' hopes up."

"Ah, the kids — as you call them — don't care. They're too busy with their own lives."

Grace smiled. "I'm not so sure."

"They're grown now and we've done our best with them, haven't we?" he said.

He moved till he was standing in front of her, then he took both her hands in his.

Grace felt a tingle of excitement at his touch. Perhaps this was crazy, but perhaps not . . .

She closed her eyes, and she didn't see Fiona watching them.

"Who's texting you?" asked Katy, leaning languorously against her new husband in the wedding car as it whisked them off to the hotel for the night.

"Fiona. She says my parents are kissing!"

Katy giggled. "I knew our wedding would change everything — didn't I tell you so?"

"Yes, you did, you genius," murmured Michael, and pretty soon there was no noise

from the back of the car, just the sound of
two people moving so they could hold each
other close.

ACKNOWLEDGEMENTS

Thanks to my readers, without whom I'd still be writing on that secondhand kitchen table. Please keep talking to me: I love your emails and messages. Thanks to Jonathan Lloyd, Lucia Rae, Melissa Pimentel, and all at Curtis Brown; thanks to my wonderful new family at Orion, especially Susan Lamb, Kate Mills, David Young, Gaby Young, Dallas Manderson, Breda Purdue, Jim Binchy, and *everyone* who has welcomed me with such warmth; thanks to all my old friends in publishing: Karen-Maree Griffiths, Christine Farmer, Thalia Suzuma, Moira Reilly, Tony Purdue, Liz Dawson, Lynne Drew, and all who have been such an important part of my life.

Thanks to all the wonderful booksellers around the world who sell my books and are such a vital part of the team. Thanks to Aileen Galvin and Terry Prone of The Communications Clinic, and thanks to Sarah Conroy for much more than organization. Thanks to

Trish Long of Buena Vista, with whom I never actually had that catch-up lunch, so all information about movies comes from my own long experience and none of hers (all hideous mistakes are mine), but we shall always remember turning up at a meeting in the same suit and how sisterhood is strong. Thanks to Chris Lennon for her wonderful advice on the fine art of being a headmistress. Again, all mistakes are mine.

Thanks to Senator Imelda Henry, who generously gave a donation to UNICEF Ireland in order to have her darling mother Mollsie's name used in the book; and thanks to Dara Car, who donated to Cancer Research UK to have her name in the book. I tried hard to make both names gloriously lovely characters to say thanks. Thanks to my friends at UNICEF Ireland, both past and present, for all the incredible work they do for children around the world.

Thanks to my dear writer friends, who are true friends and without whom I might go mad. OK, madder.

Thanks to my beloved family, as always, and thanks to my dear friends — you know who you are and are always there for me. I don't have enough room to list you and everything you do. You are all in my heart.

Finally, thanks to Dylan, Murray, and John, and the Puplets, who make it all possible.

QUESTIONS FOR FURTHER DISCUSSION

1. Though Katy and Michael's engagement fills their friends and family members with joy for them, it also brings up painful issues for Leila, who is still suffering after her heartbreak. Have you ever had a friend experience something wonderful at the same time that you were struggling? What about the reverse? How did you handle those situations?

2. Grace is a character who has spent her personal and professional lives taking care of others. Do you think she has made enough time and paid enough attention to herself? How do you see this change, and see her grow, over the course of the novel?

3. What do you make of Vonnie's decision to stay in Ireland after Joe's death rather than returning with their son Shane to Boston? What would you have done in her shoes?

4. The relationship between Leila and Susie is a difficult one; they seem to misunderstand each other's intentions frequently, and they have trouble relating to each other's lives. How is this complicated by Dolores's medical situation? Have you felt tension with a sibling as an adult, and did you resolve it?

5. When you read the emails between various characters in the novel, did you ever notice that a character was being slightly less than honest with their correspondent? Were you ever reminded of emails that you exchange with your friends and family members?

6. Jennifer Morrison is quite antagonistic throughout much of the novel. How does she express the pain that she's in following her divorce? Do you think that there was ever any hope for her and Ryan staying together?

7. On a related note, Ruby is deeply affected by her parents' separation and her mother's emotional difficulties. How did her community help her through her eating disorder?

8. One of Leila's guilty pastimes is spending time on Tynan's Facebook page. Have you ever tracked an ex-partner or an ex-friend

on social media? How did it make you feel?

9. Birdie is usually conflict-averse and eager to please. What do you think of her decision to leave Howard after so many years spent together?

10. Do you think that Leila has a bright future with Devlin? What do you think is next for Katy and Michael and their friends and family members?

ABOUT THE AUTHOR

Cathy Kelly is published around the world, with millions of copies of her books in print. A #1 bestseller in the UK, Ireland, and Australia, she is one of Ireland's best-loved storytellers. She lives with her husband, their young twin sons, and their three dogs in County Wicklow, Ireland.

The employees of Thorndike Press hope you have enjoyed this Large Print book. All our Thorndike, Wheeler, and Kennebec Large Print titles are designed for easy reading, and all our books are made to last. Other Thorndike Press Large Print books are available at your library, through selected bookstores, or directly from us.

For information about titles, please call:
  (800) 223-1244

or visit our Web site at:
  http://gale.cengage.com/thorndike

To share your comments, please write:
  Publisher
  Thorndike Press
  10 Water St., Suite 310
  Waterville, ME 04901